Math Girls

$$\sum_{k=0}^{\infty} \heartsuit^k$$

Hiroshi Yuki

Translated by Tony Gonzalez

http://bentobooks.com

MATH GIRLS by Hiroshi Yuki. Copyright © 2007 Hiroshi Yuki.
All rights reserved. Originally published in Japan by
Softbank Creative Corp., Tokyo.
English translation © 2011, 2012 Bento Books, Inc.
Translated by Tony Gonzalez with Joseph Reeder.
Additional editing by Alexander O. Smith and Brian Chandler.

Published by

Bento Books, Inc.
217 Tierra Grande Court
Austin, TX 78732-2458
USA

bentobooks.com

ISBN 978-0-9839513-1-5 (hardcover)
ISBN 978-0-9839513-0-8 (trade paperback)
Library of Congress Control Number: 2011937467

Printed in the U.S.A.
First edition, November 2011 Second edition, May 2012

Math Girls

To My Readers

This book contains math problems covering a wide range of difficulty. Some will be approachable by middle school students, while others may prove challenging even at the college level.

The characters often use words and diagrams to express their thoughts, but in some places equations tell the tale. If you find yourself faced with math you don't understand, feel free to skip over it and continue on with the story. Tetra will be there to keep you company.

If you have some skill at mathematics, then please follow not only the story, but also the math. You might be surprised at what you discover.

—Hiroshi Yuki

Contents

Prologue

We met in high school.

I'll never forget them: The brilliant Miruka, forever stunning me with her elegant solutions. The vivacious Tetra, with her earnest stream of questions. It was mathematics that led me to them.

Mathematics is timeless.

When I think back on those days, equations seem to pop into my head and fresh ideas flow like a spring. Equations don't fade with the passage of time. Even today they reveal to us the insights of giants: Euclid, Gauss, Euler.

Mathematics is ageless.

Through equations, I can share the experiences of mathematicians from ages past. They might have worked their proofs hundreds of years ago, but when I trace the path of their logic, the thrill that fills me is mine.

Mathematics leads me into deep forests and reveals hidden treasures. It's a competition of intellect, a thrilling game where finding the most powerful solution to a problem is the goal. It is drama. It is battle.

But math was too hefty a weapon for me in those days. I had only just gotten my hand around its hilt, and I wielded it clumsily—like I handled life, and my feelings for Miruka and Tetra.

It is not enough to memorize. I must also remember.

It all started my first year of high school—

CHAPTER 1

Sequences and Patterns

One, two, three. One three.
One, two, three. Two threes.

YUMIKO OSHIMA
The Star of Cottonland

1.1 BENEATH A CHERRY TREE

The entrance ceremony on my first day of high school was held on a fine spring day in April. The principal gave a speech, filled with the usual things people are supposed to say at times like these. I remember maybe half.

...unfolding blossoms that you are... on this occasion of a new beginning... the proud history of this school... excel in your studies, as you excel in sports... learn while you are young...

I pretended to adjust my glasses to hide a yawn.

On my way back to class after the ceremony, I slipped away behind the school, and found myself strolling down a row of cherry trees.

I'm 15 now, I thought. *15, 16, 17, then graduation at 18. One fourth power. One prime.*

$$15 = 3 \cdot 5$$
$$16 = 2 \cdot 2 \cdot 2 \cdot 2 = 2^4 \qquad \text{a fourth power}$$
$$17 = 17 \qquad \text{a prime}$$
$$18 = 2 \cdot 3 \cdot 3 = 2 \cdot 3^2$$

Back in class everyone would be introducing themselves. I hated introductions. What was I supposed to say?

"Hi. My hobbies include math and, uh. . . Well, mostly just math. Nice to meet you."

Please.

I had resigned myself to the idea that high school would turn out much as middle school had. Three years of patiently sitting through classes. Three years with my equations in a quiet library.

I found myself by a particularly large cherry tree. A girl stood in front of it, admiring the blossoms. Another new student, I assumed, skipping class just like me. My eyes followed her gaze. Above us, the sky was colored in blurred pastels. The wind picked up, enveloping her in a cloud of cherry petals.

She looked at me. She was tall, with long black hair brushed back from metal frame glasses. Her lips were drawn.

"One, one, two, three," she said in precise, clipped tones.

$$1 \quad 1 \quad 2 \quad 3$$

She stopped and pointed in my direction, obviously waiting for the next number. I glanced around.

"Who, me?"

She nodded silently, her index finger still extended. I was taken off guard by the pop quiz, but the answer was easy enough.

"The next number is 5. Then 8, and after that 13, and then 21. Next is, uh. . ."

She raised her palm to stop me and then issued another challenge.

"One, four, twenty-seven, two hundred fifty-six."

1   4   27   256

She pointed at me again. I immediately noticed the pattern.

"I guess the next number is 3125. After that... uh, I can't do that in my head."

Her expression darkened. "1—4—27—256—3125—46656," she said, her voice clear and confident. The girl closed her eyes and inclined her head toward the cherry blossoms above us. Her finger twitched, tapping the air.

She was by far the strangest girl I'd ever met, and I couldn't take my eyes off her.

Her gaze met mine. "Six, fifteen, thirty-five, seventy-seven."

6   15   35   77

Four numbers, again, but the pattern wasn't obvious. My head went into overdrive. *6 and 15 are multiples of 3, but 35 isn't. 35 and 77 are multiples of 7...* I wished that I had some paper to write on.

I glanced at the girl. She was still standing at attention beneath the cherry tree. A cherry petal came to rest in her hair, but she didn't brush it away. She didn't move at all. Her solemn expression made our encounter feel all the more like a test.

"Got it."

Her eyes sparkled and she showed a hint of a smile.

"6—15—35—77... and then 133!"

My voice was louder than I'd intended.

She shook her head, sending the cherry petal fluttering softly to the ground. "Check your math," she sighed, a finger touching the frame of her glasses.

"Oh. Oh right. 11 × 13 is 143, not 133."

She continued with the next problem. "Six, two, eight, two, ten, eighteen."

$$6 \quad 2 \quad 8 \quad 2 \quad 10 \quad 18$$

Six numbers this time. I thought for a bit. The 18 at the end really threw me, since I was expecting a 2. I knew there had to be another pattern, though, and it hit me when I realized that all the numbers were even.

"Next is 4—12—10—6." I frowned. "Kind of a trick question, though."

"You got it, didn't you?"

She approached, her hand extended for an unexpected handshake. I took it, still unsure exactly what was going on. Her hand was soft and warm in mine.

"Miruka," she said. "Nice to meet you."

1.2 OUTLIER

I loved nighttime. Once my family was in bed, my time was my own. I would spread books before me, and explore their worlds. I would think about math, delving deep into its forests. I would discover fantastic creatures, tranquil lakes, trees that stretched up to the sky.

But that night, I thought about Miruka. I recalled our handshake. The softness of her hand, the way she smelled. She smelled like... like a girl. It was clear that she loved math; it was also clear that she was strange—an outlier. Not many people introduced themselves with a pop quiz. I wondered if I had passed.

I laid my glasses on my desk and closed my eyes, reflecting on our conversation.

The first problem, $1, 1, 2, 3, 5, 8, 13, \cdots$, was the Fibonacci sequence. It starts with 1, 1, and each number after that is the sum of the two before it:

$$1, 1, 1 + 1 = 2, 1 + 2 = 3, 2 + 3 = 5, 3 + 5 = 8, \cdots$$

The next problem was $1, 4, 27, 256, 3125, 46656, \cdots$. That was a sequence like this:

$$1^1, 2^2, 3^3, 4^4, 5^5, 6^6, \cdots$$

The general term for this would be n^n. I could manage calculating 4^4 and even 5^5 in my head, but 6^6? No way.

The problem after that was $6, 15, 35, 77, 143, \cdots$. I got that by multiplying:

$$2 \times 3, 3 \times 5, 5 \times 7, 7 \times 11, 11 \times 13, \cdots$$

In other words <a prime number> $\times$ <the next prime number>. I couldn't believe I'd messed up multiplying 11×13. Check your math, indeed.

The last problem was $6, 2, 8, 2, 10, 18, 4, 12, 10, 6, \cdots$. In other words it was π, but with each digit doubled:

$\pi = 3.141592653\cdots$		*pi*
$\rightarrow$	$3, 1, 4, 1, 5, 9, 2, 6, 5, 3, \cdots$	digits of π
$\rightarrow$	$6, 2, 8, 2, 10, 18, 4, 12, 10, 6, \cdots$	each digit doubled

What I didn't like about this problem was that you can't solve it unless you can remember the digits of π. You need to have the pattern already in your head. It relies on memorization.

Math isn't about dredging up half-remembered formulas. It's about making new discoveries. Sure, there are some things that require rote memorization: the names of people and places, words, the symbols of the elements. But math isn't like that. With a math problem, you have a set of rules. You have tools and materials, laid out on the table in front of you. Math's not about *memorizing*, it's about *thinking*. Or at least, that's what it is to me.

I noticed something interesting about that last problem. Miruka had given me six numbers, instead of four like the rest. If she had just said, "$6, 2, 8, 2$," then the series wouldn't necessarily be a doubling of the digits of π. Another, simpler pattern might be possible. Even if she had said, "$6, 2, 8, 2, 10$," I could have answered with a series of even numbers separated by the number 2, like this:

$$6, \underline{2}, 8, \underline{2}, 10, \underline{2}, 12, \underline{2}, \cdots$$

So she knew exactly what she was doing when she made that series longer than the others. And it hadn't surprised her when I got it right. I could still see the smug curl of her mouth.

Miruka.

I remembered the way she looked, standing there in the spring light, her black hair a sharp contrast against the pink petals on the wind, slim fingers moving like a conductor's. The warmth of her hand. Her fragrance.

That night, I couldn't think of much else.

1.3 BEGINNING THE PATTERN

By May, the novelty of being in a new school, going to new classrooms, and meeting new friends had largely faded. The days of same old, same old had begun.

I didn't participate in any after-school activities, preferring instead to get away from school stuff as soon as I could. I wasn't particularly good at sports, and just hanging out with friends had never appealed to me. That's not to say I headed straight home. When classes were done, I often went to the school library to do math, a habit I picked up in middle school. No clubs for me; just reading, studying, and staring out the library window.

But my favorite thing to do was tinker with the math I learned in class. Sometimes I would start with definitions, seeing where they led me. I jotted down concrete examples, played with variations on theorems, thought of proofs. I would sit for hours, filling notebook after notebook.

When you're doing math, you're the one holding the pencil, but that doesn't mean you can write just anything. There are rules. And where there are rules, there's a game to play—the same game played by all the great mathematicians of old. All you need is some fresh paper and your mind. I was hooked.

I had assumed it was a game I would always play alone, even in high school. It turned out I was wrong.

Miruka shared homeroom with me, and she showed up in the library a few days a week. The first time she walked up, I was sitting alone, working on a problem. She took the pencil out of my hand,

and started writing in my notebook. In *my* notebook! I wasn't sure if I should be offended or impressed. I decided on the latter.

Her math was hard to follow, but interesting. Exciting, even.

"What was with the sequence quiz the other day?" I asked.

"What other day?" She looked up, hand paused in mid-calculation. A pleasant breeze drifted through the open window, carrying the indistinct sounds of baseball practice and the fragrance of sycamore trees. "I'm drawing a blank here," she said, tapping a pencil—my pencil—against her temple.

"When we first met. You know... under the cherry tree."

"Oh, that. They just popped into my head. So what?"

"I don't know. Just wondering."

"You like quizzes?"

"Sure, I guess."

"You guess, huh? Did you know there aren't any right answers to those kinds of sequence problems?"

"What do you mean?"

"Say the problem was $1, 2, 3, 4, \cdots$. What's the answer?"

"Well, 5 of course."

"Not necessarily. What if the numbers jumped after that, say to $10, 20, 30, 40$, and then $100, 200, 300, 400$? It's still a perfectly fine sequence."

"Yeah, but, you can't just give four numbers and then say the numbers jump. There's no way to know that a 10 will come after the 4."

"Well, how many numbers do you need, then?" she asked, raising an eyebrow. "If the sequence goes on forever, at what point can you figure out the rest?"

"All right, all right. So there's always a chance that the pattern will suddenly change somewhere beyond what you've seen. Still, saying that a 10 comes after 1, 2, 3, 4 makes for a pretty random problem."

"But that's the way the world works. You never know what's going to come next. Predictions fail. Check this out." Miruka started writing in my notebook. "Can you give me a general term for this sequence?"

$$1, 2, 3, 4, 6, 9, 8, 12, 18, 27, \cdots$$

"Hmmm... Maybe," I said.

"If you only saw the 1, 2, 3, 4, then you'd expect the next number to be 5. But you'd be wrong. Rules won't always reveal themselves in a small sample."

"Okay."

"And if you saw 1, 2, 3, 4, 6, 9, you'd expect the sequence to keep increasing, right? But not here. The number after the 9 is an 8. You see a pattern of increasing numbers, but then *bam*, one goes backwards. Have you found the pattern yet?"

"Well, except for the 1 they're all multiples of 2 or 3. I can't figure out why that one number becomes smaller, though."

"Here's a solution to play with," she said, writing:

$$2^0 3^0, \ 2^1 3^0, \ 2^0 3^1, \ 2^2 3^0, \ 2^1 3^1, \ 2^0 3^2, \ 2^3 3^0, \ 2^2 3^1, \ 2^1 3^2, \ 2^0 3^3, \ \cdots$$

"Look at the exponents on the 2s and 3s. That should help you see it."

"Well, I know that anything raised to the zero power is 1, so yeah, when I do the calculations I get the right sequence," I said, writing underneath:

$$2^0 3^0 = 1, \ \ 2^1 3^0 = 2, \ \ 2^0 3^1 = 3, \ \cdots$$

"But I still don't get it."

"The exponents aren't enough, huh? How about this?"

$$\underbrace{2^0 3^0}_{\text{sum}=0}, \ \underbrace{2^1 3^0, \ 2^0 3^1}_{\text{sum}=1}, \ \underbrace{2^2 3^0, \ 2^1 3^1, \ 2^0 3^2}_{\text{sum of exponents}=2}, \ \underbrace{2^3 3^0, \ 2^2 3^1, \ 2^1 3^2, \ 2^0 3^3}_{\text{sum of exponents}=3}, \ \cdots$$

"Oh, I see it now," I said.

"Hey, speaking of multiples of 2 and 3—" Miruka began, but a shout from the library entrance interrupted her.

"Are you coming, or what?"

"Oh, right. Practice today," Miruka said.

She returned my pencil and headed towards the girl standing in the doorway. On her way out, she looked back. "Remind me to tell you what the world would be like if there were only two prime numbers."

Then she was gone and I was alone again.

CHAPTER 2

Equations and Love Letters

You fill my heart.

MOTO HAGIO
Ragini

2.1 TWO PLUS ONE EQUALS THREE

My second year of high school was pretty much the same as the first, except that the "I" on my school badge became a "II." Days flowed in an endless stream, each seeming just like the one that had come before, until a cloudy morning in late April.

Less than a month had passed since the start of the new school year. I was walking through the school gates on my way to class when an unfamiliar girl called out to me.

"This is for you," she said, offering me a white envelope. Confused, I took it. She bowed curtly before scurrying off.

I peeked inside—it was a letter. But there was no time to read it. Stuffing the envelope into a pocket, I ran off to class.

It was the first time a girl had given me a letter since elementary school. I'd caught a bad cold and was absent for a couple of days. One of my classmates came by my house to drop off homework, along with a note that said "Get better soon!"

The letter felt heavy in my pocket all during class.

Just like Miruka said, you never know what's going to come next.

2.2 SOME MENTAL ARITHMETIC

I had just finished eating lunch and was pulling out the girl's letter when Miruka plopped down next to me, nibbling on a candy bar.

"Pop quiz," she announced. "1024. How many divisors?"

"I gotta do it in my head?" I asked, cramming the letter back into my pocket.

"Yep, and before I count to ten. 1, 2, 3—"

I scrambled to think of numbers that would evenly divide 1024. Definitely 1 and 2, but not 3—that would leave a remainder. I was checking 4 when it struck me that 1024 is 2^{10}. I did a quick calculation.

"—9, 10. Time's up. How many?"

"Eleven. 1024 has eleven divisors."

"Correct. How did you figure it out?" Miruka occupied herself by licking chocolate off her fingers while awaiting my answer.

"From the prime factorization of 1024, which gives you two to the tenth power," I said. "If you write it out, you get this:"

$$1024 = 2^{10} = \underbrace{2 \times 2 \times 2 \times 2 \times 2 \times 2 \times 2 \times 2 \times 2 \times 2}_{\text{ten twos}}$$

"A divisor of 1024 has to divide it evenly," I continued. "That means it has to be in the form 2^n, where n is some number from 0 to 10. So a divisor of 1024 will be one of these numbers."

Miruka nodded. "Very good. Okay, next problem. If you added up all the divisors of 1024, what would the sum—"

"Sorry," I said, abruptly standing, "but there's something I have to do before class. I'll see you later." I turned away from an obviously disgruntled Miruka and left the room.

I was already thinking of ways to find the sum of the divisors of 1024 as I headed for the roof.

2.3 THE LETTER

It was gloomy out. The usual lunchtime roof crowd was thin.

I took the envelope from my pocket and removed the letter. It was written on a sheet of white stationery in fountain pen with attractive handwriting.

Hello.

My name is Tetra. We went to the same junior high. I'm one year behind you. I'm writing to ask you for some advice about studying math.

I've been having problems with math for years. I heard that the classes get a lot harder in high school, and I'm looking for some way to get over my "math anxiety."

I know it's a lot to ask, but do you think you could spare the time to talk? I'll be in the lecture hall after school.

—Tetra

Tetra? As in mono-, di-, tri-?

I was surprised to hear that we had gone to the same middle school—I didn't remember her at all. That she was having problems with math was less surprising; lots of students did, first-year students especially.

I suppose this qualified as a bona fide letter. But somehow, it wasn't as exciting as I'd hoped my first letter from a girl would be.

I read it four times.

2.4 Ambush

Classes had finished, and I was heading to the lecture hall when Miruka ambushed me, appearing out of nowhere.

"What would the sum be?" she asked.

"2047," I answered without missing a beat.

She frowned. "I gave you too much time to think about it."

"I guess. Look, I'm—"

"Headed to the library?" Her eyes flashed.

"Not today. I have to be somewhere."

"Oh, yeah? I'll give you some homework, then."

She jotted something down on a piece of paper.

Miruka's homework

Describe a method for summing the divisors of a given positive integer n.

"You want me to give you a formula in terms of n?" I asked.

"Don't strain yourself. Just the steps of a method will do."

2.5 TETRA

The lecture hall was separate from the main school building, a short walk across the school courtyard. The room was tiered, with the podium at the bottom level so students could watch a lecturer perform experiments—ideal for physics and chemistry classes.

I found Tetra standing at the back with a nervous look on her face, a notebook and pencil case clutched tightly to her chest.

"Oh, you came. Thank you so much," she said. "Um, so, I wanted to ask you some questions, but I wasn't sure how, so I asked a friend, and she said that maybe this would be a good place to, uh, meet."

Tetra and I sat down on a bench in the very back of the hall. I took the letter she had given me that morning out of my pocket.

"I read your letter, but I have to be honest. I don't remember you from junior high."

"No, of course you don't. I wouldn't expect you to."

"So how do you know about me? I didn't exactly stand out back then." It's hard to stand out when you spend all your free time in the library.

"Actually...you were kinda famous."

"If you say so..." I held up her letter. "So, about this. You said you were having trouble with math?"

"That's right. See, back in elementary school, I liked math just fine. Doing the problems, working through things—all good. But when I got to middle school, everything changed. I felt like I wasn't really getting a lot of what I was doing, you know? My math teacher told me it would only get harder in high school, so I'd need to work at it if I wanted to keep up. And I have been. But I want to do more than regurgitate what's in the books. I want to understand."

"You're worried about your grades?"

Tetra pressed her thumbnail against her lip. "No, it's not that." Her eyes darted about beneath her bangs. She reminded me of a small, nervous animal—a kitten, maybe, or a squirrel. "When I know what's going to be on a test, I'm fine. But when they start getting creative, I do worse. A lot worse."

"You follow what your teachers go over in class?"

"More or less."

"And you can do the homework?"

"Mostly. But something's not sinking in."

"All right," I nodded. "Time to understand."

2.5.1   Defining Prime Numbers

"Let's try some specifics," I began. "Do you know what a prime number is?"

"I think so," she said.

"Prove it. Give me a definition."

"Well, 5 and 7 are prime numbers..."

"Sure, but those are just examples. I want the definition."

"A prime number is, uh, a number that can only be divided by 1 and itself, right? One of my teachers made me memorize that."

"Okay. If we write that down, we get this:"

> A positive integer p is a prime number if it can
> be evenly divided only by 1 and p.

I showed my notebook to Tetra. "So this is your definition?"

"Yeah, that looks right."

"Close, but not quite."

"But 5 is a prime number, and it can only be divided evenly by 1 and 5."

"It works for 5. But if p was 1, according to this definition 1 would be a prime number too, since it would only be divisible by 1 and p. But the list of primes starts with 2, like this:"

$$2, 3, 5, 7, 11, 13, 17, 19, \cdots$$

"Oh right, 1 isn't a prime," Tetra replied. "I remember learning that now."

"So your definition isn't perfect, but there are a few ways to fix it. You might add a qualifier at the end, like this:"

> A positive integer p is a prime number if it can be evenly divided only by 1 and p. <u>However, 1 is not a prime</u>.

"An even better way would be to put the qualifier up front:"

> An integer p <u>that is greater than 1</u> is a prime number if it can be evenly divided only by 1 and p.

"You could also give the condition as a mathematical expression:"

> An integer $p > 1$ is a prime number if it can be evenly divided only by 1 and p.

"Those definitions make sense," Tetra looked up from my notebook. "And I know that 1 isn't a prime, but I don't get it. I mean, who says 1 can't be a prime? What difference does it make? There has to be a reason."

"A reason?" I raised an eyebrow.

"Yeah, isn't there some kind of theory or something behind all this?"

This was interesting—I didn't meet a lot of people who understood the importance of being convinced.

"That was a stupid question, wasn't it." Tetra said.

"No. No, it's a great question. The primes don't include 1 because of the uniqueness of prime factorizations."

"The uniqueness of what? You lost me."

"It's a property of numbers that says that a positive integer n will only have one prime factorization. So for 24, the only prime factorization is $2 \times 2 \times 2 \times 3$. You could write it $2 \times 2 \times 3 \times 2$ or $3 \times 2 \times 2 \times 2$ if you wanted, but they're all considered the same, because the only difference is in the order of the factors. In fact, it's so important to keep prime factorizations unique that 1 isn't included in the primes, just to protect this uniqueness."

Now it was Tetra's turn to raise an eyebrow. "You mean you can define something one way just to keep it from breaking something else?"

"Kind of a harsh way of putting it, but yeah." I tapped my pencil on the notebook. "It's more like this: Mathematicians are always on the lookout for useful concepts to help build the world of mathematics. When they find something really good, they give it a name. That's what a definition is. So you *could* define the primes to include 1 if you wanted to. But there's a difference between a *possible* definition and a *useful* one. Using your definition of primes that included 1 would mean you couldn't use the uniqueness of prime factorizations, so it wouldn't be very useful. That making sense now? The uniqueness, I mean."

"I think so."

"You think so, huh? Look, it's up to you to make sure you understand something."

"If I don't know if I understand, how can I make sure?"

"With examples. An example isn't a definition, but coming up with a good example is a great way to test one out." I wrote out a problem in my notebook and handed it to Tetra:

> Give an example showing that including 1 as a prime number would invalidate the uniqueness of prime factorizations.

"Okay," Tetra replied. "If 1 was prime, then you could factorize 24 in lots of ways. Like this:"

$$2 \times 2 \times 2 \times 3$$
$$1 \times 2 \times 2 \times 2 \times 3$$
$$1 \times 1 \times 2 \times 2 \times 2 \times 3$$
$$\vdots$$

"Perfect example," I said. "See? Examples are the key to understanding." A look of relief washed over Tetra's face. "However," I continued, "instead of saying 'lots,' it would be better to say 'multiple,' or 'at least two.' Saying it that way is more..."

"Precise." Tetra finished.

"Exactly. 'Lots' isn't very precise, because there's no way to know how many it takes to become 'lots.'"

"All these words—definition, example, prime factorization, uniqueness. You don't know how much this helps. I didn't realize how important language was in math."

"That's a great point. Language is *extremely* important in mathematics. Math uses language in a very precise way to make sure there's no confusion. And equations are the most precise language of all."

"Equations are a language?"

"Not just any language. The language of *mathematics*—and your next lesson." I glanced around the lecture hall. "It'll be easier if I use the blackboard. C'mon."

I headed down the stairs at the center of the lecture hall. I had only taken a few steps when I heard a yelp, and Tetra came crashing into me, nearly sending both of us sprawling.

"Sorry!" Tetra said. "I tripped. On the step. Sorry!"

"It's cool," I said.

This is going to be more work than I thought.

2.5.2 Defining Absolute Values

We reached the blackboard without further incident, and I picked up a piece of chalk before turning to Tetra. "Do you know what absolute values are?"

"Yeah, I think so. The absolute value of 5 is 5, and the absolute value of −5 is 5 too. You just take away any negatives, right?"

"Well, sort of. Let's try a definition. Tell me if this looks good to you." I wrote on the board.

Definition of $|x|$, the absolute value of x:

$$|x| = \begin{cases} x & \text{if } x \geqslant 0 \\ -x & \text{if } x < 0 \end{cases}$$

"I remember having trouble with this. If getting the absolute value of x means taking away the minuses, why does a minus show up in the definition?"

"Well, 'taking away the minuses' is kinda vague in a mathematical sense. Not that I don't know what you mean. You're on the right track."

"Would it be better to say change minuses to pluses?"

"No, that's still pretty vague. Let's say we want the absolute value of $-x$:"

$$|-x|$$

"Well," Tetra said, "wouldn't you take the minus away, leaving x?"

$$|-x| = x$$

"Not quite. What if $x = -3$? How would you calculate that?"
Tetra picked up her own piece of chalk. "Let's see..."

$$
\begin{aligned}
|-x| &= |-(-3)| & &\text{because } x = -3 \\
&= |3| & &\text{because } -(-3) = 3 \\
&= 3 & &\text{because } |3| = 3
\end{aligned}
$$

"Right," I said. "If you use your definition, $|-x| = x$, then when $x = -3$ you would have to say that $|-x| = -3$. But in this case $|-x| = 3$. Or put another way, $|-x| = -x$."

Tetra stared at the board. "I see. Since there's no sign in front of the x, I never thought of x being a negative number like -3. But that's the whole point of using a letter like x, isn't it—it lets you define something without giving all sorts of specific examples."

"That's right," I said. "Just saying 'take off the minuses' isn't good enough. You have to be strict with yourself—you have to think about all the possibilities. No cutting corners."

Tetra nodded slowly. "Guess I'm gonna have to get used to that." She slumped into a chair and started fiddling with the corner of her notebook. "I was just wasting time in junior high," she said.

I waited quietly for her to continue.

"Not that I didn't study. But I wasn't looking at the definitions and equations the right way. I wasn't strict enough. I was too... sloppy." Tetra let out a long sigh.

"That's in the past," I said.

"Huh?"

"Just do things right from here on out."

She sat up, eyes wide.

"You're right. I can't change the past, but I can change myself."

I smiled. "Glad I could help with the breakthrough, but we should probably call it a day. It's getting dark out. We'll pick this up next time."

"Next time?"

"I'm usually in the library after school. If you have any more questions, you know where to find me."

2.6 BENEATH AN UMBRELLA

Outside the lecture hall, Tetra stopped and looked up at the sky. Clouds hung low and grey, and it had started to rain.

"Figures," she grumbled.

"No umbrella?" I asked.

"I was running late this morning. Guess I forgot it. I even watched the weather and everything!" She shrugged. "Well, it's not raining hard. I'll be okay if I run."

"You'll be soaked by the time you get to the train station. C'mon, we're going the same way. My umbrella's big enough for both of us."

She smiled. "Thanks!"

I'd never shared an umbrella with a girl before. It was a bit awkward at first, but I matched her pace and managed to keep from tripping or jabbing her with an elbow. We walked slowly through the soft spring shower. The road was quiet, the bustle of the town lost in the rain.

It was cool to have someone younger who looked up to me, and I found myself surprised by just how much I had enjoyed talking with her. She was so easy to read—when she understood something, and when she didn't.

"So how'd you know?" she asked.

"Know what?"

"How'd you know what was giving me trouble?"

"Oh, that. Well, a lot of the stuff we talked about today—prime numbers, absolute values, all that—that's stuff I wondered about too, back in the day. When I'm studying math and I don't understand something, it bugs me. I'll think about it for weeks, I'll read about it, and then suddenly I'll just *get it*. And the feeling when it happens... After you've felt that a few times you can't help but like math. And then you start getting better at it, and—oh, we should turn here."

"That's not the way to the station."

"It's a lot quicker if you cut through this neighborhood."

"Oh..."

"Yeah, it's a great shortcut."

Tetra slowed her pace to a crawl and I found myself having a hard time matching her speed the rest of the way.

The rain was still falling when we reached the station.

"I think I'm gonna hit the book store," I said. "Guess I'll see you tomorrow." I started to leave. "Oh, here," I offered her my umbrella. "Why don't you take this."

"You're going? Oh. Okay, well...thanks for all the help. It really means a lot to me." She bowed deeply.

I nodded and darted for the bookstore.

Tetra called after me. "And thanks for the umbrella!"

2.7 BURNING THE MIDNIGHT OIL

That night I sat in my room, recalling my conversation with Tetra. She had been so sincere, so enthusiastic. She definitely had potential. I hoped that she would learn to enjoy math.

When I talked to Tetra, I slipped into teacher mode. Talking with Miruka was a very different thing. With Miruka, I had to scramble to keep up. If anything, she was the one teaching me. I remembered the homework she had given me; without a doubt the first time I'd gotten homework from another student.

Miruka's homework

Describe a method for summing the divisors of a given positive integer n.

I knew that I could always solve the problem by finding all the divisors of n and adding them together, but that felt like a cheat. I wondered if I couldn't find a better way, and the prime factorization of n looked like a good place to start.

I thought back on the problem we worked on at lunch, for $1024 = 2^{10}$. Maybe there was some way to generalize this, like writing n as a power of a prime:

$$n = p^m \quad \text{for prime number p, positive integer m}$$

If $n = 1024$, then for this equation I'd have $p = 2$ and $m = 10$. If I wanted to list all the divisors of n like I did for 1024, then it would be something like this:

$$1, p, p^2, p^3, \cdots, p^m$$

So for $n = p^m$, I could find the sum of the divisors by adding them up:

$$(\text{sum of divisors of } n) = 1 + p + p^2 + p^3 + \cdots + p^m$$

That would be the answer for a positive integer n that could be written in the form $n = p^m$, at least. I pushed on to see if I couldn't generalize it for other numbers too. It shouldn't be too hard; all I needed to do was generalize prime factor decomposition.

One way to write the prime factor decomposition for a positive integer n would be to take $p, q, r, \cdots$ as primes and $a, b, c, \cdots$ as positive integers and write it like this:

$$n = p^a \times q^b \times r^c \times \cdots \times \text{whoa!}$$

Hang on. This won't work using just letters. If I went through $a, b, c, \cdots$ they'd eventually run into $p, q, r, \cdots$ and that would really confuse things.

I wanted to write an expression that looked something like $2^3 \times 3^1 \times 7^4 \times \cdots \times 13^3$, the product of a bunch of terms in the form $\text{prime}^{\text{integer}}$. So I could write the primes as $p_0, p_1, p_2, \cdots, p_m$ and the exponents as $a_0, a_1, a_2, \cdots, a_m$. Adding all of those subscripts might make things look a bit more complicated, but at least it would let me generalize. It would also let me use $m+1$ to mean the number of prime factors in the prime factor decomposition of n. I started rewriting.

Now given a positive integer n, I could generalize its prime factor decomposition:

$$n = p_0^{a_0} \times p_1^{a_1} \times p_2^{a_2} \times \cdots \times p_m^{a_m},$$

where $p_0, p_1, p_2, \cdots, p_m$ are primes and $a_0, a_1, a_2, \cdots, a_m$ are positive integers. When n was in this form, then a divisor of n would look like this:

$$p_0^{b_0} \times p_1^{b_1} \times p_2^{b_2} \times \cdots \times p_m^{b_m},$$

where $b_0, b_1, b_2, \cdots, b_m$ was an integer:

$$b_0 = \text{one of } 0, 1, 2, 3, \cdots, a_0$$
$$b_1 = \text{one of } 0, 1, 2, 3, \cdots, a_1$$
$$b_2 = \text{one of } 0, 1, 2, 3, \cdots, a_2$$
$$\vdots$$
$$b_m = \text{one of } 0, 1, 2, 3, \cdots, a_m$$

I looked back at what I had written, surprised at how messy it was to write it out precisely. All I wanted to say was that, to write a divisor, you just leave the prime factors as they are, and move through the exponents $0, 1, 2, \cdots$ for each one. But generalizing this took an alphabet soup's worth of symbols.

With things generalized to this extent, I figured the rest would be easy. To find the sum of the divisors I just had to add all of these up.

$$\begin{aligned}
(\text{sum of divisors of } n) = {} & 1 + p_0 + p_0^2 + p_0^3 + \cdots + p_0^{a_0} \\
& + 1 + p_1 + p_1^2 + p_1^3 + \cdots + p_1^{a_1} \\
& + 1 + p_2 + p_2^2 + p_2^3 + \cdots + p_2^{a_2} \\
& + \cdots \\
& + 1 + p_m + p_m^2 + p_m^3 + \cdots + p_m^{a_m}
\end{aligned}$$

I paused, realizing that what I had written was wrong. This wasn't the sum of all the divisors, it was the sum of just those divisors that

can be described as a power of a prime factor. I had said the form of
a divisor was this:

$$p_0^{b_0} \times p_1^{b_1} \times p_2^{b_2} \times \cdots \times p_m^{b_m}$$

So I had to find all the combinations of powers of prime factors,
multiply those together, and add them up. I found this easier to
write as an equation than to put into words, so that's what I did.

My answer to Miruka's homework

Write the prime factorization of the positive integer n
as follows:

$$n = p_0^{a_0} \times p_1^{a_1} \times p_2^{a_2} \times \cdots \times p_m^{a_m},$$

where $p_0, p_1, p_2, \cdots, p_m$ are prime numbers and
$a_0, a_1, a_2, \cdots, a_m$ are positive integers. Then the sum
of the divisors of n is as follows:

$$
\begin{aligned}
\text{(sum of divisors of } n) = {} & (1 + p_0 + p_0^2 + p_0^3 + \cdots + p_0^{a_0}) \\
& \times (1 + p_1 + p_1^2 + p_1^3 + \cdots + p_1^{a_1}) \\
& \times (1 + p_2 + p_2^2 + p_2^3 + \cdots + p_2^{a_2}) \\
& \times \cdots \\
& \times (1 + p_m + p_m^2 + p_m^3 + \cdots + p_m^{a_m})
\end{aligned}
$$

I went to bed wondering if there wasn't a cleaner way to write
this... and whether I was even right at all.

2.8   Miruka's Answer

"Well, it's right," Miruka said the next day, "but it's kind of a mess."

Blunt as ever, I thought, but what I said was, "Is there some
way to make it simpler?"

"Yes," she immediately replied. "First, you can use this for the long sums." Miruka started writing in my notebook as she talked. "Assuming that $1 - x \neq 0$..."

$$1 + x + x^2 + x^3 + \cdots + x^n = \frac{1 - x^{n+1}}{1 - x}$$

"Oh, of course. The formula for the sum of a geometric progression."

Miruka jotted down the proof. *Show off*.

$$1 - x^{n+1} = 1 - x^{n+1} \quad \text{equal sides}$$

$$(1-x)(1 + x + x^2 + x^3 + \cdots + x^n) = 1 - x^{n+1} \quad \text{factor left side}$$

$$1 + x + x^2 + x^3 + \cdots + x^n = \frac{1 - x^{n+1}}{1 - x} \quad \text{divide by } 1 - x$$

"You can use that to turn all your sums of powers into fractions," she continued. "You should also use Π to tidy up the multiplication." She wrote the symbol large on the page.

"That's a capital π, right?"

"Right. This one doesn't have anything to do with circles, though. Π works like Σ does, but for multiplication. Σ is a capital Greek 'S' for 'sum,' and Π is a capital Greek 'P' for 'product.' If you wanted to write out a definition for it..."

Definition of the Sigma operator

$$\sum_{k=0}^{m} f(k) = f(0) + f(1) + f(2) + f(3) + \cdots + f(m)$$

Definition of the Pi operator

$$\prod_{k=0}^{m} f(k) = f(0) \times f(1) \times f(2) \times f(3) \times \cdots \times f(m)$$

"Now, check out how much cleaner things are when you use $\prod$."

> **Miruka's answer**
>
> Write the prime factorization of the positive integer n as follows:
>
> $$n = \prod_{k=0}^{m} p_k^{a_k},$$
>
> where p_k is a prime number and a_k is a positive integer. Then the sum of the divisors of n is as follows:
>
> $$(\text{sum of divisors of } n) = \prod_{k=0}^{m} \frac{1 - p_k^{a_k+1}}{1 - p_k}.$$

"Okay," I said. "Lots of letters in there, but it is shorter. By the way, you going to the library today?"

"Nope." Miruka shook her head. "I'm off to practice with Ay-Ay. She says she has a new piece ready."

2.9 MATH BY THE LETTERS

I was working on some equations when Tetra came up to me with a smile and an open notebook.

"Look what I did! I copied all the definitions out of my math book from last year, and made my own example for every one!"

"All in one night? That's dedication."

"Oh no, I love doing stuff like this. And I thought of something when I was going through my old textbook. Maybe the difference between simple and advanced math is that, in advanced math, you use letters in the equations."

2.9.1 Equations and Identities

I nodded. "Right, and since you brought up using letters in equations, let's talk a little bit about equations and identities. You've seen equations like this: "

$$x - 1 = 0$$

"Sure. $x = 1$."

"How about this one?"

$$2(x - 1) = 2x - 2$$

She frowned. "I think I can solve that if I clean it up a little: "

$$
\begin{array}{ll}
2(x - 1) = 2x - 2 & \text{the problem} \\
2x - 2 = 2x - 2 & \text{expand the left side} \\
2x - 2x - 2 + 2 = 0 & \text{move the right side terms to the left} \\
0 = 0 & \text{simplify the left side}
\end{array}
$$

"Huh? I ended up with $0 = 0$."

"That's right, because $2(x - 1) = 2x - 2$ isn't an equation, it's an identity. See how when you expanded the $2(x - 1)$ on the left side, you got $2x - 2$ on the other? They're *identical*, right? To be precise, this is an identity in x. That means that no matter what x is, the statement will be true."

"So identities are different from equations?"

"Uh huh. An equation is a statement that's true when you replace the xs with a *certain* number. An identity is a statement that's true when you replace the xs with *any* number. When you're doing a problem that deals with an equation, you're probably trying to find the value of x that makes the statement true. When you're doing a problem that deals with an identity, you're probably trying to show that any value of x will work. Do that, and you've proven the identity."

"I get it. I guess I've always known about identities, I just never thought of them as being so different."

"Most people don't. But you use them all the time. Almost all the formulas you learn outside of math are actually identities."

"How can you tell the difference?"

"You have to look at the context and ask yourself what the person who wrote it intended it to be."

"I'm not sure I follow."

"Well, for example, if you want to change the form of a statement, you use identities. Here, look at this:"

$$(x + 1)(x - 1) = (x + 1) \cdot x - (x + 1) \cdot 1$$
$$= x \cdot x + 1 \cdot x - (x + 1) \cdot 1$$
$$= x \cdot x + 1 \cdot x - x \cdot 1 - 1 \cdot 1$$
$$= x^2 + x - x - 1$$
$$= x^2 - 1$$

"See the equals signs in each line? They're forming a chain of identities. You can follow the chain, checking everything out step by step, until you end up with this:"

$$(x + 1)(x - 1) = x^2 - 1$$

"Okay."

"Chains of identities like this give you a slow-motion replay of how a statement transforms from one thing into another. Don't freak out because there's a bunch of statements. Just follow them along, one at a time. Now take a look at this:"

$$x^2 - 5x + 6 = (x - 2)(x - 3)$$
$$= 0$$

"The first equals sign there is creating an identity. It's telling you that no matter what you stick into this x here, $x^2 - 5x + 6 = (x - 2)(x - 3)$. But that second equals sign is creating an equation. It's saying you don't have to solve $x^2 - 5x + 6 = 0$ for x, you can just solve its identity, $(x - 2)(x - 3) = 0$, instead."

"Not bad for two lines."

I nodded. "There's one more kind of equality besides equations and identities that you should know about: definitions. When you have a really complex statement, definitions let you name part of it to simplify things. You use an equals sign for this, but it doesn't mean you have to solve for anything, like with an equation, or prove anything, like with an identity. You just use them in whatever way's convenient."

"Can you give me an example?"

"Well, say you're adding together two numbers, alpha and beta. You could name them—in other words define them as—'s' like this:"

$$s = \alpha + \beta \quad \text{an example definition}$$

Tetra's hand shot up. "Question!"

"This isn't class, Tetra. You don't have to raise your hand."

She lowered her hand. "But I'm confused. Why did you name it 's'?"

"It doesn't really matter what you name it. You can use s, t, whatever you want. Then once you've said, okay, from now on $s = \alpha + \beta$, you can just write s instead of having to write $\alpha + \beta$ every time. Learn to define things, and you'll be able to write math that's easier to read *and* understand."

"So what are α and β then?"

"Well, they could be letters that you defined somewhere else. When you define something like $s = \alpha + \beta$, that usually means you're using the letter on the left side of the equals sign to name the expression on the right. So here, you'd be using s as the name of something that you made out of α and β."

"And you can name them anything you want, right?"

"Basically, yeah. Except that you shouldn't use a name that you've already used to define something else. Like, if you defined $s = \alpha + \beta$ in one place, and then turned around and redefined it as $s = \alpha\beta$, you'd start to lose your audience."

"Yeah, I can see that."

"There are also some generally accepted definitions, like using π to mean the ratio of the circumference of a circle to its diameter, or i to represent the imaginary unit, so it would be kind of weird to use those names for something else. Anyway, if you're reading through a math problem and you see a new letter popping up, don't panic, just think to yourself, 'oh, this must be a definition.' If you're reading math and it says something like 'define s as $\alpha + \beta$' or 'let s be $\alpha + \beta$' you're looking at a definition."

"Got it."

I put down my pencil. "Here's an idea. Next time you're going through your book, try looking for mathematical statements with letters in them and asking yourself if they're equations, identities, definitions, or something else altogether."

Tetra nodded enthusiastically.

"You know," I told her, "every mathematical statement you find in your textbook was written to express a thought. Just remember," I said, pausing for effect, "there's always somebody behind the math, sending us a message."

2.9.2 The Forms of Sums and Products

"Oh, one more important thing," I told her. "You should always pay attention to the overall form of a mathematical expression."

"What's that mean?"

"Take a look at this statement, for example. An equation, right?"

$$(x - \alpha)(x - \beta) = 0$$

"The expression on the left side of the equals sign is telling you to multiply. In other words, it's in multiplicative form. The things that are being multiplied together are called factors."

$$\underbrace{(x - \alpha)}_{\text{factor}} \underbrace{(x - \beta)}_{\text{factor}} = 0$$

"The same 'factor' in prime factorization?" Tetra asked.

"Sure. Factorizing something means breaking it down into a multiplicative form. Prime factorization means breaking it down into a multiplicative form where all the factors are prime numbers. Oh, and most people leave out the multiplication sign when multiplying things. So all of these are the same equation, just written different ways:"

$$(x - \alpha) \times (x - \beta) = 0 \qquad \text{using a} \times \text{sign}$$
$$(x - \alpha) \cdot (x - \beta) = 0 \qquad \text{using a} \cdot \text{sign}$$
$$(x - \alpha)(x - \beta) = 0 \qquad \text{using nothing}$$

"Okay," she said.

"Now," I added, "for $(x - \alpha)(x - \beta) = 0$ we know that at least one of the two factors has to equal zero. We can say that because it's in multiplicative form."

"So...if we multiply two things together and the result is zero, one of the factors has to be zero. That makes sense."

"Well, it's better to say that *at least* one of them has to be zero. Because they both might be, right?"

"Okay, *at least* one of them. This is that precise mathematical language thing we talked about yesterday, isn't it."

"Right. So anyway, since we know that at least one of the factors is zero, do you see how this equation is true when $x - \alpha = 0$ or $x - \beta = 0$? Another way to say this is that $x = \alpha, \beta$ is a solution to this multiplicative form equation."

"I follow."

"Okay. So let's see what happens when we expand $(x-\alpha)(x-\beta)$: "

$$(x - \alpha)(x - \beta) = x^2 - \alpha x - \beta x + \alpha\beta$$

"By the way," I asked her, "do you think this is an equation?"

"Nope!" Tetra replied quickly. "It's an identity!"

"Not bad. Okay, 'expanding something' means changing products into sums. On the left side there are two factors being *multiplied* together, and on the right side there are four terms being *added* together."

"Sorry, terms?"

"Yeah, when you add things together, you call them terms. Here, let me show you a diagram with everything labeled: "

$$\underbrace{(x - \alpha)}_{\text{factor}} \underbrace{(x - \beta)}_{\text{factor}} \quad \xrightarrow{\text{expand}} \quad = \quad \underbrace{(x^2)}_{\text{term}} + \underbrace{(-\alpha x)}_{\text{term}} + \underbrace{(-\beta x)}_{\text{term}} + \underbrace{(\alpha\beta)}_{\text{term}}$$

$$\xleftarrow{\text{factorize}}$$

"We can still do some cleanup on this expression," I continued. "It's a bit of a mess as it is: "

$$x^2 - \alpha x - \beta x + \alpha\beta$$

"Well," Tetra said, "we could take the things that have an x in them, like $-\alpha x$ and $-\beta x$..."

"Try to call them 'terms,' not 'things,' okay?" I said. "Also, terms like $-\alpha x$ and $-\beta x$ that only have one x should be called 'first degree terms of x,' or simply 'first degree terms.'"

"Okay..." Tetra scratched her head. "How 'bout we bring together the first degree terms of x. Like this:"

$$x^2 + \underbrace{(-\alpha - \beta)x}_{\text{first degree terms}} + \alpha\beta$$

"Exactly. That's a good explanation of what to do with terms, but normally you would go one more step and bring the minus sign to the outside of the parentheses:"

$$x^2 - (\alpha + \beta)x + \alpha\beta$$

"You've probably heard of that as 'combining like terms.'"
She frowned. "Heard of it, yes. Thought about it, no."
"A quick quiz, then. Is this an identity or an equality?"

$$(x - \alpha)(x - \beta) = x^2 - (\alpha + \beta)x + \alpha\beta$$

"All we've done is expand and combine like terms, right? So this should be true for any value of x... which makes it an identity!"

"Very good! Moving on, then. We started out talking about this equation, which is in multiplicative form:"

$$(x - \alpha)(x - \beta) = 0 \qquad \text{equation in multiplicative form}$$

"Using the identity that we just created, we can rewrite the equation. This is called an equation in additive form:"

$$x^2 - (\alpha + \beta)x + \alpha\beta = 0 \qquad \text{equation in additive form}$$

"These equations are in different forms, but they're the same equation. All we've done is use an identity to change the form of the left side."
"Got it."
"When we looked at the multiplicative form, we said that the solution to the equation was $x = \alpha, \beta$. That means the solution to

the equation in additive form must also be $x = \alpha, \beta$. After all, they're the same equation."

$$(x - \alpha)(x - \beta) = 0 \qquad \text{equation in multiplicative form}$$
$$\updownarrow \qquad \text{same equations, same solutions}$$
$$x^2 - (\alpha + \beta)x + \alpha\beta = 0 \qquad \text{equation in additive form}$$

"You can use this to solve some simple second degree equations just by looking at them. Here, take a look at these two. Pretty similar, aren't they?"

$$x^2 - (\alpha + \beta)x + \alpha\beta = 0 \qquad \text{(solution: } x = \alpha, \beta)$$
$$x^2 - 5x + 6 = 0$$

"Well..." She paused for a moment. "Oh, I see! You can just think of the 5 as being $\alpha + \beta$, and the 6 as $\alpha\beta$."

"Exactly. So to solve $x^2 - 5x + 6 = 0$, all you have to do is think of two numbers that equal 5 when you add them, or 6 when you multiply them. That would be $x = 2, 3$, right?"

"Makes sense."

"Mathematical expressions come in all sorts of forms. Multiplicative and additive are just two of the possibilities. Remember that solving equations like $\langle$ additive form $\rangle = 0$ can be tough, but problems like $\langle$ multiplicative form $\rangle = 0$ are super simple."

"Huh, it's like putting equations in multiplicative form is a way of solving them, isn't it," Tetra said. "You know, I think I'm getting the hang of this."

2.10 Who's Behind the Math?

"I wish my teachers taught me as well as you do," Tetra said.

I grinned. "It's a lot easier one-on-one. If I lose you, you can slow me down and ask questions. You could always try that in class sometimes."

Tetra pondered that for a moment. "What if I'm studying something and there's no one around to ask?" she asked.

"If I don't get something after a careful reading, I mark the page and move on. After a while, I'll come back to that page and read it one more time. If I still don't get it, I move on again. Sometimes I'll switch to a different book—but I keep going back to the part I didn't understand. Once, I came across an expansion of an equation that I just couldn't follow. After agonizing over it for four days, I decided there was no way it could be right, so I contacted the publisher. Turns out it was a misprint."

"Nice catch!" Tetra shook her head. "Guess it pays to keep at it."

"Well, math takes time. I mean, there's so much history to it. When you're reading math, you're trying to relive the work of countless mathematicians. Trace through the development of a formula, and you might be following *centuries* of work. With depth like that, it's not enough just to read. You have to become a mathematician yourself."

"Sounds like a tall order."

"Well, it's not like you have to get a PhD, but when you're reading math, you do have to make an effort to get into it. Don't just read it, write it out. That's the only way to be sure you really understand."

Tetra gave a slight nod. "It kind of got to me, what you said about equations being a language, and that there's somebody on the other side of the equation trying to send a message." She looked off into the distance, her words coming faster. "Maybe it's only my teacher, or the author of the textbook, but I can imagine it being a mathematician from hundreds of years ago too. It kind of makes math *real*, if you know what I mean."

She looked away and smiled. "I think I might love you—" She looked back at me, then her eyes went wide as she realized what she had just said.

I cocked an eyebrow.

"—Teaching me!" She blurted, a few seconds too late.

I looked around nervously.

Tetra's face was burning red. "Math," she whispered. "I love you teaching me math."

CHAPTER 3

Shapes in the Shadows

> The essence of mathematics is its
> freedom.
>
> ———————————
>
> GEORG CANTOR

3.1 ROTATIONS

It was summer, the last day of finals. Miruka made an immediate beeline for me when she found me sitting in the library.

"Rotations?" she asked with a glance at my notebook.

"Yeah."

The lenses in her glasses were tinted blue, inviting my gaze into the cool eyes behind them.

She looked up from the page.

"Why do it the hard way? Just think about how unit vectors on the axes move." *So much for small talk.*

"C'mon, I'm just practicing."

Miruka slid into the chair next to mine and whispered in my ear. "If you really want to have some fun, try rotating by theta twice." Her breath tickled my neck. "Consider how that's equivalent to a *single* rotation by *two* thetas. You should end up with two equalities, identities in terms of theta."

Miruka snatched my pencil away and scribbled two equations in the margin of my notebook, her hand brushing mine as she did:

$$\cos 2\theta = \cos^2 \theta - \sin^2 \theta$$
$$\sin 2\theta = 2 \sin \theta \cos \theta$$

"Tell me what these are," she said. I recognized the formulas almost at once, but couldn't get the words out in time. "Double angle formulas," she announced. Once she was in full-on lecture mode, there was no stopping her.

"You can use this matrix to represent a rotation by an angle θ," she continued:

$$\begin{bmatrix} \cos \theta & -\sin \theta \\ \sin \theta & \cos \theta \end{bmatrix}$$

"Two rotations by θ are equivalent to squaring the matrix:"

$$\begin{bmatrix} \cos \theta & -\sin \theta \\ \sin \theta & \cos \theta \end{bmatrix}^2 = \begin{bmatrix} \cos^2 \theta - \sin^2 \theta & -2 \sin \theta \cos \theta \\ 2 \sin \theta \cos \theta & \cos^2 \theta - \sin^2 \theta \end{bmatrix}$$

"But we can also think of two rotations by θ as a single rotation by 2θ. That means that the squared matrix is the same as this one:"

$$\begin{bmatrix} \cos 2\theta & -\sin 2\theta \\ \sin 2\theta & \cos 2\theta \end{bmatrix}$$

"Look at the elements in the same position in each. Since they're equal, we can write them like this:"

$$\cos 2\theta = \cos^2 \theta - \sin^2 \theta$$
$$\sin 2\theta = 2 \sin \theta \cos \theta$$

"In other words, we've got $\cos 2\theta$ and $\sin 2\theta$ in terms of $\cos \theta$ and $\sin \theta$—the double angle formulas. They come from representing a revolution as a matrix and reinterpreting its meaning."

"A single revolution by two θs, two revolutions by one θ. The equals sign shows that they're the same. What we thought were two things, we now see as one. And then, something wonderful happens. . ."

I was listening to Miruka, but my mind wasn't on the math.

A brilliant girl. A beautiful girl. What were the chances of finding both in one person?

3.2 PROJECTIONS

"Forget about the matrices for now," she said. "Here's a problem for you."

Problem 3-1

Give a general term a_n in terms of n for the following sequence:

n	0	1	2	3	4	5	6	7	$\cdots$
a_n	1	0	-1	0	1	0	-1	0	$\cdots$

"Think you can you do it?" she asked.

"Sure, that's easy. All you're doing is going back and forth between 1, 0, and −1. Sort of. . . oscillating between them."

"That's all you see?"

"Am I wrong?"

"Not wrong, exactly. Go ahead and give me a generalization."

"Like, give you an a_n for any n, right? Sure, all you have to do is break it down into cases:"

$$
a_n = \begin{cases}
1 & \text{for } n = 0, 4, 8, \ldots, 4k, \ldots \\
0 & \text{for } n = 1, 3, 5, 7, \ldots, 2k + 1, \ldots \\
-1 & \text{for } n = 2, 6, 10, \ldots, 4k + 2, \ldots
\end{cases}
$$

"Okay, that's not wrong, too. Doesn't look much like an oscillation, though, does it?" Miruka closed her eyes and traced a circle in the air. "Okay." She opened her eyes. "Generalize this for me."

Problem 3-2

Give a general term b_n in terms of n for the following
sequence:

n	0	1	2	3	4	5	6	7	$\cdots$
b_n	1	i	-1	$-i$	1	i	-1	$-i$	$\cdots$

"By i, you mean $\sqrt{-1}$?" I asked.

"What else would I mean?"

"Yeah, yeah." I took a breath. "Well, let's see. You want b_n to be
$+1$ or -1 when n is even, and $+i$ or $-i$ when n is odd. So another
oscillation?"

"Hmm. You see this sequence as an oscillation, too. Again, not
wrong."

"So how do I get from 'not wrong' to right?"

Miruka's eyes fluttered shut.

"Try thinking in the complex number plane—plot numbers with
their real part on the x-axis, and their imaginary part on the y-axis.
That lets you plot any complex number:"

$$\text{complex number} \quad \longleftrightarrow \quad \text{point}$$
$$x + yi \quad \longleftrightarrow \quad (x, y)$$

I looked at the sequence b_n again, this time as a sequence of
complex numbers. Then 1 would be $1 + 0i$, and i would be $0 + 1i$, so
the sequence would be:

$$1 + 0i, 0 + 1i, -1 + 0i, 0 - 1i, 1 + 0i, 0 + 1i, -1 + 0i, 0 - 1i, \ldots$$

Taking those values as points on the complex plane gave me a
series of points:

$$(1, 0), (0, 1), (-1, 0), (0, -1), (1, 0), (0, 1), (-1, 0), (0, -1), \ldots$$

I tried plotting them.

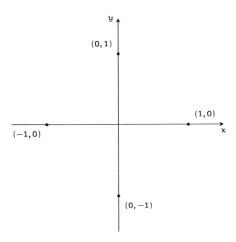

"Oh, cool. It's a diamond. Er, maybe a rotated square," I said, connecting the plotted points with lines.

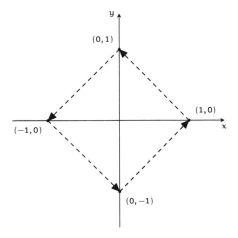

"Straight lines. Interesting. Still just 'not wrong,' though."

"So what am I supposed to see?"

"Try thinking outside the box." She grinned. "Or rotated square, in this case."

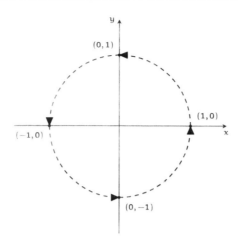

"Of course. A circle."

"Not just any circle. A circle with radius 1, centered at the origin. The unit circle, in the complex plane. So what started as a sequence of complex numbers is now a sequence of points on that circle."

"Okay, I'm with you."

"You know you can write points on the unit circle in complex form like this, right?"

$$\cos\theta + i\sin\theta$$

"Yeah, I see that. And here θ would be, uh, the angle of rotation of a unit vector $(1,0)$?"

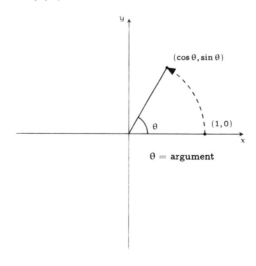

θ = argument

"That's right. When you're working in the complex plane, this θ is called the argument. Here's the correspondence between complex numbers and points:"

$$\text{complex number} \quad \longleftrightarrow \quad \text{point}$$
$$\cos\theta + i\sin\theta \quad \longleftrightarrow \quad (\cos\theta, \sin\theta)$$

"Don't think of the sequence $\{b_n\}$ in the second problem as a square, but as four points on a circle that divide it into even sections." She looked up at me. "So what complex numbers can you use to represent those points?"

"All you have to do is increase θ ninety degrees—well, $\frac{\pi}{2}$ radians—each time, so the arguments are $\theta = 0, \frac{\pi}{2}, \pi, \frac{3\pi}{2}, \cdots$. That means that these four complex numbers give you those points:"

$$\cos 0 \cdot \frac{\pi}{2} + i\sin 0 \cdot \frac{\pi}{2}$$
$$\cos 1 \cdot \frac{\pi}{2} + i\sin 1 \cdot \frac{\pi}{2}$$
$$\cos 2 \cdot \frac{\pi}{2} + i\sin 2 \cdot \frac{\pi}{2}$$
$$\cos 3 \cdot \frac{\pi}{2} + i\sin 3 \cdot \frac{\pi}{2}$$

"Right again. So now we can generalize b_n."

Answer to Problem 3-2

$$b_n = \cos n \cdot \frac{\pi}{2} + i\sin n \cdot \frac{\pi}{2} \qquad (n = 0, 1, 2, 3, \cdots)$$

"Okay, let's go back to $\{a_n\}$ in the first problem," she said. "The one you called an oscillation."

$$\{a_n\} = \{1, 0, -1, 0, 1, 0, -1, 0, \cdots\}$$

"We can deal with this the same way we dealt with b_n."

"Wait, you lost me."

"Think of it graphically, as a projection on the x-axis. That's where you get your oscillation. An oscillation is just a projection of a revolution."

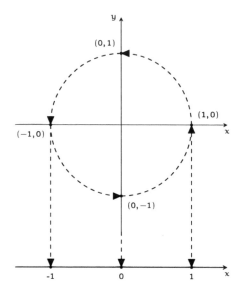

Projection on the real axis

"You can look at $\{a_n\}$ in all kinds of ways—a bunch of integers, an oscillation of points along the real number line, a point revolving in the complex plane. It's only when you realize what you're looking at is just a projection onto one dimension that you discover the two-dimensional circle that was hiding. Once you understand you're just looking at a shadow, you can find the higher dimensional form casting it. Shapes in the shadows."

Not for the first time, I realized Miruka operated on an entirely different level than me.

"So you move from integers to real numbers, from real numbers to complex numbers, on and on to higher dimensions. Seeing something from higher up can make your description simpler, and a simpler description is a sign of deeper understanding. When you look for the next number in a fragment of a sequence, you're just solving a puzzle. When you generalize the sequence, you're uncovering its hidden form. And *that's* when the magic happens."

3.3 THE OMEGA WALTZ

"Next problem," Miruka said.

Problem 3-3

Give a general term c_n in terms of n for the following sequence:

n	0	1	2	3	4	5	$\cdots$
c_n	1	$\frac{-1+\sqrt{3}\,i}{2}$	$\frac{-1-\sqrt{3}\,i}{2}$	1	$\frac{-1+\sqrt{3}\,i}{2}$	$\frac{-1-\sqrt{3}\,i}{2}$	$\cdots$

"I thought the Geneva Convention outlawed torture," I groaned.

"Oh, you've never seen this before?" Miruka's surprise was genuine.

"I guess it would be too easy to say you're repeating the numbers 1, $\frac{-1+\sqrt{3}\,i}{2}$, and $\frac{-1-\sqrt{3}\,i}{2}$ over and over." A weak answer, and I knew it.

"Of course—you haven't solved the mystery! You haven't captured the form! You haven't gotten to the heart of the problem!"

"And that would be...?"

"What these three numbers *are*, of course. But you're not there yet." She tapped the open notebook. "So, you've got a sequence you want to figure out. How do you attack it?"

"By looking at the difference between successive terms." I started writing, creating a new sequence $\{d_n\}$ based on $\{c_n\}$ from the problem:

$$d_n = c_{n+1} - c_n \qquad (n = 0, 1, 2, \cdots)$$

$$c_0 \quad c_1 \quad c_2 \quad c_3 \quad c_4 \quad c_5 \quad \cdots$$
$$d_0 \quad d_1 \quad d_2 \quad d_3 \quad d_4 \quad \cdots$$

I hurried through some calculations to find this:

n	0	1	2	3	4	5	$\cdots$
d_n	$\frac{-3+\sqrt{3}i}{2}$	$-\sqrt{3}i$	$\frac{3+\sqrt{3}i}{2}$	$\frac{-3+\sqrt{3}i}{2}$	$-\sqrt{3}i$	$\frac{3+\sqrt{3}i}{2}$	$\cdots$

Not very promising.

"Well?" Miruka asked. She could be surprisingly patient at times like this. Once the finish line was in sight she moved quickly, but she was always slow and methodical when searching for the path.

I figured an honest answer was the best approach. "I'm not seeing anything."

"Is looking at differences the only tool you have to crack open a sequence?" Miruka smiled.

"Well, if the difference between successive terms doesn't tell me much, then maybe...their ratios?"

"Get to it."

"Yes, ma'am."

So my next attempt, $\{e_n\}$, would have terms $e_n = \frac{c_{n+1}}{c_n}$. I knew that c_n was never 0, so I didn't have to worry about division errors. I calculated the values.

n	0	1	2	3	4	5	$\cdots$
e_n	$\frac{-1+\sqrt{3}i}{2}$	$\frac{-1+\sqrt{3}i}{2}$	$\frac{-1+\sqrt{3}i}{2}$	$\frac{-1+\sqrt{3}i}{2}$	$\frac{-1+\sqrt{3}i}{2}$	$\frac{-1+\sqrt{3}i}{2}$	$\cdots$

"Whoa!" A chill ran down my spine.

"Why 'whoa'?"

"Well, look. Every ratio gives me the same value."

"It does, doesn't it. That's because $\{c_n\}$ is a geometric progression with $c_0 = 1$ as its first term and $\frac{-1+\sqrt{3}i}{2}$ its common ratio. Also, the three numbers 1, $\frac{-1+\sqrt{3}i}{2}$, and $\frac{-1-\sqrt{3}i}{2}$ each equal 1 when you take their cubes. In other words, they're each solutions to the cubic equation $x^3 = 1$."

"Oh, yeah?"

"Oh, yeah. $x^3 = 1$ is a third-degree equation, so it has to have three solutions. Do you know how to find them?"

"I think so. We know that $x = 1$ is a solution, so I should be able to factor an $(x - 1)$ out."

$$x^3 = 1 \quad \text{the given equation}$$

$$x^3 - 1 = 0 \quad \text{move 1 to the left, making the right 0}$$

$$(x - 1)(x^2 + x + 1) = 0 \quad \text{factor } (x - 1) \text{ out of the left side}$$

"Okay, so what's next?" Miruka asked.

"We can find the other solutions from $x^2 + x + 1 = 0$, so now all I have to do is use the quadratic formula $x = \frac{-b + \sqrt{b^2 - 4ac}}{2a}$ to solve for x."

Sure enough I came up with:

$$x = 1, \frac{-1 + \sqrt{3}\,i}{2}, \frac{-1 - \sqrt{3}\,i}{2}$$

Miruka looked at my answer and gave a subtle nod.

"Good," she said. "Now let's define $\frac{-1+\sqrt{3}i}{2}$ as omega:

$$\omega = \frac{-1 + \sqrt{3}\,i}{2}$$

"Then ω^2 is $\frac{-1-\sqrt{3}i}{2}$, like this:"

$$
\begin{aligned}
\omega^2 &= \left(\frac{-1 + \sqrt{3}\,i}{2}\right)^2 \\
&= \frac{(-1 + \sqrt{3}\,i)^2}{2^2} \\
&= \frac{(-1)^2 - 2\sqrt{3}\,i + (\sqrt{3}\,i)^2}{4} \\
&= \frac{1 - 2\sqrt{3}\,i - 3}{4} \\
&= \frac{-2 - 2\sqrt{3}\,i}{4} \\
&= \frac{-1 - \sqrt{3}\,i}{2}
\end{aligned}
$$

"If you keep multiplying 1 by ω, you get a sequence:

$$1, \omega, \omega^2, \omega^3, \omega^4, \omega^5, \cdots$$

"But we know that $\omega^3 = 1$, so you can also write the sequence like this:"

$$1, \omega, \omega^2, 1, \omega, \omega^2, \cdots$$

"And just like that, we're back to $\{c_n\}$. Okay, now plot the three numbers $1, \omega, \omega^2$. C'mon, hurry up!"

Miruka was obviously enjoying herself.

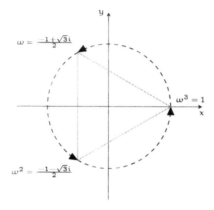

"Huh. An equilateral triangle."

"There you go again. Considering that it's cyclic, I think most people would see a circle here, too," she said. "Circles are a more natural source of repetition. People who can only see real numbers on a number line would probably call it an oscillation, but once you can see it on the complex plane you notice that it's a revolution. More hidden structure!"

Answer to Problem 3-3

$$c_n = \omega^n \qquad (n = 0, 1, 2, 3, \cdots)$$

$$\text{where } \omega = \frac{-1 + \sqrt{3}\,i}{2}.$$

Miruka's cheeks flushed, and she began to talk faster.

"We've watched three points form an equilateral triangle, and four points form a square. But we can go on, and generalize this to n points forming an n-gon. And that brings us to de Moivre's formula."

De Moivre's formula

$$(\cos\theta + i\sin\theta)^n = \cos n\theta + i\sin n\theta$$

"De Moivre's formula says that if you raise the complex number $\cos\theta + i\sin\theta$ to the nth power, you get $\cos n\theta + i\sin n\theta$. If you think of it graphically, it means that if you repeat n rotations of θ radians on a unit circle, it's the same as having rotated by $n\theta$ once. When you peek behind the equation, you see a point rotating around the unit circle."

Miruka traced a circle in the air.

"Let $n = 2$, and de Moivre's formula spits out the double angle formulas," she continued:

$$
\begin{aligned}
(\cos\theta + i\sin\theta)^n &= \cos n\theta + i\sin n\theta && \text{de Moivre's formula} \\
(\cos\theta + i\sin\theta)^2 &= \cos 2\theta + i\sin 2\theta && \text{let } n = 2 \\
\cos^2\theta + i \cdot 2\cos\theta\sin\theta - \sin^2\theta &= \cos 2\theta + i\sin 2\theta && \text{expand the left} \\
(\cos^2\theta - \sin^2\theta) + i \cdot 2\cos\theta\sin\theta &= \cos 2\theta + i\sin 2\theta && \text{rearrange the left}
\end{aligned}
$$

"Now all you have to do is look at how the real and imaginary parts correspond:"

$$
\underbrace{(\cos^2\theta - \sin^2\theta)}_{\text{real}} + i \cdot \underbrace{2\cos\theta\sin\theta}_{\text{imaginary}} = \underbrace{\cos 2\theta}_{\text{real}} + i\underbrace{\sin 2\theta}_{\text{imaginary}}
$$

"Voilà. The double angle formulas:"

$$
\begin{aligned}
\cos^2\theta - \sin^2\theta &= \cos 2\theta && \text{real parts} \\
2\cos\theta\sin\theta &= \sin 2\theta && \text{imaginary parts}
\end{aligned}
$$

"When I walked in you were playing with rotation matrices, right? That's a good start, but there's so much more. You can envision your rotating points as shapes, and as trigonometric functions, and as sequences of complex numbers... So much beauty." She shot me a look. "And you're missing all of it."

I was speechless.

"When you look at $\omega^3 = 1$, can you see how it evenly divides the unit circle into three parts?" she asked. "Can you see the $\frac{2\pi}{3}$ argument? The equilateral triangle that emerges? Can you feel the triple-time rhythm that ω is moving to? Can you see 1 and ω and ω^2, dancing in the complex plane?"

Miruka reached out and touched my hand. "Can you see the omega waltz?"

CHAPTER 4

Generating Functions

> The most powerful way to deal with
> sequences of numbers, as far as anybody
> knows, is to manipulate infinite series
> that generate those sequences.
>
> GRAHAM, KNUTH, AND PATASHNIK
> *Concrete Mathematics*

4.1 IN THE LIBRARY

It was an autumn day after class. Tetra and I were working on some simple expansions in the library. I had just gotten through showing her how $(a + b)(a - b)$ simplified to $a^2 - b^2$:

$$
\begin{aligned}
(a + b)(a - b) &= (a + b)a - (a + b)b \\
&= aa + ba - ab - bb \\
&= a^2 - b^2
\end{aligned}
$$

"All you have to remember," I said, "is that the product of a sum and a difference is a difference of squares."

"Okay." She looked up from the paper. "I can't thank you enough for helping me pull all this random stuff together into something that makes sense."

That was when Miruka showed up, walked to where we were sitting, and kicked Tetra's chair out from under her. The sound of chair and girl crashing to the floor echoed through the library. Now Tetra was on the floor and I was on my feet, unsure what to do.

Tetra picked herself up and gave Miruka a good long glare, then left without saying a word.

Miruka righted the chair as if nothing had happened, sat down, and looked at my notebook. She invited me to sit with a tug at my sleeve.

"You're doing expansions?" she asked.

"I *was*."

"You're a real boy scout." She snagged the pencil out of my hand, and gave it a quick twirl around a finger. "Let's go searching for patterns."

4.1.1 Searching for Patterns

"We'll start with $(1 + x)(1 - x)$," she said. "Think of it as a special case of your $(a + b)(a - b)$:"

$$
\begin{aligned}
(1 + x)(1 - x) &= (1 + x) \cdot 1 - (1 + x) \cdot x \\
&= (1 + x) - (x + x^2) \\
&= 1 + \underbrace{(x - x)}_{\text{cancels}} - x^2 \\
&= 1 - x^2
\end{aligned}
$$

"Now let's replace the $(1 + x)$ in $(1 + x)(1 - x)$ with $(1 + x + x^2)$:"

$$
\begin{aligned}
(1 + x + x^2)(1 - x) &= (1 + x + x^2) \cdot 1 - (1 + x + x^2) \cdot x \\
&= (1 + x + x^2) - (x + x^2 + x^3) \\
&= 1 + \underbrace{(x - x)}_{\text{cancels}} + \underbrace{(x^2 - x^2)}_{\text{cancels}} - x^3 \\
&= 1 - x^3
\end{aligned}
$$

"You see the pattern, right? Only the right and left ends stick around. Everything in the middle gets cancelled out. It's even easier to see if you write it out longhand:"

$$
\begin{array}{rrrr}
1 & +x & +x^2 & +x^3 \\
\times & & 1 & -x \\
\hline
-x & -x^2 & -x^3 & -x^4 \\
1 & +x & +x^2 & +x^3 \\
\hline
1 & & & -x^4
\end{array}
$$

"See how everything in the middle cancels? Now if we generalize this for an integer $n \geqslant 0$, we get something like:"

$$
\begin{aligned}
(1)(1-x) &= 1-x^1 \\
(1+x)(1-x) &= 1-x^2 \\
\left(1+x+x^2\right)(1-x) &= 1-x^3 \\
\left(1+x+x^2+x^3\right)(1-x) &= 1-x^4 \\
\left(1+x+x^2+x^3+x^4\right)(1-x) &= 1-x^5 \\
&\vdots \\
\left(1+x+x^2+x^3+x^4+\cdots+x^n\right)(1-x) &= 1-x^{n+1}
\end{aligned}
$$

"Got it?"

I got it, but I was more interested in what had happened to Tetra than the generalization of a pretty boring expansion. I soon discovered that it took more than disinterest to stop Miruka.

4.1.2 Sums of Geometric Progressions

"Up to now this has been pretty straightforward stuff. But we're just getting started. Here's where we are:"

$$
\left(1+x+x^2+x^3+x^4+\cdots+x^n\right)(1-x) = 1-x^{n+1}
$$

"Now, let's divide both sides by $(1-x)$. We'll assume that $(1-x) \neq 0$ so we don't have to worry about division errors:"

$$
1+x+x^2+x^3+x^4+\cdots+x^n = \frac{1-x^{n+1}}{1-x}
$$

"What we had before looked like a rule for finding products, but now it looks more like a rule for finding sums, doesn't it? And it is—this is the formula for the sum of a geometric progression. To be precise, if you have a geometric progression $\left\{1, x, x^2, x^3, \cdots, x^n, \cdots\right\}$ that starts with 1 and has x as its common ratio, then $\frac{1-x^{n+1}}{1-x}$ gives the sum of the first n terms," Miruka finished. "So, where do we go next?"

"We pull out all the stops." I was along for the ride whether I liked it or not. "We let it run forever."

4.1.3 Infinite Geometric Series

"So let's talk about infinite series," she began. "The series $1 + x + x^2 + x^3 + \cdots$ is defined as the limit of the partial sums, each a geometric progression like this:"

$$1 + x + x^2 + x^3 + \cdots + x^n = \frac{1 - x^{n+1}}{1 - x}$$

"When the absolute value of x is less than 1, then x^{n+1} approaches 0 as n approaches infinity, so we get this:"

$$1 + x + x^2 + x^3 + \cdots = \frac{1}{1 - x}$$

"There's our infinite series. The condition that $|x| < 1$ is important, though. That ensures that x^{n+1} fades away into nothingness. Here, I'll sum it up."

Formula for a geometric series

$$1 + x + x^2 + x^3 + \cdots = \frac{1}{1 - x}$$

for 0th term 1, common ratio x, and $|x| < 1$.

"Isn't that just *cool*? On the left you're adding up an infinite number of terms. An *infinite number*. It seems like it should be impossible. But on the right you've got one little fraction that does the whole job. No muss, no fuss."

Miruka and I were the only ones left in the library. It was already getting dark outside, but Miruka was oblivious.

4.1.4   Creating Generating Functions

"Let's take a look at generating functions," she said. "Just assume the conditions for convergence. We'll start with the same geometric series, but let's think of it as a function of x:"

$$f(x) = 1 + x + x^2 + x^3 + \cdots$$

"Since we're going to talk about the function's coefficients, I'll go ahead and write them out:"

$$f(x) = \underline{1}x^0 + \underline{1}x^1 + \underline{1}x^2 + \underline{1}x^3 + \cdots$$

"If you look at just the coefficients, they form an infinite sequence $\{1, 1, 1, 1, \cdots\}$. So we can make a correspondence like this:"

sequence	$\longleftrightarrow$	function
$\{1, 1, 1, 1, \cdots\}$	$\longleftrightarrow$	$f(x) = 1 + x + x^2 + x^3 + \cdots$

"In other words, we're considering the sequence $\{1, 1, 1, 1, \cdots\}$ and the function $f(x) = 1 + x + x^2 + x^3 + \cdots$ to be the same thing. But since we said $1 + x + x^2 + x^3 + \cdots = \dfrac{1}{1-x}$, we can substitute:"

sequence	$\longleftrightarrow$	function
$\{1, 1, 1, 1, \cdots\}$	$\longleftrightarrow$	$f(x) = \dfrac{1}{1-x}$

"Now, we can go even further and generalize a correspondence between any series and a function that generates it:"

sequence	$\longleftrightarrow$	function
$\{a_0, a_1, a_2, a_3, \cdots\}$	$\longleftrightarrow$	$f(x) = a_0 + a_1 x + a_2 x^2 + a_3 x^3 + \cdots$

"Functions like this, ones where the coefficients form a sequence, are called 'generating functions.' They take all the countless terms in an infinite sequence and tidy them up into a single function. Technically, a generating function is defined as an infinite sum of powers of x. In other words, a power series."

Miruka stopped. She knit her eyebrows and closed her eyes. *Perfect lips. Functions with corresponding sequences. Metal frame glasses. Infinite geometric series and their generating functions...*

Miruka opened her eyes.

"We were talking about generating functions for a given sequence, weren't we." Her voice grew softer. Warmer. "About how a closed expression for a generating function lets you create a correspondence with a sequence—and it got me thinking..."

She leaned towards me and lowered her voice just above a whisper. The delicate citrus of her perfume wafted around me.

"I want to go on a hunt," she said, "between two realms."

Huh?

"What are you talking about?"

"We're after a sequence, but they're hard to catch head on. We have to leave the realm of sequences, and cross over into the realm of generating functions. Once we have what we need, we jump back into the realm of sequences and grab the sucker. First—"

"The library is closed!" a voice boomed, startling us both. We had gotten so caught up in our discussion that we hadn't noticed the librarian, Ms. Mizutani, approach. She wanted us to leave, and what Ms. Mizutani wanted, Ms. Mizutani got.

4.2 CAPTURING THE FIBONACCI SEQUENCE

We moved to a nearby coffee shop and ordered just enough to keep the barista from shooting rude glances our way.

"So what's this about capturing sequences?" I asked. "Something about two realms?"

"That's why we're here," Miruka began, a finger on the frame of her glasses.

4.2.1 The Fibonacci Sequence

"Maybe I got a bit carried away with the analogy," she said. "All that stuff about the realms, what I meant was using generating functions to find the general term for a sequence." She pulled out her notepad. "Here's a little roadmap."

A map for finding the general term of a sequence using generating functions

sequence $\longrightarrow$ generating function

$\downarrow$

general term $\longleftarrow$ closed form

"First, we find a generating function that corresponds to the sequence. Then, we transform the generating function so that it's in a closed form. Finally, we expand that closed form into a power series to get a general term for the sequence." She glanced at me to make sure I was following. "In other words, we're going to use a generating function to find the general term. Let's start with an example. We'll make the Fibonacci sequence our first quarry. I know you know the Fibonacci sequence:"

$$\{0, 1, 1, 2, 3, 5, 8, \cdots\}$$

"To find the next term in the sequence, you just add the two that came before. A lot of the time you start with 1, but let's start from 0. We'll call the general term for the Fibonacci sequence F_n. So F_0 equals 0, F_1 is 1, and when $n \geqslant 2$, $F_n = F_{n-2} + F_{n-1}$. In other words, F_n can be defined as what's called a 'recurrence relation.'"

Definition of the Fibonacci sequence as a recurrence relation

$$F_n = \begin{cases} 0 & \text{for } n = 0 \\ 1 & \text{for } n = 1 \\ F_{n-2} + F_{n-1} & \text{for } n \geqslant 2 \end{cases}$$

"This is an okay way to define it, since it's easy to see the most important feature of the sequence: that the sum of two adjacent terms gives you the next term. It also lets you calculate the terms of the sequence in order, $F_0, F_1, F_2, \cdots$, which is fine. But this F_n isn't in closed form. I can't just hand it an n and get back a value. We haven't captured the sequence quite yet."

"Hmm. Not sure I'm following you," I said.

"Okay, say that you wanted to know the one-thousandth term in the Fibonacci sequence. If this recurrence relation is all you had, then you'd have to add F_0 and F_1 to find F_2, then F_1 and F_2 to find F_3, and so on and so on until you finally added F_{998} and F_{999} to find F_{1000}. If you're stuck with just a recurrence relation to find Fibonacci numbers, then finding F_n will require $n - 1$ additions. Totally inelegant. So I want to represent F_n as a closed equation in terms of n. I want a function that only uses a handful of simple operations a limited number of times to give me an answer. When we have that, then we've tamed the Fibonacci sequence."

Problem 4-1

Represent the general term F_n for the Fibonacci sequence as a closed form expression in terms of n.

4.2.2 A Generating Function

"So we're after the generating function for the Fibonacci sequence. Let's call that $F(x)$," she said. "That means the function and the sequence correspond like this:"

$$\text{sequence} \qquad \longleftrightarrow \qquad \text{generating function}$$
$$\{F_0, F_1, F_2, F_3, \cdots\} \qquad \longleftrightarrow \qquad F(x)$$

"F_n is the coefficient of the x^n term for $F(x)$:"

$$
\begin{aligned}
F(x) &= F_0 x^0 + F_1 x^1 + F_2 x^2 + F_3 x^3 + F_4 x^4 + \cdots \\
&= 0x^0 + 1x^1 + 1x^2 + 2x^3 + 3x^4 + \cdots \\
&= x + x^2 + 2x^3 + 3x^4 + \cdots
\end{aligned}
$$

"So this is how we enter the realm of generating functions?" I asked.

"Exactly. Now we need to look at the properties of $F(x)$. We know that a coefficient F_n of $F(x)$ is the nth term of the Fibonacci sequence, so we should be able to use that to find some interesting stuff. And what's the most important property of the Fibonacci sequence? The recurrence relation $F_n = F_{n-2} + F_{n-1}$, of course. That's going to be the key. Coefficients F_{n-2}, F_{n-1}, and F_n will show up in $F(x)$ like this:"

$$F(x) = \cdots + F_{n-2}x^{n-2} + F_{n-1}x^{n-1} + F_n x^n + \cdots$$

"We want to add F_{n-2} and F_{n-1}, but we can't, because the degree of the terms is different. So what do we do?"

Miruka stopped and looked at me. I knew you can only add like terms, not terms with different exponents, so we couldn't just mash them together. What I couldn't see was why we were bothering with generating functions, corresponding sequences, and all that in the first place. Was it really worth the trouble?

4.2.3 Searching for a Closed Expression

"It's not as bad as it looks," Miruka said. "When you have an x that's a power you don't like, just multiply it by more xs until it falls into line. When you multiply factors you add their exponents. You remember that from the power laws, right?"

$$x^{n-2} \cdot x^2 = x^{n-2+2} = x^n$$

"For example, if we multiply $F_{n-2}x^{n-2}$ by x^2 then we get $F_{n-2}x^n$. So, with a bit of multiplication magic—*poof*— x^ns everywhere."

$$\begin{cases} F_{n-2}x^{n-2} \cdot x^2 = F_{n-2}x^n \\ F_{n-1}x^{n-1} \cdot x^1 = F_{n-1}x^n \\ F_{n-0}x^{n-0} \cdot x^0 = F_{n-0}x^n \end{cases}$$

"I wrote 1 as x^0, just to keep everything clean. Now we're almost ready to use the recurrence relation on our function $F(x)$. Let's multiply $F(x)$ by x^2, x^1, and x^0 and see what happens:"

Eq. A: $F(x) \cdot x^2 = \qquad\qquad F_0 x^2 + F_1 x^3 + F_2 x^4 + \cdots$

Eq. B: $F(x) \cdot x^1 = \qquad F_0 x^1 + F_1 x^2 + F_2 x^3 + F_3 x^4 + \cdots$

Eq. C: $F(x) \cdot x^0 = F_0 x^0 + F_1 x^1 + F_2 x^2 + F_3 x^3 + F_4 x^4 + \cdots$

"Now we have our degrees all sorted out. Next we're going to perform a calculation to put things in a form that will let us use the recurrence relation for F_n on coefficients of the xs of the same degree:"

$$\text{Eq. A} + \text{Eq. B} - \text{Eq. C}$$

"Here's what happens on the left side:"

$$(\text{left side}) = F(x) \cdot x^2 + F(x) \cdot x^1 - F(x) \cdot x^0$$
$$= F(x) \cdot \left(x^2 + x^1 - x^0\right)$$

"And here's what happens on the right:"

$$(\text{right side}) = F_0 x^1 - F_0 x^0 - F_1 x^1$$
$$+ (F_0 + F_1 - F_2) \cdot x^2$$
$$+ (F_1 + F_2 - F_3) \cdot x^3$$
$$+ (F_2 + F_3 - F_4) \cdot x^4$$
$$+ \cdots$$
$$+ (F_{n-2} + F_{n-1} - F_n) \cdot x^n$$
$$+ \cdots$$

"The only thing that's going to stick around on the right is that $F_0 x^1 - F_0 x^0 - F_1 x^1$ at the beginning. Everything else is going to disappear, because the recurrence relation of the Fibonacci sequence will make the $F_{n-2} + F_{n-1} - F_n$ bits all equal to 0."

Miruka paused and stretched a little before continuing. "I'm tired of writing x^0 and x^1 all the time, so I'm just going to write 1 and x like normal from now on," she said. "I'm also going to make use of the fact that we know that $F_0 = 0$ and $F_1 = 1$. Now, when we write the left and right sides together, we get this:"

$$F(x) \cdot \left(x^2 + x - 1\right) = -x$$

"Now we just divide both sides by $x^2 + x - 1$, and $F(x)$ in closed form is ours at last:"

$$F(x) = \frac{x}{1 - x - x^2}$$

"Isn't it amazing how simple the generating function for the Fibonacci sequence is? I mean, look at it! It's so compact! That little thing puts an infinite number of Fibonacci numbers right in our hands:"

$$\{0, 1, 1, 2, 3, 5, 8, \ldots\} \quad \longleftrightarrow \quad \frac{x}{1 - x - x^2}$$

A generating function $F(x)$ for the Fibonacci numbers in closed form

$$F(x) = \frac{x}{1 - x - x^2}$$

4.2.4 On to the Infinite Series

"So now we have a generating function $F(x)$ for the Fibonacci sequence," Miruka said, "which means if we wrote the closed form of $F(x)$ as an infinite series, then the coefficient of the nth degree term should be F_n.

"Our next goal is to take $\frac{x}{1-x-x^2}$ and represent it as an infinite series. Remember how we did that for this fraction before?"

$$\frac{1}{1 - x} = 1 + x + x^2 + x^3 + \cdots$$

"Well, now we want to see if we can find a way to do the same thing to $\frac{x}{1-x-x^2}$ that we did to $\frac{1}{1-x}$. If we can, then we can escape from the realm of generating functions, and make it back to the realm of sequences. Not only that, but we'll be bringing back a general term for the Fibonacci sequence as a souvenir. Sound good?"

I stared at the generating function she had come up with, trying to see it with my mind's eye, imagining how we could write it as a series, and thereby come up with a general term:

$$F(x) = \frac{x}{1 - x - x^2}$$

The denominator was a second degree equation, so my first instinct was to try factoring it. Miruka watched intently as I scratched in the notebook, thinking aloud as I wrote.

"Well, I guess there will be two constants—let's call them r and s—that would allow us to factor the denominator:"

$$1 - x - x^2 = (1 - rx)(1 - sx)$$

"If we had factored it that way," I continued, "the common denominator would have been $1 - x - x^2$ when we added the two fractions together. Something like this:"

$$\frac{1}{1 - rx} + \frac{1}{1 - sx} = \frac{(\text{something})}{(1 - rx)(1 - sx)}$$
$$= \frac{(\text{something})}{1 - x - x^2}$$

"So what we need to do is figure out what r and s need to be so that, in the end, we get $\frac{x}{1-x-x^2}$. Here goes nothing..."

$$\frac{1}{1 - rx} + \frac{1}{1 - sx} = \frac{1 - sx}{(1 - rx)(1 - sx)} + \frac{1 - rx}{(1 - rx)(1 - sx)}$$
$$= \frac{2 - (r + s)x}{1 - (r + s)x + rsx^2}$$
$$= \text{hmmm...}$$

"Wait a minute. I'm pretty sure that I can figure out r and s so that the denominator comes out to be $1 - x - x^2$, but how am I going to get the numerator to become just x? How on earth can I get rid of that constant 2? It feels like I'm really close, but I'm missing something."

4.2.5   The Solution

"Try this," Miruka said. "Make the numerators variables, too. Use four unknowns instead of two—R, S, r, and s:"

$$\frac{R}{1 - rx} + \frac{S}{1 - sx}$$

"When you work that out, you get this:"

$$\frac{R}{1-rx} + \frac{S}{1-sx} = \frac{R(1-sx)}{(1-rx)(1-sx)} + \frac{S(1-rx)}{(1-rx)(1-sx)}$$
$$= \frac{(R+S)-(rS+sR)x}{1-(r+s)x+rsx^2}$$

"So now we need to find four constants that make the equation work:"

$$\frac{(R+S)-(rS+sR)x}{1-(r+s)x+rsx^2} = \frac{x}{1-x-x^2}$$

"Look at both sides of the equation. See how we have to solve these four simultaneous equations?"

$$\begin{cases} R+S \ = \ 0 \\ rS+sR = -1 \\ r+s \ = \ 1 \\ rs \ \ \ = -1 \end{cases}$$

"Four equations with four unknowns. This might take a bit of work, but at least we know it's possible. First off, let's get R and S in terms of r and s:"

$$R = \frac{1}{r-s}, \qquad S = -\frac{1}{r-s}$$

"Actually, this gives us a hint how we're going to represent $F(x)$ as a series... Let's worry about finding r and s later, and forge ahead with the calculations."

$$F(x) = \frac{x}{1-x-x^2}$$
$$= \frac{x}{(1-rx)(1-sx)}$$
$$= \frac{R}{1-rx} + \frac{S}{1-sx}$$

"Now we're going to take advantage of the fact that $R = \frac{1}{r-s}$ and $S = -\frac{1}{r-s}$:"

$$= \frac{1}{r-s} \cdot \frac{1}{1-rx} - \frac{1}{r-s} \cdot \frac{1}{1-sx}$$

$$= \frac{1}{r-s} \left(\frac{1}{1-rx} - \frac{1}{1-sx} \right)$$

"All right, now you should see how $\frac{1}{1-rx} = 1+rx+r^2x^2+r^3x^3+\cdots$ and $\frac{1}{1-sx} = 1 + sx + s^2x^2 + s^3x^3 + \cdots$. And since they do, we can write this:"

$$= \frac{1}{r-s} \Big(\left(1 + rx + r^2x^2 + r^3x^3 + \cdots\right)$$
$$- \left(1 + sx + s^2x^2 + s^3x^3 + \cdots\right) \Big)$$

$$= \frac{1}{r-s} \Big((r-s)x + \left(r^2 - s^2\right)x^2 + \left(r^3 - s^3\right)x^3 + \cdots \Big)$$

$$= \frac{r-s}{r-s}x + \frac{r^2 - s^2}{r-s}x^2 + \frac{r^3 - s^3}{r-s}x^3 + \cdots$$

"When we pull it all together, here's what we get:"

$$F(x) = \underbrace{0}_{F_0} + \underbrace{\frac{r-s}{r-s}x}_{F_1} + \underbrace{\frac{r^2 - s^2}{r-s}x^2}_{F_2} + \underbrace{\frac{r^3 - s^3}{r-s}x^3}_{F_3} + \cdots$$

"So now we have a general term for the Fibonacci sequence in terms of r and s:"

$$F_n = \frac{r^n - s^n}{r-s}$$

"All that's left to do is find r and s, using this from our system of simultaneous equations:"

$$\begin{cases} r + s = 1 \\ rs = -1 \end{cases}$$

"We could solve this like any other system of equations, but we know that the sum of r and s is 1, that their product is -1, and that they solve the equation $x^2 - (r+s)x + rs = 0$, right? So we just have

to look at this as the relationship between the solution to a quadratic
equation and its coefficients, since we can factor it like this:"

$$x^2 - (r+s)x + rs = (x-r)(x-s)$$

"You follow? Since we know $r+s = 1$ and $rs = -1$, that means r
and s must be the solutions to this quadratic:"

$$x^2 - (r+s)x + rs = x^2 - x - 1$$
$$= 0$$

"Now, when we use the quadratic equation to solve, we get this:"

$$x = \frac{1 \pm \sqrt{5}}{2}$$

"If we assume that $r > s$, then this must be true:"

$$\begin{cases} r = \dfrac{1+\sqrt{5}}{2} \\ s = \dfrac{1-\sqrt{5}}{2} \end{cases}$$

"Since $r - s = \sqrt{5}$, we can say:"

$$\frac{r^n - s^n}{r - s} = \frac{1}{\sqrt{5}}\left(\left(\frac{1+\sqrt{5}}{2}\right)^n - \left(\frac{1-\sqrt{5}}{2}\right)^n\right)$$

"So, there we have it. A general term F_n for the Fibonacci sequence:"

$$F_n = \frac{1}{\sqrt{5}}\left(\left(\frac{1+\sqrt{5}}{2}\right)^n - \left(\frac{1-\sqrt{5}}{2}\right)^n\right)$$

"Whew! Wasn't that *fun?*"

Answer to Problem 4-1
(A general term for the Fibonacci sequence)

$$F_n = \frac{1}{\sqrt{5}}\left(\left(\frac{1+\sqrt{5}}{2}\right)^n - \left(\frac{1-\sqrt{5}}{2}\right)^n\right)$$

4.3   REFLECTIONS

To be honest, there was something about this equation that didn't sit well with me. Something I didn't trust. The Fibonacci numbers are all *integers*. So what was that $\sqrt{5}$ doing in there?

Miruka sat back with a satisfied look and took a sip of her coffee. "Go ahead," she said, reading the doubt on my face. "Try it."

Unable to resist, I gave the first few values a shot:

$$F_0 = \frac{1}{\sqrt{5}}\left(\left(\frac{1+\sqrt{5}}{2}\right)^0 - \left(\frac{1-\sqrt{5}}{2}\right)^0\right) = \frac{0}{\sqrt{5}} = 0$$

$$F_1 = \frac{1}{\sqrt{5}}\left(\left(\frac{1+\sqrt{5}}{2}\right)^1 - \left(\frac{1-\sqrt{5}}{2}\right)^1\right) = \frac{\sqrt{5}}{\sqrt{5}} = 1$$

$$F_2 = \frac{1}{\sqrt{5}}\left(\left(\frac{1+\sqrt{5}}{2}\right)^2 - \left(\frac{1-\sqrt{5}}{2}\right)^2\right) = \frac{4\sqrt{5}}{4\sqrt{5}} = 1$$

$$F_3 = \frac{1}{\sqrt{5}}\left(\left(\frac{1+\sqrt{5}}{2}\right)^3 - \left(\frac{1-\sqrt{5}}{2}\right)^3\right) = \frac{16\sqrt{5}}{8\sqrt{5}} = 2$$

$$F_4 = \frac{1}{\sqrt{5}}\left(\left(\frac{1+\sqrt{5}}{2}\right)^4 - \left(\frac{1-\sqrt{5}}{2}\right)^4\right) = \frac{48\sqrt{5}}{16\sqrt{5}} = 3$$

"$0, 1, 1, 2, 3, \cdots$," I listed off. "That's the Fibonacci sequence, all right. Cute trick, how those $\sqrt{5}$s always manage to cancel out."

As I finished my coffee, I reflected back on what we had just done. Figuring out a general term for the Fibonacci sequence as a closed-form expression in n was an impressive feat, and I wanted to be sure I could duplicate it myself. I jotted down some notes:

1. Think of a generating function $F(x)$ that has the terms of the Fibonacci sequence as its coefficients.

2. Find a closed form of $F(x)$ in terms of x. (Note: use the Fibonacci sequence as a recurrence relation to do that.)

3. Express the closed form of $F(x)$ as an infinite series. The coefficient for the x^n term will be the general term for the Fibonacci sequence.

So we'd used a generating function—a function that uses the elements in a sequence as its coefficients—to capture the Fibonacci sequence. We'd followed her roadmap—and what a road it was!

A map for finding the general term of a sequence using generating functions

the Fibonacci sequence $\xrightarrow{1.}$ its generating function $F(x)$

$\downarrow 2.$

general term for the sequence $\xleftarrow[3.]{}$ closed form of $\Gamma(x)$

"Generating functions are a powerful way to deal with sequences," Miruka said. "They let us bring all of our tools for analyzing and working with functions into the realm of sequences, and that's a pretty big toolbox. Handy, huh?"

I nodded, but something else had already started to bug me. "I thought changing the order of the terms when you're adding up an infinite series was off limits. You sure we haven't broken any rules here?"

"You *do* have to be careful about stating conditions. I promise that we're okay as far as what we did today, though. If you want to be really paranoid, don't tell people you found the solution using a generating function, and use mathematical induction to prove the general term that pops out."

Easy for you to say.

...the point of the rather long derivation above was to show how it would be possible to discover the equation in the first place, using the important method of generating functions, which is a valuable technique for solving so many problems.

DONALD KNUTH
The Art of Computer Programming,
Vol. I

CHAPTER 5

Arithmetic and Geometric Means

The joy of any kind of creation is in
playing at the boundaries of what has
been done.

DOUGLAS HOFSTADTER
Metamagical Themas

5.1 THE SECOND NOTE

The next day after school I found myself hurrying down the tree-lined
path that cut through our campus. As I walked, I pulled the note
out of my pocket and reread it for the hundredth time.

Meet me after school in the student lounge—Tetra

The path led straight to the lounge, where I found her waiting
for me just outside the doors.

She bowed her head. "I'm sorry about yesterday."

"No, I'm the one who should be apologizing," I said. "But *in*side.
It's freezing out here."

Tetra opened the door and I followed her in.

The lounge served several functions: The first floor held the school store and a large seating area with tables and chairs, making it a good place to hang out. Upstairs were rooms for club meetings.

The lounge was almost empty, but I could hear the intermittent squawking of someone practicing the flute. We bought coffee from a vending machine and sat down across from each other at the nearest table.

"Sorry for running off like that. I really didn't know what else to do."

"I'm sorry, too. For... for everything."

Tetra peered at me over her cup of coffee. Something about the way she held it reminded me of a squirrel gnawing on a walnut. The image of her with a big, fluffy tail rose in my mind, and I stifled a laugh.

"So, you two. Is she your, uh..."

"Tutor?" I offered.

"Girlfriend," she blurted over me.

I shook my head. "Miruka? No, we're just friends."

Tutor, possibly. Girlfriend, definitely not.

"I just thought that maybe," Tetra said, "since we were studying together, she got the wrong idea or something." She inclined her head. "You can still teach me math, can't you? I mean, if you don't mind, of course."

"Yeah, sure. You know where to find me." I put the note on the table. "Is that all this was about?" I asked.

Tetra nodded. "I thought about looking for you in the library, but after yesterday..."

I couldn't blame her for being a bit embarrassed. Terrified, even.

"If she sees us together, do you think she might, you know—freak out again?"

"Miruka's hard to read," I said. "But I wouldn't be surprised. How about I talk to her and make sure it doesn't happen again."

Tetra smiled for the first time that day.

5.2 QUESTIONS

"As long as we're here," Tetra said, "there's something I've been wondering for a long time, but never got a good answer for. You remember helping me with $(a+b)(a-b) = a^2 - b^2$? Well, I found it in my textbook, only there it was written as $(x+y)(x-y) = x^2 - y^2$."

"Right. It's the same equation," I said. "What about it?"

"Well, this is probably stupid, but when I see things like that, I get confused. How do I know when to use a and b or x and y?"

"Ah, right. . ."

"I get hung up on things like this, and while I'm trying to figure it out the teacher moves on and then I'm really lost. And when I try to ask a teacher about it, I'm not even sure what to ask. It makes me—I don't know, *frustrated.*"

I nodded to indicate I was listening.

"I already feel like it takes me twice as long as anybody else to understand something," she went on. "So why am I wasting time trying to figure out stuff that no one even cares about?"

"Who says no one cares about it?"

"All my friends who are good at math, for starters. They tell me not to worry about stuff like this—that it's not important. So then I try ignoring things that bother me, and they say I'm not paying enough attention. How can I learn anything when I can't even tell the difference between the important stuff and useless details?"

"You know," I said, "all this worrying about *the details* makes me think you might really have an eye for math."

If she picked up the compliment, she didn't let on.

"When I study a foreign language, if there's a word I don't know, I look it up. If there's a phrase I don't understand, I can memorize it. Grammar is kind of a pain, but all it takes is a few examples to see how it works. The more I study, the more I understand."

That seemed like an oversimplification, but I didn't say anything.

"Math is different. When I get it, I totally get it. When I don't, I'm clueless. There's no in-between."

"Well, when you get stuck working on an equation, sometimes if you go back and check for mistakes—"

"No, that's not what I mean. It's like—wait, I'm sorry. You didn't come here to listen to me rant. It's just, I want to get better. I really do!"

I noticed Tetra's hands were balled into fists.

"This is a great high school. I was so happy when I got accepted," she said. "When I go to college, I want to study computer science—who knows, I'll probably change my mind by then, but whatever I end up doing, I know math will be important. I can't just give up." Tetra shook her head. "Maybe I'm doing it wrong." She paused. "How do *you* study math?"

"Sometimes I do textbook problems, but most of the time I just mess around with whatever," I said. "Like... Well, why don't I just show you?"

Another smile lit up Tetra's face. "Perfect!"

5.3 INEQUALITIES

Tetra moved to the seat next to me and leaned over to look at the notebook I'd pulled out. She smelled different from Miruka. Sweet. Less imposing.

"Okay, say you have a real number r. What can we say about its square?"

$$r^2$$

Tetra thought for a moment. "Well, since we squared it, we know it has to be greater than 0... right?"

"You're on the right track, but if you say *greater than* 0 then you haven't included 0 itself. Couldn't that be a problem?"

Tetra nodded to herself. "If r was 0, then r^2 would be 0, too. So we have to say that r^2 is greater than *or equal to* 0."

"Right. So no matter what the value of r is, would you agree we can write this inequality?"

$$r^2 \geqslant 0$$

"Um, yeah...yeah sure. If r is a real number, then r^2 is greater than or equal to 0."

"Good. A real number has to be positive, or negative, or 0, and in any of those cases if you square it you get a number greater than or equal to 0. That's where our statement $r^2 \geqslant 0$ comes from. This is an important property, and one that you should keep in mind anytime you're told that a number is a real number. The only time you would get an equals sign instead is when r was 0 to begin with."

"That... seems kind of obvious, doesn't it?"

"It does, and that's a good thing. When you're doing math, it's always best to start from the obvious. The statement will be true for any real number r. An inequality like this, one that's true for any real number, is called an 'absolute inequality.' "

"Absolute inequality," Tetra said, writing in her notebook.

"Since they're statements that are true for any number, you can say that absolute inequalities are kinda like identities. Except that absolute inequalities are a kind of inequality, and identities are a kind of equation."

"That makes sense."

"Okay, this time, let's say we have two real numbers a and b. Do you see how this inequality will always be true?"

$$(a - b)^2 \geqslant 0$$

"I do! Because a − b will be a real number, too, and the square of a real number is greater than or equal to 0, right? But wait, there it is again. Before, you wrote $r^2 \geqslant 0$, but now you're using a and b. Why the change?"

"No particular reason. I used an 'r' before because it's the first letter in the word 'real.' I could have used an 'x,' though, or a 'w.' Anything, really. You'll usually see people using letters like 'a,' 'b,' or 'c' to represent constant values, and letters like 'x,' 'y,' and 'z' to represent variables, but it doesn't really matter. Well, some people might think it's weird if you said, 'let n be a real number,' because n is usually used for integers, or natural numbers, but that's more of an exception. Okay, you good so far?"

"Yeah, much better. I always wondered how people chose what letters to use."

There was a gleam in Tetra's eye. I loved that she didn't want to move ahead until she'd figured everything out.

"Where to next?" I asked.

Tetra swallowed. "What do you mean?"

"Well, we know that $(a - b)^2 \geqslant 0$, so what kind of equation do you want to look at next? You name it. Better yet," I said, handing her my pencil, "you write it."

"Um, okay. I guess I'll expand:"

$$(a - b)^2 = (a - b)(a - b)$$
$$= (a - b)a - (a - b)b$$
$$= aa - ba - ab + bb$$
$$= a^2 - 2ab + b^2$$

"Did I do it right?"

"Perfect. Now when you compare this with what we did before, do you see anything new?"

$$(a - b)^2 \geqslant 0, \qquad (a - b)^2 = a^2 - 2ab + b^2$$

"Uh..."

"It doesn't have to be complicated. Here's something simple. We can say that for any real numbers a and b:"

$$a^2 - 2ab + b^2 \geqslant 0$$

"Since $(a - b)^2$ has to be greater than or equal to 0, then its expanded version has to be, too."

Tetra looked up from the equation and blinked. "Right! I see that!" A smile spread across her face. "Okay, what's next?"

"Well, let's mess around and see what happens. Try moving that $-2ab$ term over to the other side of the inequality sign. That will flip its sign from negative to positive."

"Okay:"

$$a^2 + b^2 \geqslant 2ab$$

"Now what happens if you divide both sides by 2?"

"I get this:"

$$\frac{a^2 + b^2}{2} \geqslant ab$$

"And what does this equation say?"

"No clue."

"Look at the left side. Doesn't $\frac{a^2 + b^2}{2}$ look like the average of a^2 and b^2?"

"You're right! We're adding two things and then dividing by 2—an average!"

"So now the left side of the equation is written using a^2 and b^2. I'd like to write the ab on the right side as a^2 and b^2, too."

"Is that some sort of rule?"

"No, just something I want to try. Now, this is going to be a little trickier than what we've done so far. To write the ab on the right side using a^2 and b^2 we need to change some things." I returned my attention to the notebook. "First off, will this equality always work?"

$$ab = \sqrt{a^2 b^2}$$

"Well, we're squaring something and then taking its root. I guess that would just turn it back into what it was before. So I'd have to say yes."

"Not quite. Let's look at an example. What if $a = 2$ and $b = -2$? Then the left side would be $ab = 2 \cdot (-2) = -4$, but the right would be $\sqrt{a^2 b^2} = \sqrt{2^2 \cdot (-2)^2} = \sqrt{16} = 4$."

Tetra ran her finger along what I had written. "You got me again."

"Only numbers that are greater than or equal to 0 go back to what they were after squaring and taking their root. But since ab could be a negative number, we have to add a condition if we always want this equation to be true. So if we add a condition that $ab \geqslant 0$, we're still good."

$$ab = \sqrt{a^2 b^2} \qquad \text{for } ab \geqslant 0$$

"Then we can write the inequality we were talking about before: "

$$\frac{a^2 + b^2}{2} \geqslant \sqrt{a^2 b^2} \qquad \text{for } ab \geqslant 0$$

"Okay..." Tetra's face clouded.

"Wait a minute," she said. "Do we really still need this condition that $ab \geqslant 0$? Won't this inequality be true even if $ab < 0$? Here, let me try something. If $a = 2$ and $b = -2$, then this is what we get on each side: "

$$\text{left side} = \frac{a^2 + b^2}{2}$$

$$= \frac{2^2 + (-2)^2}{2}$$

$$= 4$$

$$\text{right side} = \sqrt{a^2 b^2}$$

$$= \sqrt{2^2 \cdot (-2)^2}$$

$$= \sqrt{16}$$

$$= 4$$

"Nice catch," I said. "Looks like we don't need the condition in this case. So what do you think we should do?"

Tetra thought for a moment then shook her head. "I don't know."

"If we want to get rid of the condition that $ab \geqslant 0$, all we have to do is show that the inequality is true even when $ab < 0$, so let's do that. We know that if $ab < 0$, then one of either a or b is positive, and the other is negative. Let's assume that a is the positive one, which means that $a > 0$ and $b < 0$. Now we're going to introduce a new number c, where $c = -b$. Since $b < 0$, we know that $c > 0$. We said before that $\frac{a^2 + b^2}{2} \geqslant ab$ for any number, so we know that it will be true for a and c, too. So it's safe to say this:"

$$\frac{a^2 + c^2}{2} \geqslant ac$$

"Now let's look at the left and right sides of this equation, just like you did a minute ago:"

$$\text{left side} = \frac{a^2 + c^2}{2}$$

$$= \frac{a^2 + (-b)^2}{2} \qquad \text{because } c = -b$$

$$= \frac{a^2 + b^2}{2}$$

right side $= ac$

$$= \sqrt{a^2 c^2} \qquad \text{because } ac > 0$$

$$= \sqrt{a^2(-b)^2} \qquad \text{because } c = -b$$

$$= \sqrt{a^2 b^2}$$

"When we combine the two, we get this:"

$$\frac{a^2 + b^2}{2} \geqslant \sqrt{a^2 b^2} \qquad \text{for } a > 0 \text{ and } b < 0$$

"We have to write it that way because up to now we've been assuming that a is positive and b is negative, but you can repeat the whole process after switching them. So in the end, we get the following inequality:"

$$\frac{a^2 + b^2}{2} \geqslant \sqrt{a^2 b^2} \qquad \text{for given real numbers } a, b$$

Tetra stared intently at the equations I had written. Eventually she nodded and looked up.

"I get it. Just one more question, though. What does 'given' mean here?"

"Oh, that just means that it's true no matter what the number is. You can also say "for all' instead."

"Gotcha. I think I like 'for all real numbers' better."

"Now that we finally have both sides of the equation using a^2 and b^2, I want to rename a^2 as x, and b^2 as y. Do you remember how to do that?"

"I do!" Tetra wrote the definitions:

$$x = a^2 \qquad y = b^2$$

"Good. Now x and y are squared real numbers, so we know that they're both greater than or equal to 0. In other words, we know that $x \geqslant 0$ and $y \geqslant 0$. So now we can rewrite the inequality we just came up with like this:"

$$\frac{x + y}{2} \geqslant \sqrt{xy} \qquad \text{for } x \geqslant 0, y \geqslant 0$$

"I've seen this!" Tetra said. "This is...uh...the arithmetic-geometric mean inequality!"

"Exactly. The left side of the inequality is the arithmetic mean, $\frac{x+y}{2}$, where you're adding two numbers and dividing them by 2. On the right is the geometric mean, $\sqrt{xy}$, where you're multiplying two numbers and taking their square root. The relationship says that the arithmetic mean will always be at least as large as the geometric mean."

"Wow. We got a real formula just playing around with $r^2 \geqslant 0$."

"When most people hear the word 'formula,' I think they imagine something that's written in stone, something to be memorized but never questioned. Once you start playing around with math, you see them in a different light. They're more like clay than stone: the more you work with them, the softer they get."

"Until you can make your own?"

" 'Derive' is probably a better word to use than 'make.' Actually, your textbooks and teachers have probably been showing you how the formulas you're learning are derived, but you may not have noticed. Sometimes the derivations are disguised as examples, or problems."

"Huh. I'll watch out for that. Up to now, when I saw a formula, I just took it for granted. Guess I'm one of the memorizers."

"You can memorize formulas, but it's hard to memorize their derivations. The first thing you need to do is work through them yourself and make sure you understand everything that's going on. Memorization without comprehension is the *hardest* way to do math."

"I'm starting to see that."

"So, when do you think the arithmetic mean will equal the geometric mean? In other words, when could we write this?"

$$\frac{x+y}{2} = \sqrt{xy}$$

"Um... when x and y are both 0?"

"Okay, but that's only part of the answer."

"Why? When $x = 0$ and $y = 0$ both sides will equal 0, right?"

"Sure. But that's not the only time both sides will be equal. Check what happens when $x = y$."

"Okay. Let's see what happens when $x = 3$ and $y = 3$... On the left we get $\frac{x+y}{2} = \frac{3+3}{2} = 3$, and on the right we get $\sqrt{xy} = \sqrt{3 \times 3} = 3$. It worked!"

"It did. Testing things with concrete examples like that is really important. Examples are the key to understanding, right?"

"Let me try it one more time then. How about when $x = -2$ and $y = -2$? Then the left is $\frac{x+y}{2} = \frac{(-2)+(-2)}{2} = -2$ and on the right it's $\sqrt{xy} = \sqrt{(-2) \times (-2)} = 2$. What went wrong?"

"You forgot about the condition that $x \geqslant 0$ and $y \geqslant 0$."

"Oh, yeah." Tetra said, blushing. "I do that all the time. I get so focused on one thing that I forget about everything else."

"Well, if you go all the way back to what we started out with, that $(a - b)^2 \geqslant 0$, then it's probably easier to see why we get an equality when $x = y$, in other words, when $a = b$."

Arithmetic-geometric mean inequality

$$\frac{x + y}{2} \geqslant \sqrt{xy}$$

for $x \geqslant 0, y \geqslant 0$.
Note that equality occurs when $x = y$.

5.4   FORGING AHEAD

"We're getting a little sidetracked," I said, "but since it came up, let's talk a little more about the arithmetic-geometric mean inequality. It's easy enough to prove. All we need to do is expand the left side of the inequality $\left(\sqrt{x} - \sqrt{y}\right)^2 \geqslant 0$, where $x \geqslant 0$ and $y \geqslant 0$:"

$$
\begin{aligned}
\left(\sqrt{x} - \sqrt{y}\right)^2 &= \left(\sqrt{x}\right)^2 - 2\sqrt{x}\sqrt{y} + \left(\sqrt{y}\right)^2 \\
&= x - 2\sqrt{x}\sqrt{y} + y \\
&= x - 2\sqrt{xy} + y \qquad \text{from } x \geqslant 0, y \geqslant 0 \\
&\geqslant 0 \qquad\qquad\quad \text{from } \left(\sqrt{x} - \sqrt{y}\right)^2 \geqslant 0
\end{aligned}
$$

"Which gets us this:"

$$x - 2\sqrt{xy} + y \geqslant 0$$

"Now all we have to do is move the $2\sqrt{xy}$ term over and divide both sides by 2, and we get this inequality:"

$$\frac{x + y}{2} \geqslant \sqrt{xy} \qquad \text{for } x \geqslant 0, y \geqslant 0$$

"Wait. Where did the conditions that $x \geqslant 0$ and $y \geqslant 0$ come from this time?"

"Since we're only talking about real numbers right now, values that we take the square root of have to be 0 or greater."

"What happens if we take the square root of a negative number?"

"Then we would get an imaginary number."

"Right. Let's not do that."

"Fine by me! Okay, let's play around with the inequality of arithmetic and geometric means just a little bit more then. The way we wrote the terms before doesn't really capture their symmetry."

"What symmetry?"

"I'll show you. First, I want to change the way that we're writing sums, products, and square roots. Well, we can keep writing $x + y$ for sums, but let's start explicitly writing out multiplication signs, like $x \times y$. I'm also going to start writing division by 2 as multiplication by $\frac{1}{2}$, and the square root of something as raising it the power of $\frac{1}{2}$. When we write it that way, the inequality of arithmetic and geometric means looks like this:"

$$(x + y) \cdot \frac{1}{2} \geqslant (x \times y)^{\frac{1}{2}} \qquad (x \geqslant 0, y \geqslant 0)$$

"It's still the same inequality. We just made things a little more symmetrical, which looks better."

"Question." Tetra raised her hand. "What do you mean, writing the square root of something as raising it to the power of $\frac{1}{2}$?"

"Technically, that's what a square root is. It might look weird if you've never seen fractional exponents, but that's how they're defined. It makes sense if you think about the exponent laws."

"I don't see anything that makes sense about a $\frac{1}{2}$ power."

"Okay, then let's take an $x \geqslant 0$, and I'll show you that its square root is the same thing as $x^{\frac{1}{2}}$. First off, what is $(x^3)^2$?"

"Um... that's the same as saying $(x \cdot x \cdot x)^2$, so you're multiplying six xs together, so that means that $(x^3)^2 = x^6$, right?"

"Right. If you want to generalize it, you could say:"

$$(x^a)^b = x^{ab}$$

"Sure, I've seen that before."

"Keeping that in mind, what value would work for a in this equation?"

$$(x^a)^2 = x^1$$

"Hm. Since we multiply the exponents, we need something that equals 1 when you double it. So... $a = \frac{1}{2}$."

"Everything makes sense so far, right? But look at that equation. Since x^1 just means x, this equation is asking for something that equals x when x^a is squared. If that's the case, then what does have to equal?"

"A number that equals x when you square it? Well, that would be—hey, that's the square root of x! Oh, cool!"

"It *is* cool. So now does it make more sense to think of a number being raised to the $\frac{1}{2}$ power as being the same as its square root?"

Square roots as $\dfrac{1}{2}$ powers

$$x^{\frac{1}{2}} = \sqrt{x} \qquad (x \geqslant 0)$$

"It actually does."

I smiled. "I just thought of something fun we could do. Let's try to derive a generalization of the inequality of arithmetic and geometric means. All we have to do is prove this inequality:"

$$(x_1 + x_2 + \cdots + x_n) \cdot \frac{1}{n} \geqslant (x_1 \times x_2 \times \cdots \times x_n)^{\frac{1}{n}} \qquad (x_k \geqslant 0)$$

"Let's start by cleaning this up using Σ and Π:"

$$\left(\sum_{k=1}^{n} x_k\right) \cdot \frac{1}{n} \geqslant \left(\prod_{k=1}^{n} x_k\right)^{\frac{1}{n}} \qquad (x_k \geqslant 0)$$

"The symbol on the left is the summation operator, by the way, and the symbol on the right is the product operator." I stopped, realizing something myself. "That means that the inequality of arithmetic and geometric means is really a relationship between sums and products. That's so cool! Now let's—"

"Whoa, time out!" Tetra held up her hands. "Maybe it's cool for *you*, but just looking at this is giving me a headache."

5.5   A GLIMPSE BEHIND THE CURTAIN

We decided to take a break, and Tetra moved back to the seat across the table.

"The thing that's hard about math for me," she said, "is that I don't see the big picture, and my teachers aren't trying to help me see it, either. It's like... I've been tossed into a pitch-black room with a tiny flashlight. I have just enough light to inch forward, but I can't see where I'm going. All I can see is the narrow circle I'm focused on. The part I'm looking at makes sense, but I still can't figure out what the room looks like."

Tetra leaned back in her chair and sighed.

"You know, you're the only person I can talk to like this. I have a friend who's great at math, but he makes fun of me when I tell him how I feel. He thinks I worry too much. His answer to everything is 'just memorize it.'" Tetra laughed. "Makes me want to kick his chair out from under him."

"Well, I don't know how other people feel," I said, "but I love math. I love staring at equations, pulling apart the ones we learn in class to see how they work; I love the feeling I get when I know for sure that I understand something new, and I love it when I can do it on my own."

I meant every word, and it must have showed. Tetra listened in silence.

"School only teaches you the bare minimum; most teachers don't think much beyond what you need to know to get into college. And that's fine for most people, I guess, but I love this stuff, so I want to know more. No one makes me do it—my parents don't have a clue about what I'm studying, so as long as it looks like I'm doing homework they're happy. That leaves me free to study what I like."

"Easy for you—you have good grades. Mine suck, so my parents are always on my case to study. They never shut up about it. But you must study a lot—you're always in the library."

"Yeah, but I'm not really studying. I'm just messing around in my notebook, playing with formulas that I've picked up or rewriting definitions to see what happens. The point is, you have to do all the important stuff yourself. You said that every time you see an equation you wonder why it's written the way it is, right? That's a wonderful thing. It's really important to question things, to think things through, even if it takes longer that way. That's what real learning is." My voice had risen to what would pass for loud, even in the lounge, but I didn't care. "Your parents, your friends—even your teachers—they won't have the answers for you. Not all the answers, at least. And it's okay to get frustrated when you hit something you can't figure out. That's just part of the process."

"Is this the kind of stuff you two talk about?"

I blinked.

"You know—you and Miruka."

"Well, our talks tend to be a little more... specific. She usually tracks me down in the library, sees what I'm working on, and takes it from there. She's the one who ends up doing most of the talking. She's really smart—way beyond me. And not just in math."

"I could have sworn that you two were... well... a couple. You're together all the time."

"Well, we *do* have classes together."

"But I always see you in the library."

"I guess."

"You're the top in your class, right?"

"No. Miruka has me beat in math. And there's Kaito. He's probably got the best grades all around."

"I wonder what it is that makes you different from the rest of us."

"Well, I can't speak for Miruka, but I think we all have our weak points, too. I suck at giving presentations, public speaking, anything like that. And Kaito has both of us beat, since he's even good at sports. But we're all just doing what we love. What do you love, Tetra?"

"Me? Languages, I guess."

"Then I'll bet when you go to a bookstore, you go straight for the foreign language section. Am I right?"

"Pretty much."

"I'm the same way. Except when I go to a bookstore, I head for the technical section. I could probably find it blindfolded in any bookstore in town. If it's a place I go often enough, I can glance at the shelves and pick out the new arrivals. That's what I'm talking about. When you really love something, you go deep. You can't stop thinking about it, and you wouldn't want to if you could. Isn't everybody like that? Isn't that what love is all about?"

Something had flipped a switch inside me. I rarely talked this much, but now I couldn't shut up.

"School is such a small, narrow world, Tetra. It's filled with fluff for kids. There's a lot of fluff outside of school, too, but there's a lot more real stuff. *Really real* stuff."

"School seems real enough."

"Maybe I'm not explaining it right. Take teachers, for example. You know Mr. Muraki, right? Everybody says how weird he is, but he really knows a lot. Miruka and Kaito will tell you the same thing. You wouldn't believe some of the stuff he's taught us. And he knows the coolest books no one else has even heard of."

Tetra tilted her head, listening.

"When you keep plugging away at something you love, you learn to tell the difference between what's important and what's fluff. I've had math teachers that try to impress their students by talking really loud, or by acting smarter than they are. I guess they want to be the center of attention, like it's an ego thing, or something. But someone who's used to thinking about things, someone who knows what's *real*, doesn't act like that. You can't figure out a recurrence relation by shouting at it. You can't solve an equation by pretending you're a genius. So no matter what people say to you, no matter what people think about you, just do your own thing until you figure it out. I think that's really important. You have to follow what you love. You have to chase after—"

I cut myself off. I was monologuing. Worse, for one horrible moment, I felt like I had become just the sort of person I was describing, shouting and pretending to know things I didn't.

The flutist was practicing trills now.

"Would it be okay if... uh... I mean would you mind if I..."

The lounge was filling up with students, and the drone of other conversations drowned out Tetra's voice.

"What's that?"

"Is it okay if... if I keep bugging you with my stupid questions?"

"Of course. Keep thinking about this stuff, and let me know what you come up with. And they aren't stupid questions. I enjoy talking with you."

"I'm so jealous. I try so hard, I really do, but you're on a whole other level." Tetra glanced down at her hands. "No, that's the wrong attitude to take, isn't it. I shouldn't be trying to be like someone else. I should be chasing after what's real for me. And that's what I'll do!" Tetra looked up at me, a deep earnestness in her eyes. "But I still want to talk sometimes, okay?"

"No problem." At least, I hoped it wouldn't be a problem. I glanced at the clock.

"Are you going to the library today?" Tetra asked.

"Yeah, I guess."

"Could I go with you?" Then, after a brief reconsideration, "Actually, I think I'll just head home. But it's okay if I come to you with questions again, right? Maybe in the library. Or in your homeroom?"

That was the third—or maybe fourth—time she'd asked permission to come talk to me. Clearly the encounter with Miruka had left her shaken.

"Sure. Anytime."

"Hey, Tetra! S'up," came a voice from behind her. I looked up to see three girls passing by our table.

Tetra twisted around in her chair. "S'up, girlfriend!"

"Friends of yours?" I asked, laughing.

She spun back around, her hand clapped to her mouth with embarrassment. It was as though she had let the façade slip for a moment and I'd gotten a glimpse behind the curtain. I'd never seen her so, well, like a *girl*.

"Oh, no! I mean, yes! I mean, oh..." A blush spread from her cheeks all the way back to her ears.

I'm not sure exactly what image she had been trying to project before, but I liked this one better.

CHAPTER **6**

The Discrete World

The fusion of analysis and number
theory... Only a fool would waste time
on such a combination. Only a fool... or
a genius.

WILLIAM DUNHAM
Euler: The Master of Us All

6.1 DERIVATIVES

I was sitting in the library, studying math as usual. Miruka came
and sat right next to me, a citrus-scented breeze announcing her
presence.

She peeked at my notebook.

"Derivatives?"

"Yeah."

Miruka propped her head on her hands, staring intently as I went
through my calculations.

"What's wrong?" she asked.

Like many things, math is harder to do while someone is watching.

"Nothing. Just wondering what you're staring at."

"Your math."

"I figured that much."

Miruka had this special brand of no-holds-barred, full-contact
observation. I'd think that there was no way she could possibly invade

my space any further, then my hand would move so that it hid her view of the equation I was working on and, right on cue, her face would drift closer until we were practically cheek-to-cheek.

I remembered the promise I had made to Tetra.

"Hey, Miruka, about the other day—"

"Wait," she said, closing her eyes, those perfect lips mouthing the words to an inner dialogue. She had latched on to some interesting idea, and I knew better than to try and interrupt her.

Precisely seven seconds later, her eyes opened. "Derivatives are nothing but a measure of change."

She snatched my notebook and began writing. "Say that x is your current location on a straight line, and just a wee bit away is some other location, $x + h$. Now h isn't all that big—it's just enough to get you away from x."

"So let's look at some function f. The value of f corresponding to x is $f(x)$, and the value corresponding to $x + h$ is $f(x + h)$. We want to see how much of a difference that h makes.

"I'm going to use some explicit zeros to make the comparison clearer. If our current location is $x + 0$, then the value of f is $f(x + 0)$. When we move to $x + h$, then our location will be $f(x + h)$. The change in x when we move from $x + 0$ to $x + h$ is:

(its position after the move) − (its position before the move)

In other words, $(x + h) - (x + 0)$, which is just h. And the amount of change in f is $f(x + h) - f(x + 0)$:"

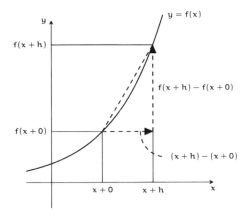

"What we really want to see is how f is changing when it's at x. Not just *around* x, but the very moment that it's there—its instantaneous rate of change. Now if there's a big difference in the value of f where it is—that's at $x + 0$—and where it's going—that's at $x + h$—then f might be making some big changes too, so we want to look at the ratio of the two. If you remember all that 'rise over run' stuff they made us learn, you can see that the ratio is the same as the slope of the diagonal line in the graph:"

$$\frac{\text{change in } f}{\text{change in } x} = \frac{f(x + h) - f(x + 0)}{(x + h) - (x + 0)}$$

"Since we're interested in the change that's happening right at x, we want to make h as small as possible. I mean, *really* small. So we look at the limit as h approaches 0, which we write as $\lim_{h \to 0}$:"

$$\lim_{h \to 0} \frac{f(x + h) - f(x + 0)}{(x + h) - (x + 0)}$$

"This is called the derivative of f. Graphically, it's the slope of the tangent line at the point $(x, f(x))$:"

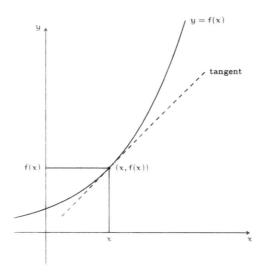

"When the tangent slopes steeply up and to the right, that means that $f(x)$ is increasing really fast. In other words, the rate of change at that point is very large.

"Now we could write that limit every time, but it's a pain, so let's write the derivative of f as Df instead. D is what's called the 'differential operator.'"

The differential operator D

$$Df(x) = \lim_{h \to 0} \frac{f(x+h) - f(x+0)}{(x+h) - (x+0)}$$

"And of course we can simplify this by getting rid of the zeros and cleaning up the denominator:"

$$Df(x) = \lim_{h \to 0} \frac{f(x+h) - f(x)}{h}$$

"The important thing to remember is that the derivative is a higher order function—a function created from another function.

"So everything we've talked about so far has been taking place in a world of continuity; we've been letting x glide smoothly from place to place. Now I want to take a trip to a different world, the discrete world. One where you have to jump from number to number, like stepping stones. In a continuous world we can let h get as close to x as we want—*arbitrarily close*. That's why we were able to use the limit $h \to 0$ to define the derivative of f. So what happens to derivatives when we carry them over to the discrete world?"

Problem 6-1

Develop a definition for the differential operator D in discrete space, corresponding to the definition of the differential operator in continuous space.

6.2 DIFFERENCES

I considered Miruka's problem, assuming the solution depended on figuring out what it meant to be "close" in a discontinuous world in the same way you could be "close" in a continuous one.

My eyes wandered around the library before returning to Miruka, sitting beside me. *Aha.*

"Instead of talking about things being *close* to each other, you talk about them being *next* to each other."

"Exactly," she said. "In a discrete world you can't get arbitrarily close to something. The best you can do is be adjacent to it. In other words, we can't talk about $h \to 0$ any more, we have to talk about $h = 1$. *Adjacency* is the fundamental property of the discrete world. Once you realize that, everything else falls into place."

The continuous world (arbitrarily close locations)

The discrete world (adjacent locations)

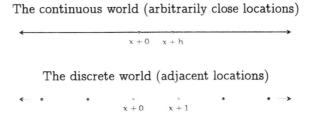

"The change in x when it moves from x+0 to x+1 is $(x+1)-(x+0)$, and the change in f is $f(x+1)-f(x+0)$. The next step is just like before—take the ratio of the two. Of course, it isn't much of a ratio, since the denominator will always be 1:"

$$\frac{f(x+1)-f(x+0)}{(x+1)-(x+0)}$$

"There's no need for limits in the discrete world, so this equation is already the derivative of f. Another name for it is the difference of f. We can define the difference operator, delta, like this."

Answer to Problem 6-1
(Definition of the difference operator delta (Δ))

$$\Delta f(x) = \frac{f(x+1)-f(x+0)}{(x+1)-(x+0)}$$

"Since the denominator is just 1, a simpler way to write it would be:"

$$\Delta f(x) = f(x+1) - f(x)$$

"Here's a discrete world version of our graph of the derivative for good measure. Now let's compare the derivative operator of the continuous world with the difference operator of the discrete world."

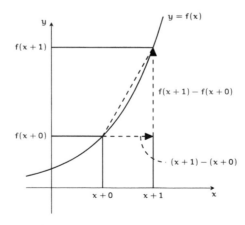

$$\text{Derivative (continuous)} \quad \longleftrightarrow \quad \text{Difference (discrete)}$$

$$Df(x) \quad \longleftrightarrow \quad \Delta f(x)$$

$$\lim_{h \to 0} \frac{f(x+h) - f(x+0)}{(x+h) - (x+0)} \quad \longleftrightarrow \quad \frac{f(x+1) - f(x+0)}{(x+1) - (x+0)}$$

6.3 Bringing Them Together

Miruka had a big grin on her face. I was already one foot in the world she was describing, and was about to bring in the other foot—but our talk about Tetra couldn't wait.

"You know that girl that was sitting next to me the other day..."

She looked up from the notebook. A look of irritation flashed across her face before she turned her eyes back to her equations.

"She's from my old junior high."

"I know."

"You do?"

"You told me that already."

Her eyes were still fixed on the page.

"Anyway, I've been helping her with her math—"

"I know."

I blinked. I hadn't been expecting that.

"We need to get into specifics here," Miruka continued.

"We—huh?"

"Well, we're not going to make much progress as long as we're talking abstractly now, will we."

6.3.1 Linear Functions

"So how about some concrete examples. Some *real* functions. Let's start with a simple linear function, $f(x) = x$.

"Here's the derivative—"

$$\begin{aligned} Df(x) = Dx & \quad \text{from } f(x) = x \\ &= \lim_{h \to 0} \frac{(x+h) - (x+0)}{(x+h) - (x+0)} \quad \text{definition of D} \\ &= \lim_{h \to 0} 1 \\ &= 1 \end{aligned}$$

"—and here's the difference:"

$$\Delta f(x) = \Delta x \qquad \qquad \text{from } f(x) = x$$
$$= \frac{(x+1) - (x+0)}{(x+1) - (x+0)} \qquad \text{definition of } \Delta$$
$$= 1$$

"So in the case of the function $f(x) = x$, the derivative and the difference are the same: 1."

6.3.2 Quadratic Functions

"Let's try a simple quadratic function like $f(x) = x^2$. First, the derivative:"

$$Df(x) = Dx^2 \qquad \qquad \text{from } f(x) = x^2$$
$$= \lim_{h \to 0} \frac{(x+h)^2 - (x+0)^2}{(x+h) - (x+0)} \qquad \text{definition of } D$$
$$= \lim_{h \to 0} \frac{2xh + h^2}{h} \qquad \text{cleaned up}$$
$$= \lim_{h \to 0} 2x + h \qquad \text{cancelled an } h$$
$$= 2x$$

"Now, the difference:"

$$\Delta f(x) = \Delta x^2 \qquad \qquad \text{from } f(x) = x^2$$
$$= \frac{(x+1)^2 - (x+0)^2}{(x+1) - (x+0)} \qquad \text{definition of } D$$
$$= (x+1)^2 - x^2 \qquad \text{cleaned up}$$
$$= 2x + 1$$

"So the derivative of x^2 is $2x$, but the difference is $2x + 1$. They didn't come out the same this time. But that's no fun. We want to bring these two worlds together. How are we going to do that?"

Problem 6-2

Define a discrete space function corresponding to the continuous space function

$$f(x) = x^2$$

I tried to think of an answer to Miruka's challenge, but I had no idea how to correspond derivatives with differences. Once she was sure I was stumped, she continued.

"Okay, I'll admit I was being a bit tricky on that one. I shouldn't have implied that we're going to make a correspondence between the continuous world x^2 and the discrete world x^2. On the discrete side, try using $f(x) = (x - 0)(x - 1)$ in place of x^2. Here's how you calculate the difference:"

$$\begin{aligned}
\Delta f(x) &= \Delta(x - 0)(x - 1) \\
&= ((x + 1) - 0)((x + 1) - 1) - ((x + 0) - 0)((x + 0) - 1) \\
&= (x + 1) \cdot x - x \cdot (x - 1) \\
&= 2x
\end{aligned}$$

"See? Same derivative. So what we really wanted to do was create a correspondence between x^2 in the continuous world and $(x - 0)(x - 1)$ in the discrete world. We need something new, the falling factorial, so that we can be clear about the correspondence with powers like x^n. The falling factorial is written $x^{\underline{n}}$. Here's the relationship:"

$$\begin{array}{ccc}
\text{exponent} & \longleftrightarrow & \text{falling factorial} \\
x^2 = x \cdot x & \longleftrightarrow & x^{\underline{2}} = (x - 0)(x - 1)
\end{array}$$

"It's easier to see how they're similar if you write it:"

$$x^2 = \lim_{h \to 0} (x - 0)(x - h) \qquad \longleftrightarrow \qquad x^{\underline{2}} = (x - 0)(x - 1)$$

> **Answer to problem 6-2**
> **(A discrete world equivalent of x^2)**
>
> $$x^{\underline{2}} = (x-0)(x-1)$$

"While we're at it, how about if we write up a formal definition of the falling factorial."

> **Definition of the falling factorial**
> **(for positive integer n)**
>
> $$x^{\underline{n}} = \underbrace{(x-0)(x-1)\cdots(x-(n-1))}_{n \text{ factors}}$$

"Here, I'll work out a few to give you some examples:"

$$x^{\underline{1}} = (x-0)$$
$$x^{\underline{2}} = (x-0)(x-1)$$
$$x^{\underline{3}} = (x-0)(x-1)(x-2)$$
$$x^{\underline{4}} = (x-0)(x-1)(x-2)(x-3)$$

6.3.3   Cubic Functions

"Now let's try it for a cubic function, $f(x) = x^3$. Differentiation first:"

$$Df(x) = Dx^3$$
$$= \lim_{h \to 0} \frac{(x+h)^3 - (x+0)^3}{(x+h) - (x+0)}$$
$$= \lim_{h \to 0} \frac{(x^3 + 3x^2h + 3xh^2 + h^3) - x^3}{h}$$
$$= \lim_{h \to 0} \frac{3x^2h + 3xh^2 + h^3}{h}$$
$$= \lim_{h \to 0} 3x^2 + 3xh + h^2$$
$$= 3x^2 \qquad\qquad\qquad \text{terms with } h \text{ go away}$$

"In the discrete world, we want to use the function corresponding with x^3, which would be $x^{\underline{3}} = (x-0)(x-1)(x-2)$. Okay then, let's find its difference:"

$$\Delta f(x) = \Delta x^{\underline{3}}$$
$$= \Delta(x-0)(x-1)(x-2)$$
$$= ((x+1)-0)((x+1)-1)((x+1)-2)$$
$$\quad - ((x+0)-0)((x+0)-1)((x+0)-2)$$
$$= (x+1)(x-0)(x-1)$$
$$\quad - (x-0)(x-1)(x-2)$$
$$= \Big((x+1)-(x-2)\Big)\underbrace{(x-0)(x-1)}_{\text{factored out}}$$
$$= 3(x-0)(x-1)$$
$$= 3x^{\underline{2}}$$

"If you use falling factorials, the derivatives and the differences both come out the same:"

$$x^3 \quad\longleftrightarrow\quad x^{\underline{3}} = (x-0)(x-1)(x-2)$$
$$Dx^3 = 3x^2 \quad\longleftrightarrow\quad \Delta x^{\underline{3}} = 3x^{\underline{2}}$$

"Here's a generalization:"

$$\text{derivative of } x^n \quad\longleftrightarrow\quad \text{difference of } x^{\underline{n}}$$
$$Dx^n = nx^{n-1} \quad\longleftrightarrow\quad \Delta x^{\underline{n}} = nx^{\underline{n-1}}$$

6.3.4 Exponential Functions

"So, we have a definition of the difference operator Δ that corresponds with the differential operator D. We pulled these two worlds even closer together by defining the falling factorial $x^{\underline{n}}$ to correspond with the more familiar x^n. What we want to do next is find a discrete world equivalent for the exponential function e^x."

Problem 6-3

Define a discrete space function corresponding with the continuous space exponential function e^x.

"e^x does just what it looks like—it raises the constant e to the x power. The constant e is an irrational number, also called the base of the natural logarithm. Its value is 2.718281828. Rounded off, of course.

"Important stuff, but it's not what we're interested in right now. We want to talk about how e^x behaves in the continuous world, and what happens when we take its derivative."

"Good question," I said. "What does happen?"

"This is the fun part. The derivative of e^x is...wait for it...e^x! In other words, nothing happens. Of course, it's less surprising when you learn it was intentionally defined that way, but still. . .

"Anyway, we can summarize that very important property, that the derivative of the thing is the thing itself, using the D operator:"

$$D e^x = e^x$$

"Okay, enough of the exponential function in the continuous world. Time to head back to the discrete world. Let's call the discrete world equivalent of the exponential function $E(x)$. We want to make sure that when we take the difference of $E(x)$ we just get $E(x)$ back. We can express this property using the difference operator:"

$$\Delta E(x) = E(x)$$

"This is called a difference equation, by the way. Let's expand the left side, using the definition of the Δ operator:"

$$E(x + 1) - E(x) = E(x)$$

"Then we clean it up and get this recurrence relation:"

$$E(x + 1) = 2E(x)$$

"The recurrence relation will hold for an integer x that is greater than or equal to 0. It's easy to solve the recurrence relation by repeatedly decreasing the value in the pardenthesesby 1, multiplying by 2 each time we do:"

$$
\begin{aligned}
E(x+1) &= 2 \cdot E(x) \\
&= 2 \cdot 2 \cdot E(x-1) && \text{because } E(x) = 2 \cdot E(x-1) \\
&= 2 \cdot 2 \cdot 2 \cdot E(x-2) && \text{because } E(x-1) = 2 \cdot E(x-2) \\
&= 2 \cdot 2 \cdot 2 \cdot 2 \cdot E(x-3) && \text{because } E(x-2) = 2 \cdot E(x-3) \\
&= \cdots \\
&= 2^{x+1} \cdot E(0)
\end{aligned}
$$

"In other words, we get this equation:"

$$E(x+1) - 2^{x+1} \cdot E(0)$$

"So, how should we define $E(0)$? Well, since $e^0 = 1$, it makes sense to define it as $E(0) = 1$, doesn't it? And from that, we find that the function $E(x)$ corresponding to the exponential function e^x is:"

$$E(x) = 2^x$$

Answer to problem 6-3 (the exponential function)

continuous world	$\longleftrightarrow$	discrete world
e^x	$\longleftrightarrow$	2^x

"Doesn't it seem somehow *perfect* that the exponential function in the discrete world is a power of 2?

6.4   TRAVELING BETWEEN TWO WORLDS

"Okay, so we've talked about the correspondence between derivatives and differences. Now let's talk about the correspondence between integrals and sums:"

$$\int 1 = x \qquad \longleftrightarrow \qquad \sum 1 = x$$

$$\int t = \frac{x^2}{2} \qquad \longleftrightarrow \qquad \sum t = \frac{x^2}{2}$$

$$\int t^2 = \frac{x^3}{3} \qquad \longleftrightarrow \qquad \sum t^2 = \frac{x^3}{3}$$

$$\int t^{n-1} = \frac{x^n}{n} \qquad \longleftrightarrow \qquad \sum t^{\underline{n-1}} = \frac{x^{\underline{n}}}{n}$$

$$\int t^n = \frac{x^{n+1}}{n+1} \qquad \longleftrightarrow \qquad \sum t^{\underline{n}} = \frac{x^{\underline{n+1}}}{n+1}$$

"Oh, assume that all the $\int$ symbols mean $\int_0^x$ and all the $\sum$ symbols mean $\sum_{t=0}^{x-1}$. Or if you want a more abstract correlation:"

$$D \qquad \longleftrightarrow \qquad \Delta$$

$$\int \qquad \longleftrightarrow \qquad \sum$$

"The comparison is even more fun when you consider that the $\int$ symbol is a stretched-out Roman 'S,' and the $\sum$ symbol is a Greek 'S.' Maybe people were highly connected in Rome, but more discrete in Greece?"

As Miruka smiled at her own joke, I let it all sink in. We had used what we knew about the continuous world to explore a whole new realm: the discrete world. I was used to making *precise* definitions, but now we were making *useful* definitions. We came up with differences to use in place of derivatives, and, based on that, found $x^{\underline{n}}$ as a replacement for x^n. We had created not differential equations, but *difference* equations to find that e^x in one world corresponded with 2^x in the other.

Back and forth, between two worlds. I had never felt so free. I had never had so much *fun*.

I knew then that even if I couldn't get arbitrarily close to Miruka, I always wanted to be next to her.

"Miruka, this is all incredible, but what I was trying to say before—I'm helping Tetra with her math—"

"Tetra? Is that her name?"

"Yeah. So when she comes by for help, I—"

"—don't want me to sit next to you anymore?"

Miruka's pencil never stopped moving as she spoke.

"Wha—? No. I want you to—you can sit next to me anytime. It's just... maybe you could, y'know, not kick her chair out from under her?"

"Fine." Miruka's pencil stopped. She looked up from the notebook, smiling. "Her name is Tetra. You're teaching her math. I can sit next to you. Got it."

I blinked, a deer in the headlights.

"Back to math," she said. "Where do you want to go next?"

CHAPTER 7

Generalizations

> Yes, the solution seems to work, it
> appears to be correct; but how is it
> possible to invent such a solution?
> Yes, this experiment seems to work, this
> appears to be a fact; but how can
> people discover such facts? And how
> could I invent or discover such things by
> myself?
>
> GEORGE POLYA
> *How to Solve It*

7.1 BACK IN THE LIBRARY

7.1.1 With Miruka

I was at my favorite seat on a bright winter day when Miruka strode in and slapped a piece of paper on the table in front of me.

"Started on it yet?" she asked, standing with her arms crossed.

"Started on what?"

"The problem from Mr. Muraki!"

Every school has at least one teacher who's kind of, well, *weird*, and at our school that was Mr. Muraki, our math teacher. He seemed to like Miruka and me, though, and would sometimes give us...unusual problems to work on. Apparently Miruka had his latest.

Problem 7-1

$$0 + 1 = (0 + 1)$$
$$\text{1 way for 1 } (C_1 = 1)$$

$$0 + 1 + 2 = (0 + (1 + 2))$$
$$= ((0 + 1) + 2)$$
$$\text{2 ways for 2 } (C_2 = 2)$$

$$0 + 1 + 2 + 3 = (0 + (1 + (2 + 3)))$$
$$= (0 + ((1 + 2) + 3))$$
$$= ((0 + 1) + (2 + 3))$$
$$= ((0 + (1 + 2)) + 3)$$
$$= (((0 + 1) + 2) + 3)$$
$$\text{5 ways for 3 } (C_3 = 5)$$

$$0 + 1 + 2 + 3 + \cdots + n = ?$$
$$\text{? ways for } n \ (C_n = ?)$$

"Would it kill him to give us a shorter problem?" I said.

"Write no more than necessary. Use formulas. Define your terms. Eschew obfuscation. Write with grandeur, drama, and Zen-like simplicity. That's what you want?"

"Exactly," I said.

"Glad that's settled." Miruka tapped the paper in front of me. "Better get to it. I already have the recurrence relation."

"How long have you had this?"

"Since lunch. I dropped by the teacher's lounge. Think you can catch up?" Miruka glided off with a wave. "I'll be over here if you need me."

I watched her take a seat by the window. Outside, the bare branches of a sycamore traced a delicate pattern against the clear winter sky. The brilliant afternoon sun belied the cold.

If this had been a problem I'd discovered, Miruka would have walked in, snatched the pencil from my hand, and started lecturing me as she worked it out in my notebook. Not that I would have minded much. I always enjoyed watching her as she talked. One moment her eyes burned with fire, the next they were closed in intense thought.

Those long eyelashes. The line of her jaw—

I snapped back to the problem at hand. Miruka had already come up with a recurrence relation, and knowing her it wouldn't be long before she had a solution.

Okay, let's have at it.

The problem gave a series of equalities for $0 + 1, 0 + 1 + 2, 0 + 1 + 2 + 3, \cdots$, with different arrangements of parentheses. From the lines "1 way for 1," "2 ways for 2" and the like, I figured the idea was to find the number of ways that parentheses could be assigned. In other words, how many ways could parentheses be put around the terms in a sum $0 + 1 + 2 + 3 + \cdots + n$?

Checking to see what n meant here, I saw that since $0 + 1 + 2 + 3 + \cdots + n$ starts with a 0, this was a sum of $n + 1$ terms. I could also think of n as the number of plus signs in that sum.

So what were the rules for adding parentheses? I noticed that each plus sign had a single expression to its left and right. It looked like I was allowed to combine sums of two terms, like $(0 + 1)$, or combinations of sums of two terms, like $(0 + (1 + 2))$, but not sums of three or more terms, like $(1 + 2 + 3)$.

I decided to apply this to one more concrete example. The problem gave solutions for $n = 1, 2, 3$, so I tried it for $n = 4$:

$$\begin{aligned} 0 + 1 + 2 + 3 + 4 &= (0 + (1 + (2 + (3 + 4)))) \\ &= (0 + (1 + ((2 + 3) + 4))) \\ &= (0 + ((1 + 2) + (3 + 4))) \\ &= (0 + ((1 + (2 + 3)) + 4)) \\ &= (0 + (((1 + 2) + 3) + 4)) \end{aligned}$$

$$= ((0 + 1) + (2 + (3 + 4)))$$
$$= ((0 + 1) + ((2 + 3) + 4))$$
$$= ((0 + (1 + 2)) + (3 + 4))$$
$$= (((0 + 1) + 2) + (3 + 4))$$
$$= ((0 + (1 + (2 + 3))) + 4)$$
$$= ((0 + ((1 + 2) + 3)) + 4)$$
$$= (((0 + 1) + (2 + 3)) + 4)$$
$$= (((0 + (1 + 2)) + 3) + 4)$$
$$= ((((0 + 1) + 2) + 3) + 4)$$

Wow, fourteen of them, huh? I jotted down "14 ways for 4."

My hand nearly cramped writing all that down, but it helped me see the pattern to assigning parentheses. That was good, because finding a pattern is the first step to stating a recurrence relation.

Next up was generalizing this. What I was verbosely calling "the number of ways to add parentheses for a sum with n plus signs" was just called C_n in the problem. I had come up with 14 ways when there are four plus signs, so that meant $C_4 = 14$. I knew $C_1 = 1$, $C_2 = 2$, $C_3 = 5$, and $C_4 = 14$, and it would probably be safe to assume that $C_0 = 1$. I summarized what I knew in a table:

n	0 1 2 3 4 $\cdots$
C_n	1 1 2 5 14 $\cdots$

From the look of things C_5 would be pretty huge.

Now for the tricky part: finding a recurrence relation for C_n, and ultimately a closed equation for it.

Just as I was hunkering down to get to work, Tetra came bounding through the library door.

7.1.2   With Tetra

"Hey," she said between gasps for breath. "Am I interrupting?"

"Well, sorta. Something important?"

"No, not really." Tetra retreated a few steps. "Nothing that can't wait. Maybe I'll catch you on the way home. You'll be here till the library closes, right?"

"Yeah, until Ms. Mizutani kicks me out. Wanna walk to the station together?"

I glanced towards the window. Miruka sat still as a stone, intent on the notebook in front of her.

"That would be great! See you then!"

Tetra snapped her heels together, gave an exaggerated bow, and spun towards the exit. She cast a glance in Miruka's direction as she walked out the door.

7.1.3 Recurrence

I returned my attention to finding a recurrence formula for the number of ways to add parentheses to a sum.

When you add up five numbers, 0 through 4, you'll get four plus signs. It occurred to me that the only thing that mattered was the number of terms being added, not the terms themselves. So even though the problem gave specific statements like $((0 + 1) + (2 + (3 + 4)))$, they could just as easily be written more generally, like $((A + A) + (A + (A + A)))$.

To find a recurrence formula I would have to nail down the structure behind the process of adding parentheses. I knew there was a pattern in here somewhere, and this was my ticket to finding it. This statement had four plus signs, so I tried reducing it to cases of three plus signs or less. In other words, I took this:

$$\underbrace{((A + A) + (A + (A + A)))}_{\text{4 plus signs}}$$

And looked at it like this:

$$\underbrace{((A + A)}_{\text{1 plus sign}} + \underbrace{(A + (A + A)))}_{\text{2 plus signs}}$$

Now I was getting somewhere! *I need to pay attention to the last-used plus sign—the last one you use when working out the sum—and its position.* In the case of this statement, that would be the second plus from the left, which was the very same plus sign that separated the statement into left and right parts. By starting at the left and moving that last-used plus sign to the right, one space at a time, I could be sure to find every possible case. I wrote down each pattern for a statement with four plus signs, circling the plus that would be used last in each:

$$((A) \oplus (A + A + A + A))$$
$$((A + A) \oplus (A + A + A))$$
$$((A + A + A) \oplus (A + A))$$
$$((A + A + A + A) \oplus (A))$$

What I wrote included sums of three or four terms that didn't have parentheses yet, like $(A + A + A + A)$. That was okay, though—I could easily go back and do those separately as a new sub-problem with fewer plus signs.

Yep, this is starting to smell like a recurrence equation all right.

The patterns for four plusses—the $(A + A + A + A + A)$ patterns—could be broken up into cases like this:

an $(A + A + A + A)$ pattern for each (A) pattern
an $(A + A + A)$ pattern for each $(A + A)$ pattern
an $(A + A)$ pattern for each $(A + A + A)$ pattern
an (A) pattern for each $(A + A + A + A)$ pattern

I focused on finding the number of patterns, pretty sure that would lead me to a recurrence relationship for C_n.

"For each" is usually a sign that we'll be multiplying, and in this case it signaled a product of the number of cases. That meant that for $n = 4$ we would be finding the sum of these four terms:

$$C_0 \times C_3, C_1 \times C_2, C_2 \times C_1, C_3 \times C_0$$

Writing that as an equation gave this:

$$C_4 = C_0 C_3 + C_1 C_2 + C_2 C_1 + C_3 C_0$$

Getting close now. I wrote a generalization:

$$C_{n+1} = C_0 C_{n-0} + C_1 C_{n-1} + \cdots + C_k C_{n-k} + \cdots + C_{n-0} C_0$$

My, what a pretty equation.

Next, a rewrite using sigma notation to make the structure even clearer:

$$C_0 = 1$$

$$C_{n+1} = \sum_{k=0}^{n} C_k C_{n-k} \quad (n \geq 0)$$

And there it was: the recurrence equation. I took it for a test drive to make sure it was working:

$$C_0 = 1$$

$$C_1 = \sum_{k=0}^{0} C_k C_{0-k} = C_0 C_0 = 1$$

$$C_2 = \sum_{k=0}^{1} C_k C_{1-k} = C_0 C_1 + C_1 C_0 = 1 + 1 = 2$$

$$C_3 = \sum_{k=0}^{2} C_k C_{2-k} - C_0 C_2 + C_1 C_1 + C_2 C_0 = 2 + 1 + 2 = 5$$

$$C_4 = \sum_{k=0}^{3} C_k C_{3-k} = C_0 C_3 + C_1 C_2 + C_2 C_1 + C_3 C_0 = 5 + 2 + 2 + 5 = 14$$

Sure enough, the answers I got were the same as the brute force examples from before. It had taken all afternoon, but at least I'd finally caught up with Miruka.

"The library is closed!" a voice boomed behind me. Good old Ms. Mizutani. She spent most of the day hidden in the recesses of her office, but, like clockwork, at the end of the day she would walk quietly to the middle of the library for her ritual announcement.

I hadn't realized the time. I looked towards the window to find Miruka, but she was gone.

A recurrence relation for C_n

$$\begin{cases} C_0 = 1 \\ C_{n+1} = \displaystyle\sum_{k=0}^{n} C_k C_{n-k} \quad (n \geqslant 0) \end{cases}$$

7.2 HEADING HOME

"You use this word 'generalize' a lot," Tetra said, big eyes shining. "What does it mean?"

We walked side by side on our way to the train station. I had checked our homeroom for Miruka, but her bag was gone, so I assumed she'd already gone; maybe she'd solved Mr. Muraki's problem. Either way, I was annoyed she had left without saying goodbye.

The sun had almost set, but the streetlights were still dark, leaving the winding shortcut to the station in a dim twilight. Tetra flit about like a butterfly during the day—the effort must have left her exhausted, because she moved at a snail's pace in our walks to the station after school.

"Well, it's kind of hard to generalize generalization," I said. Tetra didn't even blink—so much for math humor. "Okay, say you have some equation with specific numbers like 2 or 3 in it. A typical example of generalization would be to rewrite the equation so that it was true for any integer n, not just those numbers."

"Why would you want to do that?"

"Well, maybe you have an equation that works for other numbers, too. There's an infinite number of integers, so you could never give examples for *all* of them. Instead, you create an equation with a variable n that would make the equation true for any number you want. That's what it means to be 'an equation that holds for a given integer n,' or 'an equation that's true for all integers.'"

"So you're generalizing equations by replacing constants with variables?"

"Yup. If you want to get more technical, you'd call that 'generalization through the introduction of a variable.'"

A sudden sneeze burst from Tetra.

"Are you cold? What happened to that scarf you always wear?"

"I must've left it at home."

This all sounded strangely familiar.

"Here, take mine," I said, unwinding it from around my neck.

"Thanks, but—what about you?"

"Nah, I'm fine."

"Too bad we can't share a scarf."

"What would people say?" I joked.

"Huh? Oh, no, I didn't mean—"

I grinned as Tetra stumbled over her words.

"Tell me more about those equations for a given integer," she said, retreating back to the safer waters of math.

"Sure, but it's kind of hard if I can't write. Do you have some time? We could drop by Beans."

"Time? I have time!" she half shouted. Tetra's pace quickened until she was ahead of me. She looked cute with my scarf wrapped around her neck.

She turned and called with a puff of white breath, "C'mon! Let's go!"

7.3 THE BINOMIAL THEOREM

We continued our discussion of generalizations at Beans, a coffee shop next to the train station. I started with this equation:

$$(x + y)^2 = x^2 + 2xy + y^2$$

"Specific examples like this are fine," I said, "but let's take a shot at generalizing this for *any* exponent. Instead of using a specific number like 2, we want to use n as a placeholder for any number you might want to use."

Problem 7-2

Expand $(x + y)^n$, where n is a positive integer.

"Before we start on that, though, let's get a good grasp of what we already know by working out some examples and seeing what happens. It's also a great way to make sure we really understand the problem. Examples are the key to understanding, right? We'll start by letting the n in $(x + y)^n$ be 1, 2, 3, and 4:"

$$(x + y)^1 = x + y$$
$$(x + y)^2 = x^2 + 2xy + y^2$$

$$(x + y)^3 = x^3 + 3x^2y + 3xy^2 + y^3$$
$$(x + y)^4 = x^4 + 4x^3y + 6x^2y^2 + 4xy^3 + y^4$$

"See the pattern those x^n and y^n terms fall into? We can already see that our generalization is going to look something like this:"

$$(x + y)^n = x^n + \cdots + y^n$$

"Now we just need to fill in the stuff that goes in the middle."
"That's the part I never remember how to do," Tetra said.
"Don't remember. *Think.* Try looking at it like this:"

$$(x + y)^1 = (x + y)$$
$$(x + y)^2 = (x + y)(x + y)$$
$$(x + y)^3 = (x + y)(x + y)(x + y)$$
$$(x + y)^4 = (x + y)(x + y)(x + y)(x + y)$$
$$\vdots$$
$$(x + y)^n = \underbrace{(x + y)(x + y)(x + y) \cdots (x + y)}_{n \text{ factors}}$$

"Sure, that makes sense," Tetra said. "$(x + y)^n$ just means to multiply $(x + y)$ by itself n times."

"That's right. Do you see how when we multiply these out, we'll be choosing one of either the x or the y in each $(x + y)$ to multiply?"

"Um..."

"Here, let me write that out for a cube:"

$$(\underline{x} + y)(\underline{x} + y)(\underline{x} + y) \quad \rightarrow \quad xxx = x^3$$
$$(\underline{x} + y)(\underline{x} + y)(x + \underline{y}) \quad \rightarrow \quad xxy = x^2y$$
$$(\underline{x} + y)(x + \underline{y})(\underline{x} + y) \quad \rightarrow \quad xyx = x^2y$$
$$(\underline{x} + y)(x + \underline{y})(x + \underline{y}) \quad \rightarrow \quad xyy = xy^2$$
$$(x + \underline{y})(\underline{x} + y)(\underline{x} + y) \quad \rightarrow \quad yxx = x^2y$$
$$(x + \underline{y})(\underline{x} + y)(x + \underline{y}) \quad \rightarrow \quad yxy = xy^2$$
$$(x + \underline{y})(x + \underline{y})(\underline{x} + y) \quad \rightarrow \quad yyx = xy^2$$
$$(x + \underline{y})(x + \underline{y})(x + \underline{y}) \quad \rightarrow \quad yyy = y^3$$

"That's all the possible cases, and I've underlined the x or the y that we're multiplying for each one. Next, we add them all together:"

$$xxx + xxy + xyx + xyy + yxx + yxy + yyx + yyy$$
$$= x^3 + x^2y + x^2y + xy^2 + x^2y + xy^2 + xy^2 + y^3$$
$$= x^3 + 3x^2y + 3xy^2 + y^3$$

"By the way, we started out with a product of sums, $(x + y)(x + y)(x + y)$, and we ended up with a sum of products, $x^3 + 3x^2y + 3xy^2 + y^3$. That's called expanding. When you go the other way, from a sum of products to a product of sums, it's called factorization."

"Gotcha. Is it just me, or does it look like there's a pattern behind all those xs and ys?"

"Good catch. There *is* a pattern."

"Oh, cool!"

"Let's find it. First, how many ways are there to choose only xs from the three factors?"

"Um... if you're only going to choose xs, then there's only one way to do that, right?"

"Good. So how many ways are there to choose $n - 1$ xs and one y?"

"Let's see... Since we only want one y, we could choose either the first one, or the second one, or the third one, and so on up to n. So there must be n ways."

"Right. Now let's take the generalization one step further. How many ways are there to choose $n - k$ xs and k ys?"

"Oh, wow. Uh... n is the number of terms. But what's k?"

"Great question. k is a variable we're introducing so we can generalize everything. It just means 'the number of ys that we choose.' We know that it has to be an integer, and that $0 \leqslant k \leqslant n$. The examples we just talked about were the cases where $k = 0$, when we chose all xs, and where $k = 1$, when we chose just one y."

"Oh, okay, so then k is the number of things that you've taken out of n things. Since the order doesn't matter, that's called a combination, right?"

"Exactly, a combination. There's a formula for finding the number of ways to choose k ys and $n - k$ xs:"

$$\binom{n}{k} = \frac{(n-0)(n-1)\cdots(n-(k-1))}{(k-0)(k-1)\cdots(k-(k-1))}$$

"Calculating that gives you the coefficient for the $x^{n-k}y^k$ term."

"Question," Tetra said, her hand shooting straight up. "What's that $\binom{n}{k}$? I thought that combinations were written as $_nC_k$. At least, that's what I've seen before."

"They both mean the same thing. You'll see combinations written as $\binom{n}{k}$ in a lot of math books. You'll also see matrices and vectors written that way, but those don't have anything to do with combinations."

"One more question, then. When we studied combinations before, I memorized this formula:"

$$_nC_k = \frac{n!}{k!(n-k)!}$$

"Why is yours different?"

"They're the same," I said. "Just cancel a bunch of terms and you'll see. Here, let's look at what happens when you choose 3 objects out of 5:"

$$\begin{aligned}
_5C_3 &= \frac{5!}{3!(5-3)!} \\
&= \frac{5!}{3! \cdot 2!} \\
&= \frac{5 \cdot 4 \cdot 3 \cdot \cancel{2} \cdot \cancel{1}}{3 \cdot 2 \cdot 1 \cdot \cancel{2} \cdot \cancel{1}} \\
&= \frac{5 \cdot 4 \cdot 3}{3 \cdot 2 \cdot 1} \\
&= \binom{5}{3}
\end{aligned}$$

"See? It works out the same. Combinations are even simpler to write if you use something called 'falling factorials.' A falling factorial is written $x^{\underline{n}}$, and it means to multiply n values, starting with x and decreasing by 1 each time:"

$$x^{\underline{n}} = \underbrace{(x-0)(x-1)(x-2)\cdots(x-(n-1))}_{n \text{ factors}}$$

"If you write a normal factorial $n!$ as a falling factorial, you get this:"

$$n! = n^{\underline{n}}$$

"Look how clean $\binom{n}{k}$ is when you write it as a falling factorial:"

$$\binom{n}{k} = \frac{n^{\underline{k}}}{k^{\underline{k}}}$$

**Number of ways of selecting k items
from among n items**

$$\begin{aligned}
{}_nC_k &= \binom{n}{k} \\
&= \frac{n!}{k!(n-k)!} \\
&= \frac{(n-0)(n-1)\cdots(n-(k-1))}{(k-0)(k-1)\cdots(k-(k-1))} \\
&= \frac{n^{\underline{k}}}{k^{\underline{k}}}
\end{aligned}$$

"Uh. . . okay."

"Sorry, sorry. Got a little sidetracked there. So where were we?" I glanced back at my notes. "Right, we had almost gotten our equation for expanding $(x + y)^n$. Let me write it out in a kind of wordy way so that it's easier to see the pattern:"

$$(x + y)^n = \binom{n}{0}x^{n-0}y^0 \qquad \text{choose 0 ys}$$

$$+ \binom{n}{1}x^{n-1}y^1 \qquad \text{choose 1 y}$$

$$+ \cdots$$

$$+ \binom{n}{k}x^{n-k}y^k \qquad \text{choose k ys}$$

$$+ \cdots$$

$$+ \binom{n}{n}x^{n-n}y^n \qquad \text{choose n ys}$$

"If you look closely at what's changing with each term, you'll see that we can use the Σ operator to write the equation out like this, what's called the binomial theorem."

Answer 7-2

Expansion of $(x + y)^n$ (the binomial theorem)

$$(x + y)^n = \sum_{k=0}^{n} \binom{n}{k}x^{n-k}y^k$$

"It's practically impossible to look at a formula like that and just memorize it, but once you've derived it yourself it's not so bad. Funny thing is, once you've run through the derivation a few times you end up remembering it, and then you never need to derive it again. Cool, huh?"

Tetra spoke up. "Something about the Σ makes things look so advanced all of a sudden."

"If you ever see one that confuses you, try writing out a few of the terms that it's adding up. Start with 0, then 1, then 2, and by then you'll probably get it. That's a great exercise to do until you get comfortable with it."

"Kinda weird, having combinations pop up in what I thought was an algebra problem. I remember talking about this when we studied probability—something about red balls and white balls, and lots and lots of multiplication. It all felt like just practicing canceling out fractions. I had no idea you could use it for something like this. Pretty cool!"

"We aren't done yet. Remember, after you come up with a generalization you have to put it through its paces with some test calculations. Never skip that step! Why don't you try this one out with $n = 1, 2, 3, 4$."

Tetra worked carefully though each test, nodding to herself as she went:

$$(x+y)^1 = \sum_{k=0}^{1} \binom{1}{k} x^{1-k} y^k$$
$$= \binom{1}{0} x^1 y^0 + \binom{1}{1} x^0 y^1$$
$$= x + y$$

$$(x+y)^2 = \sum_{k=0}^{2} \binom{2}{k} x^{2-k} y^k$$
$$= \binom{2}{0} x^2 y^0 + \binom{2}{1} x^1 y^1 + \binom{2}{2} x^0 y^2$$
$$= x^2 + 2xy + y^2$$

$$(x+y)^3 = \sum_{k=0}^{3} \binom{3}{k} x^{3-k} y^k$$
$$= \binom{3}{0} x^3 y^0 + \binom{3}{1} x^2 y^1 + \binom{3}{2} x^1 y^2 + \binom{3}{3} x^0 y^3$$
$$= x^3 + 3x^2 y + 3xy^2 + y^3$$

$$(x+y)^4 = \sum_{k=0}^{4} \binom{4}{k} x^{4-k} y^k$$
$$= \binom{4}{0} x^4 y^0 + \binom{4}{1} x^3 y^1 + \binom{4}{2} x^2 y^2 + \binom{4}{3} x^1 y^3 + \binom{4}{4} x^0 y^4$$
$$= x^4 + 4x^3 y + 6x^2 y^2 + 4xy^3 + y^4$$

Tetra looked over what she had written. "Usually when I see a bunch of letters in an equation it kind of scares me away, but when I think of all this as the result of the generalization we just did, it's not such a big deal. There's still a bunch of letters, but at least now I know what they're all for."

"And hopefully why they're needed, too—the n lets you write just this one equation, instead of having to create an infinite number of examples. Do you see how the right side of the equation is generalized, too, using k?"

"Yeah. But it gets messy with all those k and $n - k$ bits. This is going to be hard to remember."

"It'll probably be easier if you don't think of k and $n - k$ as unrelated numbers, but as parts of a sum of n. You're going from 0 to n, changing the balance of the sum at each step. When you start out, the exponent for x is n, its biggest value, and y's exponent is 0, its smallest value. Each time you add on a new term, the value of the x exponent goes down one, and the value of the y exponent goes up until it maxes out at n. Like k's moving along to keep track of where you are:"

$$k = 0 \quad x \quad x \quad x \quad x \quad x \quad x \mid$$
$$k = 1 \quad x \quad x \quad x \quad x \quad x \mid y$$
$$k = 2 \quad x \quad x \quad x \quad x \mid y \quad y$$
$$k = 3 \quad x \quad x \quad x \mid y \quad y \quad y$$
$$k = 4 \quad x \quad x \mid y \quad y \quad y \quad y$$
$$k = 5 \quad x \mid y \quad y \quad y \quad y \quad y$$
$$k = 6 \mid y \quad y \quad y \quad y \quad y \quad y$$

"Oh, neat! The xs are scooting over, making room for the ys."

"Exactly. They're sharing the nth power of the binomial equally." I paused before adding, "Kinda like sharing a scarf."

7.4 Convolution

That night, after my family was in bed, I was finally able to concentrate on Mr. Muraki's problem again. So far, I had managed to find a recurrence relation for C_n:

$$C_0 = 1$$

$$C_{n+1} = \sum_{k=0}^{n} C_k C_{n-k} \quad (n \geqslant 0)$$

My next challenge was going from that to a solution using a
generating function, something that Miruka and I had done once
before. She had shown me how to create a correspondence between
sequences and generating functions, and use that as a way to travel
between what she called "the realm of sequences" and "the realm of
generating functions."

I opened my notebook, recalling how we had done that.

First, when given a sequence $\{a_0, a_1, a_2, \cdots, a_n, \cdots\}$, we want to
think of a power series $a_0 + a_1 x + a_2 x^2 + \cdots + a_n x^n + \cdots$ that has
the elements of the sequence as coefficients for each term. That's our
generating function. The two are in correspondence like this, and for
practical purposes we can treat them as the same thing:

$$\text{sequence} \quad \longleftrightarrow \quad \text{generating function}$$
$$\{a_0, a_1, a_2, \cdots, a_n, \cdots\} \quad \longleftrightarrow \quad a_0 + a_1 x + a_2 x^2 + \cdots + a_n x^n + \cdots$$

Doing it this way lets us treat an infinitely long sequence like
a single function. But things really come together when we find a
closed form for the generating function, since that gives us a general
term for the series.

When Miruka and I did this to find a general term for the Fibonacci sequence, we had succeeded in taking an unruly herd of wild
numbers, and wrangling them into a generating function. Thinking
about it still gave me chills.

Question was, could I do it again? I jotted down a quick map for
the journey.

A map for finding a closed form of C_n

sequence C_n $\longrightarrow$ generating function $C(x)$

$\downarrow$

closed form of C_n $\longleftarrow$ closed form of $C(x)$

In this problem, C_n was the number of ways to assign parentheses to a sum with n plus signs, so my sequence would be $\{C_0, C_1, C_2, \cdots, C_n, \cdots\}$. Now I needed a generating function $C(x)$ for the sequence, though the x would just be a dummy variable to keep track of the elements of the sequence. The exponent n on each term would correspond to the subscript n of C_n, so $C(x)$ would look something like this:

$$C(x) = C_0 + C_1 x + C_2 x^2 + \cdots + C_n x^n + \cdots$$

So far this was all straight out of the generating function playbook, no thought involved. It's easy to step into the realm of generating functions. The problem is thinking your way back out.

The only weapon I had at my disposal was a recurrence relation for C_n. I needed to use it to carve out a closed form of $C(x)$ in terms of just x, no ns. Unfortunately, this recurrence relationship was nowhere near as simple as the one for the Fibonacci sequence. In that case we had just multiplied the generating function by some xs, and after some repositioning of the coefficients and a bit of clever arithmetic the ns went poof.

It was hard to see how things could go so smoothly with a recurrence relation like $C_{n+1} = \sum_{k=0}^{n} C_k C_{n-k}$, which was basically a bunch of $C_k C_{n-k}$ products summed up with a Σ. What had I gotten myself into? Then I saw it.

Of course, a sum of products!

My smile widened as I noticed that the sum of the subscripts on C_k and C_{n-k} was n.

I had told Tetra not to think of $n-k$ and k as unrelated numbers, but as parts of a sum of n. You had to imagine it as going from 0 to n, changing the balance of the sum at each step.

This recurrence relation had me in a similar situation. The equation $C_{n+1} = \sum_{k=0}^{n} C_k C_{n-k}$ told me that if I ever came across a sum of products that looked like $\sum_{k=0}^{n} C_k C_{n-k}$, I could replace it with the relatively simple C_{n+1}.

I leaned back in my chair, remembering what I'd told Tetra. "We started out with a product of sums, $(x+y)(x+y)(x+y)$, and we ended up with a sum of products, $x^3 + 3x^2 y + 3xy^2 + y^3$." That was the key here, too—expanding a product of sums to get a sum of products.

The question was, *what* product?

I decided to look for a product involving my generating function, hoping that would give me a clue. Since $C(x)$ was the only generating function I had, I tried squaring it:

$$C(x) = C_0 + C_1 x + C_2 x^2 + \cdots + C_n x^n + \cdots$$
$$C(x)^2 = (C_0 C_0) + (C_0 C_1 + C_1 C_0)x + (C_0 C_2 + C_1 C_1 + C_2 C_0)x^2 + \cdots$$

That gave me a constant $C_0 C_0$ term, followed by a coefficient $C_0 C_1 + C_1 C_0$ on the x term, and a coefficient $C_0 C_2 + C_1 C_1 + C_2 C_0$ on the x^2 term. *Hmm. . .*

I generalized the coefficient for x^n in the squared generating function $C(x)^2$. The only sound in my room was the scratching of my pencil. When I was finished, this is what I had:

$$C_0 C_n + C_1 C_{n-1} + \cdots + C_k C_{n-k} + \cdots + C_{n-1} C_1 + C_n C_0$$

I should show this to Tetra.

Focusing on the subscripts, I noticed a familiar pattern—$C_k C_{n-k}$, with the left subscript k getting bigger and bigger as it moved from 0 to n, and the right subscript $n-k$ getting smaller and smaller.

Writing everything out just made it harder to see the pattern, so I tidied everything up using sigma notation. Now I had my generalization for the coefficient of x^n:

$$\sum_{k=0}^{n} C_k C_{n-k}$$

Since this was the coefficient of x^n when $C(x)$ was squared, I could rewrite $C(x)^2$ as a double summation:

$$C(x)^2 = \sum_{n=0}^{\infty} \underbrace{\left(\sum_{k=0}^{n} C_k C_{n-k} \right)}_{\text{coefficient of } x^n} x^n$$

This is it... This is it!

I had found an equation with the $\sum_{k=0}^{n} C_k C_{n-k}$ in it. That meant that I could use the recurrence relation to replace that chunk with just C_{n+1}, and doing that would really clean up my squared version of $C(x)$:

$$C(x)^2 = \sum_{n=0}^{\infty} \underbrace{\left(\sum_{k=0}^{n} C_k C_{n-k} \right)}_{\text{replace this}} x^n$$

$$= \sum_{n=0}^{\infty} \underbrace{C_{n+1}}_{\text{with this}} x^n$$

Look at that! No more double summation!

I could feel the hope swelling inside me, until I noticed that the subscript of the C_{n+1} and the exponent for x^n were out of sync. Thankfully, I remembered how we took care of that when "capturing" the Fibonacci sequence: multiply the part that's lagging behind by x to make it catch up. Well, that and the other side of the equation:

$$x \cdot C(x)^2 = x \cdot \sum_{n=0}^{\infty} C_{n+1} x^n$$

Then with a little luck—and the rules of sigma notation—I was able to move the x inside the Σ:

$$x \cdot C(x)^2 = \sum_{n=0}^{\infty} C_{n+1} x^{n+1}$$

Next I rewrote the starting point for the summation as $n+1$ to get everything to match up:

$$x \cdot C(x)^2 = \sum_{n+1=1}^{\infty} C_{n+1} x^{n+1}$$

With everything in agreement, I could just replace all the $n + 1$ bits with ns:

$$x \cdot C(x)^2 = \sum_{n=1}^{\infty} C_n x^n$$

So now the stuff on the right was almost the same as the generating function $C(x)$. The only thing left to do was subtract a C_0 out of the sigma to fix the index:

$$x \cdot C(x)^2 = \sum_{n=0}^{\infty} C_n x^n - C_0$$

And what do you know, now I could zap all of the ns!

$$x \cdot C(x)^2 = C(x) - C_0$$

Then for a bit of cleanup, taking advantage of the fact that $C_0 = 1$:

$$x \cdot C(x)^2 - C(x) + 1 = 0$$

I was left with a simple quadratic equation in terms of $C(x)$. Making the safe assumption that $x \neq 0$, it was time for my old friend the quadratic formula:

$$C(x) = \frac{1 \pm \sqrt{1 - 4x}}{2x}$$

I pushed back from my desk and breathed out. I had done it.

Using a product of generating functions allowed me to find just the right sum of products, and thus a closed equation. Definitely one to remember.

Of course, I had no idea what that $\pm$ sign was doing there, much less the $\sqrt{1 - 4x}$. Mysteries within mysteries. But at least I'd rid the thing of ns. And more importantly, I'd come up with a closed form of the generating function $C(x)$.

But it was late. Expanding the closed equation as a power series would wait till morning.

7.5 MIRUKA'S SOLUTION

7.5.1 A Different Approach

The next day after school, I didn't have to wait long for Miruka to show up in the library.

"So I started out with the recurrence relation," she said, pulling up a chair, "but then I changed my mind."

"You—what? You didn't use the recurrence relation?"

"I found a better way."

Just when I thought I'd caught up with her...

I opened my notebook, and Miruka helped herself to it.

"Watch. Let's use $n = 4$ as an example:"

$$((0 + 1) + (2 + (3 + 4)))$$

"If you think about it," she continued, "we don't really need the closing parentheses. We can always figure out where they go because of the rule that says you can only have pairs of things connected by plus signs:"

$$((0 + 1 + (2 + (3 + 4$$

"Hey, yeah," I said. "If you wanted to put them back, you could just look at the second term of each pair." I considered this for a bit. "And I thought I was being slick by rewriting it as $((A+A)+(A+(A+A)))$. I should have kept simplifying."

The corners of Miruka's mouth turned up in a smile.

"Here's simple for you. You don't even need *numbers* for this problem:"

$$((+ + (+ (+$$

"All you have to do to get them back is stick a number in front of every plus sign. Oh, and one on the end, of course."

"Wow."

"So it turns out figuring out how many ways there are to assign parentheses boils down to the number of ways you can line up left parentheses and plus signs. When $n = 4$, like the example we just did, we're looking for the number of ways to line up four left parentheses and four plus signs. Here, let's use asterisks as placeholders:"

* * * * * * * *

"Now we just need to choose four of those to become left parentheses:"

((* * (* (*

"After we've done that, we know the remaining asterisks have to be plus signs:"

((+ + (+ (+

"So it turns out this is actually all about counting the number of ways to choose four out of eight locations to place the left parentheses, which in this case we can calculate as $\binom{8}{4}$. Generalizing that, we're looking for the number of ways of putting n parentheses into $2n$ locations, which would be $\binom{2n}{n}$. If you want to think about it graphically, you can use a diagram:"

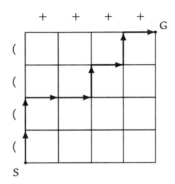

"Start at S, and make your way to G moving only up or to the right. When you move up, write a left parenthesis. When you move right, write a plus sign. The number of ways you can do that will give you the number of possible combinations. See the line I drew? That's the path that describes ((+ + (+ (+. Now, there's one more—"

"Wait, not so fast. You can't just choose *any* four locations for the parentheses. Look, here's a pattern that wouldn't work:"

((+ + + + ((

I wrote the path for this pattern using Miruka's graph:

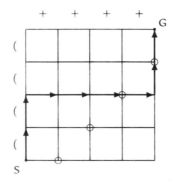

"In fact, you can't count any path that goes through the intersections I circled here. The parentheses would be all messed up."

Miruka was not pleased.

"You didn't let me finish. There's one more rule you have to follow—as you're building the pattern, you can't let the number of plus signs become greater than the number of parentheses. And where does that happen?"

"Uh... in the places where I drew the circles."

"Right. So the number of ways you can get from S to G while following the rule will be equal to C_n. The number of ways you can get there if you ignore the rule is $\binom{2n}{n}$. So we need to subtract the number of paths that will pass through a circle at least once.

"Say that P is the first circle that a path passes through. When that happens, we're going to treat every advance after that as the opposite of what was going to happen."

Miruka drew a dotted line through the circles in the graph:

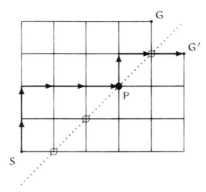

"Think of this diagonal line as a mirror that reflects the path from P on. If the path was going to go right, we'll move it up instead. If it was going up, we'll send it right. When we do that, the path won't end up at G, it will end up at this other location G' instead, the mirrored location of G. The result is that a path like ((+ + + + ((will morph into the path ((+ + + (+ +.

"If you think about it, the number of paths that pass through a circle will be equal to the number of paths that move from S to G'. The number of ways to do that is the same as the number of ways to choose $n + 1$ paths that go off to the side from among $2n$ horizontal and vertical paths. In other words, $\binom{2n}{n+1}$.

"So here's the equation we need to find C_n:"

$$C_n = (\text{the \# of paths from S to G}) - (\text{the \# of paths from S to G}')$$

"Time for some serious falling factorial action:"

$$
\begin{aligned}
C_n &= \binom{2n}{n} - \binom{2n}{n+1} \\
&= \frac{(2n)^{\underline{n}}}{(n)^{\underline{n}}} - \frac{(2n)^{\underline{n+1}}}{(n+1)^{\underline{n+1}}} \qquad \text{using } \binom{n}{k} = \frac{n^{\underline{k}}}{k^{\underline{k}}} \\
&= \frac{(n+1) \cdot (2n)^{\underline{n}}}{(n+1) \cdot (n)^{\underline{n}}} - \frac{(2n)^{\underline{n}} \cdot (n)}{(n+1) \cdot (n)^{\underline{n}}} \qquad \text{like denominators}
\end{aligned}
$$

"Do you understand what I'm doing in that last line there, especially the second term? It should be pretty clear if you think about how falling factorials work."

"Er..."

"Let me run through it, just in case. I transformed the numerator, exposing an n:"

$$(2n)^{\underline{n+1}} = (2n) \cdot (2n - 1) \cdot (2n - 2) \cdots (n + 1) \cdot (n)$$
$$= (2n)^{\underline{n}} \cdot (n)$$

"Then I did something similar with the denominator, this time yanking out an $(n + 1)$:"

$$(n + 1)^{\underline{n+1}} = (n + 1) \cdot (n) \cdot (n - 1) \cdots 2 \cdot 1$$
$$= (n + 1) \cdot (n)^{\underline{n}}$$

"Makes sense." I nodded.

"Okay, let's get back to working out C_n. I'll pick up where I left off:"

$$
\begin{aligned}
C_n &= \frac{(n + 1) \cdot (2n)^{\underline{n}} - (2n)^{\underline{n}} \cdot (n)}{(n + 1) \cdot (n)^{\underline{n}}} \\[2mm]
&= \frac{((n + 1) - (n)) \cdot (2n)^{\underline{n}}}{(n + 1) \cdot (n)^{\underline{n}}} \qquad \text{factoring out a } (2n)^{\underline{n}} \\[2mm]
&= \frac{1}{n + 1} \cdot \frac{(2n)^{\underline{n}}}{(n)^{\underline{n}}} \qquad \text{cleaning up} \\[2mm]
&= \frac{1}{n + 1} \binom{2n}{n} \qquad \text{from } \frac{n^{\underline{k}}}{k^{\underline{k}}} = \binom{n}{k}
\end{aligned}
$$

"And there we have it. The number of ways to assign parentheses in an equation with n plus signs:"

$$C_n = \frac{1}{n + 1} \binom{2n}{n}$$

"I'll leave the test calculations up to you."

I wrote a few test cases out, shocked at the simplicity of Miruka's answer:

$$C_1 = \frac{1}{1+1}\binom{2}{1} = \frac{1}{2}\cdot\frac{2}{1} \qquad = 1$$

$$C_2 = \frac{1}{2+1}\binom{4}{2} = \frac{1}{3}\cdot\frac{4\cdot 3}{2\cdot 1} \qquad = 2$$

$$C_3 = \frac{1}{3+1}\binom{6}{3} = \frac{1}{4}\cdot\frac{6\cdot 5\cdot 4}{3\cdot 2\cdot 1} \qquad = 5$$

$$C_4 = \frac{1}{4+1}\binom{8}{4} = \frac{1}{5}\cdot\frac{8\cdot 7\cdot 6\cdot 5}{4\cdot 3\cdot 2\cdot 1} = 14$$

"I can't believe it," I said. "It works."

Answer to problem 7-1

$$C_n = \frac{1}{n+1}\binom{2n}{n}$$

Miruka grinned.

"Okay," she said. "I showed you mine, now you show me yours."

7.5.2 Confronting Generating Functions

I was equal parts stunned and embarrassed by the elegance of Miruka's solution. My idea of using generating functions wasn't necessarily a bad one, but the closed form equation it had given me was a horrible mess, and there wasn't much more I could do with it. Maybe I'd bitten off more than I could chew. Squaring the generating function, which had seemed so cool the night before, was starting to look pretty weak.

How frustrating.

Miruka read the expression on my face with concern. "C'mon, tell me," she prodded. "What did you do after you found the recurrence relation?"

I told her about my plan for finding the generating function, how I squared the generating function to create a "just right" sum of factors, and then forced the generating function into a closed form. I had made it into the realm of generating functions in one piece, but my return journey to the realm of sequences had been a rough one.

How truly, incredibly frustrating.

"Well? What did you end up with?"

I winced.

"It can't be *that* bad. C'mon, show me!"

Reluctantly, I wrote the equation in my notebook:

$$C(x) = \frac{1 \pm \sqrt{1-4x}}{2x}$$

"Hmm. We've gotta do something about that $\pm$ sign, don't we. And the $\sqrt{1-4x}$, too."

"I know, I know. Totally inelegant."

Miruka continued on stoically, unfazed by the annoyance in my tone.

"Let's start with the $\pm$," she said.

Miruka stared at the equation for a time, then closed her eyes and tilted her head back. She held up a finger and traced out a zero, then another zero, then an infinity symbol before opening her eyes again.

"Let's go back to your definitions. This is what you got for the generating function, right?"

$$C(x) = C_0 + C_1 x + C_2 x^2 + \cdots + C_n x^n + \cdots$$

"If you pass that function a 0, then all of the terms with an x will go away, so we know that $C(0) = C_0$. Now back to the closed form you found: "

$$C(x) = \frac{1 \pm \sqrt{1-4x}}{2x}$$

"What happens when you calculate $C(0)$?"

"Well, you can't," I said. "You'd end up dividing by zero, so it becomes infinitely large." I had calmed down a bit now—there was no point taking out my frustration on Miruka.

She shook her head. "Not quite. One form of the function becomes infinity, but the other is indeterminate. Let's split the $\pm$ cases into two, calling the one that uses a plus sign $C_+(x)$, and the one that uses a minus sign $C_-(x)$:

$$C_+(x) = \frac{1 + \sqrt{1-4x}}{2x}$$

$$C_-(x) = \frac{1 - \sqrt{1-4x}}{2x}$$

"We can sidestep the division by zero problem by getting rid of the denominators:"

$$2x \cdot C_+(x) = 1 + \sqrt{1-4x}$$

$$2x \cdot C_-(x) = 1 - \sqrt{1-4x}$$

"Now when $x = 0$, the left side will be 0 in both cases, and on the right $1 + \sqrt{1-4x}$ will be 2, and $1 - \sqrt{1-4x}$ will be 0. So what does that tell us?"

"That $C_+(x)$ isn't a valid function, I guess."

"Good guess. I can't say for sure based on what I know about generating functions, but my bet is that $C_+(x)$ is a dead end. So we've narrowed down the generating function we're interested in to $C_-(x)$."

A closed form for the generating function $C(x)$

$$C(x) = \frac{1 - \sqrt{1-4x}}{2x}$$

"So what's next?"

"Figure out how to deal with that $\sqrt{1-4x}$," I answered.

Miruka smiled. She knew I couldn't say no to math.

But her smile didn't last long.

7.5.3   The Scarf

I glanced up to find Tetra in the library doorway, watching us work.
She was standing motionless, clutching a small paper bag in both
hands. I wondered how long she'd been there.

I gave her a feeble wave. She walked towards us, all signs of her
normal exuberance gone. Her face was deadly serious.

"Uh, hi. Thanks for the other day," she mumbled. She bowed, and
held out the bag. I took it, and saw my scarf inside, neatly folded.

"Oh, yeah, sure. Don't mention it. I hope you didn't catch cold."

"No, I was fine... Thanks to your scarf. And the coffee."

Tetra's eyes slipped over to Miruka as she said this. I couldn't
help but take a look, too. Her pencil was still. She glanced at the
bag, and then up at Tetra. Both of them remained silent, their eyes
locked.

An eternity seemed to pass.

Tetra started breathing again and looked back towards me.

"I should probably be going. I look forward to our next lesson."
She bowed again and headed out of the library, pausing at the door
to look back and give another quick bow.

Miruka had already returned her attention to the notebook.

"Find anything?" I asked.

"No. But *you* will," she replied, her pencil scratching and her
head down.

"Huh?"

"A note."

"What note?"

"In the bag," she said, pencil moving furiously.

I stuck a hand in the bag and dug around. My fingers touched
something beneath the scarf—an elegant beige card. *How did she
know?* The note was short, and in Tetra's handwriting:

> *Thanks for the warm scarf!*
>
> *P.S.—Take me to Beans again sometime!*

7.5.4   The Final Hurdle

Miruka and I got back to the problem. I looked again at the new
closed form of the generating equation.

> ### A closed form for the generating function $C(x)$
>
> $$C(x) = \frac{1 - \sqrt{1 - 4x}}{2x}$$

"This is where things went off the tracks," I said. "I got a closed form of the equation, but wasn't sure where to go from there. What did we do at this point when we were working on the Fibonacci sequence?"

"Well, the whole point of getting a closed form of $C(x)$ is to find the coefficients of x^n. In other words, we need to expand it as a power series."

"Well that $\sqrt{1 - 4x}$ isn't making things any easier, but I'm not sure what to do about it."

"Like I said, expand a power series. What else is there to do? You could create a new sequence of coefficients $\{K_n\}$, and handle the expansion like this: "

$$\sqrt{1 - 4x} = K_0 + K_1 x + K_2 x^2 + \cdots + K_n x^n + \cdots$$
$$= \sum_{k=0}^{\infty} K_k x^k$$

"This is your original generating function, right?" Miruka pointed at the equation in my notebook.

$$C(x) = \frac{1 - \sqrt{1 - 4x}}{2x}$$

"And when we got rid of the denominator we ended up with this: "

$$2x \cdot C(x) = 1 - \sqrt{1 - 4x}$$

"We can make $C(x) = \sum_{k=0}^{\infty} C_k x^k$ and $\sqrt{1 - 4x} = \sum_{k=0}^{\infty} K_k x^k$ play nicely with each other by writing something like this: "

$$2x \sum_{k=0}^{\infty} C_k x^k = 1 - \sum_{k=0}^{\infty} K_k x^k$$

"Now we want to move the 2x inside the sigma on the left, and pull the K_0 term out of the sigma on the right:"

$$\sum_{k=0}^{\infty} 2C_k x^{k+1} = 1 - K_0 - \sum_{k=1}^{\infty} K_k x^k$$

"Our indices are out of sync, so lets get the left sigma to start from $k = 1$:"

$$\sum_{k=1}^{\infty} 2C_{k-1} x^k = 1 - K_0 - \sum_{k=1}^{\infty} K_k x^k$$

"Now gather the sigmas on the left side..."

$$\sum_{k=1}^{\infty} 2C_{k-1} x^k + \sum_{k=1}^{\infty} K_k x^k = 1 - K_0$$

"...and bring them together:"

$$\sum_{k=1}^{\infty} (2C_{k-1} + K_k) x^k = 1 - K_0$$

"Since this is an infinite sequence, if we change the order of the summation, then technically speaking we have to add some conditions, but right now we're just looking for another equation so we can skip that in this case.

"What we have now is an identity in terms of x, so we can compare the coefficients of both sides to find a relationship between K_n and C_n:"

$$0 = 1 - K_0 \qquad \text{compare the } x^0 \text{ coefficients}$$
$$2C_0 + K_1 = 0 \qquad \text{compare the } x^1 \text{ coefficients}$$
$$2C_1 + K_2 = 0 \qquad \text{compare the } x^2 \text{ coefficients}$$
$$\vdots$$
$$2C_n + K_{n+1} = 0 \qquad \text{compare the } x^{n+1} \text{ coefficients}$$
$$\vdots$$

"Here's what we have when the dust settles:"

$$\begin{cases} K_0 = 1 \\ C_n = -\dfrac{K_{n+1}}{2} \quad (n \geq 0) \end{cases}$$

"In other words, if you find K_n then you're also going to get C_n as a bonus. Okay, now it's finally time to leap over our final hurdle, expanding $\sqrt{1-4x}$."

Wherever we were going, I could tell that Miruka was eager to get there.

7.5.5 The Leap

"Here we go," she said. "Say that $K(x) = \sqrt{1-4x}$. Then what we're after is the sequence $\{K_0, K_1, \cdots, K_n, \cdots\}$ that we get when we rewrite it like this:"

$$K(x) = \sum_{k=0}^{\infty} K_k x^k$$

"So where should we start?" she asked.

"Probably from something obvious."

"Good answer. Is it obvious what we should do with K_0?"

"Let $x = 0$," I answered immediately. "That will nuke all of the terms in $\sum_{k=0}^{\infty} K_k x^k$ other than the constant, leaving us with this:"

$$K(0) = K_0$$

"So what comes after that?"

"You mean, what should we try setting x to next?"

"Don't just guess at stuff." Miruka was growing impatient. "Pull out some real tools for analyzing functions."

"Like what?"

"How about derivatives? Think of what happens when you take the derivative of $K(x)$ with respect to x. The entire sequence is going to shift over, and K_1 will become your constant term:"

$$K(x) = K_0 + K_1 x^1 + K_2 x^2 + K_3 x^3 + \cdots + K_n x^n + \cdots$$
$$K'(x) = 1K_1 + 2K_2 x^1 + 3K_3 x^2 + \cdots + nK_n x^{n-1} + \cdots$$

"So now we've learned something else:"

$$K'(0) = 1K_1$$

"You see why I'm explicitly writing the 1s out, right?" Miruka asked.

"To show the pattern of exponents coming down to become coefficients."

"Exactly. Once you see the pattern, this isn't so tough. Let's take the derivative of $K'(x)$ just for fun:"

$$K''(x) = 2 \cdot 1K_2 + 3 \cdot 2K_3 x^1 \cdots + n \cdot (n-1)K_n x^{n-2} + \cdots$$

"When we let $x = 0$ again, here's what we get:"

$$K''(0) = 2 \cdot 1K_2$$

"Wash, rinse, repeat. If we write the nth derivative of $K(x)$ as $K^{(n)}(x)$, then we can generalize:"

$$K^{(n)}(x) = n(n-1)(n-2)\cdots 2 \cdot 1K_n$$
$$+ (n+1)n(n-1)(n-2)\cdots \qquad \ldots \text{ugh} \ldots \text{gross}$$

"Never mind. That's just ugly. Back to the falling factorials:"

$$K^{(n)}(x) = n^{\underline{n}}K_n$$
$$+ (n+1)^{\underline{n}}K_{n+1}x^1$$
$$+\cdots$$
$$+ (n+k)^{\underline{n}}K_{n+k}x^k$$
$$+\cdots$$

"So when $x = 0$, we get this:"

$$K^{(n)}(0) = n^{\underline{n}}K_n$$

"Look what we can do now—express K_n using $K^{(n)}(0)$. We've stumbled onto a Taylor series:"

$$K_n = \frac{K^{(n)}(0)}{n^{\underline{n}}}$$

"Okay," she said, "time for a breather."

Miruka took herself literally, drawing in a long, deep breath.

"But we can't go anywhere from here," I said. "This is a dead end."

"What do you mean, a dead end? We've been using $K(n)$ as a power series, right? So let's shift gears and try treating it like a normal function."

"Uh, how?"

"By going back to our toolbox for analyzing functions and whipping out the derivative again."

Miruka surprised me by winking.

"Remember how we defined $K(x)$?"

$$K(x) = \sqrt{1 - 4x}$$

"Let's rewrite that as a fractional exponent:"

$$K(x) = (1 - 4x)^{\frac{1}{2}}$$

"Now pay attention to what happens when we keep taking its derivative:"

$$K(x) = (1 - 4x)^{\frac{1}{2}}$$
$$K'(x) = -2 \cdot (1 - 4x)^{-\frac{1}{2}}$$
$$K''(x) = -2 \cdot 2 \cdot (1 - 4x)^{-\frac{3}{2}}$$
$$K'''(x) = -2 \cdot 4 \cdot 3 \cdot (1 - 4x)^{-\frac{5}{2}}$$
$$K''''(x) = -2 \cdot 6 \cdot 5 \cdot 4 \cdot (1 - 4x)^{-\frac{7}{2}}$$
$$\vdots$$
$$K^{(n)}(x) = -2 \cdot (2n - 2)^{\underline{n-1}} \cdot (1 - 4x)^{-\frac{2n-1}{2}}$$
$$K^{(n+1)}(x) = -2 \cdot (2n)^{\underline{n}} \cdot (1 - 4x)^{-\frac{2n+1}{2}}$$

"When we substitute $x = 0$, that last equation becomes this:"

$$K^{(n+1)}(0) = -2 \cdot (2n)^{\underline{n}}$$

"Now go back and grab the equation that we got when we were playing with the power series, the one that you called a 'dead end,' and see what happens with $n + 1$:"

$$K_{n+1} = \frac{K^{(n+1)}(0)}{(n+1)^{\underline{n+1}}}$$

"When we combine the two, here's what we get:"

$$K_{n+1} = \frac{-2 \cdot (2n)^{\underline{n}}}{(n+1)^{\underline{n+1}}}$$

"Well, now, look at that. We have K_{n+1}. Maybe this is going to lead us somewhere after all. Remember the relationship between K_n and C_n?"

$$C_n = -\frac{K_{n+1}}{2}$$

"We're in the home stretch now:"

$$C_n = -\frac{K_{n+1}}{2}$$
$$= \frac{(2n)^{\underline{n}}}{(n+1)^{\underline{n+1}}}$$

"We can transform the denominator as $(n+1)^{\underline{n+1}} = (n+1) \cdot n \cdot (n-1) \cdots 1 = (n+1) \cdot n^{\underline{n}}$, right?"

$$= \frac{(2n)^{\underline{n}}}{(n+1) \cdot n^{\underline{n}}}$$
$$= \frac{1}{n+1} \cdot \frac{(2n)^{\underline{n}}}{(n)^{\underline{n}}}$$
$$= \frac{1}{n+1} \cdot \binom{2n}{n}$$

"And there it is. The C_n that we've been chasing all this time."

$$C_n = \frac{1}{n+1} \binom{2n}{n}$$

"Done and done. See? We ended up with the same equation after all. We've made it back from the realm of generating functions to the realm of sequences."

Miruka put down her pencil and smiled.

"Now that was fun."

7.5.6   A Circle with Zero Radius

"Wow," I said. "Thanks... I guess."

"My pleasure."

I looked at Miruka. She was blunt, yet kind. Cool, yet simmering. Whether I wanted to admit it or not, I was falling for her.

Miruka's eyes narrowed and she stood up.

"Dance with me," she said. "To celebrate."

Speechless, I stood.

Miruka gracefully extended her left arm towards me. I took her hand in mine as gently as cradling a baby bird.

So warm...

We moved to an open space in front of a bookshelf. Miruka began walking in a circle around me. One step. Another. Halting motion blended into the glide of a dance.

We were the only ones in the library, the only sound the light steps of Miruka's feet.

"A rotation about a fixed point, me at the origin," I said. "Are you dancing on the unit circle?"

Did I really just say that?

Miruka stopped and smiled. "Only if you take the sum of the lengths of our arms as 1," she replied, closing her eyes.

Even if I can't get arbitrarily close to Miruka, I want to be next to her.

Miruka opened her eyes. She pulled me towards her.

"So what happens when the radius becomes zero?"

Miruka's face came closer and closer. Our glasses were practically touching.

It's still a circle. A circle with zero radius. A single point...

"The library is closed!" Ms. Mizutani's voice rang out like a gong.

The radius between us jumped back to the length of our arms.

Turns out the numbers in that sequence $\{C_n\} = \{1, 1, 2, 5, 14, ...\}$ Miruka and I derived today are called the "Catalan numbers". I also found out that my trick of finding just the right sum of products has a name, too: "convolution".

If we consider a correspondence between sequences and generating functions, we can also consider a correspondence between sequences convolved with other sequences and functions derived from a multiple of the original generating function. i.e., if you represent the convolution of sequences $\{a_n\}$ and $\{b_n\}$ as $\{a_n\} * \{b_n\}$, then you get a correspondence like this:

sequence	generating function
$\{a_n\} = \{a_0, a_1, ..., a_n, ...\}$	$a(x) = \sum_{k=0}^{n} a_k x^k$
$\{b_n\} = \{b_0, b_1, ..., b_n, ...\}$	$b(x) = \sum_{k=0}^{n} b_k x^k$
$\{a_n\} * \{b_n\} = \left\{ \sum_{k=0}^{n} a_k b_{n-k} \right\}$	$a(x) \cdot b(x) = \sum_{n=0}^{\infty} \left(\sum_{k=0}^{n} a_k b_{n-k} \right) x^n$

I was up half the night trying to think of exactly this kind of correspondence. Turns out that convolutions in the realm of sequences are products in the realm of generating functions. Absolutely beautiful...

CHAPTER 8

Harmonic Numbers

He regarded his musical parts as so
many persons engaged in conversation.
If there are three, each of them on
occasion may be silent and listen to the
others until it finds something relevant
to say itself.

JOHANN NIKOLAUS FORKEL
*Johann Sebastian Bach: His Life, Art
and Work*

8.1 TREASURE HUNT

8.1.1 Tetra

"Hey!" Tetra came running up to me after school, in front of the
school gates. "There you are! I didn't see you in the library, so I
wondered what was wrong. You on your way home? Would it be
okay if I—hey, what's that?"

I handed her the card I was holding.

My card

$$H_\infty = \sum_{k=1}^{\infty} \frac{1}{k}$$

"It's a challenge. The starting point for a hunt."

"Huh?" Tetra looked puzzled.

"Think of it as a... a forest with a hidden treasure. You know it's in there, the trick is finding it. Mr. Muraki gives us problems like this all the time."

"A treasure hunt!" Tetra looked down at the card again.

"Right, and that equation's the compass. I use it to make up some problems of my own, see what I can find."

"Have you found the treasure yet?"

"No, but I've got some clues. I already know that it's a definition of something called H_∞, and that the $\sum_{k=1}^{\infty} \frac{1}{k}$ on the right—"

"Nonononono!" Tetra held up her hands. "Don't say anything else. Just tell me one thing: do you think I could find the treasure?"

"What do you mean?"

"I want to roll up my sleeves and start digging—unless you think it's too hard."

"You can probably handle it. If you find anything interesting, you should write it up and give it to Mr. Muraki."

"To Mr. Muraki? Oh I couldn't do that." She shook her head. "No way."

"Well, hang onto the card. Think about it tonight, and come by the library tomorrow to show me what you find."

"Will do!" Tetra's eyes gleamed.

"You know," she continued, "you're so—uh oh."

Tetra's gaze shifted to something over my shoulder. I turned and saw Miruka standing behind me.

8.1.2 Miruka

"There you are," Miruka said, all smiles.

It's amazing how uncomfortable it can be to stand between two attractive girls.

"Oh, you were waiting for—" Tetra said, flustered. "You two were going to—I'm sorry, I'm leaving now. Catch you later." She gave a quick bow and prepared to scurry off.

Miruka looked at Tetra, then at me, then back at Tetra.

"No, you stay," she said. "I think I'd rather be alone today after all."

Miruka reached out and gently patted Tetra on the head—the girl instinctively ducked—before passing between the two of us. Tetra stood there blinking as she watched Miruka head off.

Miruka waved farewell over her shoulder and disappeared around the corner, leaving us to stand there in silence: Tetra speechless, and me holding back a scream.

As she walked by, Miruka had stomped on my foot. *Hard.*

8.2 For Every Library There Exists a Dialogue...

The next day the library was nearly empty, as usual. Tetra looked close to tears as she opened her notebook.

"Didn't go so well, huh?"

"It's like I thought. I'm just no good at math," she said.

I looked at what she had written, a single line on the page:

$$\sum_{k=1}^{\infty} \frac{1}{k} = \frac{1}{1} + \frac{1}{2} + \frac{1}{3} + \cdots$$

"That's a good start. You tried to capture the essence of the equation, right? There's nothing wrong with this."

"But that's *all* I could do. I really wanted to find something interesting, but after I wrote this, I had no idea where to go."

"Well, it's hard to handle something that's infinitely large, even when you're pretty sure you know what it means. Still, you gave it a shot, and that's what matters. How about we work on it together for a while?"

"Sure, I'd love to, but I know you're busy, and I wouldn't want to—"

"Don't worry about it. Let's see what we can find."

8.2.1 Partial Sums and Infinite Series

"Okay," I began, "let's start by taking a close look at the summation, $\sum_{k=1}^{\infty} \frac{1}{k}$." I pointed at the infinity symbol. "This is probably the trickiest part about it."

"That's the number infinity, right?"

"Well, yeah, except that infinity isn't really a number, and most of the time you can't treat it like one."

"Oh."

"Yeah. When you see something like $\sum_{k=1}^{\infty} \frac{1}{k}$, it's tempting to read that as 'add up $\frac{1}{k}$ for ks from 1 up to infinity,' but actually there's no such thing as 'up to' infinity. $\sum_{k=1}^{\infty} \frac{1}{k}$ is what's called an infinite series, and what you really have to do is think of it as the limit of the partial sums $\sum_{k=1}^{n} \frac{1}{k}$, like this:"

$$\sum_{k=1}^{\infty} \frac{1}{k} = \lim_{n \to \infty} \sum_{k=1}^{n} \frac{1}{k}$$

"And 'lim' is for limit?" Tetra asked.

"That's right. It would take a while to give you a real mathematical definition of a limit, but here's the basics. Say you have a sequence $\{a_0, a_1, a_2, \cdots\}$. Then $\lim_{n \to \infty} a_n$ asks what happens to a_n when n gets big. Sometimes a_n gets big, too. But not always. It could be that a_n gets bigger, and then smaller again. Other times a_n gets closer and closer to some specific number. I guess another way to put it is that $\lim_{n \to \infty} a_n$ asks where a_n is heading. If it's heading for a specific location, you say that a_n converges."

"Hmm. I'm not sure I got all that, but I did get the part about figuring out what a_n is when n is really, really big."

"Yeah, this isn't easy stuff to put into words. Which is why we usually use equations. One thing that's important to understand, though, is that our destination is something that's *defined*. That means it isn't necessarily something that's easy to have a natural feel for, so it's best to think of it as the limit of a sequence of partial sums as n heads off towards infinity, and not as something to add up directly."

"Sorry, you're still losing me. What's an infinite series, and what's a partial sum?"

"Here's an example of an infinite series. You can also just call it 'a series':"

$$\sum_{k=1}^{\infty} (\text{some expression involving k})$$

"And here's a partial sum:"

$$\sum_{k=1}^{n} (\text{some expression involving k})$$

"Do you see the difference?" I asked.

"I guess the n and the infinity sign are the only difference, but why is that such a big deal? Since n is just a variable, aren't these the same if you let n be infinity?"

"No, these are very different ideas. You're right saying that n is a variable, but it's a finite number, which means that $\sum^n$ will involve adding up some finite number of terms. That means you'll always be able to find an answer. But when you try to add up an infinite number of terms like $\sum^\infty$ is telling you to do, then sometimes you just can't do it. Like I said before, sometimes you'll find that the sum gets bigger and bigger, or it might get bigger and then smaller. In either case, there's no specific target that the sum is heading for, right? And if there's no target, then there's no number we can find, and we can't treat 'no number' as if it *were* a number. In cases like that we say that the sum diverges. When you're dealing with an infinite number of things, that's a risk you have to take."

"Okay, I'll be sure to be careful with those infinities." Tetra wrote in her notebook—*Equations with infinities in them might not lead to definite answers.*

"Good. Now a word of warning about notation. Take a look at these two expressions:"

$$\frac{1}{1} + \frac{1}{2} + \frac{1}{3} + \cdots + \frac{1}{n} \qquad (1)$$

$$\frac{1}{1} + \frac{1}{2} + \frac{1}{3} + \cdots \qquad (2)$$

"Both of them have an ellipsis, right? But the meaning is a little bit different. Do you see which one means 'infinity'?"

"The second one, right?"

"Exactly. The ellipsis in the top equation doesn't mean to go on forever, it's just an abbreviation. That sum only has a finite number of terms in it. You can definitely find an answer to a sum like that, no worries. The ellipsis in the second equation is an infinite number of additions, though. There's a limit hiding in there. It's a hint that you might be able to find an answer, and you might not. So be careful—there's a big difference between a finite ellipsis and an infinite one."

Tetra nodded.

"That's a whole lot of meaning in just three little dots."

8.2.2 *Starting with the Obvious*

"Looks like I got carried away with infinities again," I said. "We should be sure that you're comfortable with finite sums before we move on to infinite series, though. Let's do a little exercise to help you get used to sigma notation. Can you write $\sum_{k=1}^{n} \frac{1}{k}$ where n equals 1 through 5?"

"Sure!"

$$\sum_{k=1}^{1} \frac{1}{k} = \frac{1}{1}$$

$$\sum_{k=1}^{2} \frac{1}{k} = \frac{1}{1} + \frac{1}{2}$$

$$\sum_{k=1}^{3} \frac{1}{k} = \frac{1}{1} + \frac{1}{2} + \frac{1}{3}$$

$$\sum_{k=1}^{4} \frac{1}{k} = \frac{1}{1} + \frac{1}{2} + \frac{1}{3} + \frac{1}{4}$$

$$\sum_{k=1}^{5} \frac{1}{k} = \frac{1}{1} + \frac{1}{2} + \frac{1}{3} + \frac{1}{4} + \frac{1}{5}$$

"Good," I said. "Now let's look at these finite sums in a little more detail. The first thing to notice is that the value of $\sum_{k=1}^{n} \frac{1}{k}$ is determined by n, right? So that means we could also write this as something like H_n:"

$$H_n = \sum_{k=1}^{n} \frac{1}{k} \qquad \text{(definition of } H_n\text{)}$$

"Hang on a sec," Tetra interrupted, "I don't understand what you mean when you say that the value is determined by n."

"It just means that once you've given n some specific value like 5 or 1000 or whatever, then you can calculate what the final value of $\sum_{k=1}^{n} \frac{1}{k}$ will be. So its value is determined by n, right? That also means that we can write H with n as a subscript, like H_n, and when n is assigned a value then it becomes something like H_5 or H_{1000}. It's just a convenient way of naming the thing."

"Why did you name it H?"

"Just because the card said H_∞. It seemed natural to name its partial sums H_n."

"Oh, I see. But what happened to the k? There's a k in the equation, but not in H_n."

"Because the k in $\sum_{k=1}^n \frac{1}{k}$ is just a temporary thing that's only used inside the sigma. It isn't really visible from the outside. A variable like that is called a 'bound variable.' In this case, it's bound up inside the sigma. Of course, we didn't have to name it k. We could have named it anything at all, though it's pretty common to use the letters i, j, k, l, m, and n. Oh, but don't forget that i is also used to represent the imaginary number $\sqrt{-1}$, so you would only use it in situations where that wouldn't be confusing. Normally we could have used n instead of k, but we can't here because we already have another variable named n. If you wrote $\sum_{n=1}^n \frac{1}{n}$ instead of $\sum_{k=1}^n \frac{1}{k}$ then nobody would understand what you meant."

"Okay, got it. Sorry I got you off track like that."

"Not at all. It's easier to go on to something new when I'm sure that you understood everything leading up to it."

8.2.3 Propositions

"Okay, so let's summarize what we know about $H_n = \sum_{k=1}^n \frac{1}{k}$. Examples are the key to understanding, right?" I started a list in the notebook. "Would you say that this is a true statement:"

If $n = 1$, then $H_n = 1$.

"Sure, it's true, but it's a little obvious," Tetra said. "Oh, of course. Always start from the obvious."

"Exactly. Don't forget that. Okay, how about this one?"

$H_n > 0$ for all positive integers n.

"Sure, that works, too."

"Good. When you make a statement like this, one that can be mathematically proven or disproven, it's called a 'proposition.' You can either make propositions using words, or as an equation. So what do you think about this proposition:"

For all positive integers n, as n becomes larger
H_n, too, becomes larger.

"Hmm, let's see... Yeah, I think that's right. Because if n is bigger then there's going to be more terms added."

"That's right, and if you add a positive value to something, then that something has to get bigger. We could have also written that statement a little more precisely by using mathematical notation:"

For all positive integers n, $H_n < H_{n+1}$.

"I see how that works, but they're both true propositions, right? What do you get out of writing it the harder way? Why is that more precise? Oh, hang on..."

I waited while Tetra thought it through.

"I get it! Saying that something 'gets bigger' is the imprecise part. The difference is in the declarative expression 'is larger' that the inequality represents, versus the process described by a phrase like 'to become larger.' It's just like action verbs and linking verbs."

"It's... huh?" I blinked, surprised by Tetra's take on the whole thing. *Action verbs? Linking verbs?* Though it took me a little time, once I'd figured out what she said, I realized that not only was she right, but that Mr. Muraki had mentioned something very similar. What was it...? Something about sequences, and how you could either make a procedural statement from the point of view of the changes occurring within the sequence, or a declarative statement about the relationship between each term...

"Are you okay?" Tetra asked.

"Oh, yeah, sorry. I was just thinking about what you said. I was going to say that mathematical statements carry a more precise meaning than everyday speech, but that works too. Where on earth did you get that from?"

"Get what from?" Tetra cocked her head and looked up at me with those big eyes.

"Never mind. Let's move on to the next one. What do you think of this?"

For all positive integers n, $H_{n+1} - H_n = \frac{1}{n}$.

"I think that works. We got H_n by adding up a bunch of fractions, so it makes sense that when you subtract them you get another fraction."

"No, not quite. This one isn't true—the denominator on the right should look like this:"

For all positive integers n, $H_{n+1} - H_n = \frac{1}{n+1}$.

"Oh, come on—that's so close. No fair!"

"I just wanted to show you that it's important to check things out before answering."

"Yeah, I know." Tetra frowned. "But still..."

"Try checking it yourself by calculating $H_{n+1} - H_n$."

"Okay..."

She started with this:

$$H_{n+1} - H_n = \sum_{k=1}^{n+1} \frac{1}{k} - \sum_{k=1}^{n} \frac{1}{k}$$

"That's just from the definition of H_n," she said. "Now I guess I need to write that out explicitly:"

$$= \left(\frac{1}{1} + \frac{1}{2} + \cdots + \frac{1}{n} + \frac{1}{n+1}\right) - \left(\frac{1}{1} + \frac{1}{2} + \cdots + \frac{1}{n}\right)$$

"Okay, there's that. Next, let's see... I guess I could rearrange the terms:"

$$= \left(\frac{1}{1} - \frac{1}{1}\right) + \left(\frac{1}{2} - \frac{1}{2}\right) + \cdots + \left(\frac{1}{n} - \frac{1}{n}\right) + \frac{1}{n+1}$$

"And there's where the answer comes from, right?"

$$= \frac{1}{n+1}$$

"Perfect," I said. "Why don't you take a turn at stating a new proposition."

"Well, let's see. We talked about $H_{n+1} - H_n$, so how about something like this?"

> For all positive integers n, as n becomes larger
> $H_{n+1} - H_n$ becomes smaller.

"Hey, good one! Can you write that using mathematical notation?"
She mulled it over for a moment. "Something like this?"

> For all positive integers n, $H_{n+1} - H_n > H_{n+2} - H_{n+1}$.

"Exactly! You're on a roll!"

"Nah, I just did the same thing as last time. Instead of talking about the numbers $\frac{1}{2}, \frac{1}{3}, \frac{1}{4}, \cdots$ 'getting smaller,' I reworded it as 'are smaller' using an inequality."

8.2.4 For All...

"The deeper you get into math, the more important it becomes to write everything as symbols," I said, "so it's probably a good idea to get in the habit, even with really simple stuff. Like doing drills when you learn a new language."

"So why didn't you write the 'for all positive integers n' part in symbols?"

"You can if you want to, like this:"

$$\forall n \in \mathbb{N} \quad H_{n+1} - H_n > H_{n+2} - H_{n+1}$$

"How do you read that first part?"

"You say 'for all n in $\mathbb{N}$.' That first symbol is an upside down 'A,' for 'all.' The capital $\mathbb{N}$ is an abbreviation for 'natural numbers,' another name for the positive integers."

"Why did you write it funny like that?"

"If you just write a normal 'N' people might think you meant a number. This is actually a set, so it's pretty common to write it that way to emphasize that."

"What about this round 'E' looking thing?"

"Actually it really is an 'E,' for 'element,' turned into a math symbol. If you write something like this..."

> element $\in$ set

" ...you're saying that 'element' is in 'set.' So this..."

$$\forall n \in \mathbb{N} \cdots$$

"...means 'for any element n that you could choose from the set $\mathbb{N}$.'"

"And any element that you could choose would mean all of them, right? This is cool! It's like writing in a foreign language, putting all of these strange parts together into something that makes a sentence."

"Math is a lot like that. Most of the time an equation is a short sentence, but there's a lot of information squeezed into all of those symbols. Remember that the next time you're trying to decipher a hard equation, and just take it slow."

"Oooh, like concentrated orange juice! You'll gag on it if you try to gulp it all down at once!"

"Uh... yeah. Sooo, let's write out some concrete examples of H_n. The final term in each line is the increase over the one before it:"

$$H_1 = \frac{1}{1}$$
$$H_2 = \frac{1}{1} + \frac{1}{2}$$
$$H_3 = \frac{1}{1} + \frac{1}{2} + \frac{1}{3}$$
$$H_4 = \frac{1}{1} + \frac{1}{2} + \frac{1}{3} + \frac{1}{4}$$
$$H_5 = \frac{1}{1} + \frac{1}{2} + \frac{1}{3} + \frac{1}{4} + \frac{1}{5}$$

"That's the same as $H_{n+1} - H_n$, right?"

$$H_2 - H_1 = \frac{1}{2}$$
$$H_3 - H_2 = \frac{1}{3}$$
$$H_4 - H_3 = \frac{1}{4}$$
$$H_5 - H_4 = \frac{1}{5}$$
$$H_6 - H_5 = \frac{1}{6}$$

"So $H_{n+1} - H_n$ gets smaller and smaller, just like your proposition says."

"Right!"

"We also said that $H_1, H_2, H_3, H_4, H_5, \cdots$ keeps getting bigger and bigger, but now we know that it's getting bigger and bigger by less and less."

"Hold up!" Tetra said. "The proposition that I wrote before says the same thing, that it's getting bigger and bigger by less and less, right? Um, this one here." Tetra pointed to a line in the notebook:

For all positive integers n, $H_{n+1} - H_n > H_{n+2} - H_{n+1}$.

"Exactly. 'Bigger and bigger by less and less' is a pretty vague expression, but when you put everything into symbols, there's no question about the meaning. A lot of people think that writing things out like this is a pain, but in most cases math would be a lot harder to understand if you wrote it using words. Math is a language. Learn to speak it, and you'll not only understand it better, you'll be able to express your ideas more clearly."

"You told me to practice whenever I can, so I'm going to rewrite this one in math language. Is this right?"

$$\forall n \in \mathbb{N} \quad H_{n+1} - H_n > H_{n+2} - H_{n+1}$$

"Perfect," I said.

Tetra beamed.

8.2.5 There Exists...

"I'm starting to see something here," I said. "The first glimmer of the treasure that we're after."

"Where?" Tetra replied.

"Let's see if we can find out. Define $H_n = \sum_{k=1}^{n} \frac{1}{k}$, like we've been doing. We already know that as n gets bigger, H_n does too. But we also said that the bigger it gets, the smaller its next increase will be. That leads to an interesting question: Can we make H_n as big as we want, by adding more of the sequence to it? If not, just how big *can* it become?"

"So what you're asking," Tetra said, her head resting on her hand, "is if this sequence hits a wall somewhere?"

$$\frac{1}{1} + \frac{1}{2} + \frac{1}{3} + \frac{1}{4} + \frac{1}{5} + \cdots$$

"Yeah, I think that's where the problem on the card is leading us. We need to find out if this sequence converges or diverges. I'll write it out formally."

> ### Problem 8-1
>
> Let $\mathbb{R}$ be the set of real numbers, and $\mathbb{N}$ the set of positive integers. Determine the validity of the following statement.
>
> $$\forall M \in \mathbb{R} \quad \exists n \in \mathbb{N} \quad M < \sum_{k=1}^{n} \frac{1}{k}$$

"You wrote this 'E' backwards."

"Well, that is an 'E'—it means 'exists' here—but you write it backwards like that when you use it in a math statement."

"Ooookay... So you would read this, 'For all M in $\mathbb{R}$, an n exists in $\mathbb{N}$...'?"

"Something like that. You can say 'n exists,' but most times people say 'there exists n.' You'll also hear people add in a 'such that' to make things clearer. So the whole thing would become, 'For all M in $\mathbb{R}$, there exists n in $\mathbb{N}$ such that $M < \sum_{k=1}^{n} \frac{1}{k}$.'"

"Wow, there's a lot packed in there. But I think I get it."

I wrote two more statements in the notebook, labeling them (a) and (b):

$$\forall M \in \mathbb{R} \quad \exists n \in \mathbb{N} \quad M < \sum_{k=1}^{n} \frac{1}{k} \qquad \text{(a)}$$

$$\exists n \in \mathbb{N} \quad \forall M \in \mathbb{R} \quad M < \sum_{k=1}^{n} \frac{1}{k} \qquad \text{(b)}$$

"These two lines look similar, but they mean very different things. Can you spot the difference?"

When I could see she didn't have the answer, I said, "Here, since these are kind of long statements, let me add some brackets to help clear things up:"

$$\underbrace{\left[\forall M \in \mathbb{R} \; \exists n \in \mathbb{N} \underbrace{\left[M < \sum_{k=1}^{n} \frac{1}{k}\right]}_{\text{scope of } n}\right]}_{\text{scope of } M} \quad \text{(a)}$$

$$\underbrace{\exists n \in \mathbb{N} \; \forall M \in \mathbb{R} \underbrace{\left[M < \sum_{k=1}^{n} \frac{1}{k}\right]}_{\text{scope of } M}}_{\text{scope of } n} \quad \text{(b)}$$

Another pause.

"It might help if I write them out into words, too:"

For all M in $\mathbb{R}$, there exists n in $\mathbb{N}$ such that $M < \sum_{k=1}^{n} \frac{1}{k}$ (a)

There exists n in $\mathbb{N}$ such that for all M in $\mathbb{R}$, $M < \sum_{k=1}^{n} \frac{1}{k}$ (b)

Tetra's lips moved as she read through the lines.

"I think I understand," she finally said. "The order changes things. In (a), you have an M and you're looking for an n. M won't change when you try different ns. But in (b) you're starting out with an n, and saying that something is true for any M you try."

"That's right. In (a) you're going to choose an M, and then find an n that makes the statement true, and the statement says that you can always find one. With (b), though, you find an n first, a pretty amazing n that will make the inequality true for any real number M. In (b), that n will just sit there, unchanging, regardless of what M becomes. The problem that we're working on is the (a) version. Got it?"

"I think so."

"When you try to pin down the difference between the two text versions, things can get kind of slippery. Once you're comfortable with the mathematical statements things are a lot more precise."

"All the more reason to stick to symbols, I guess," Tetra said. "What's the M in that inequality, anyway?"

"What do you think it is?"

"Um... some really big number?"

"Close. Remember, we were talking about things getting as big as we want, and making a statement about something being bigger than that. But it's clearer to name 'as big as we want' M. If there's some n like the one the problem describes, no matter what we pick to be our M, then we can always make H_n bigger than M. But if we can find an M so that H_n never reaches M, no matter how big we make n, that would mean that we can't make H_n as big as we want."

"There's a lot in there to chew on."

"You want to stop?"

"No... Well, maybe. I'm definitely expanding my math vocabulary, though."

"Why don't we call it quits for today. It's about time for Ms. Mizutani to make her appearance, anyway. Want to meet again tomorrow and open up this treasure chest together?"

"Sure thing!"

"I bet you never knew math could be so exciting," I grinned.

Tetra blushed. "I can hardly wait till tomorrow."

8.3   An Infinite Upward Spiral

The next day I ate lunch in the music room, which was much more crowded than usual—an impromptu piano recital by two attractive pianists had drawn a crowd.

One was Miruka; the other was her friend Ay-Ay, keyboard wizard and president of "Fortissimo," the school piano club. She was a second year student, like Miruka and me, but she had a different homeroom.

Miruka and Ay-Ay were playing a piece based on rising scales. Their hands worked in marvelous synchronization, taking turns playing a similar rapid phrase that went further and further up the scale with each repetition. At least that was my first impression, but the scale had gone on for so long that it would have been off the top of the keyboard by now. Then I noticed that the key was lower than it had been just moments before. When had it gone down? This continued in bewildering fashion, as if progressing through an infinite number of octaves without getting any higher, an eternal variation. I was amazed a piano could produce such an effect.

From where I stood I could see Miruka's fingers—those soft, warm fingers—as they danced up the keyboard. Watching closely, I finally caught the moment when her hand moved back to a lower position. Yet despite what my eyes told me, my ears heard only the incessant climb of the music.

The piece came to an end, fading out in a decrescendo. As the last notes died away, everyone around the piano erupted in cheers and applause. Miruka and Ay-Ay stood and took a bow.

Miruka walked over to me as the crowd began to disperse. "Well?" she asked. "What did you think?"

"That was. . . really weird. Like you're using a finite number of notes to create an infinite number of keys."

"Pretty cool contradiction, huh? A divergence to infinity within limited bounds."

"You do it using notes separated by an octave?"

"Right. Multiple notes being played one octave apart, going up in parallel. The higher a note goes, though, the softer you play it. Just as it disappears off the top, you softly bring in a lower note. The notes are loudest in the middle. That tricks your ear into thinking you're hearing the sound get higher and higher, an infinite ascension. You can't pull it off with two hands, though, so it takes two people to play."

Ay-Ay hit Miruka playfully on the back of the head. "Hey, stop giving away my secrets! Do you have any idea how long I spent writing that to keep it from sounding like a boring scale? Not easy keeping the audience's attention with something so simple. But it's only the really simple pieces that let the magic shine through, you know? Seriously, though, thanks for the help. I might need those fingers again, so don't let anything happen to them."

"Next time'll cost you: I want a piece based on the Möbius strip."

"Don't hold your breath." Ay-Ay walked off towards her classroom.

Miruka walked with me back to our room, twirling a finger as she hummed.

8.4 An Ill-Tempered Zeta

During what was left of lunch, Miruka sat at the desk in front of me, nibbling on a candy bar.

"Have you seen the latest from Muraki?" she asked, pulling out a card.

Miruka's card

$$\zeta(1)$$

The card was different from the one he'd given me.

"I guess he wants me to learn about the zeta function," she said, "but everybody knows $\zeta(1)$ diverges to positive infinity, and it's a really easy proof. Yawn town. So I decided to look for something with a slightly different rhythm. First—"

I nodded in all the right places as Miruka began her rapid-fire exposition. I'd heard of the zeta function, and knew that it had something to do with modern mathematical research, so I figured Mr. Muraki was raising the bar for Miruka. *And not for me, apparently.*

I wondered if Tetra had figured out anything about the problem Mr. Muraki had given me. She had shown real insight—anyone who could use procedural and declarative statements had serious math potential, whether she admitted it or not.

At first I had seen our relationship as teacher-student, but something had changed. The more we talked, the more I realized she was teaching me, too—a new recurrence relation, you might say. Minor changes with every step, checking what we'd done as we moved along. And those eyes . . .

"Hey."

Miruka glared at me.

Oops. I wasn't paying attention to a word she said. That was probably a mistake.

The bell rang, signaling the end of lunch. Miruka stood up without a word and marched back to her seat.

Yep. Big mistake.

8.5 OVERESTIMATING INFINITY

The library was closed for inventory, so I met Tetra in the student lounge. We headed to some seats at the side of the room, and Tetra sat primly beside me. The flutist had brought a friend today, and they were playing a duet.

"Sorry I was late," she said. Whatever perfume she was wearing, it smelled wonderful.

I opened my notebook and started working the answer to the problem we had begun the day before.

Problem 8-1

Let $\mathbb{R}$ be the set of real numbers, and $\mathbb{N}$ the set of positive integers. Determine the validity of the following statement.

$$\forall M \in \mathbb{R} \quad \exists n \in \mathbb{N} \quad M < \sum_{k=1}^{n} \frac{1}{k}$$

Tetra leaned in to watch as I wrote:

$$
\begin{aligned}
H_8 &= \sum_{k=1}^{8} \frac{1}{k} \\
&= \frac{1}{1} + \frac{1}{2} + \frac{1}{3} + \frac{1}{4} + \frac{1}{5} + \frac{1}{6} + \frac{1}{7} + \frac{1}{8} \\
&= \frac{1}{1} + \underbrace{\left(\frac{1}{2}\right)}_{1 \text{ term}} + \underbrace{\left(\frac{1}{3} + \frac{1}{4}\right)}_{2 \text{ terms}} + \underbrace{\left(\frac{1}{5} + \frac{1}{6} + \frac{1}{7} + \frac{1}{8}\right)}_{4 \text{ terms}} \\
&\geqslant \frac{1}{1} + \left(\frac{1}{2}\right) + \left(\frac{1}{4} + \frac{1}{4}\right) + \left(\frac{1}{8} + \frac{1}{8} + \frac{1}{8} + \frac{1}{8}\right) \\
&= \frac{1}{1} + \left(\frac{1}{2} \times 1\right) + \left(\frac{1}{4} \times 2\right) + \left(\frac{1}{8} \times 4\right) \\
&= \frac{1}{1} + \frac{1}{2} + \frac{1}{2} + \frac{1}{2} \\
&= 1 + \frac{3}{2}
\end{aligned}
$$

"Okay, let me explain what we've got so far. Part way down the line we get a $\geqslant$ sign, and that breaks the chain of identities. Now we've got two chains, linked like this:"

$$\underbrace{a = b = c = d}_{\text{chain 1}} \geqslant \underbrace{e = f = g = h}_{\text{chain 2}}$$

"From this we know that:"

$$a \geqslant h$$

"To create the first line of chain 2, I replaced some of the numbers in the last line of chain 1 with smaller values, so we know that chain 2 has to be less than chain 1. When we put the actual values we were working with back in, we get $H_8 \geqslant 1 + \frac{3}{2}$. We only did this for H_8, but we could do the same thing for $H_1, H_2, H_4, H_8, H_{16}$ which would give us this:"

$$H_1 \geqslant 1 + \frac{0}{2}$$

$$H_2 \geqslant 1 + \frac{1}{2}$$

$$H_4 \geqslant 1 + \frac{2}{2}$$

$$H_8 \geqslant 1 + \frac{3}{2}$$

$$H_{16} \geqslant 1 + \frac{4}{2}$$

$$\vdots$$

"Generalizing this is easy," I said. "We let m be some number 0 or greater, and then the following will be true:"

$$H_{2^m} \geqslant 1 + \frac{m}{2}$$

"But that's an inequality, not an equation," Tetra said. "Doesn't that mean we can't find the value of H_{2^m}?"

"That's not what we're trying to do here. We just want to know if we can make H_{2^m} as big as we want. Think about what happens to this inequality when m becomes really big."

Tetra paused to think. "Oh, okay... Hey, I get it! We can! We *can* make it as big as we want! Just make m bigger, and then $1 + \frac{m}{2}$ will get bigger too! And the inequality says that making m bigger will make H_{2^m} bigger!"

"Okay, let's do it right, using the problem. The question we need to answer is, when somebody gives us an M, how will we find an n so that $M < \sum_{k=1}^{n} \frac{1}{k}$?"

"We can do that. No matter how big M is, we just have to make an m that's big enough so this works:"

$$M < 1 + \frac{m}{2}$$

"We can just let m be some integer greater than 2M," she continued. "Then, once we have that, m, we let $n = 2^m$. Basically we're using m to create the n. That would mean this:"

$$M < 1 + \frac{m}{2} \leqslant H_{2^m} = H_n = \sum_{k=1}^{n} \frac{1}{k}$$

"That's right," I said. "So here's the answer to the problem."

Answer to Problem 8-1

Let $\mathbb{R}$ be the set of real numbers, and $\mathbb{N}$ the set of positive integers. *Then the following statement is true.*

$$\forall M \in \mathbb{R} \quad \exists n \in \mathbb{N} \quad M < \sum_{k=1}^{n} \frac{1}{k}$$

"Wow, that's the first math problem I've ever done where I didn't need to solve for some specific value. All we had to do was use the inequality to push things up from underneath." Tetra raised both hands in an exaggerated stretch.

"And it's pushed up our first treasure," I said. "We found out that we can make $\sum_{k=1}^{n} \frac{1}{k}$ as big as we want."

"It's kinda weird. There's this number out there, $1 + \frac{m}{2}$, getting bigger and bigger, using an inequality to push this other number, H_{2^m}, up along with it. I'm okay with that part, but where it gets confusing is that even though $\frac{1}{k}$ is getting smaller and smaller, we can still pile enough of them up to make $\sum_{k=1}^{n} \frac{1}{k}$ as big as we want it to be. It just seems like it shouldn't work that way."

"I know what you mean. Let's take that phrase 'as big as we want it to be' and write it down using mathematical notation. To keep things simple, we'll just talk about sequences that only have positive terms." I started scribbling in my notebook as I spoke. "Say that we have a sequence of elements $a_k > 0$ $(k = 1, 2, 3, \cdots)$, and a partial sum $\sum_{k=1}^{n} a_k$. Now check out this statement:"

$$\forall M \in \mathbb{R} \quad \exists n \in \mathbb{N} \quad M < \sum_{k=1}^{n} a_k$$

"When this is true, we're going to say that as $n \to \infty$, then $\sum_{k=1}^{n} a_k$ diverges towards infinity. That's a definition that we're assigning, right? And when that happens, we can also say this:"

$$\sum_{k=1}^{\infty} a_k = \infty$$

"That last problem that we were working on was like this, but for the specific case where $a_k = \frac{1}{k}$. Now that we've defined what it means to diverge to infinity, we can make statements about it, like 'the infinite series $\sum_{k=1}^{\infty} \frac{1}{k}$ diverges towards infinity.' "

Tetra stared at what I had written with a serious look on her face.

"So I guess if you keep adding positive numbers up, you can pile them as high as you want. But that makes sense, right? I mean, there's an infinite number of them, after all."

"Maybe, maybe not. How would you answer a problem like this?"

Problem 8-2

Let $\mathbb{R}$ be the set of real numbers, let $\mathbb{N}$ be the set of positive integers, and assume that $\forall k \in \mathbb{N} \; a_k > 0$. Determine the validity of the following statement.

$$\forall M \in \mathbb{R} \;\; \exists n \in \mathbb{N} \;\; M < \sum_{k=1}^{n} a_k$$

"That should be true," Tetra replied. "If the a_ks are all positive numbers, then adding a whole bunch of them together—in other words, making n big enough—will make the sum $\sum_{k=1}^{n} a_k$ keep getting bigger and bigger, right? So you just keep making it bigger and bigger until you go past M."

"I see why you'd think that, but believe it or not, you're overestimating the size of your infinities, if that makes any sense."

"I'm not sure it does. How can I keep adding positive numbers forever and ever but not get anywhere?"

"Let's try an example. What happens if we defined a_k like this?"

$$a_k = \frac{1}{2^k}$$

"No clue."

"Well, you see that the a_k for any positive integer k will be positive, right? But it turns out $\sum_{k=1}^{n} a_k$ can't get very big. Take a look."

$$\sum_{k=1}^{n} a_k = \sum_{k=1}^{n} \frac{1}{2^k}$$

"That's just from the definition of a_k. Next, let's write the sum out explicitly:"

$$= \frac{1}{2^1} + \frac{1}{2^2} + \cdots + \frac{1}{2^n}$$

"Now let's simplify the calculation, first by adding and subtracting a $\frac{1}{2^0}$…"

$$= \left(\frac{1}{2^0} + \frac{1}{2^1} + \frac{1}{2^2} + \cdots + \frac{1}{2^n} \right) - \frac{1}{2^0}$$

"…and then by using the formula for a geometric series:"

$$= \frac{1 - \frac{1}{2^{n+1}}}{1 - \frac{1}{2}} - 1$$

"We can take the $-\frac{1}{2^{n+1}}$ term out of the numerator by making this an inequality:"

$$< \frac{1}{1 - \frac{1}{2}} - 1$$

"Now all that's left is a bit of arithmetic:"

$$= 2$$

"I don't think you simplified that last line right," Tetra said.

"Really? Oh, good catch. That 2 should be a 1. So we end up with this:"

$$\sum_{k=1}^{n} \frac{1}{2^k} < 1$$

"The fraction $\frac{1}{2^k}$ approaches 0 so fast that $\sum_{k=1}^{n} a_k = \sum_{k=1}^{n} \frac{1}{2^k}$ is never going to reach 1, no matter how big you make n. You can find an n that will reach any $M < 1$, but no n will ever give you an $M \geqslant 1$. That means that $a_k = \frac{1}{2^k}$ is a counterexample to the statement in our problem, so that statement isn't necessarily true."

Answer to Problem 8-2

Let $\mathbb{R}$ be the set of real numbers, let $\mathbb{N}$ be the set of positive integers, and assume that $\forall k \in \mathbb{N} \ a_k > 0$. *Then the following does not necessarily hold.*

$$\forall M \in \mathbb{R} \ \exists n \in \mathbb{N} \ M < \sum_{k=1}^{n} a_k$$

"Okay, my mind is officially blown. How can you add up an infinite number of things, but depending on what you add you might head off towards infinity, or you may never even reach 1?" She crossed her arms in a defiant pose. "Oh, and while we're on the subject of mind blowing, two minus one equals two? I expected better."

"We all make mistakes," I smiled. "At least that one didn't throw off the proof too much."

"Just saying. You're the one always talking about checking your work."

8.6 HARMONY IN THE CLASSROOOM

I stopped Miruka on her way out of class after school the next day. She hadn't said a word to me since storming off the day before.

"Hey, Miruka. About yesterday...the zeta function. Sorry I zoned out like that. I don't really know much about that function. Could you tell me a little more about it? How $\zeta(1)$ diverges to positive infinity?"

Cold silence.

"Please?"

Finally she went to the blackboard, picked up a piece of chalk, and began writing:

$$\zeta(s) = \sum_{k=1}^{\infty} \frac{1}{k^s} \qquad \text{(definition of the zeta function)}$$

"There. The zeta function $\zeta(s)$, also called the Riemann zeta function. It's defined as an infinite series. If you let $s = 1$, then the result is what's called the harmonic series, which is normally written as H_∞:"

$$H_\infty = \sum_{k=1}^{\infty} \frac{1}{k} \qquad \text{(definition of the harmonic series)}$$

"In other words, the zeta function with $s = 1$ and the harmonic series are equivalent."

So Mr. Muraki had given Miruka and me the same problem after all. Mine was just presented as the harmonic series.

Miruka continued scribbling equations on the board.

"A partial sum H_n like this is called a harmonic number:"

$$H_n = \sum_{k=1}^{n} \frac{1}{k} \qquad \text{(definition of a harmonic number)}$$

"As n approaches ∞, the harmonic numbers H_n approach the harmonic series H_∞:"

$$H_\infty = \lim_{n \to \infty} H_n$$

The squeak of chalk on blackboard filled the room.

"Also, as $n \to \infty$ the harmonic numbers diverge towards positive infinity:"

$$\lim_{n \to \infty} H_n = \infty$$

"That means that the harmonic series also diverges towards infinity:"

$$H_\infty = \infty$$

"And from that, we get that $\zeta(1)$ must diverge towards infinity:"

$$\zeta(1) = \infty$$

The zeta function, the harmonic series, and harmonic numbers

$$\zeta(s) = \sum_{k=1}^{\infty} \frac{1}{k^s} \qquad \text{(definition of the zeta function)}$$

$$H_\infty = \sum_{k=1}^{\infty} \frac{1}{k} \qquad \text{(definition of the harmonic series)}$$

$$H_n = \sum_{k=1}^{n} \frac{1}{k} \qquad \text{(definition of a harmonic number)}$$

"But what lets us say that all this diverging is going on in the first place?" Miruka glanced at me and smiled. It was good to have her back.

Relieved, I told her about the proof that Tetra and I had worked out, how we had shown that when m was an integer 0 or greater, the inequality $H_{2^m} \geqslant 1 + \frac{m}{2}$ would always be true.

"Right," Miruka said. "That's the same proof that Oresme gave in the fourteenth century."

Miruka closed her eyes, shaped her left hand into an L, and waved it as if conducting an orchestra.

A moment later her eyes popped open. "Remember when we went to the discrete world looking for exponential functions?"

"Sure. We solved them using difference equations."

"We have unfinished business there. We need to go back and look for the inverse of the exponential functions. We have to find the discrete world equivalent of the natural logarithm."

Problem 8-3

Define a discrete world function $L(x)$ corresponding to the continuous world logarithmic function $\ln x$.

$$\text{continuous world} \quad \longleftrightarrow \quad \text{discrete world}$$
$$\ln x \quad \longleftrightarrow \quad L(x) = ?$$

"But not now," she said. "I'm going home. Think about it, see what you come up with."

Miruka brushed the chalk dust from her fingers as she walked towards the door. Reaching it, she turned back towards me. "And a piece of advice: draw more graphs. Math isn't all equations, you know."

8.7 Two Worlds, Four Operators

That night I sat at my desk, notebook open in front of me, and thought about Miruka's problem: finding a discrete world equivalent to the natural logarithm function $\ln x$.

When we looked for the exponential function, we created a correspondence between the equations $De^x = e^x$ and $\Delta E(x) = E(x)$. In other words, we had associated derivatives with differences.

I decided to try something similar, starting with the derivative of ln. I remembered its derivative from one of my books:

$$f(x) = \ln x$$
$$\downarrow \text{ differentiate}$$
$$f'(x) = \frac{1}{x}$$

I hoped that I could use this property as the criterion to evaluate the function I was after. Since $\frac{1}{x}$ can also be written as x^{-1}, I thought it might be better to say that the derivative of the function I wanted was x^{-1}. When I wrote that using the D notation that Miruka had used, this is what I got:

$$D \ln x = x^{-1} \qquad \text{derivative of the lnfunction}$$

We had found that the discrete world didn't have exponents, though—its equivalent was the falling factorial. Also, the discrete version of differentiation was difference equations. So, by analogy, I figured that the discrete world function $L(x)$ I was looking for should be equivalent to $\ln x$ if it fulfilled a condition like this:

$$\Delta L(x) = x^{\underline{-1}} \qquad \text{difference equation for } L(x)$$

That's where I hit my first snag. When I looked back at my notes, I saw that Miruka and I had only used falling factorials in cases where $n > 0$.

**Definition of the falling factorial
(for positive integer n)**

$$x^{\underline{n}} = \underbrace{(x-0)(x-1)\cdots(x-(n-1))}_{n\ factors}$$

Now I had to rework our definition of the falling factorial so I could use it with negative exponents. I wrote out a few explicit $x^{\underline{n}}$s while I thought about this:

$$x^{\underline{4}} = (x-0)(x-1)(x-2)(x-3)$$
$$x^{\underline{3}} = (x-0)(x-1)(x-2)$$
$$x^{\underline{2}} = (x-0)(x-1)$$
$$x^{\underline{1}} = (x-0)$$

After staring at these for a while, I noticed something interesting. Underneath, I wrote:

· Dividing $x^{\underline{4}}$ by $(x-3)$ gives $x^{\underline{3}}$

· Dividing $x^{\underline{3}}$ by $(x-2)$ gives $x^{\underline{2}}$

· Dividing $x^{\underline{2}}$ by $(x-1)$ gives $x^{\underline{1}}$

This led to a natural pattern:

· Dividing $x^{\underline{1}}$ by $(x-0)$ gives $x^{\underline{0}}$

· Dividing $x^{\underline{0}}$ by $(x+1)$ gives $x^{\underline{-1}}$

· Dividing $x^{\underline{-1}}$ by $(x+2)$ gives $x^{\underline{-2}}$

· Dividing $x^{\underline{-2}}$ by $(x+3)$ gives $x^{\underline{-3}}$

I rewrote my discovery as equations:

$$x^{\underline{0}} = 1$$

$$x^{\underline{-1}} = \frac{1}{(x+1)}$$

$$x^{\underline{-2}} = \frac{1}{(x+1)(x+2)}$$

$$x^{\underline{-3}} = \frac{1}{(x+1)(x+2)(x+3)}$$

Now I could write out my extended definition.

Definition of the falling factorial (for integer n)

$$x^{\underline{n}} = \begin{cases} (x-0)(x-1)\cdots(x-(n-1)) & \text{for } n > 0 \\ 1 & \text{for } n = 0 \\ \dfrac{1}{(x+1)(x+2)\cdots(x+(-n))} & \text{for } n < 0 \end{cases}$$

With that done, it was back to logarithms. My goal was to solve this difference equation:

$$\Delta L(x) = x^{\underline{-1}}$$

The definition of the Δ operator said that the left side would be $L(x+1) - L(x)$. My new and improved definition of the falling factorial said that the right side would be $\frac{1}{x+1}$, allowing me to rewrite the equation:

$$L(x+1) - L(x) = \frac{1}{x+1} \qquad \text{difference equation for } L(x)$$

Now all I had to do was solve for $L(x)$. *Déjà vu all over again.*

I thumbed back through my notebook to the pages Tetra and I had been working on the other day, and found our recurrence relation for the harmonic number H_n:

$$H_{n+1} - H_n = \frac{1}{n+1}$$

The difference equation for $L(x)$ was exactly the same as the recurrence relation for harmonic numbers. That meant I could just define $L(1) = 1$, and simplify all the rest:

$$L(x) = \sum_{k=1}^{x} \frac{1}{k}$$

And even simpler using the H_n notation of harmonic numbers:

$$L(x) = H_x \qquad \text{for positive integer } x$$

Thanks to my notes, the answer to this problem had fallen into my lap.

Answer to Problem 8-3

$$L(x) = \sum_{k=1}^{x} \frac{1}{k}$$
$$= H_x \qquad \text{(a harmonic number)}$$

I wrote out the correspondence, just to be complete.

Correspondence between logarithms and harmonic numbers

continuous world $\longleftrightarrow$ discrete world

$$\ln x \quad \longleftrightarrow \quad H_x = \sum_{k=1}^{x} \frac{1}{k}$$

Something about this didn't feel right, though. Why should there be such a close association between logarithms and harmonic numbers?

Then I remembered something Miruka had mentioned in passing as we were finishing our discussion of derivatives and differences. Something about integrals and summations, and how they had a similar correspondence between the continuous world and the discrete world. We had talked about four operations in all: differentiating, taking differences, integrating, and summing. I drew a chart to help me organize my thoughts.

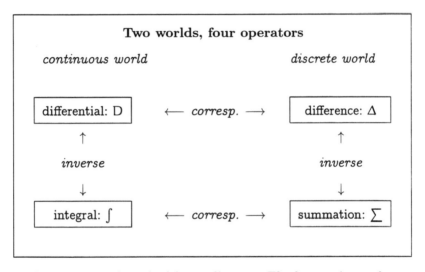

I was pretty pleased with my diagram. The harmonic numbers I was working with would go with the "summation: Σ" block in the lower right. So when I moved that over to the left, back to the continuous world—

Of course! Differentiating $\ln x$ gives $\frac{1}{x}$, which means that integrating $\frac{1}{x}$ would give $\ln x$, so there was even a correspondence between integrating and summing reciprocals. Things felt weird because I had written the correspondence as $\ln x$. I should have written it as $\int_1^x \frac{1}{t}$, giving me an updated correspondence.

Correspondence between logarithms and harmonic numbers

continuous world $\longleftrightarrow$ discrete world

$$\ln x = \int_1^x \frac{1}{t} \quad \longleftrightarrow \quad H_x = \sum_{k=1}^{x} \frac{1}{k}$$

Much better.

The integral looked naked without a trailing dt, though. I wondered if that would carry over into the discrete world as δk. It made sense to define $\delta k = 1$, and include it that way:

$$\int_1^x \frac{1}{t}\,dt \quad \longleftrightarrow \quad \sum_{k=1}^{n} \frac{1}{k}\delta k$$

If there was ever a beautiful correspondence, this was it.

I remembered Miruka's admonition to use more graphs—she knew exactly how to get to me, and it wasn't by stomping on my foot.

Okay, then. Let's draw some graphs. I needed something that would show both integrations and summations, and the areas they cover.

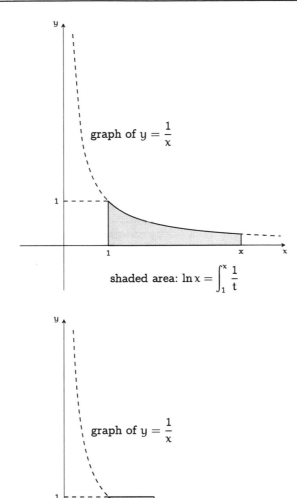

graph of $y = \dfrac{1}{x}$

shaded area: $\ln x = \displaystyle\int_1^x \dfrac{1}{t}$

graph of $y = \dfrac{1}{x}$

shaded area: $H_n = \displaystyle\sum_{k=1}^n \dfrac{1}{k}$

I stared at what I'd created, enthralled at this glimpse into two worlds.

8.8   KEYS TO THE KNOWN, DOORS TO THE UNKNOWN

"...and then I had a correspondence between natural logarithms in the continuous world and harmonic numbers in the discrete world."

I was giving Tetra a rundown of Miruka's problem as we walked our familiar path to the station after school.

"Now that I think about it, it would have been obvious if I'd paid more attention to Oresme's proof. Remember how we grouped things into 2^m-sized chunks of terms—1, 2, 4, 8—when we were showing that $\sum_{k=1}^{\infty} \frac{1}{k}$ diverges to infinity? The size of the groupings was increasing exponentially. That should have clued me in to the possibility of a similarity between harmonic numbers and logarithms, since logs are the inverse of exponentials." I didn't mention that a simple graph would have been enough to answer Miruka's problem as soon as she'd given it to me. *Another point for Miruka.*

Suddenly Tetra stopped, her face grim.

"I'm the one who asked to take on the challenge, but I didn't find a single thing. I only saw what you showed me. Guess I'm just not a math person."

"I don't think that's true at all," I said, stopping beside her. "You gave it a shot. That's the important thing. You may not have found anything, but the work you did let you understand my explanation every step of the way."

I looked down into those big eyes.

"Most people turn and run as soon as they see an equation like that. But there'll always be equations you won't understand completely. At least you're getting to where you can see the parts you get, and the parts you don't. If you just throw your hands up in the air and say it's hopeless, you'll never get anywhere. It's okay if you don't understand something. It's *not* okay if you give up before you even try."

"I don't know," she said. "I can follow along with you just fine, but there's no way I'd ever be able to do that on my own. I wouldn't know where to start."

"It's not like I'm doing anything super-original," I said. "All the problems I work on are things I've read somewhere, or variations on things I've solved in the past—problems that we did in class, examples from books, methods I talked about with friends—that kind of stuff."

I started walking again, and Tetra followed.

"When you're working on math, your mind should be thinking more like an inequality than an equation. Answers won't always be obvious and absolute, like an equals sign. You have to feel out your answers based on whatever clues you've collected. That's the key to unlocking the door to the unknown."

Some of the sparkle returned to Tetra's eyes.

"You know how you have those 'I get it!' moments when you're studying math? Just keep piling those up for now. Don't worry if it isn't stuff you figured out for yourself. Reading through a well-written proof and seeing why it's so amazing is a valuable experience, too."

"I think I know what you mean," Tetra said. "It's like listening to a native speaker when I'm studying a foreign language. Talking like they do seems like such a distant goal, but every little thing I learn helps me get a little bit closer." She smiled. "Thanks for the pep talk. I feel a lot better now. You're always so... I mean, I... Umm..."

Her feet slowed to a tortoise's pace.

"Oh, that reminds me," I said, breaking the silence. "You want to go to the planetarium this Saturday?"

"With you?"

"Kaito gave me some extra tickets. He says the show's pretty cool, but if you're not into that kind of thing—"

"Are you kidding!? I'd love to go! But... shouldn't you be taking... you know, Miruka?"

"I guess I could, if you'd rather not go."

"I'd rather! I'd rather!"

8.9   IF THERE WERE ONLY TWO PRIMES

There's just too many people in the world. Wars? Starvation? Not a problem with fewer people. Like, say, two. Adam and Eve. Okay, bad example. Though I suppose you could argue that the snake made three—lousy snake. I guess two's the limit? But, who knows. With enough time they'd probably get into trouble anyway, not to mention make more people! Increased variation brings increased opportunity for conflict—

"What are you daydreaming about?" Miruka asked.

I looked up from my notebook.

"I was just wondering what the world would be like if there were only two people."

"I don't know about only two people, but what about only two primes? I never got around to telling you about that, did I."

Miruka grabbed my notebook and started writing.

"Let's see, where to start?" she said. "I know, take a look at this formal product:"

$$\left(2^0 + 2^1 + 2^2 + \cdots\right) \cdot \left(3^0 + 3^1 + 3^2 + \cdots\right)$$

"Of course the whole thing would shoot off to infinity—that's why I called it a formal product. But we can just take the first few terms and play with those:"

$$2^0 3^0 + 2^0 3^1 + 2^1 3^0 + 2^0 3^2 + 2^1 3^1 + 2^2 3^0 + \cdots$$

"It's easier to see the pattern if you group things up as a sum of exponents:"

$$\left(2^0 3^0\right) + \left(2^0 3^1 + 2^1 3^0\right) + \left(2^0 3^2 + 2^1 3^1 + 2^2 3^0\right) + \cdots$$

"See how that lets us write this as a double summation?"

$$\sum_{n=0}^{\infty} \sum_{k=0}^{n} 2^k 3^{n-k}$$

I realized what she was doing right away. "That's a convolution. The n on the outer sigma will advance through $0, 1, 2, \cdots$, and for each step the inner sigma will generate all the exponents for the 2 and the 3 that add up to n, like they're...sharing it."

"Sharing it? Hmm, I guess you could say that. Do you see why any positive integer that has only 2s and 3s as prime factors has to appear somewhere in this sum exactly once? After all, any combination of integers 0 or greater will have to show up just once as exponents on the 2s and 3s, right?"

"Yeah, I'm with you."

8.9.1 Converging Geometric Progressions

"Okay," Miruka continued, "Now let's do the same thing with a product of infinite series, like this one, which I'll name Q_2:"

$$Q_2 = \left(\frac{1}{2^0} + \frac{1}{2^1} + \frac{1}{2^2} + \cdots \right) \cdot \left(\frac{1}{3^0} + \frac{1}{3^1} + \frac{1}{3^2} + \cdots \right)$$

"The first example we looked at headed towards infinity, but this one doesn't because the two factors are converging geometric progressions. We can use the geometric progression formula to rewrite this as a simple product:"

$$Q_2 = \left(\frac{1}{2^0} + \frac{1}{2^1} + \frac{1}{2^2} + \cdots \right) \cdot \left(\frac{1}{3^0} + \frac{1}{3^1} + \frac{1}{3^2} + \cdots \right)$$

$$= \left(\frac{1}{1 - \frac{1}{2}} \right) \cdot \left(\frac{1}{1 - \frac{1}{3}} \right) \qquad \text{(as a product)}$$

"Let's also try expanding Q_2, starting from the top, to get a sum instead:"

$$Q_2 = \left(\frac{1}{2^0} + \frac{1}{2^1} + \frac{1}{2^2} + \cdots \right) \cdot \left(\frac{1}{3^0} + \frac{1}{3^1} + \frac{1}{3^2} + \cdots \right)$$

$$= \underbrace{\left(\frac{1}{2^0 3^0} \right)}_{n=0} + \underbrace{\left(\frac{1}{2^0 3^1} + \frac{1}{2^1 3^0} \right)}_{n=1} + \underbrace{\left(\frac{1}{2^0 3^2} + \frac{1}{2^1 3^1} + \frac{1}{2^2 3^0} \right)}_{n=2} + \cdots$$

$$= \sum_{n=0}^{\infty} \sum_{k=0}^{n} \frac{1}{2^k 3^{n-k}} \qquad \text{(as a sum)}$$

"Two different ways of expressing Q_2, but they're both describing the same thing. So we can write an equation:"

$$\left(\frac{1}{1 - \frac{1}{2}} \right) \cdot \left(\frac{1}{1 - \frac{1}{3}} \right) = \sum_{n=0}^{\infty} \sum_{k=0}^{n} \frac{1}{2^k 3^{n-k}}$$

"Product on the left, sum on the right," I said. "No problem."

8.9.2 The Uniqueness of Prime Factorizations

"Let's pretend," Miruka said, "that we're in a world where 2 and 3 are the only prime numbers. That would mean that every positive integer would appear exactly once somewhere in the denominator $2^k 3^{n-k}$ of $\sum_{n=0}^{\infty} \sum_{k=0}^{n} \frac{1}{2^k 3^{n-k}}$."

"Huh?" I said. "Wait, not *every* integer is going to show up. Just the ones that have only 2 and 3 as prime factors. You aren't going to get a 5, or a 7, or a 10—"

"No, no, no. In a world where 2 and 3 are the only primes, those numbers *don't exist.* Are you still not getting this?"

"You're talking about the uniqueness of prime factorizations, right? You're saying that if every integer greater than 1 can be uniquely written as a product of primes, and if the only prime numbers were 2 and 3, then there are no integers 5 and 7 and so on. But, I dunno... What's the point?"

"Okay, so you don't like the world of two primes. Sure, it seems kind of silly since we know that there are more than two." A sly smile lit her face. "Can I interest you in a trip to a world with only m primes?"

What was she up to?

"How's that any different? Whether you say two or twenty or m, you're still talking about a finite number of primes, right? It's the same thing—there is no such world."

"Oh, yeah?" Miruka said. "Prove it."

8.9.3 The Infinitude of Primes

"Okay, I get it," I said. Miruka's smirk had tipped me off. "A proof by contradiction, right?"

Proof by contradiction is one of the fundamental ways to develop a mathematical proof. You make a statement that denies exactly what you want to prove, but then you turn around and show that the denial leads to some contradiction. At first it might seem like playing dirty, but there's no arguing with the results.

Proof by contradiction

> Proposition: A negation of the statement you wish to prove

$$\downarrow$$

Leads to a contradiction

$$\downarrow$$

The proposition must be false

$$\downarrow$$

> Conclusion: The statement you wish to prove must be true

"Good, you're finally caught up. Now let's contradict ourselves into a proof showing that there are an infinite number of primes."

"Hang on. If you're about to walk me through Euclid's proof then that's old territory. You assume that there are a finite number of primes, then multiply all of them together and add 1 to get a new prime, which—"

Miruka silenced me with the wag of a finger.

"Assume," she began, "that there are a finite number of primes. m of them, let's say. Then we could line them all up, smallest to largest, like this:"

$$p_1, p_2, \ldots, p_k, \ldots, p_m$$

"The first three primes would be $p_1 = 2$, $p_2 = 3$, and $p_3 = 5$, right? So let's look at this finite product of infinite sums, Q_m:"

$$
\begin{aligned}
Q_m &= \left(\frac{1}{2^0} + \frac{1}{2^1} + \frac{1}{2^2} + \cdots \right) \times \left(\frac{1}{3^0} + \frac{1}{3^1} + \frac{1}{3^2} + \cdots \right) \\
&\quad \times \cdots \times \left(\frac{1}{p_m{}^0} + \frac{1}{p_m{}^1} + \frac{1}{p_m{}^2} + \cdots \right) \\
&= \prod_{k=1}^{m} \left(\frac{1}{p_k{}^0} + \frac{1}{p_k{}^1} + \frac{1}{p_k{}^2} + \cdots \right) \\
&= \prod_{k=1}^{m} \frac{1}{1 - \frac{1}{p_k}} \qquad \text{(as a product)}
\end{aligned}
$$

"All I've done here is beef up the Q_2 expansion that we did for two primes so it can handle m primes. Since we're just multiplying m terms, and m is a finite number, then Q_m must be finite, too."

I traced through the equations and let it settle in.

"Right... Okay, I see that. A prime p_k will be 2 or greater, so the geometric series $\frac{1}{p_k{}^0} + \frac{1}{p_k{}^1} + \frac{1}{p_k{}^2} + \cdots$ will converge towards $\frac{1}{1 - 1/p_k}$, which is some finite number. Got it."

"Good. Okay, now here's where things get interesting."

Miruka wet her upper lip with the tip of her tongue.

"Keeping in mind that m is some finite number, we need to 'share' the exponents, as you like to put it, not between two primes, but among m primes. Here's how:"

$$
Q_m = \left(\frac{1}{2^0} + \frac{1}{2^1} + \frac{1}{2^2} + \cdots \right) \times \left(\frac{1}{3^0} + \frac{1}{3^1} + \frac{1}{3^2} + \cdots \right)
$$

$$
\times \cdots \times \left(\frac{1}{p_m{}^0} + \frac{1}{p_m{}^1} + \frac{1}{p_m{}^2} + \cdots \right)
$$

$$
= \underbrace{\left(\frac{1}{2^0 3^0 5^0 \cdots p_m^0} \right)}_{\text{sum of exponents} = 0} + \underbrace{\left(\frac{1}{2^1 3^0 5^0 \cdots p_m^0} + \cdots + \frac{1}{2^0 3^0 5^0 \cdots p_m^1} \right)}_{\text{sum of exponents} = 1} + \cdots
$$

$$
= \sum_{n=0}^{\infty} \underbrace{\sum \frac{1}{2^{r_1} 3^{r_2} 5^{r_3} \cdots p_m^{r_m}}}_{\text{sum of exponents} = n} \qquad \text{(as a sum)}
$$

"I'm stuck on that last line," I said. "For one thing, why doesn't the inner sigma have any limits on it?"

"Just assume it means that we're taking the total sum of all $r_1, r_2, \cdots, r_m$ that meet the condition $r_1 + r_2 + \cdots + r_m = n$."

"Which would mean all combinations where the sum of the exponents is n?"

"Right, writing the exponent for prime p_k as r_k, and summing up $\frac{1}{\text{product of primes}}$ for every combination like that. Now, pay attention to the denominator, the part that's a product of primes. It looks like this, right?"

$$
2^{r_1} 3^{r_2} 5^{r_3} \cdots p_m^{r_m}
$$

"According to our proposition, the one we want to contradict, there's only m primes in the world. So the uniqueness of prime factorizations says that all positive integers can be factored into some unique form of $p_1^{r_1} p_2^{r_2} p_3^{r_3} \cdots p_m^{r_m}$. That means that if we expand Q_m, then every positive integer will show up exactly once in the denominator of the resulting $\frac{1}{\text{product of primes}}$ terms."

"The same as we did in the case where 2 and 3 were the only primes."

Miruka nodded. "Now since every positive integer will appear exactly once, that means Q_m expands like this:"

$$Q_m = \frac{1}{1} + \frac{1}{2} + \frac{1}{3} + \frac{1}{4} + \cdots$$

"That's... the harmonic series!"

"Imagine that."

"Q_m is supposed to be finite, but the harmonic series diverges to infinity."

"Exactly. And we know that Q_m is finite, because we showed that using a converging infinite geometric series:"

$$Q_m = \prod_{k=1}^{m} \frac{1}{1 - \frac{1}{p_k}} \qquad \text{(a finite value)}$$

"But we've also shown that Q_m is equivalent to the harmonic series:"

$$Q_m = \sum_{k=1}^{\infty} \frac{1}{k} \qquad \text{(the harmonic series)}$$

"Which means we can equate them like this:"

$$\prod_{k=1}^{m} \frac{1}{1 - \frac{1}{p_k}} = \sum_{k=1}^{\infty} \frac{1}{k}$$

"A finite number on the left, infinity on the right. That enough of a contradiction for ya?"

I nodded. "Yeah, that would do it."

"And there you have it. The proposition that there are a finite number of primes is false, so it follows that there are indeed an infinite number of primes." Miruka held up a finger and announced, "*Quod erat demonstrandum.*"

Fantastic! She had given me a real treasure, showing how the divergence of harmonic series shows up in the proof of an infinite number of primes.

"A beautiful proof, isn't it?" Miruka said. "It was passed down to us from the master."

"The master?"

"The greatest mathematician of the eighteenth century. Someone once said he did calculations like a man breathes, or an eagle glides on the wind. It was second nature to him." Miruka looked me in the eye. "Leonhard Euler."

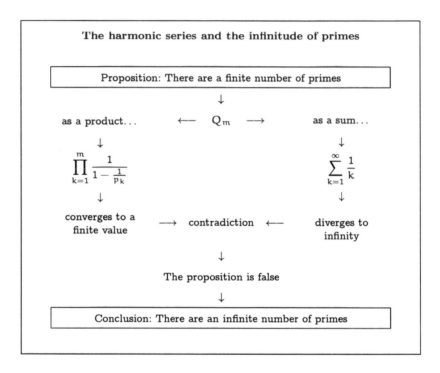

The harmonic series and the infinitude of primes

Proposition: There are a finite number of primes

$\downarrow$

as a product... $\longleftarrow \quad Q_m \quad \longrightarrow$ as a sum...

$$\prod_{k=1}^{m} \frac{1}{1 - \frac{1}{p_k}} \qquad\qquad \sum_{k=1}^{\infty} \frac{1}{k}$$

converges to a $\longrightarrow$ contradiction $\longleftarrow$ diverges to
finite value   infinity

$\downarrow$

The proposition is false

$\downarrow$

Conclusion: There are an infinite number of primes

8.10 UNDER THE STARS

The planetarium was filled with the usual weekend crowd of couples and families. After a long wait in line, Tetra and I finally made it inside and settled into our seats. A black, misshapen projector crouched in the middle of the domed room.

Tetra stifled a yawn. "Sorry. I woke up super early this morning. I was so excited about coming here today. With you."

The lights went down, and twilight surrounded us. The sun set and a star appeared, then another, and another. Gradually the room fell into darkness, and points of light filled the sky.

"Wow," Tetra sighed.

A recorded voice announced, "Let us take you on a journey...to the North Pole."

The heavens shuddered, and the stars streaked as we took off. My body tensed with the illusion of being catapulted into space.

A pale light waxed and waned, surrounding us in a multilayered curtain of pulsing gradations. A child shouted "The aurora!" and was quickly shushed. The crowd was silent after that, bathing in a luminous harmony.

We had left our world, and now Tetra and I floated in some other place, some other time. We were alone, just the two of us gazing into space. What should have been a finite number of stars invoked images of infinity.

My heart skipped a beat as I felt Tetra press against my arm, her sweet fragrance settling around me.

Tetra...?

The narration described the constellations above us, the axial tilt of the Earth, the midnight sun, but I was unable to follow any of it. The constellations no longer resembled fantastic beasts and heroes, but rather the many faces of Tetra. Tetra smiling when I called her name. Tetra scurrying about at school. Tetra working hard to understand a problem. Tetra engaged in her studies. Single-minded, focused, ebullient Tetra.

Was it possible? Was that very same Tetra...in love with me?

My mind spun.

Our feelings for each other may never reach equivalence, but maybe we could approach some common point. Maybe we could find some recurrence relation that, given enough time, would bring us parallel. We share a common point in time. Ahead of us there is little that we can see, so many unknowns, but we can reach for infinity. We can use what we find, use the knowledge that we gain. We have no wings, but we have words.

I'm not sure how long I sat there, staring at the whirling stars, but eventually the aurora faded and the narration pulled me back to reality.

"We hope that you have enjoyed this journey. . ."

The lights came up, erasing the stars. What had been a night sky teeming with stars transformed once again into the rough screen of the dome above us. The other viewers returned from their own fantasies, though not without relief that the world they knew was still here. People coughed, and stretched, and collected their things, and trudged back to their daily lives.

I, however, remained sitting. Tetra still pinned me down, keeping us in that faraway land beneath a rippling curtain of light.

I turned my head toward her, frantically searching for the right words, acutely aware of her weight on my arm.

I looked down.

She was sound asleep.

partial sum

$$\sum_{k=1}^{n} a_k = a_1 + a_2 + a_3 + \cdots + a_n$$

infinite series

$$\sum_{k=1}^{\infty} a_k = a_1 + a_2 + a_3 + \cdots$$

harmonic number

$$H_n = \sum_{k=1}^{n} \frac{1}{k} = \frac{1}{1} + \frac{1}{2} + \frac{1}{3} + \cdots + \frac{1}{n}$$

harmonic series

$$H_\infty = \sum_{k=1}^{\infty} \frac{1}{k} = \frac{1}{1} + \frac{1}{2} + \frac{1}{3} + \cdots$$

zeta function

$$\zeta(s) = \sum_{k=1}^{\infty} \frac{1}{k^s}$$

zeta function as harmonic series

$$\zeta(1) = \sum_{k=1}^{\infty} \frac{1}{k}$$

zeta function as Euler product

$$\zeta(s) = \prod_{\text{prime } p} \frac{1}{1 - \frac{1}{p^s}}$$

CHAPTER 9

Taylor Series and the Basel Problem

> Several chapters have been included in which I have examined the properties and summation of many infinite series; some of these are arranged in such a way that it can be seen that they could hardly be investigated without the aid of analysis.
>
> LEONHARD EULER
> *Introduction to Analysis of the Infinite*

9.1 TWO CARDS

9.1.1 *One for Tetra*

"Special delivery!" Tetra shouted, bounding through the library waving two cards in the air.

"This may not be the best place to be shouting."

"Oh, sorry," she whispered, scanning the room. "Wait, we're the only ones here."

"Tell that to Ms. Mizutani."

"I know, I know." Tetra checked the cards she held and offered one to me.

"One for you." She pressed the other against her chest. "And one for me."

"Mr. Muraki gave you a card, too?"

"I told him you were helping me with math!" Tetra was positively beaming. "Feel free to thank me for the same-day delivery service."

I looked at my card.

My card

$$\sum_{k=1}^{\infty} \frac{1}{k^2}$$

"Check out my research assignment." Tetra held out her card so I could see it.

Tetra's card

$$\sin x = \sum_{k=0}^{\infty} a_k x^k$$

Tetra sat down next to me. Her expression turned serious.

"Well, I doubt he really means for these to be assignments. They're more like a starting point for us to play around with, see what we can find."

She held her card in both hands, staring the problem down.

"I'm already stuck. How am I supposed to solve this?"

"I don't think you're supposed to. It isn't an equation."

"It's not?"

"I'm pretty sure that's supposed to be an identity. He probably wants you to look for a sequence of a_ks that would make the identity true for every value of x."

"Okay. Hmm. . ." Tetra thought for a moment. "Can you give me a hint, just to get me started? I want to figure it out on my own, but maybe you could just," she made a pushing motion, "give me a little nudge."

9.1.2 Polynomials of Infinite Degree

"How about I flesh things out a bit." I took Tetra's card, and added a bit to it.

Problem 9-1

Assume that the function $\sin x$ can be written as the power series shown below. Find the sequence $\{a_k\}$.

$$\sin x = \sum_{k=0}^{\infty} a_k x^k$$

"What's a power series?"

"It's a polynomial of infinite degree, like the right side of your identity there. You know what a polynomial is, right? As in, a second-degree polynomial of x? A quadratic?"

"Something like this?" Tetra scribbled in her notebook:

$$ax^2 + bx + c \qquad \text{a second-degree polynomial}$$

"Almost. You have to add a condition that says a can't be 0, otherwise you might have a case like $a = 0, b \neq 0$, and you'd end up with a first-degree polynomial instead. Go ahead and add that."

"Sure." Tetra amended her definition:

$$ax^2 + bx + c \qquad \text{a second-degree polynomial } (a \neq 0)$$

"So would I write a polynomial of infinite degree like this?" she asked.

$$ax^{\infty} + bx^{\infty-1} + cx^{\infty-2} + \cdots \qquad \text{an infinite-degree polynomial}$$

"I can see why you might think so," I said, "but no, you can't do it that way."

"Yeah," she agreed. "Something about that doesn't look right."

"You have to write the terms starting with the smallest exponent. That way you avoid weird things like using an infinity symbol. The 'infinity' part is already implied by the three dots. See how these two are different?"

$$a_0 + a_1x + a_2x^2 \qquad \text{second-degree polynomial } (a_2 \neq 0)$$
$$a_0 + a_1x + a_2x^2 + \cdots \quad \text{infinite-degree polynomial (power series)}$$

"That makes sense. But why'd you use $a_0, a_1, a_2, \cdots$ for the coefficients? Couldn't you have just written $a, b, c, \cdots$?"

"Well, that might work for the first twenty-six—no, twenty-five, I guess, since x is already being used as the variable—but we need to describe an infinite number of terms. Also, using subscripts makes it easier to generalize, since we can use a new variable like k to take the place of the number. Remember how we talked about generalization through the introduction of a variable?"

"Right! I get it now."

"Okay, so let's rewrite the problem without the sigma:"

$$\sin x = a_0 + a_1x + a_2x^2 + \cdots + \underbrace{a_kx^k}_{\text{general term}} + \cdots$$

"Is that the sequence $\{a_k\}$?" Tetra asked.

"No, this is still just the original problem. All I did was expand it to get rid of the sigma. You have to use the behavior of $\sin x$ as a clue to figure out what $\{a_k\}$ looks like. You have to figure out what the actual values of $a_0, a_1, a_2, \cdots$ are."

"The actual values? For all of them?"

"Yep, all of them. You've seen a graph of $\sin x$ before, right? A sine curve?" I sketched one out in her notebook:

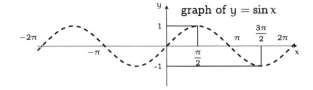

graph of $y = \sin x$

"Think about what this graph tells you. If nothing else, you should be able to find the value for a_0."

"Easy for *you* to say."

"Come on, give it a shot."

Tetra hunkered down in front of her notebook, one finger resting on the expanded identity, the other on the graph of $\sin x$. Her face was an open book of joy, confusion, wonder—and her emotions were more contagious than a smile. Part of it was her eyes, and her exaggerated body language that drew me in. But more than anything else, it was the childlike innocence with which she approached the world. Tetra was just... Tetra, and there was no one else like her.

She looked up, a huge grin on her face.

"It's 0. $a_0 = 0$!"

"Good. How'd you figure it out?"

"The curve on the graph goes through $x = 0$, $y = 0$, which means that $\sin 0$ is 0. Since the left side equals the right, the $a_0 + a_1 x + a_2 x^2 + \cdots$ on the right side has to equal 0, too. And because we know x is 0, everything with an x in it will get multiplied by 0, so a_0 will be the only thing left. That means a_0 has to equal 0!"

"Tetra, you should never shout 0."

"Oops, sorry. I forgot we were in the library."

"It's not that. If you shout a 0, it becomes a 1. See?" I wrote in the notebook:

$$0!$$

Tetra returned my expectant grin with a blank stare.

"Forget I said anything." I erased what I'd written, banishing it to the realm of bad math jokes. "Can you figure out any other values?"

Tetra directed her attention back to the graph, encouraged by her initial success. As disjointed as her thoughts could be at times, I envied the deep concentration she could summon when needed.

Now oblivious of me, Tetra scribbled calculations. I pulled out my own notebook and favorite mechanical pencil. Taking another look at the card Mr. Muraki had sent along, I started working out some concrete examples. The library settled back into silence.

9.2 Learning on Your Own

Tetra and I wound our way along the backstreet shortcut to the station, me struggling as usual to match her languid pace.

"So how far'd you get with the power series of $\sin x$?"

"Well," Tetra said, "since I got a $0 = 0$ from $x = 0$, I tried plugging in some other values for x, like $x = \frac{\pi}{2}$ and $x = \pi$, but it didn't get me anywhere. I only know a few things about the sine function, like $\sin \frac{\pi}{2} = 1$ and $\sin \pi = 0$. And that it goes up and down and up and down." Tetra traced a sine wave in the air.

I laughed. "Well, it's a start."

"Doesn't help much, though. Setting x to 0 was an easy one, since that gets rid of almost everything on the right side of the equation, but things get ugly when I start messing around with $\frac{\pi}{2}$."

"Okay to give you a hint?"

"Sure."

"One word: differentiation."

"Differentiation... I've always wondered what that was."

"Why stop at wondering? Go to a bookstore or a library—you'll find a million books that explain it. School is a good start, but you can't just sit there like a baby bird with its mouth open, waiting to be fed."

"Oh." Tetra looked a bit wounded.

"You said you like studying languages, right? Do you read any foreign books?"

"Sure. I'm always working my way through something."

"When you hit a word you don't know, do you wait until you learn it in class?"

"Okay, okay, you made your point."

"Look, if you're learning something because you enjoy it, you can't let something like school hold you back. Study as deep, as wide, and as far as you can."

"It's so weird. When I'm reading a book in another language, I can't wait to get to the next page. I don't just look words up in a dictionary, I look them up in a thesaurus to find their synonyms too. But I never even thought about doing the same thing with math. I always felt like you weren't allowed to go off on your own and study things that you hadn't seen in class yet."

"Yeah...but I got us off topic, didn't I. What were we talking about?"

"Not a clue. But I bet a cup of coffee at Beans would remind me."

Who could resist an invitation like that?

9.3   GETTING CLOSER

9.3.1   Differentiation Rules

Tetra and I had become regulars at Beans. When we first started coming we always sat across from each other, but somewhere along the way we had begun sitting side by side—easier to work on math that way. Or at least that's what I told myself.

I pulled my notebook out as we sat down.

"It'll be hard to understand what I want to do without knowing how to differentiate polynomials and trigonometric functions, so let's go over the basics of how to do that."

"I'm ready," Tetra said, fists clenched.

"Say that we can represent the sine function as a power series:"

$$\sin x = a_0 + a_1 x + a_2 x^2 + \cdots$$

"Now, it's not exactly obvious that you can do that, so really we should start out by proving that you can. Let's skip that for now, though. Instead, our first goal is to dig a bit deeper into this infinite sequence $\{a_k\} = \{a_0, a_1, a_2, \cdots\}$. We need to expand $\sin x$ into that series by creating something called the power series expansion of a function. With me so far?"

Tetra gave a determined nod.

"So you've already found the value of a_0 by setting x to 0. Since $\sin 0 = 0$, you got this:"

$$a_0 = 0$$

Tetra nodded again.

"Okay, you haven't studied differentiation yet, and it would take too long to start from scratch on that, so for now just think of it as a set of rules. A set of rules that takes one function, and creates another function out of it."

"You aren't changing the function, you're making a new one?"

"Right. When you differentiate a function $f(x)$, you get a new function called the derivative of $f(x)$, which you write as $f'(x)$. Well, I guess there are other ways to write it, but $f'(x)$ is the most common:"

$f(x)$ a function $f(x)$

$\downarrow$ differentiate

$f'(x)$ the derivative of $f(x)$

"Now I'm going to list some rules for creating derivatives. Once you learn the formal definition of the derivative, you'll see why things work out this way. For now you'll have to take my word on it."

"*A priori*, got it."

"Whattiori?"

"Just using one of those words I looked up once," she smiled. "Go on."

I wrote down the rules in my notebook.

Differentiation Rule #1:
The derivative of a constant is 0

$$(a)' = 0$$

Differentiation Rule #2:
The derivative of x^n is nx^{n-1}

$$(x^n)' = nx^{n-1} \quad \text{(exponent drops down)}$$

Differentiation Rule #3:
The derivative of $\sin x$ is $\cos x$

$$(\sin x)' = \cos x$$

"So," I said, "let's find the derivative of both sides of this equation:"

$$\sin x = a_0 + a_1 x + a_2 x^2 + a_3 x^3 + a_4 x^4 + \cdots$$

$$\downarrow$$

$$(\sin x)' = (a_0 + a_1 x + a_2 x^2 + a_3 x^3 + a_4 x^4 + \cdots)'$$

"Using those rules I get this:"

$$\cos x = a_1 + 2a_2 x + 3a_3 x^2 + 4a_4 x^3 + \cdots$$

"Hmm..." Tetra's eyes jumped between equations and rules. "So you got the left side of the equation from rule three, which says that the derivative of sine is cosine, and all the terms on the right are coming from rule two, right?"

"Right. If we wanted to be really thorough, we would prove the linearity of the derivative operator, and that you can apply it to a power series. But we don't."

"Oh, what happened to the a_0?"

"That's a constant, just some number without an x, so it got zapped. The derivative of a constant is 0, right?"

"Rule number one," she said. "I think I've got it."

9.3.2 Looping Derivatives

"Okay, take a look at this new equation we just found, and see if you can't figure out what a_1 is. Looking at a graph of $\cos x$ should help:"

$$\cos x = a_1 + 2a_2 x + 3a_3 x^2 + 4a_4 x^3 \cdots$$

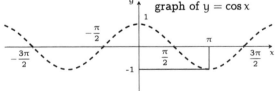

"So I can just do it the same as before? By substituting a 0 in for the xs like this?"

$$\cos 0 = a_1 + 2a_2 \cdot 0 + 3a_3 \cdot 0^2 + 4a_4 \cdot 0^3 \cdots$$

$$= a_1$$

"If that's right," she continued, "then the graph says that $\cos 0 = 1$, so this should be the answer: "

$$a_1 = 1$$

I nodded. "Uh huh."

"I think I've got this figured out! Next we're going to take the derivative of $\cos x$, right?"

"Exactly. I guess we need a new differentiation rule to cover that one, don't we." I added a new rule to our list.

Differentiation Rule #4:
The derivative of $\cos x$ is $-\sin x$

$$(\cos x)' = -\sin x$$

"Now we just do the same thing we did before: "

$$\cos x = a_1 + 2a_2 x + 3a_3 x^2 + 4a_4 x^3 + \cdots$$
$$\downarrow$$
$$(\cos x)' = (a_1 + 2a_2 x + 3a_3 x^2 + 4a_4 x^3 + \cdots)'$$

"Hey, I can do this!" Tetra said, flushed with excitement.

$$-\sin x = 2a_2 + 6a_3 x + 12a_4 x^2 + \cdots$$

"Very good," I said. "And what do we get from that?"

"The coefficient a_2. We just substitute a 0 like we've been doing." Tetra scrawled in the notebook:

$$-\sin x = 2a_2 + 6a_3 x + 12a_4 x^2 + \cdots \qquad \text{from deriving}$$
$$-\sin 0 = 2a_2 \qquad \text{substitute } x = 0$$
$$a_2 = 0 \qquad \text{use } \sin 0 = 0, \text{ clean up}$$

"Now we have a_2," Tetra said. "Let's keep going! What's the next differentiation rule we need?"

"Actually, we don't need any more."

"Why not? We have to find the derivative of $-\sin x$... Oh, we can just use the $\sin x$ rule for that one."

"Right. After this we're just going to keep running in circles, repeating ourselves."

Tetra glanced back over the rules. "Hey, you're right. When you take the derivative of $\sin x$ you get $\cos x$, and when you take the derivative of $\cos x$ you get $-\sin x$. Then you get $-\cos x$, and after that you're back to $\sin x$."

"That's one of the cool things about differentiating the trig functions."

Differentiation of the sine and cosine functions

$$\sin x \quad \xrightarrow{\text{differentiate}} \quad \cos x$$

$$\text{differentiate} \uparrow \qquad\qquad\qquad \downarrow \text{differentiate}$$

$$-\cos x \quad \xleftarrow{\text{differentiate}} \quad -\sin x$$

"Guess a_3's next," she said.

$-\sin x = 2a_2 + 6a_3x + 12a_4x^2 + \cdots$	what we got before
$(-\sin x)' = (2a_2 + 6a_3x + 12a_4x^2 + \cdots)'$	differentiate both sides
$-\cos x = 6a_3 + 24a_4x + \cdots$	differentiation rules
$-\cos 0 = 6a_3$	substitute $x = 0$
$a_3 = -\dfrac{1}{6}$	use $\cos 0 = 1$, clean up

"So it looks like $a_3 = -\frac{1}{6}$. Now on to a_4—"

"Hold on," I said. "We could keep finding the coefficients one at a time, but maybe we can find a way to get them all at once. Want to give it a shot?"

"You bet!"

9.3.3 The Taylor Series for $\sin x$

I took a sip of cold coffee and turned to a fresh page in the notebook. Tetra and I agreed that I would give her some hints, but that she should work things out herself.

"Okay, so your goal is to expand a power series for $\sin x$," I said. "You've worked out what the first four coefficients are, now you want to find the rest. Why don't you start by writing out the generalization of the equation that you're looking for."

"That's this, right?"

$$\sin x = a_0 + a_1 x + a_2 x^2 + a_3 x^3 + a_4 x^4 + a_5 x^5 + \cdots$$

"You might want to go ahead and add the 1 exponent here." I pointed to the second term, and Tetra added a 1:

$$\sin x = a_0 + a_1 x^1 + a_2 x^2 + a_3 x^3 + a_4 x^4 + a_5 x^5 + \cdots$$

"Now I want you to differentiate both sides like you did before, only this time, don't work out the calculations."

"Why not?"

"Because that'll let you see the form of the products. You can bet that there's going to be a pattern there, and this should let you find it. Go ahead and give it a try, and pay close attention to what happens with the constant terms."

"Okay, here goes." Tetra's pencil raced across the page.

$$\sin x = \underline{a_0} + a_1 x^1 + a_2 x^2 + a_3 x^3 + a_4 x^4 + a_5 x^5 + \cdots$$
$$\downarrow \text{differentiate}$$
$$\cos x = \underline{1 \cdot a_1} + 2 \cdot a_2 x^1 + 3 \cdot a_3 x^2 + 4 \cdot a_4 x^3 + 5 \cdot a_5 x^4 + \cdots$$
$$\downarrow \text{differentiate}$$
$$-\sin x = \underline{2 \cdot 1 \cdot a_2} + 3 \cdot 2 \cdot a_3 x^1 + 4 \cdot 3 \cdot a_4 x^2 + 5 \cdot 4 \cdot a_5 x^3 + \cdots$$
$$\downarrow \text{differentiate}$$
$$-\cos x = \underline{3 \cdot 2 \cdot 1 \cdot a_3} + 4 \cdot 3 \cdot 2 \cdot a_4 x^1 + 5 \cdot 4 \cdot 3 \cdot a_5 x^2 + \cdots$$
$$\downarrow \text{differentiate}$$
$$\sin x = \underline{4 \cdot 3 \cdot 2 \cdot 1 \cdot a_4} + 5 \cdot 4 \cdot 3 \cdot 2 \cdot a_5 x^1 + \cdots$$
$$\downarrow \text{differentiate}$$

$$\cos x = \underline{5 \cdot 4 \cdot 3 \cdot 2 \cdot 1} \cdot a_5 + \cdots$$

↓ differentiate

$$\vdots$$

"Got it." Tetra said. "Here's the pattern, this $5 \cdot 4 \cdot 3 \cdot 2 \cdot 1$ here. It comes from the second differentiation rule, right? Because the exponents keep 'falling down.' That's what's causing the pattern in the multiplication."

"See how much clearer it is when you write it all out instead of just reading through the equations?"

"Yeah, I see what you mean."

"Okay, so now let's start substituting 0s and watch what happens."

"Oh, cool. It's like performing a chemistry experiment or something. Let's see, I know that $\sin 0 = 0$ and $\cos 0 = 1$, so..."

$$0 = a_0$$
$$+1 = 1 \cdot a_1$$
$$0 = 2 \cdot 1 \cdot a_2$$
$$-1 = 3 \cdot 2 \cdot 1 \cdot a_3$$
$$0 = 4 \cdot 3 \cdot 2 \cdot 1 \cdot a_4$$
$$+1 = 5 \cdot 4 \cdot 3 \cdot 2 \cdot 1 \cdot a_5$$

$$\vdots$$

"Definitely a pattern there," Tetra said.

"Yeah. So what we're after is the sequence $\{a_k\}$. You can get each of these terms by rearranging things so the a_ks are on the left, and rewriting things like $5 \cdot 4 \cdot 3 \cdot 2 \cdot 1$ in factorial form."

I waited while she worked through the calculations:

$$a_0 = 0$$
$$a_1 = \frac{+1}{1!}$$
$$a_2 = \frac{0}{2!}$$
$$a_3 = \frac{-1}{3!}$$

$$a_4 = \frac{0}{4!}$$

$$a_5 = \frac{+1}{5!}$$

$$\vdots$$

"Almost there," I continued. "Now that you have the a_ks in a better form, go ahead and replace the coefficients in the original power series expansion you worked out." I tapped the equation at the top of the page:

$$\sin x = a_0 + a_1 x^1 + a_2 x^2 + a_3 x^3 + \cdots$$

"All the terms with even numbers became 0," she said. "I can skip those, right? So let's see... Okay, done."

I looked over what she had written. "Check it out. You've just found the Taylor series for $\sin x$."

The Taylor series for $\sin x$

$$\sin x = +\frac{x^1}{1!} - \frac{x^3}{3!} + \frac{x^5}{5!} - \frac{x^7}{7!} + \cdots$$

"Hey, I did all the work. Can't I call it the Tetra series?"

"Uh... no. No you can't."

"Well, it was worth a shot. How'm I going to remember this, though? It's so complicated."

"Depends on how you look at it. There's lots of stuff left over from the differentiation—the factorials in the denominators from bringing down exponents, the cycling positive and negative signs—which is also why there aren't any even numbers, and the signs keep alternating. Work it out a couple more times and you'll know it by heart."

"When you break it down like that, I guess it's not so bad."

"You could also write it out without using factorials and exponents. You can see a kind of pattern when you do it that way."

Tetra wrote the new version:

$$\sin x = +\frac{x}{1} - \frac{x \cdot x \cdot x}{1 \cdot 2 \cdot 3} + \frac{x \cdot x \cdot x \cdot x \cdot x}{1 \cdot 2 \cdot 3 \cdot 4 \cdot 5} - \frac{x \cdot x \cdot x \cdot x \cdot x \cdot x \cdot x}{1 \cdot 2 \cdot 3 \cdot 4 \cdot 5 \cdot 6 \cdot 7} + \cdots$$

"I like that. It's almost... pretty."

"Don't be scared to play around with what you find. It's a fun way to get to know it better. Even Euler wrote out things like x^2 as xx in his books sometimes. Might not want to do that on a math test, though. Oh, by the way, you've solved the problem that's on your card."

"Wow, the card. I completely forgot about it." Tetra fished the card out of her bag.

Problem 9-1

Assume that the function $\sin x$ can be expanded as the power series shown below. Find the sequence $\{a_k\}$.

$$\sin x = \sum_{k=0}^{\infty} a_k x^k$$

"You can write the answer by breaking it up into cases, based on the remainder when you divide k by 4."

Answer to Problem 9-1

$$a_k = \begin{cases} 0 & \text{if } k \div 4 \text{ leaves a remainder of } 0 \\ +\dfrac{1}{k!} & \text{if } k \div 4 \text{ leaves a remainder of } 1 \\ 0 & \text{if } k \div 4 \text{ leaves a remainder of } 2 \\ -\dfrac{1}{k!} & \text{if } k \div 4 \text{ leaves a remainder of } 3 \end{cases}$$

9.3.4 Taking Equations to the Limit

"Let's talk a little bit more about what the Taylor series for $\sin x$ means," I said, turning to a new page. "Go ahead and write it out one more time."

"Can I write the long version? I like that one:"

$$\sin x = +\frac{x}{1} - \frac{x \cdot x \cdot x}{1 \cdot 2 \cdot 3} + \frac{x \cdot x \cdot x \cdot x \cdot x}{1 \cdot 2 \cdot 3 \cdot 4 \cdot 5} - \frac{x \cdot x \cdot x \cdot x \cdot x \cdot x \cdot x}{1 \cdot 2 \cdot 3 \cdot 4 \cdot 5 \cdot 6 \cdot 7} + \cdots$$

"See how this is an infinite series, a sum of an infinite number of terms? Let's pull out some finite chunks to play with, some partial sums. When we add up the terms from x^1 to x^k, we'll call that $s_k(x)$. That's going to be a function of x, too, just like the full thing. Try writing out the first few."

"Sure," Tetra said.

$$s_1(x) = +\frac{x}{1}$$

$$s_3(x) = +\frac{x}{1} - \frac{x \cdot x \cdot x}{1 \cdot 2 \cdot 3}$$

$$s_5(x) = +\frac{x}{1} - \frac{x \cdot x \cdot x}{1 \cdot 2 \cdot 3} + \frac{x \cdot x \cdot x \cdot x \cdot x}{1 \cdot 2 \cdot 3 \cdot 4 \cdot 5}$$

$$s_7(x) = +\frac{x}{1} - \frac{x \cdot x \cdot x}{1 \cdot 2 \cdot 3} + \frac{x \cdot x \cdot x \cdot x \cdot x}{1 \cdot 2 \cdot 3 \cdot 4 \cdot 5} - \frac{x \cdot x \cdot x \cdot x \cdot x \cdot x \cdot x}{1 \cdot 2 \cdot 3 \cdot 4 \cdot 5 \cdot 6 \cdot 7}$$

I pulled some graph paper out of my backpack.

"Okay, give me a minute," I said. "I'm going to graph these functions along with $\sin x$:"

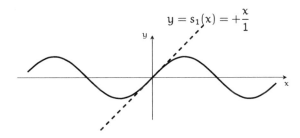

$$y = s_1(x) = +\frac{x}{1}$$

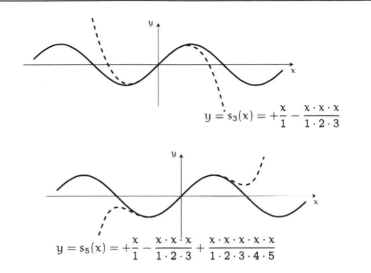

$$y = s_3(x) = +\frac{x}{1} - \frac{x \cdot x \cdot x}{1 \cdot 2 \cdot 3}$$

$$y = s_5(x) = +\frac{x}{1} - \frac{x \cdot x \cdot x}{1 \cdot 2 \cdot 3} + \frac{x \cdot x \cdot x \cdot x \cdot x}{1 \cdot 2 \cdot 3 \cdot 4 \cdot 5}$$

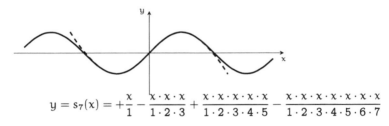

$$y = s_7(x) = +\frac{x}{1} - \frac{x \cdot x \cdot x}{1 \cdot 2 \cdot 3} + \frac{x \cdot x \cdot x \cdot x \cdot x}{1 \cdot 2 \cdot 3 \cdot 4 \cdot 5} - \frac{x \cdot x \cdot x \cdot x \cdot x \cdot x \cdot x}{1 \cdot 2 \cdot 3 \cdot 4 \cdot 5 \cdot 6 \cdot 7}$$

"See how in each graph the function you wrote is a closer approximation of $\sin x$?"

"Cool. So this is what it means to represent $\sin x$ as a power series. Before, I understood how we got all this using derivatives and stuff, but I was like, 'so what?' Now it all makes sense. When k gets bigger, $s_k(x)$ gets closer and closer to $\sin x$. Like it's trying to snuggle up to it."

"Yeah, uh, snuggle. Sure."

"To me, $\sin x$ is just the name of some weird function. It doesn't really mean anything. This Taylor series feels different, though. I know it's just the same function written a different way, so I guess in a sense they're the same thing, but when you write it like this—as a power series, right?—it seems more, I don't know, useful. Sorry, I'm probably not making any sense."

"No, that makes perfect sense. It also shows that you're really seeing into the heart of all this. If you want to study a function, and it can be rewritten as a Taylor series, then a lot of times things get easier to deal with, because you're just working with something that behaves a lot like a polynomial. Like what we just did with $s_k(x)$, for example, seeing how one function can approximate another one. You do have to be careful, since they have infinite order and that can present some issues, but like you said, writing things as a power series can be very useful. Speaking of which, we used power series when we were looking at the Fibonacci sequence, didn't we? The Catalan numbers, too."

Tetra fidgeted with my notebook.

"This is all so different from what we do in class. It's all trees, no forest there. We spend so much time on details I forget what we're doing, and why we're doing it. But with you it's the exact opposite." She looked up and our eyes met. "With you, I actually *understand*."

"I think you're giving me too much credit."

"I'm not so sure. When we walked in here today, I had no idea what differentiation was, and I hadn't even heard of a Taylor series. Now I know that Taylor series let you study functions like they were plain old polynomials. I may not be able to do it on my own yet, but that's not the point. I know that when you want to use some difficult function, you can turn it into an infinite order polynomial—a power series, or an infinite sum of x^ks, or whatever you want to call it—and go from there. I really get it. Here." She tapped her chest. "And I owe it all to you."

Tetra looked away, staring blankly at the graph paper on the table. Her cheeks were flushed.

"It's just that I... I love—" Tetra gulped. "I love the way you teach me things."

9.4   THE PROBLEM WITHIN

Back home that night, I looked at the card from Mr. Muraki. I had spent so much time with Tetra on her problem that I hadn't even touched my own.

Problem 9-2

If the following infinite series converges, find the value it converges to. Otherwise, prove that it diverges.

$$\sum_{k=1}^{\infty} \frac{1}{k^2}$$

I started with the usual, expanding the sigma for a few terms to get a feel for the equation:

$$\sum_{k=1}^{\infty} \frac{1}{k^2} = \frac{1}{1^2} + \frac{1}{2^2} + \frac{1}{3^2} + \frac{1}{4^2} + \frac{1}{5^2} + \cdots$$

I spent a few minutes playing with this, but didn't find anything that would make the problem an easy one. I decided to try some calculations—not tackling the entire infinite series yet, but just working out $\sum_{k=1}^{n} \frac{1}{k^2}$ for a few values of n. Boring, but who knows? Time for number crunching mode:

$$\sum_{k=1}^{1} \frac{1}{k^2} = \qquad \frac{1}{1^2} = 1$$

$$\sum_{k=1}^{2} \frac{1}{k^2} = \qquad 1 + \frac{1}{2^2} = 1.25$$

$$\sum_{k=1}^{3} \frac{1}{k^2} = \qquad 1.25 + \frac{1}{3^2} = 1.3611\cdots$$

$$\sum_{k=1}^{4} \frac{1}{k^2} = \quad 1.3611\cdots + \frac{1}{4^2} = 1.423611\cdots$$

$$\sum_{k=1}^{5} \frac{1}{k^2} = 1.423611\cdots + \frac{1}{5^2} = 1.463611\cdots$$

$$\sum_{k=1}^{6} \frac{1}{k^2} = 1.463611\cdots + \frac{1}{6^2} = 1.491388\cdots$$

$$\sum_{k=1}^{7} \frac{1}{k^2} = 1.491388\cdots + \frac{1}{7^2} = 1.511797\cdots$$

$$\sum_{k=1}^{8} \frac{1}{k^2} = 1.511797\cdots + \frac{1}{8^2} = 1.527422\cdots$$

$$\sum_{k=1}^{9} \frac{1}{k^2} = 1.527422\cdots + \frac{1}{9^2} = 1.539767\cdots$$

$$\sum_{k=1}^{10} \frac{1}{k^2} = 1.539767\cdots + \frac{1}{10^2} = 1.549767\cdots$$

Maybe something there, maybe not. Having learned my lesson about the importance of graphing, I decided to sketch this. I dug around in my backpack for my graph paper, but came up empty. *Must've left it at school.*

Well, whatever. From the look of things, the partial sums weren't preparing for a launch off to infinity. Not that that meant they converged. As I'd seen working on the harmonic series, the number could be diverging, only very, very slowly.

The harmonic series.

Now that I thought about it, this statement looked awfully similar. The only difference was the exponent in the denominator:

$$\sum_{k=1}^{\infty} \frac{1}{k^2} \qquad \text{my problem}$$

$$\sum_{k=1}^{\infty} \frac{1}{k} \qquad \text{the harmonic series}$$

Looking at it another way, the harmonic series was just a series of inverse ks with an exponent of 1, and my problem was a series of inverse ks with an exponent of 2. All of a sudden this was starting to sound like a problem related to the zeta function that Miruka had mentioned.

I thumbed back through my notes and found the definition of the zeta function:

$$\zeta(s) = \sum_{k=1}^{\infty} \frac{1}{k^s} \qquad \text{(definition of the zeta function)}$$

By this definition, the harmonic series could be written $\zeta(1)$:

$$\zeta(1) = \sum_{k=1}^{\infty} \frac{1}{k^1} \quad \text{(the harmonic series as a zeta function)}$$

Of course, I could do the same thing with my problem. Since the exponent was 2, I could write this as $\zeta(2)$:

$$\zeta(2) = \sum_{k=1}^{\infty} \frac{1}{k^2} \quad \text{(my problem as a zeta function)}$$

At least I had a name for the thing. Now I just had to solve it.

9.5 The Fundamental Theorem of Algebra

The next morning I arrived at my classroom to find Kaito cornered by Miruka. Upon seeing me he gave a "she's all yours" look and backed away. Following his gaze, Miruka rounded on me and jabbed a finger in my face.

"Please tell me you know the fundamental theorem of algebra," she said.

This was actually a fairly typical conversation starter for her. She was too talented to waste her time with the material we were studying at school. Miruka had a different process: She read books, found her own problems, and solved them. I had the first two steps down, but the last, well... let's just say I was nowhere near Miruka's level.

Not that I had an inferiority complex, but I'll admit to a tinge of jealousy. And why not? She could see a world I couldn't.

I knew enough math to know how much I didn't know. I would stand in the bookstore, painfully aware that I couldn't understand even half of what surrounded me. From time to time I caught glimpses of the awe that math could invoke, the beauty it could describe. Then I would think of Miruka, and how much further her view must reach. Her work was smart and elegant. Everything I did seemed juvenile and clumsy by comparison.

Time to take a page from Tetra's book; I'd clench my fists and do my best.

"The fundamental theorem of algebra says that an nth-degree equation has n solutions, right?"

"Partial credit. It says that an nth-degree equation with complex coefficients has n complex solutions, with the caveat that multiple roots are counted to their multiplicity."

"That's... long."

"Gauss was only twenty-two when he discovered that. It was his graduation thesis. Can you believe it? The guy picked up a fundamental problem in math, and did it for *homework*. Sheesh."

Something had obviously switched Miruka into power lecture mode. She continued her lesson at the blackboard.

"Actually, the classic version of the theorem just says that any nth degree equation with complex coefficients has at least one solution. That's all you need, because once you have a solution, call it α, then you can just divide the polynomial by $x - \alpha$, right? Okay, so let's say that I have an nth degree equation, $a_n x^n + a_{n-1} x^{n-1} + \cdots + a_1 x^1 + a_0 = 0$. Let's prove that it has at least one solution. Start by making a function $f(x) = a_n x^n + a_{n-1} x^{n-1} + \cdots + a_1 x^1 + a_0$. Next, take its absolute value, $|f(x)|$, and think about how small we can make that. If we can squeeze it down to 0, then we'll know we have a solution. But before we do that, maybe we should have a quick review of complex numbers. Ready?"

Miruka blasted through Gauss's proof in a cloud of chalk dust. My main takeaway was a deepened feeling of inadequacy, brought on by my woefully shallow understanding of complex numbers. I got the gist of what she was saying, but having something explained to me was never enough to make me feel like I really understood it. I had to do it on my own, first writing out the proof myself, and then working it out without looking back at anything. Working through a difficult proof while explaining it to someone else would have to wait until I'd leveled up a bit more.

As I ruminated on my shortcomings, equations flowed through Miruka's fingertips onto the board. She had worked her way though the fundamental theorem of algebra and the factor theorem, and was now factoring out her nth degree polynomial using the solution she had found.

"—write that out in detail. Going back to our nth degree equation, $a_n x^n + a_{n-1} x^{n-1} + \cdots + a_1 x^1 + a_0 = 0$, and taking $\alpha_1, \alpha_2, \cdots, \alpha_n$ as our n solutions, we can factor the left side of the equation like this." Bang, bang, bang on the board:

$$a_n x^n + a_{n-1} x^{n-1} + \cdots + a_1 x^1 + a_0 = a_n (x - \alpha_1)(x - \alpha_2) \cdots (x - \alpha_n)$$

"So factorization is directly related to the solutions of equations. Check out the constant a_n at the beginning of the right side. See how that becomes the coefficient of x^n, the term with the highest degree? That means that we could have just divided both sides by a_n, and then made the nth degree coefficient 1. No worries about dividing by zero, since we said this was an nth degree equation. That rules out a_n being 0."

Kaito tapped me on the shoulder, snapping me out of my stupor.

Someone shouted, "Your dorky little sister's here."

All eyes were on Tetra—it wasn't common to see a younger student in our classroom. She walked up to me, face burning scarlet, clutching my graph paper.

"Um, hi. You left this yesterday. I just wanted to give it back." She added, "If I'm your dorky little sister, I guess that makes you my nerdy big brother."

"Hey, I never—"

"I'll bet he'd like that," Miruka said without turning from the board.

Great. *Now* they team up.

Tetra looked at the blackboard and gasped. "Did you write all this?"

Miruka turned and pointed at her. "Please tell me that you know the fundamental theorem of algebra."

Somehow Tetra's arrival hit Miruka's reset button, and the lecture started over from the beginning. Tetra got a whirlwind tour of everything Miruka had just explained to me.

"—so taking α and β as the solutions to the quadratic $ax^2 + bx + c = 0$, we know that $ax^2 + bx + c = a(x - \alpha)(x - \beta)$ holds. Factorization leads us directly to solving the equation. Here's how you get the coefficients:"

$$-\frac{b}{a} = \alpha + \beta$$

$$+\frac{c}{a} = \alpha\beta$$

"Similarly, if α, β, and γ are the solutions to the third degree equation $ax^3 + bx^2 + cx + d = 0$, we do this:"

$$-\frac{b}{a} = \alpha + \beta + \gamma$$

$$+\frac{c}{a} = \alpha\beta + \beta\gamma + \gamma\alpha$$

$$-\frac{d}{a} = \alpha\beta\gamma$$

"Now you probably want a generalization. Take $\alpha_1, \alpha_2, \cdots, \alpha_n$ as the solutions to the nth degree equation $a_n x^n + a_{n-1} x^{n-1} + \cdots + a_1 x + a_0 = 0$. Ready for the coefficients?"

$$-\frac{a_{n-1}}{a_n} = \alpha_1 + \alpha_2 + \cdots + \alpha_n$$

$$+\frac{a_{n-2}}{a_n} = \alpha_1\alpha_2 + \alpha_1\alpha_3 + \cdots + \alpha_{n-1}\alpha_n$$

$$-\frac{a_{n-3}}{a_n} = \alpha_1\alpha_2\alpha_3 + \alpha_1\alpha_2\alpha_4 + \cdots + \alpha_{n-2}\alpha_{n-1}\alpha_n$$

$$\vdots$$

$$(-1)^k \frac{a_{n-k}}{a_n} = \text{(the sum of every product of k factors from } \alpha_1, \alpha_2, \cdots, \alpha_n)$$

$$\vdots$$

$$(-1)^n \frac{a_0}{a_n} = \alpha_1\alpha_2\cdots\alpha_n$$

"And there you have it. The coefficients for every nth degree equation."

The warning bell rang. Tetra staggered off to class, mumbling about how her head was going to explode.

"Cute little sister you've got." Miruka pushed her glasses back with her middle finger and tucked her long hair behind an ear. My eyes followed the graceful curve her finger traced through the air, the outline of her face... Those lips, too, and the beautiful voice that passed between them. Rich and resonating, like some exotic musical instrument. Like—

"You got a zeta, right?"

"Huh?"

"Your follow-up problem from Muraki. Was it a zeta function?" Miruka showed me her latest card.

Miruka's card

$$\zeta(2)$$

I had seen this coming. When Mr. Muraki gave me a problem about harmonic numbers, he gave Miruka one about the zeta function. Given my current assignment, I wasn't surprised to see Miruka working on $\zeta(2)$. Apparently Mr. Muraki was guiding us towards the same problem from different angles. *Strange that Tetra's doesn't seem to be related...*

"You solved yours yet?" I asked.

"Well, not so much solved it as answered it. I knew the solution to the Basel problem, so I was able to give him an answer as soon as I got the card."

"What's the Basel problem?"

"Basically just a solution to $\zeta(2)$. Muraki just laughed at me, though. 'Everybody knows the answer,' he said. He told me to look for something more interesting." Miruka shrugged.

"It's a famous problem or something?"

"It was all the rage in the eighteenth century. Nobody could figure it out. Nobody until Euler, that is. Solving that problem made him famous overnight."

"Wait a minute, a problem that hard, and Mr. Muraki expects us to solve it?"

"Sure, no sweat. I mean, it was hard three hundred years ago, but we've made some progress since then."

"And you just remembered the answer?"

"Yeah, well, things stick with me. I'm going to keep messing with it, though. It would be a shame to waste a card. I'm playing with changing the x to a z, and expanding the scope to the complex numbers."

"So this $\zeta(2)$—the Basel problem—does it diverge?"

"You really want me to tell you?" Miruka said, surprised. The light flashed off her glasses as she looked at me.

"No, no spoilers."

I did jot down 'cf. the Basel problem' on my card, though.

9.6   Tetra's Attempt

9.6.1   Trial and Error

I had just sat down in the library when Tetra came bouncing along.

"I found the coolest thing!"

"Yeah?"

Lately I'd been spending time with Tetra almost every day, so to be honest I'd been looking forward to getting back to my own stuff.

"Remember how we worked out the Taylor series for the sine function yesterday? Well, I got to thinking. You know how $\sin x$ keeps coming back to 0 as x changes?"

Tetra pulled out her notebook and opened it to a page with a series of equations:

$$\sin \pi = 0, \sin 2\pi = 0, \sin 3\pi = 0, \cdots, \sin n\pi = 0, \cdots$$

"Yeah, it does that." I made no effort to conceal my annoyance. "You left out the cases where n is negative, though. If you're trying to generalize that, you need to write it like this:"

$$\sin n\pi = 0 \qquad n = 0, \pm 1, \pm 2, \cdots$$

"Oops, you're right. I guess n could be negative, couldn't it."

"Or 0," I said. "C'mon, Tetra, just draw a graph and see where it crosses the x axis:"

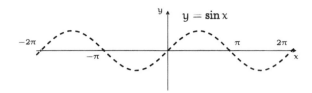

"Sorry, maybe this wasn't the best time. I'll get out of your way."

I immediately regretted my choice of words, and moved to salvage the situation.

"Nah, it's okay. So, did you figure something out about yesterday's problem?"

"Yeah. Well, maybe. Nothing major, I guess." Tetra glanced at me. "I tried factoring sin x."

"Oh, you—wait, what? You *factored* it?"

"Well, I thought, I have all these values for x that make sin x = 0 true, right? Doesn't that make them solutions to the equation? And today Miruka was talking about how there's a direct relationship between finding the solution to equations and their factorization, so. . . "

Miruka did say something like that, but factoring sin x? I tried to think of where to begin explaining how that wasn't possible. Tetra took my silence as a cue to continue her explanation.

"Like you said, the solutions are $x = 0, \pm\pi, \pm 2\pi, \pm 3\pi, \cdots$, so doesn't that mean that we can factor it out like this?"

$$\sin x = x(x + \pi)(x - \pi)(x + 2\pi)(x - 2\pi)(x + 3\pi)(x - 3\pi) \cdots$$

I could see where she was coming from, and sure enough substituting $x = n\pi$ would give 0, but something about this didn't feel right. It took me a minute to figure out why.

"I don't think this works, Tetra. There's a famous limit involving sin x that goes like this:"

$$\lim_{x \to 0} \frac{\sin x}{x} = 1$$

"This says that when x gets really, really close to 0, then $\frac{\sin x}{x}$ will get really, really close to 1. But as long as x isn't exactly 0, then we could divide both sides of your equation by x:"

$$\frac{\sin x}{x} = (x + \pi)(x - \pi)(x + 2\pi)(x - 2\pi)(x + 3\pi)(x - 3\pi) \cdots$$

"If we took the limit on both sides of that, then the left should be approaching 1, but I don't see how the stuff on the right could, too. I think that means something is wrong here."

9.6.2   A Solution Emerges

"Tetra?" The voice from behind startled us both. I ducked, and Tetra let out a small yelp. "You're working on the Basel problem, too?"

We turned and saw Miruka standing there. Tetra jerked back, knocking her notebook and pencil case off the table. Pens, erasers, and highlighters flew everywhere.

"Oh, hey," I said. "No, Tetra isn't working on the Basel problem. She thinks she found a way to factor $\sin x$."

"What's this Basel problem?" Tetra asked, groping for a pencil.

I showed Tetra the card, and explained that the Basel problem had to do with the $\sum_{k=1}^{\infty} \frac{1}{k^2}$ on my card, and the $\zeta(2)$ on Miruka's card. In other words, finding the value of a series of inverse squares—if the sum converged, at least.

Tetra listened politely, but she didn't seem to follow my explanation. Not surprising, I guess. It was a lot to take in.

During this, Miruka fished under the table and retrieved Tetra's notebook. She began flipping through the pages.

"Hmm..."

"Oh, that's my—" Tetra reached out to take her notebook back, but a single glance from Miruka was enough to deflect Tetra's hand. Miruka looked back at its pages and spoke to me.

"You were teaching her the Taylor series for $\sin x$. Hmph. Muraki knows what he's doing." Miruka read a line off the page. "What do we have here? 'I'll never forget this!' Never forget what, Tetra?"

"Nothing!" Tetra squealed. Her hand darted out and snatched the notebook.

Miruka closed her eyes and traced a finger through the air. Tetra and I stared spellbound.

Miruka opened her eyes.

"Let's start with the Taylor series for $\sin x$," she said. She grabbed my mechanical pencil and notebook, and got to work:

$$\sin x = +\frac{x}{1!} - \frac{x^3}{3!} + \frac{x^5}{5!} - \frac{x^7}{7!} + \cdots \qquad \text{the Taylor series for } \sin x$$

"Assume that $x \neq 0$, and divide both sides by x:"

$$\frac{\sin x}{x} = 1 - \frac{x^2}{3!} + \frac{x^4}{5!} - \frac{x^6}{7!} + \cdots \qquad \text{divide both sides by } x$$

"You see that we're representing $\frac{\sin x}{x}$ as a sum here?"

We nodded.

"Okay. You," she pointed at Tetra, "were playing with this equation, right?"

$$\sin x = 0$$

"And you," pointing at me, "said the solutions to the equation were this:"

$$x = n\pi \qquad (n = 0, \pm1, \pm2, \pm3, \cdots)$$

Again, we nodded.

"And using this to 'factor out' $\sin x$ was Tetra's idea?"

I actually heard Tetra gulp when Miruka said that. She was still clutching her notebook to her chest, Taylor series and "I will never forget this!" pressed over her heart.

"Yeah, but it didn't work. Something about a limit going to 1 on the left, but not for my factorization, so—"

"In that case," Miruka interrupted, a gleam in her eye, "why don't you try factoring like this instead?"

$$\sin x = x \left(1 + \frac{x}{\pi}\right) \left(1 - \frac{x}{\pi}\right) \left(1 + \frac{x}{2\pi}\right) \left(1 - \frac{x}{2\pi}\right) \left(1 + \frac{x}{3\pi}\right) \left(1 - \frac{x}{3\pi}\right) \cdots$$

Tetra and I looked at each other, then back at what Miruka had written. Tetra opened her notebook and began writing.

"Yay, it works!" exclaimed Tetra. "Of course it's 0 when $x = 0$, and no matter what other value n is for the $x = n\pi$ solutions, there's bound to be a $(1 - \frac{x}{n\pi})$ factor in there somewhere, which will make the whole thing 0."

"Not only that," I said, "but it looks like the limit works, too:"

$$\frac{\sin x}{x} = \left(1 + \frac{x}{\pi}\right) \left(1 - \frac{x}{\pi}\right) \left(1 + \frac{x}{2\pi}\right) \left(1 - \frac{x}{2\pi}\right) \left(1 + \frac{x}{3\pi}\right) \left(1 - \frac{x}{3\pi}\right) \cdots$$

"See? When x approaches 0, I think the right side will approach 1 along with the $\frac{\sin x}{x}$."

"Tetra," Miruka said, her voice soft yet forceful, "see if you can't simplify the right side of what he just wrote."

"Simplify it? Uh, okay, let's see... Oh, look, the product of a sum and a difference is a difference of squares, right?" Tetra glanced at me. "So $\left(1 + \frac{x}{\pi}\right)\left(1 - \frac{x}{\pi}\right) = 1^2 - \frac{x^2}{\pi^2}$, which means, uh... something like this?"

$$\frac{\sin x}{x} = \left(1 - \frac{x^2}{\pi^2}\right)\left(1 - \frac{x^2}{2^2\pi^2}\right)\left(1 - \frac{x^2}{3^2\pi^2}\right)\cdots$$

Miruka turned to me. "So Tetra has just written $\frac{\sin x}{x}$ as a product. No big surprise there, I guess, since that's what factoring something out is. But before, you wrote out its Taylor series. A sum, right? Well that means," she took a deep breath, "we can set those equivalent to each other:"

$$\frac{\sin x}{x} \text{ as a product} = \frac{\sin x}{x} \text{ as a sum}$$

$$\left(1 - \frac{x^2}{1^2\pi^2}\right)\left(1 - \frac{x^2}{2^2\pi^2}\right)\left(1 - \frac{x^2}{3^2\pi^2}\right)\cdots = 1 - \frac{x^2}{3!} + \frac{x^4}{5!} - \frac{x^6}{7!} + \cdots$$

Miruka seemed pretty sure of herself, but I was on edge. Where was she taking us? And why had she mentioned the Basel problem? I felt something building here. Something big.

Tetra had been peering at the notebook as Miruka worked. Now Miruka moved closer to her, until their faces were almost touching, and said, "Do you see it?"

Tetra pulled back. "See... see what?"

Miruka put her arms around both of us and whispered.

"A comparison of the coefficients of x^2."

I looked at the equation. *A comparison of the coefficients?*

I did a quick calculation. *A comparison of the coefficients!*

My breath caught in my throat.

No way.

I looked at Miruka. Miruka was looking at Tetra. Tetra was looking confused.

"What? What's going on?"

"Do you see what the coefficient for the x^2 term on the left will be?" Miruka asked her.

"Huh? No. How could I see that? We're multiplying an infinite number of things, right?"

"Let's walk through it, starting by expanding this:"

$$\left(1 - \frac{x^2}{1^2\pi^2}\right)\left(1 - \frac{x^2}{2^2\pi^2}\right)\left(1 - \frac{x^2}{3^2\pi^2}\right)\left(1 - \frac{x^2}{4^2\pi^2}\right)\cdots$$

"Kind of a mess, isn't it? All those πs and stuff in there," Miruka said. "So let's set up some definitions to clean things up:"

$$a = -\frac{1}{1^2\pi^2}, \quad b = -\frac{1}{2^2\pi^2}, \quad c = -\frac{1}{3^2\pi^2}, \quad d = -\frac{1}{4^2\pi^2}, \cdots$$

"Doesn't that look better?"

$$(1 + ax^2)(1 + bx^2)(1 + cx^2)(1 + dx^2)\cdots$$

"Okay, now we're going to expand, starting on the left:"

$$\underbrace{(1 + ax^2)(1 + bx^2)}_{\text{expand the 1st two terms}} (1 + cx^2)(1 + dx^2)\cdots$$

$$= \underbrace{\left(1 + (a + b)x^2 + abx^4\right)}_{\text{expanded}}(1 + cx^2)(1 + dx^2)\cdots$$

$$= \underbrace{\left(1 + (a + b)x^2 + abx^4\right)(1 + cx^2)}_{\text{expand the new 1st two terms}}(1 + dx^2)\cdots$$

$$= \underbrace{\left(1 + (a + b + c)x^2 + (ab + ac + bc)x^4 + abcx^6\right)}_{\text{expanded}}(1 + dx^2)\cdots$$

$$\vdots$$

"It looks like there's a pattern there..." Tetra said, watching Miruka work.

"There is," Miruka said. "It's the relationship between solutions and coefficients that we talked about this morning. Now do you see what's happening to the coefficient of x^2?"

I noticed that Miruka had slowed down from her normal pace. She was expanding the equation more methodically than she normally would, too.

"Sure. It's going to be $a + b + c + d + \cdots$, right?"

"That's right. Every one of the coefficients on the x^2s in the infinite product is going to be combined into an infinite sum after this is expanded. Okay, back to our factorization:"

$$\frac{\sin x}{x} \text{ as a product} = \frac{\sin x}{x} \text{ as a sum}$$

$$\left(1 - \frac{x^2}{1^2\pi^2}\right)\left(1 - \frac{x^2}{2^2\pi^2}\right)\left(1 - \frac{x^2}{3^2\pi^2}\right)\cdots = 1 - \frac{x^2}{3!} + \frac{x^4}{5!} - \frac{x^6}{7!} + \cdots$$

"Now we know that to get the coefficient for the x^2 term after the left side is expanded, we just need to add up all of the coefficients on the x^2s before the expansion. We just did that as $a+b+c+d+\cdots$, but without the renaming that would be $-\frac{1}{1^2\pi^2} - \frac{1}{2^2\pi^2} - \frac{1}{3^2\pi^2} - \frac{1}{4^2\pi^2} -\cdots$, right? Finding x^2's coefficient on the right is super easy, since it's right there, so we can compare the coefficients from both sides, like this:"

$$-\frac{1}{1^2\pi^2} - \frac{1}{2^2\pi^2} - \frac{1}{3^2\pi^2} - \frac{1}{4^2\pi^2} - \cdots = -\frac{1}{3!}$$

Tetra pored over what Miruka had written. "This coefficient from here, and this stuff from there... Okay, I get that."

"Still not seeing it?"

"Not seeing what?"

Miruka gave a reassuring smile and started writing again. "We can clean this equation up some more:"

$$\frac{1}{1^2\pi^2} + \frac{1}{2^2\pi^2} + \frac{1}{3^2\pi^2} + \frac{1}{4^2\pi^2} + \cdots = \frac{1}{6}$$

"After that, if we multiply both sides by π^2..."

$$\frac{1}{1^2} + \frac{1}{2^2} + \frac{1}{3^2} + \frac{1}{4^2} + \cdots = \frac{\pi^2}{6}$$

A cry of joy burst from Tetra, library be damned. Not that I didn't need to resist the urge myself.

"You solved it," I said. "That's the answer to the Basel problem!"

Tetra looked from Miruka to me.

Miruka nodded. "That's the solution to one of the greatest math problems of the eighteenth century. Isn't it beautiful?"

Tetra was still bewildered. "But how—? When did—? Huh—?"

Miruka polished things off by writing the final answer.

Answer to Problem 9-2 (the Basel problem)

$$\sum_{k=1}^{\infty} \frac{1}{k^2} = \frac{\pi^2}{6}$$

"Of course," she said, "we could also write it like this:"

$$\zeta(2) = \frac{\pi^2}{6}$$

"Done and done," Miruka said. She cocked her head and smiled. Oh, how I loved that smile.

9.6.3 Defying Infinity

"The master, Leonhard Euler gave us that proof," Miruka said. "He was the first person in the world to solve it. That was in 1735, when he was 28 years old."

I sat there, savoring the aftertaste of this delicacy, prepared for us over two and a half centuries ago. When Euler found this, he was only about ten years older than we were.

"Can we say that we solved it, too?" Tetra asked.

"Well, I wouldn't go that far. It's more like we retraced one of the proofs that he gave. This is just one of several."

"I got lost somewhere in the middle," Tetra said, "but I'm still impressed. The solution just seemed to pop up out of nowhere. When I thought about $x = n\pi$ being a solution to $\sin x = 0$, I thought that maybe we could factor out $\sin x$ somehow, and that it would be super cool if we could, but that's as far as I got. But that other way of factoring you showed us—once we had that, everything else just fell into place."

Tetra stared at the solution. "What I still can't get over is, what's π doing in there?"

"Hmm, good question," Miruka said. "How could the ratio of a circle's circumference to its diameter have anything to do with a sum of inverse squares?"

We all fell quiet, enjoying this new mysterious spice.

I broke the silence. "Why didn't Tetra's factorization work? It looks like just as good a solution as the one we used." I flipped to the page with the equation:

$$\frac{\sin x}{x} = (x + \pi)(x - \pi)(x + 2\pi)(x - 2\pi)(x + 3\pi)(x - 3\pi) \cdots$$

"Well," Miruka said, "$n\pi$ works fine as a solution to $\frac{\sin x}{x} = 0$, but the factoring isn't tight enough. There're too many degrees of freedom in there. If your only condition is that $x = n\pi$ is a solution, then that works when the right side is multiplied by a constant, right?"

$$\frac{\sin x}{x} = C \cdot (x + \pi)(x - \pi)(x + 2\pi)(x - 2\pi)(x + 3\pi)(x - 3\pi) \cdots$$

"Ah, I see. That's why it failed the limit test. Because $\lim_{x \to 0} \frac{\sin x}{x} = 1$ isn't going to work here."

"Exactly. If it was just an nth order polynomial then you could use the nth coefficient to play with the constant. Things aren't so nice when you're messing with infinities, though—no highest order coefficient anymore. So instead of starting with $(x - n\pi)$ and going from there, you need to rig things so that you know the limit is going to work. That's where the $(1 - \frac{x}{n\pi})$ factors came from. Never start off on an infinite journey unprepared."

Miruka adjusted her glasses and continued.

"If you really want to be picky, there's a hole in the logic of this proof. We used a graph of the sine curve to get our solutions to $\sin x = 0$, looking at where it crossed the x-axis. But that ignores complex number solutions, so we can't say anything about those yet. That's why Euler wrote more than one proof of this problem. I kind of like this one, though, because I have this thing about power series. Also, in this one we compared the x^2 coefficients to find $\zeta(2)$, right? Well, you can do something similar using any even exponent on x to find the answer to the zeta function for that exponent.

"I did some cleanup at the end, but that's only because I already knew the solution. Your idea to try factoring $\sin x$ was wonderful, Tetra, even if it didn't work out like you wanted. I love a girl who defies infinity."

Miruka stood.

"A round of applause," she said. "To Euler and Tetra."

Miruka began clapping, and I stood up and joined her. Flustered by her standing ovation, Tetra put both hands on her reddening cheeks.

"Hey, c'mon guys, it's the library!"

Yes, it was the library. Maybe it wasn't the best place.

But Tetra deserved it.

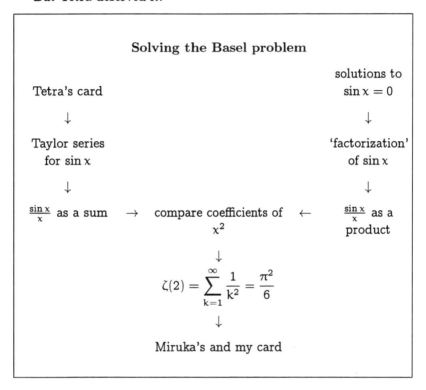

Solving the Basel problem

Tetra's card

solutions to
$\sin x = 0$

$\downarrow$

$\downarrow$

Taylor series
for $\sin x$

'factorization'
of $\sin x$

$\downarrow$

$\downarrow$

$\frac{\sin x}{x}$ as a sum $\quad\rightarrow\quad$ compare coefficients of $\quad\leftarrow\quad$ $\frac{\sin x}{x}$ as a
x^2 product

$\downarrow$

$$\zeta(2) = \sum_{k=1}^{\infty} \frac{1}{k^2} = \frac{\pi^2}{6}$$

$\downarrow$

Miruka's and my card

It is clear that any infinite series of the form $1 + 1/2^n + 1/3^n + 1/4^n + \cdots$, provided n is an even integer, can be expressed in terms of π, since it always has a sum equal to a fractional part of a power of π.

LEONHARD EULER
Introduction to Analysis of the Infinite

CHAPTER 10

Partitions

> I confess my love
> and your answer lies beyond
> the edges of space
>
> ___
>
> MIWA KOBAYASHI
> from *Youth in Seventeen Syllables*

10.1 PARTITION NUMBERS

10.1.1 Ways to Pay

"Here it is." Miruka slapped a sheet of paper on the table. "Muraki's latest."

Problems from Mr. Muraki

Assume that there exist coins for any denomination of yen. Consider how many combinations of coins you could use to pay ¥n. Let that number be P_n. (Note: Each way of paying ¥n is called a "partition" of n, and the number of possible ways of paying, P_n, is called the "partition number" of n.)

> **Example.** ¥3 can be paid using one ¥3 coin, one ¥2 coin and one ¥1 coin, or three ¥1 coins. Since there are three ways of paying, $P_3 = 3$.
>
> **Problem 10-1**
> Find P_9.
>
> **Problem 10-2**
> Is $P_{15} < 1000$?

"We just have to find out how many ways there are to pay for something?" Tetra asked. "Sounds easy enough."

"I don't know..." I said.

"What's not to know? P_9 just means the number of ways to pay ¥9, right? All we have to do is go in order, using ¥1 coins, ¥2 coins, and so on."

"It's not that simple," I said. "We can use the same denomination coin any number of times. So in every case where we use, say, ¥1 coins, we have to consider how many of them we're going to use."

"Sure, but can't we just take our time and count out each case separately?"

"We could, but we'd probably miss at least a couple of cases. And even if we did manage it for P_9, finding all the ways for P_{15} would be pretty rough. Coming up with a general solution is much safer."

"You think? I mean, we're just talking about paying out ¥15 yen here, right? How hard could it—"

Bang!

Miruka slammed her hand down on the table.

"Tetra, over to that corner! You, over by the window! I'll stay here. It's time for thinking, not talking."

Tetra and I managed two small nods—the response least likely to further incur her wrath, we hoped.

"Well, what are you waiting for? *Move!*"

10.1.2 Some Concrete Examples

I began as I usually do, by figuring out some simple concrete examples to give me a better feel for the problem.

The simplest case would be to pay ¥0—or should I say to not pay anything?—and there's only one way to do that:

$$P_0 = 1 \qquad \text{1 way to pay ¥0}$$

The next case was easy too. The only way to pay ¥1 is with a single ¥1 coin:

$$P_1 = 1 \qquad \text{1 way to pay ¥1}$$

I had a choice in the case of paying ¥2—I could either use one ¥2 coin, or two ¥1 coins:

$$P_2 = 2 \qquad \text{2 ways to pay ¥2}$$

I started to copy the answer for ¥3 from the example on Mr. Muraki's card—one ¥3 coin, one ¥2 coin and one ¥1 coin, or three ¥1 coins—but all of these words and numbers were getting confusing. Since I was really just doing an addition problem, why not write it like that? So instead of "one ¥2 coin and one ¥1 coin," I could just write:

$$\underbrace{2}_{\text{one ¥2 coin}} + \underbrace{1}_{\text{one ¥1 coin}}$$

Then I could write the different ways of paying ¥3 like this:

$$
\begin{aligned}
3 &= 3 \\
&= 2 + 1 \\
&= 1 + 1 + 1
\end{aligned}
$$

Three lines, so the next answer was 3:

$$P_3 = 3 \qquad \text{3 ways to pay ¥3}$$

I'd been thinking of this as "the number of ways to pay ¥n," but looking back at Mr. Muraki's note, it occurred to me that I could also think of it as "the number of ways to partition the number n into positive integers." In other words, the partition number of n.

I moved on to $n = 4$, which had five partitions:

$$
\begin{aligned}
4 &= 4 \\
&= 3 + 1 \\
&= 2 + 2 \\
&= 2 + 1 + 1 \\
&= 1 + 1 + 1 + 1
\end{aligned}
$$

That gave the answer for P_4:

$$P_4 = 5 \qquad \text{5 ways to pay ¥4}$$

I found seven partitions for $n = 5$:

$$
\begin{aligned}
5 &= 5 \\
&= 4 + 1 \\
&= 3 + 2 \\
&= 3 + 1 + 1 \\
&= 2 + 2 + 1 \\
&= 2 + 1 + 1 + 1 \\
&= 1 + 1 + 1 + 1 + 1
\end{aligned}
$$

$$P_5 = 7 \qquad \text{7 ways to pay ¥5}$$

I was finally getting to big enough values of n to see a pattern emerging. Like Miruka had once said, rules won't always show themselves in a small sample. Still, creating a big sample with this problem was getting harder and harder. I gritted my teeth and moved on to $n = 6$:

$$
\begin{aligned}
6 &= 6 \\
&= 5 + 1 \\
&= 4 + 2 \\
&= 4 + 1 + 1 \\
&= 3 + 3
\end{aligned}
$$

$$= 3 + 2 + 1$$
$$= 3 + 1 + 1 + 1$$
$$= 2 + 2 + 2$$
$$= 2 + 2 + 1 + 1$$
$$= 2 + 1 + 1 + 1 + 1$$
$$= 1 + 1 + 1 + 1 + 1 + 1$$

$P_6 = 11$ 11 ways to pay ¥6

So far, I had found that $\{P_2, P_3, P_4, P_5, P_6\} = \{2, 3, 5, 7, 11\}$. Intrigued by all those primes, I decided to press on to see if P_7 would be 13:

$$7 = 7$$
$$= 6 + 1$$
$$= 5 + 2$$
$$= 5 + 1 + 1$$
$$= 4 + 3$$
$$= 4 + 2 + 1$$
$$= 4 + 1 + 1 + 1$$
$$= 3 + 3 + 1$$
$$= 3 + 2 + 2$$
$$= 3 + 2 + 1 + 1$$
$$= 3 + 1 + 1 + 1 + 1$$
$$= 2 + 2 + 2 + 1$$
$$= 2 + 2 + 1 + 1 + 1$$
$$= 2 + 1 + 1 + 1 + 1 + 1$$
$$= 1 + 1 + 1 + 1 + 1 + 1 + 1$$

$P_7 = 15$ 15 ways to pay ¥7

Oh, well. It was a good guess, but the series of primes was broken.

Having come this far, I figured that I might as well work out $n = 8$ and $n = 9$, but I was starting to get worried about missing a case or two. Not that worrying was going to get me anywhere. I began to write:

$$8 = 8$$
$$= 7 + 1$$
$$= 6 + 2$$
$$= 6 + 1 + 1$$
$$= 5 + 3$$
$$= 5 + 2 + 1$$
$$= 5 + 1 + 1 + 1$$
$$= 4 + 4$$
$$= 4 + 3 + 1$$
$$= 4 + 2 + 2$$
$$= 4 + 2 + 1 + 1$$
$$= 4 + 1 + 1 + 1 + 1$$
$$= 3 + 3 + 2$$
$$= 3 + 3 + 1 + 1$$
$$= 3 + 2 + 2 + 1$$
$$= 3 + 2 + 1 + 1 + 1$$
$$= 3 + 1 + 1 + 1 + 1 + 1$$
$$= 2 + 2 + 2 + 2$$
$$= 2 + 2 + 2 + 1 + 1$$
$$= 2 + 2 + 1 + 1 + 1 + 1$$
$$= 2 + 1 + 1 + 1 + 1 + 1 + 1$$
$$= 1 + 1 + 1 + 1 + 1 + 1 + 1 + 1$$

$$P_8 = 22 \qquad \text{22 ways to pay ¥8}$$

The numbers were starting to get pretty big, but I was in the home stretch now:

$$9 = 9$$
$$= 8 + 1$$

$= 7 + 2$

$= 7 + 1 + 1$

$= 6 + 3$

$= 6 + 2 + 1$

$= 6 + 1 + 1 + 1$

$= 5 + 4$

$= 5 + 3 + 1$

$= 5 + 2 + 2$

$= 5 + 2 + 1 + 1$

$= 5 + 1 + 1 + 1 + 1$

$= 4 + 4 + 1$

$= 4 + 3 + 2$

$= 4 + 3 + 1 + 1$

$= 4 + 2 + 2 + 1$

$= 4 + 2 + 1 + 1 + 1$

$= 4 + 1 + 1 + 1 + 1 + 1$

$= 3 + 3 + 3$

$= 3 + 3 + 2 + 1$

$= 3 + 3 + 1 + 1 + 1$

$= 3 + 2 + 2 + 2$

$= 3 + 2 + 2 + 1 + 1$

$= 3 + 2 + 1 + 1 + 1 + 1$

$= 3 + 1 + 1 + 1 + 1 + 1 + 1$

$= 2 + 2 + 2 + 2 + 1$

$= 2 + 2 + 2 + 1 + 1 + 1$

$= 2 + 2 + 1 + 1 + 1 + 1 + 1$

$= 2 + 1 + 1 + 1 + 1 + 1 + 1 + 1$

$= 1 + 1 + 1 + 1 + 1 + 1 + 1 + 1 + 1$

$P_9 = 30$ 30 ways to pay ¥9

That took care of Mr. Muraki's first problem, at least. There are 30 different ways of paying ¥9. In other words, the number 9 has 30 partitions.

Now I had the second problem to tackle. From the look of things, counting out P_{15} by hand would be all kinds of painful. No doubt finding the general term for P_n would be the easier route.

"The library is closed!"

I jolted upright in my chair. Ms. Mizutani had snuck up on me again. Today her glasses were jet-black wraparounds, and I imagined laser-scoped android eyes behind them, scanning the library for stragglers.

I was surprised at how late it was. I still wasn't sure how I was going to tackle Mr. Muraki's second problem, but at least I had managed to get one of them done.

Answer to Problem 10-1

$$P_9 = 30$$

10.2   THE FIBONACCI SIGN

The three of us set off towards the train station. We had been walking for a few minutes when I noticed Tetra waggling her hand, as if playing some bizarre solitaire version of rock-paper-scissors.

"What are you doing?" I asked.

"The Fibonacci sign," she replied simply.

"The what?"

"You don't know it yet, because I just made it up."

"Um, okay..."

"It's a sign for math lovers to flash to each other to show their street cred. No words, just gestures, transcending language barriers. It can mean 'hello,' 'goodbye'—anything you want it to."

I gave her my best dubious look.

"Here's how it goes. Ready?" Tetra flicked her fingers in front of my face. "You get that?"

"Get what?"

"C'mon, pay attention! It's all in the number of fingers. One, one, two, three." Tetra repeated the gesture.

"Uh, okay. Yeah, that's—"

"Then, after someone gives you the Fibonacci sign," she continued, "you answer like this." She held her hand up, palm facing me. "Five fingers, right? 1, 1, 2, 3, 5. And that's the Fibonacci sign!"

"So, Miruka, about the P_9 problem..."

I looked over at Miruka to find her gesturing wildly.

"Not you, too," I said.

"What do you do after five, Tetra? Use three fingers from your other hand to make eight? Ooh, and you could switch bases to do thirteen—"

"No, you just stop at five," Tetra said. "Okay, we all ready? I give the sign, you two give the response. Go!"

Tetra's fingers flipped out a 'one-one-two-three.' Miruka laughed and held up a 'five.'

"Guys, c'mon," I said.

But Tetra stood holding up three fingers, staring at me with those big doe-eyes.

"Okay, okay..." *What the heck.* I held up my hand.

* * *

We made our way out of the side streets and onto the main road where a guardrail encroached on the sidewalk, forcing us to walk single file. Tetra took the lead, but spent half her time walking backwards so that she could talk to us. Miruka walked behind me, which made me oddly self-conscious.

"The first problem was exercise for our hands," Miruka said. "The second one will be exercise for our heads."

Tetra spun around to face us. "I finished the first problem, but I'm still working on the second one. I'm trying to write out all the combinations for P_{15}, but I'm starting to see why that might not be the best way. I'm already up to fifty, and I still have a ton to go. No way there's going to be a thousand, though."

"Tetra! Telephone pole!"

She stepped deftly to one side, still walking backward. "I see it, I see it. You got 29 for the first problem, right?" Tetra opened her notebook and held it out for me to see.

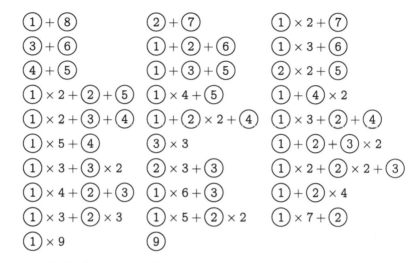

"Huh? Wasn't it 30?" I said. "Hang on, how do you read this?"

"What do you mean? The circles are coins, of course. So ① × 3 means three ¥1 coins."

"Ah, I see. Yeah, I guess that works, too."

"You forgot ②+③+④," Miruka said, peering over my shoulder. Her long hair tickled my neck.

"Aww, after all those times I double—" *BANG*. "Ouch!" A low-hanging sign swung as Tetra stumbled past, rubbing the back of her head.

* * *

"I'm off," Miruka said when we arrived at the station. "See you guys tomorrow."

Miruka gave Tetra a pat on the head as she headed towards her platform.

"Yo," Tetra called after her, "Fibonacci!"

Tetra flicked her fingers, *one-one-two-three*. Miruka waved five fingers at us over her shoulder.

10.3 CONFESSIONS

Tetra suggested that we have a cup of coffee before leaving, so we ducked into Beans.

She poured cream into her coffee and then sat in silence, forgetting to even stir it. Something was obviously on her mind. Finally she muttered something down at her cup.

"I wish I was better at math. If I can't even get P_9 right, how am I ever going to get P_{15}? How am I ever going to get *him*?"

"Huh?" I said.

"Huh?" Tetra said back. "I didn't say anything!" she blurted, her face a deep crimson. "I mean I did, but I didn't—Uh..." She groaned, waving her hands in frantic denial. I half expected her to throw a new gang sign.

Tetra collected her thoughts, and tried a new tack. "Do you remember back in your last year of junior high, when you gave that presentation about binary numbers?" she asked. "You talked about how all those mathematicians studied them so long ago, but how their work is still alive today. How what Leibniz did in the seventeenth century lies at the heart of every twenty-first century computer. You said, 'Mathematics is timeless.' That really stuck with me."

I smiled, remembering that day, amazed that she remembered it too.

Tetra continued. "I started hanging out in the library after that, because... well, I wanted to be closer to you, I guess. You probably never even noticed me. I was always back in a corner reading books, and you were always doing your math." She looked up and gave a self-conscious laugh.

"Wow," I said. "You're right, I didn't notice. I always thought I was alone."

"I was there almost every day that winter." She smiled. "I was so happy when I got into the same high school as you. It took me a while to get up the nerve, but I'm glad I wrote you that note, too, and that you agreed to help me with math. I'm even glad I got to know Miruka."

Tetra looked back at her coffee and assumed a more somber tone. "But, sometimes I get frustrated. I love talking about math with you two, but I know that when I'm there you have to bring things down to my level. I can't do anything right, and I can't do anything on my own."

Exactly how I feel when I'm talking to Miruka.

"I guess what I'm trying to say is, I know I'm just some third wheel, but. . . I don't know. I just hope you'll always have a place for me. Even if it's just to teach me math."

I had never thought of myself as a limited space, one that would require a domain for Tetra to occupy. But I understood what she meant—or so I thought.

"I'll teach you anytime you want, just like I promised. I love talking with you. You're honest, and you're smarter than you give yourself credit for. Besides, I could never go back to messing with my equations alone in the library now. It's so much more fun to have friends, somebody to share all this with. You're part of that, and you always will be."

"Stop right there," Tetra said, holding up a hand. "Don't get me wrong, hearing you say that means so much to me. But if we keep going, I'm afraid I'll say something I'll regret."

That's when something clicked and I finally understood why Tetra walked so slowly on our way to the train station after school. It was her way of expanding the domain that we shared. Her way of extending a finite space.

10.4 MAKING SELECTIONS

I looked at the digital clock on my desk. 11:59 pm. *Two primes*. My family was asleep, and I was doing math. Everything was perfect.

My parents never understood what math meant to me. At times I was so overjoyed at some discovery that I tried to show them—to *make* them understand—but the best response they could manage was, "Wow, that's great."

I thought about how important my new friends were to me, and the times we shared: Working on problems and solving them together, combining our wits and improving each others' solutions, communicating through the language of math. . . Things were so different now than back in junior high, when I spent so much time alone. Well, at least I had *thought* I was alone.

I shook my head to clear it, determined to get at least some work done on Mr. Muraki's second problem. Back to partitions and P_n.

I had decided to try using generating functions as a way to see if P_{15} would be less than 1000. They'd been a useful tool when Miruka and I tackled the Fibonacci sequence and the Catalan numbers, so I hoped they might lead me to a general term for this sequence. If I could find a closed form of P_n, then the problem was as good as solved.

I started by making a table summarizing what I had found so far:

n	0	1	2	3	4	5	6	7	8	9	$\cdots$
P_n	1	1	2	3	5	7	11	15	22	30	$\cdots$

I called the sequence's generating function $P(x)$, which, by definition, would have a form like this:

$$P(x) = P_0 x^0 + P_1 x^1 + P_2 x^2 + P_3 x^3 + P_4 x^4 + P_5 x^5 + \cdots$$

Replacing the coefficients with the values from the table gave me an explicit equation:

$$P(x) = 1x^0 + 1x^1 + 2x^2 + 3x^3 + 5x^4 + 7x^5 + \cdots$$

The next step was to find a closed form, a generating function in terms of x. When we worked on the Fibonacci sequence we did that using its recurrence relation—I still got chills when I remembered our trick of shifting coefficients to do that. When we conquered the Catalan numbers, we used a product of generating functions and made them "share" an exponent.

But what to do with partition numbers? Setting up a generating function is easy; finding its closed form takes some work. I needed to make some kind of essential discovery about the nature of this beast.

I glanced at the clock and decided that sleep could wait a bit longer.

I paced in my room, my thoughts tracing a pattern on the floor. Working things out by hand is important, but I had taken that as far as I could—the number of combinations was just getting to be too big. I had to make the leap to a general solution. Miruka was right. It was time to exercise my head, not my hands.

Think, think. . .

I opened my window and inhaled the night air. A dog barked in the distance. My mind wandered, and I began to think about math in more general terms. Why did I like it so much? Just what is math, anyway?

My thoughts went to something Miruka had told me once.

"Cantor said that the essence of mathematics is its freedom. If that's right, then Euler must have been the freest person who ever lived. Infinities and infinitesimals were like toys to him. He gave the world π and i and e. When he came to rivers that no one had crossed before, he built bridges."

I wondered if the day would ever come when I would build some bridges of my own.

Resuming my pacing, I decided to take a step back from generating functions to look at the problem in a new light. I tried to recall if I had ever solved anything similar, which brought to mind something I had told Tetra: "Don't remember, *think*." I made a mental note to tell Tetra that sometimes remembering is important, too.

That had been when we were talking about the binomial theorem. I recalled her surprise at seeing combinations appear when we calculated $(x + y)^n$. We had talked about how when you take the nth power of $(x + y)$, you had to choose an x or a y from among each of the n factors, and how collecting like terms made the number of possible choices appear as coefficients.

For example, when expanding $(x + y)^3$ you would find all possible combinations of xs and ys, giving these eight terms:

$$
\begin{aligned}
(\underline{x} + y)\,(\underline{x} + y)\,(\underline{x} + y) &\quad\rightarrow\quad xxx = x^3 y^0 \\
(\underline{x} + y)\,(\underline{x} + y)\,(x + \underline{y}) &\quad\rightarrow\quad xxy = x^2 y^1 \\
(\underline{x} + y)\,(x + \underline{y})\,(\underline{x} + y) &\quad\rightarrow\quad xyx = x^2 y^1 \\
(\underline{x} + y)\,(x + \underline{y})\,(x + \underline{y}) &\quad\rightarrow\quad xyy = x^1 y^2 \\
(x + \underline{y})\,(\underline{x} + y)\,(\underline{x} + y) &\quad\rightarrow\quad yxx = x^2 y^1 \\
(x + \underline{y})\,(\underline{x} + y)\,(x + \underline{y}) &\quad\rightarrow\quad yxy = x^1 y^2 \\
(x + \underline{y})\,(x + \underline{y})\,(\underline{x} + y) &\quad\rightarrow\quad yyx = x^1 y^2 \\
(x + \underline{y})\,(x + \underline{y})\,(x + \underline{y}) &\quad\rightarrow\quad yyy = x^0 y^3
\end{aligned}
$$

Adding them all up and collecting like terms would give you the expanded form:

$$(x + y)(x + y)(x + y) = \underline{1}x^3 y^0 + \underline{3}x^2 y^1 + \underline{3}x^1 y^2 + \underline{1}x^0 y^3$$

The coefficients 1, 3, 3, and 1 are equivalent to the number of ways to choose 3, 2, 1, and 0 xs. That meant that they could be written in $\binom{n}{k}$ form, like this:

$$(x + y)(x + y)(x + y) = \binom{3}{3}x^3 + \binom{3}{2}x^2y + \binom{3}{1}xy^2 + \binom{3}{0}y^3$$

As I smiled at the thought of the look on Tetra's face when she saw that, something flitted through my mind and I halted midstride. I was on the verge of a major realization.

The look on Tetra's face? No, before that.

Don't remember, think? No, after that.

Number of possible choices appear as coefficients? That's it!

I could use Tetra's groupings, pick up what I needed from the factors...then just change the infinite sum to an infinite product and...done.

Miruka's voice tickled the back of my mind. "Well, what are you waiting for? *Move!*"

I hurried to my desk and began writing. I wasn't sure if an infinite product would technically classify as a closed form of the function, but I was pretty sure I was on the right track.

Problem 10-3 (Self-assigned)

Let $P(x)$ be a generating function for partition numbers. Express $P(x)$ as a product.

10.5 THREE SOLUTIONS

I met Miruka and Ay-Ay in the music room the next day after school.

"I'll stop telling you to play Bach when you stop telling me to read Euler," Ay-Ay said, her fingers moving across the piano keys. She was playing one of the *Goldberg Variations*.

"I don't mind Bach at all," Miruka said. She was walking around the room, hands laced behind her back. She was obviously in a good mood, a broad smile on her face as she bounced along with the music.

"Hey, where's Tetra?" Ay-Ay asked me. "I thought you two were joined at the hip."

"Come on, it's not like she follows me *everywhere*."

Just then Tetra appeared in the doorway, notebook clutched to her chest.

"Oh, there you are," she said. "When I didn't see you in the library, I started to get worried."

"You were saying?" Ay-Ay whispered to me.

Tetra scanned our group. "Am I interrupting something?"

"Nah," I said, "we're just hanging out."

"I think you meant to say," Ay-Ay purred, "we were just being blown away by Ay-Ay's performance."

"That's what I meant." I smiled. "Actually, your timing is perfect, Tetra. Is it okay with everyone if we slip into math mode for a while? I want to tell you about some stuff I figured out last night. I made progress with the partition numbers problem."

Miruka's eyes narrowed.

"Don't tell me you found a closed form..."

"No, I went a different route. I wrote the generating function as an infinite product instead."

"Then by all means." Miruka's smile returned.

I walked to the sliding chalkboard at the front of the room and got ready. Miruka and Tetra followed.

"Oh, boy." Ay-Ay said, giving the keys a final tinkle. "Here comes the math."

10.5.1 Using Generating Functions

I wrote the generating function on the board, beginning my explanation as I did:

$$P(x) = P_0 x^0 + P_1 x^1 + P_2 x^2 + P_3 x^3 + P_4 x^4 + P_5 x^5 + \cdots$$

"To solve the second problem, we need to find a general term P_n for the partition numbers. In order to do that, we want to find this generating function. I wasn't sure how to get beyond this definition form here, so I assigned myself a new problem, finding a way to write $P(x)$ as a product. Before I get into that, though, let's warm up by working through this example. Think of it as a constrained version of the bigger problem, one where there's a limited number of coins and types of coins."

> **Problem 10-4 (A constrained partition number)**
>
> Assume that you have one ¥1 coin, one ¥2 coin, and one ¥3 coin. How many ways are there to pay ¥3?

"Of course, this isn't very hard. There are only two solutions: either pay with the ¥1 coin and the ¥2 coin, or pay with the ¥3 coin."

> **Answer to Problem 10-4**
>
> 2 ways

"This problem gives a good way to look at the generating function, though. Let's make a list of what you can use each coin for:"

· The ¥1 coin can by used to pay ¥0 or ¥1
· The ¥2 coin can by used to pay ¥0 or ¥2
· The ¥3 coin can by used to pay ¥0 or ¥3

"But check this out:"

$$(x^0 + x^1)(x^0 + x^2)(x^0 + x^3)$$

"This says the same thing. The xs here are just formal variables. We're using the exponents as placeholders for the values we can pay."

"I think I'm going to like this," Miruka said.

"I thought you might," I smiled.

"Wait," Tetra said, pouting, "I'm lost. What does Miruka like? Why did you think she would like it? Don't leave me behind here, guys."

Ay-Ay accompanied Tetra with a bar of droll music.

"Patience, grasshopper," Miruka said.

"Yeah, I think you'll get it in the next step, Tetra," I reassured her. "First, think of each factor as being related to a single coin:"

$$\underbrace{(x^0 + x^1)}_{\yen 1\ \text{coin}}\,\underbrace{(x^0 + x^2)}_{\yen 2\ \text{coin}}\,\underbrace{(x^0 + x^3)}_{\yen 3\ \text{coin}}$$

"When we expand this out, then the role of each coin is expressed in the exponents. Not only that, but every possible way of paying is going to show up as a coefficient:"

$$
\begin{aligned}
(x^0 + x^1)(x^0 + x^2)(x^0 + x^3) = {}& x^{0+0+0} \\
& + x^{0+0+3} \\
& + x^{0+2+0} \\
& + x^{0+2+3} \\
& + x^{1+0+0} \\
& + x^{1+0+3} \\
& + x^{1+2+0} \\
& + x^{1+2+3}
\end{aligned}
$$

"Take the x^{1+2+0} as an example. You read the exponent like this:"

$$1 \longrightarrow \quad \text{used the } \yen 1 \text{ coin to pay } \yen 1$$
$$2 \longrightarrow \quad \text{used the } \yen 2 \text{ coin to pay } \yen 2$$
$$0 \longrightarrow \quad \text{used the } \yen 3 \text{ coin to pay } \yen 0$$

"Hang on," Tetra said. "I still don't get it. You wrote $1 + 2 + 0$. But if you used one $\yen 1$ coin, one $\yen 2$ coin, and no $\yen 3$ coins, shouldn't that exponent be $1 + 1 + 0$?"

"No, not here. We aren't keeping track of how many coins we used, we want to know how much we paid when we used them."

"I'd call it the contribution of a $\yen k$ coin, myself," Miruka added.

"Okay, I'm getting there," Tetra said. "So the exponents in the expanded equation are showing you all the ways of paying with the $\yen 1$, $\yen 2$, and $\yen 3$ coins. I got that part. What I'm still not seeing is where the original $(x^0 + x^1)(x^0 + x^2)(x^0 + x^3)$ came from."

"From the way that you expand products. It works out just the same as figuring out all the ways of paying with coins. When you expand $(x^0 + x^1)(x^0 + x^2)(x^0 + x^3)$, what you're doing is this:"

- Choose a term from $x^0 + x^1$
- Choose a term from $x^0 + x^2$
- Choose a term from $x^0 + x^3$

"Once you've made your choices, you multiply them together. It's exactly the same as if you had done this:"

- Choose an amount to pay with the ¥1 coin
- Choose an amount to pay with the ¥2 coin
- Choose an amount to pay with the ¥3 coin

"Aha! So to make all the possible combinations, the coins are riding piggyback on the xs. Gotcha!" Tetra appeared satisfied at last.

"So after we expand the equation, combine the terms with the same exponent, and order them from smallest exponent to largest, here's what we end up with:"

$$(x^0 + x^1)(x^0 + x^2)(x^0 + x^3) \qquad \text{original expression}$$
$$= x^{0+0+0} + x^{0+0+3} + x^{0+2+0} + x^{0+2+3} \qquad \text{expand}$$
$$+ x^{1+0+0} + x^{1+0+3} + x^{1+2+0} + x^{1+2+3}$$
$$= x^0 + x^3 + x^2 + x^5 + x^1 + x^4 + x^3 + x^6 \qquad \text{add up exponents}$$
$$= x^0 + x^1 + x^2 + 2x^3 + x^4 + x^5 + x^6 \qquad \text{combine and sort}$$

"See how the coefficient on the x^3 term is 2, Tetra? What do you think that means?"

"Well, it must mean that there were two x^3 terms after we expanded. That would be the x^{0+0+3} and the x^{1+2+0}, *here* and *here*. And there's two of them because there's two ways to pay ¥3, right?"

"Exactly. Now think about what you just said. We're adding up exponents on all these dummy xs, and the coefficient on each x^n term tells you the number of ways you can pay ¥n. What's another way to describe the number of ways to pay ¥n?"

"Another way? Hmm... Oh, I know! The partition number!"

"Right. Now we haven't quite answered Mr. Muraki's problem yet, because this one only used a limited number of coins. It's pretty close, though, and we should be able to solve the real problem by doing the same thing—adding up the exponents on some dummy x variables, and looking at the coefficients of what we end up with. In other words, we'll have our generating function, just like we now have a generating function for our limited case."

A generating function for Problem 10-4

$$(x^0 + x^1)(x^0 + x^2)(x^0 + x^3)$$

"Oh, cool! I always think of generating functions as these big huge things with infinite series in them, but this little one doesn't seem so scary. It's small enough to stick in my pocket!" Tetra mimed doing just that.

"Now," I continued, "what we have to do is get rid of these limitations, since the real problem wants us to think about what happens when we could pay anything, using any kind of coin. We're going to do it in pretty much the same way, but this time we'll be dealing with an infinite number of infinite sums, like this:"

$$
\begin{aligned}
&(x^0 + x^1 + x^2 + x^3 + \cdots) && \text{contribution of ¥1 coins} \\
&\times (x^0 + x^2 + x^4 + x^6 + \cdots) && \text{contribution of ¥2 coins} \\
&\times (x^0 + x^3 + x^6 + x^9 + \cdots) && \text{contribution of ¥3 coins} \\
&\times (x^0 + x^4 + x^8 + x^{12} + \cdots) && \text{contribution of ¥4 coins} \\
&\times \cdots \\
&\times (x^{0k} + x^{1k} + x^{2k} + x^{3k} + \cdots) && \text{contribution of ¥kcoins} \\
&\times \cdots
\end{aligned}
$$

"Do you see where all that's coming from? The exponents are an infinite series because there's no limit to the *number* of coins we can use, and there's an infinite number of factors because there's no limit to the *kind* of coins we can use. If we can expand all that, then we'll have captured every possible way of paying any amount of money in one fell swoop, because we'll be able to find the coefficient on the x^n term, which will be the partition number of n. In other words, the number of ways to pay out ¥n."

I picked up a fresh piece of chalk before continuing.

"Okay, so we've figured out that our generating function for the partition numbers is going to be an infinite product of infinite sums. You could also call it a formal power series with partition numbers as its coefficients. That means we can write $P(x)$ like this:

$$
\begin{aligned}
P(x) =&(x^0 + x^1 + x^2 + x^3 + \cdots) \\
&\times (x^0 + x^2 + x^4 + x^6 + \cdots) \\
&\times (x^0 + x^3 + x^6 + x^9 + \cdots) \\
&\times (x^0 + x^4 + x^8 + x^{12} + \cdots) \\
&\times \cdots \\
&\times (x^{0k} + x^{1k} + x^{2k} + x^{3k} + \cdots) \\
&\times \cdots
\end{aligned}
$$

"Now we're going to play a little trick here. Since the xs are just dummy variables anyway, let's go ahead and assume that every one is a real number where $0 \leqslant x < 1$, which lets us use the geometric series formula. Then we can rewrite the contribution of each kind of coin like this:"

$$
x^{0k} + x^{1k} + x^{2k} + x^{3k} + \cdots = \frac{1}{1 - x^k}
$$

"Now all of those infinite sums that popped up in $P(x)$ become fractions:"

$$
\begin{aligned}
P(x) =&\frac{1}{1 - x^1} \\
&\times \frac{1}{1 - x^2} \\
&\times \frac{1}{1 - x^3} \\
&\times \frac{1}{1 - x^4} \\
&\times \cdots \\
&\times \frac{1}{1 - x^k} \\
&\times \cdots
\end{aligned}
$$

"And with that we've changed our infinite product of infinite sums into an infinite product of fractions, so we have $P(x)$ in the form we wanted."

Answer to Problem 10-3
(The generating function $P(x)$ of the partition numbers P_n as a product)

$$P(x) = \frac{1}{1-x^1} \cdot \frac{1}{1-x^2} \cdot \frac{1}{1-x^3} \cdots$$

"Okay, let's see where we stand," I said. "Our goal is to solve P_{15} to get an answer to Mr. Muraki's second problem, and to do that we want to find a general term P_n. That means we need to find a good form for the generating function $P(x)$, which is why we did my problem. Working that out, we got a version of $P(x)$ that's written as a product. So I propose we work on a new problem."

Problem X
Find the coefficient for x^n when the following function $P(x)$ is expanded as a power series.

$$P(x) = \frac{1}{1-x^1} \cdot \frac{1}{1-x^2} \cdot \frac{1}{1-x^3} \cdots$$

"The coefficient of x^n will be P_n, so if we can find the general term then we'll be able to verify the inequality $P_{15} < 1000$ in Mr. Muraki's problem."

A map for finding a general term P_n for partition numbers

partition numbers $\longrightarrow$ generating function $P(x)$

$\downarrow$ Prob. 10-3

General term for P_n $\xleftarrow[\text{Prob. X}]{}$ $P(x)$ as a product

I turned from the blackboard and held my breath. Miruka was the first to speak.

"So you want to attack the problem head-on."

"What do you mean?"

"Well, there's no real need to find P_n to answer the problem, is there?"

"Since it's an inequality, no, I guess not..." My palms started to feel clammy.

"Just making sure, because I solved it without using a general term or the value of P_{15}."

"Wait, you *solved* it?"

10.5.2   Using an Upper Bound

Miruka took my place at the blackboard.

"As Tetra discovered, the partition numbers get big fast, so writing them out is less than ideal. And we all agree there's no need to calculate the value of P_{15} to show that it's less than 1000. That's why I decided to tackle this by looking for an upper bound on the partition numbers."

"What does that mean, exactly?" Tetra asked.

"It means that I wanted to find a function $M(n)$ so that anytime you gave me some number n, I could tell you if P_n was less than $M(n)$. When n gets bigger we know that P_n gets bigger, too, I just want to be sure that it never gets bigger than $M(n)$."

"I guess that's why it's called an upper bound," Tetra said, placing her hand on top of her head.

"Right. Sometimes you'll see constants that are called upper bounds, too, but this is a little bit different. $M(n)$ is a function of n." Miruka started to scribble on the chalkboard, talking as she did. "One interesting thing I noticed was that the first five partition numbers, P_0 through P_4, were the same as the first five Fibonacci numbers: "

$$P_0 = F_1 = 1$$
$$P_1 = F_2 = 1$$
$$P_2 = F_3 = 2$$
$$P_3 = F_4 = 3$$
$$P_4 = F_5 = 5$$

Miruka paused to flash Tetra a quick Fibonacci sign.

"That's as far as that went, though, since the next partition number was 7 and the next Fibonacci number is 8. That does lead to an interesting inequality, though: "

$$P_5 < F_6$$

"So I wasn't able to get an equality like $P_n = F_{n+1}$, but I wondered if I couldn't pull off an inequality like: "

$$P_n \leqslant F_{n+1}$$

"Turns out I could, so I used $M(n) = F_{n+1}$ as my upper bound. Here, I'll show you a proof using mathematical induction."

Miruka wrote her proposition on the board.

Fibonacci numbers as an upper bound for the partition number P_n

Let $\{P_n\} = \{1, 1, 2, 3, 5, 7, \cdots\}$ be partition numbers, and $\{F_n\} = \{0, 1, 1, 2, 3, 5, 8, \cdots\}$ be the Fibonacci numbers. Then for all integers $n \geqslant 0$, $P_n \leqslant F_{n+1}$.

"First, from what we already know we can see that $P_n \leqslant F_{n+1}$ is true when n is 0 or 1. So now we have to show that this will be true for any positive integer k: "

$$P_k \leqslant F_{k+1} \quad \overset{\text{and}}{\wedge} \quad P_{k+1} \leqslant F_{k+2} \quad \overset{\text{implies}}{\Longrightarrow} \quad P_{k+2} \leqslant F_{k+3}$$

"Do you see why?" Miruka asked.

I began to answer yes, before Tetra interrupted with a resounding no!

Miruka explained. "Because if we knew that statement was true, then we could say things like this: "

· $P_0 \leqslant F_1$ and $P_1 \leqslant F_2$, so $P_2 \leqslant F_3$
· $P_1 \leqslant F_2$ and $P_2 \leqslant F_3$, so $P_3 \leqslant F_4$
· $P_2 \leqslant F_3$ and $P_3 \leqslant F_4$, so $P_4 \leqslant F_5$
· $P_3 \leqslant F_4$ and $P_4 \leqslant F_5$, so $P_5 \leqslant F_6$

"—and so on and so on—" I said.

"—forever and ever," Miruka finished. "That's basically how you do a proof by mathematical induction.

"So let's say that you're thinking of some way to pay ¥$k + 2$. Whatever that way is, we could classify it into one of these three cases, according to the smallest denomination coin that you used: "

(1) The case where the smallest coin you used was a ¥1 coin,
(2) The case where the smallest coin you used was a ¥2 coin, or
(3) The case where the smallest coin you used was a ¥3 or higher coin

"Next we're going to convert your way of paying ¥$k + 2$ into a way of paying either ¥$k + 1$ or ¥k. If the smallest coin you used was a ¥1 coin, then we're going to take away one ¥1 coin, which makes what's left a way to pay ¥$k + 1$. If the smallest coin you used was a ¥2 coin, then we're going to take away one ¥2 coin, which makes what's left a way to pay ¥k. Whatever that way is, we know that the smallest coin won't be a ¥1 coin, right? If the smallest coin you used was a ¥3 coin or higher, then let's say that the smallest coin was for ¥m, and exchange it out like this:"

$$¥2 + \underbrace{¥1 + ¥1 + \cdots + ¥1}_{m-2 \text{ coins}}$$

"Next we'll take out that ¥2 coin, which will make what's left a way to pay ¥k with a ¥1 coin as the lowest denomination.

"So in the end, whichever way we're working with, we've taken some way of paying ¥k + 2 and changed it into a way of paying either ¥k + 1 or ¥k, like I said we would. Not only that, but every new way of paying that we generate will be unique. Got it?"

A stunned silence filled the room.

"Okay, maybe that was kind of hard to follow. Let's work out an example. Say we're looking for partitions of k + 2 = 9, which would give us cases like this." Miruka began writing long columns of calculations at a blistering pace. "These numbers that I'm crossing out are the coins that we're taking away, and the underlined parts are exchanged coins. These dots here are just to skip a bunch of ones:"

P_9	(1) Part of P_8	(2) Part of P_7	(3) Part of P_7
9			~~2~~+1+···+1
8+1	8+~~1~~		
7+2		7+~~2~~	
7+1+1	7+1+~~1~~		
6+3			6+~~2~~+1
6+2+1	6+2+~~1~~		
6+1+1+1	6+1+1+~~1~~		
5+4			5+~~2~~+1+1
5+3+1	5+3+~~1~~		
5+2+2		5+2+~~2~~	
5+2+1+1	5+2+1+~~1~~		
5+1+1+1+1	5+1+1+1+~~1~~		
4+4+1	4+4+~~1~~		
4+3+2		4+3+~~2~~	
4+3+1+1	4+3+1+~~1~~		
4+2+2+1	4+2+2+~~1~~		
4+2+1+1+1	4+2+1+1+~~1~~		
4+1+···+1+1	4+1+···+1+~~1~~		
3+3+3			3+3+~~2~~+1
3+3+2+1	3+3+2+~~1~~		

P_9	(1) Part of P_8	(2) Part of P_7	(3) Part of P_7
$3+3+1+1+1$	$3+3+1+1+\not{1}$		
$3+2+2+2$		$3+2+2+\not{2}$	
$3+2+2+1+1$	$3+2+2+1+\not{1}$		
$3+2+1+1+1+1$	$3+2+1+1+1+\not{1}$		
$3+1+\cdots+1+1$	$3+1+\cdots+1+\not{1}$		
$2+2+2+2+1$	$2+2+2+2+\not{1}$		
$2+2+2+1+1+1$	$2+2+2+1+1+\not{1}$		
$2+2+1+\cdots+1+1$	$2+2+1+\cdots+1+\not{1}$		
$2+1+\cdots+1+1$	$2+1+\cdots+1+\not{1}$		
$1+\cdots+1+1$	$1+\cdots+1+\not{1}$		

"Since we can always split the partition like this, we know that the number of ways to pay ¥$k+2$ will never be greater than the number of ways to pay ¥$k+1$ plus the number of ways to pay ¥k. And that means that we've gotten this inequality:"

$$P_{k+2} \leqslant P_{k+1} + P_k$$

"So assume we have this:"

$$P_k \leqslant F_{k+1} \overset{\text{and}}{\wedge} P_{k+1} \leqslant F_{k+2}$$

"If we combine that with the inequality we just got, then that would imply this:"

$$P_{k+2} \leqslant F_{k+2} + F_{k+1}$$

"But check out the right side there. It's a new Fibonacci number, right? So we can rewrite it like this:"

$$P_{k+2} \leqslant F_{k+3}$$

"Bring it all together and what do we have? The statement that we wanted to show is true:"

$$P_k \leqslant F_{k+1} \overset{\text{and}}{\wedge} P_{k+1} \leqslant F_{k+2} \overset{\text{implies}}{\Longrightarrow} P_{k+2} \leqslant F_{k+3}$$

"There it is. We've used mathematical induction to show that, for any positive integer n, $P_n \leqslant F_{n+1}$. The Fibonaccis have their thumb on the partition numbers."

Miruka dusted chalk from her hands.

"Done and—no, wait. The fun isn't over yet. We still haven't taken care of Muraki's second problem. Let's make a table of Fibonacci numbers:"

n	0	1	2	3	4	5	6	7	8	9	10	11	12	13	14	15	16	...
F_n	0	1	1	2	3	5	8	13	21	34	55	89	144	233	377	610	987	...

"From this we know that $F_{16} = 987$, so we can write this:"

$$P_{15} \leqslant F_{16} = 987 < 1000$$

"Cutting out the stuff in the middle, we get the answer that we wanted:"

$$P_{15} < 1000$$

"And that's it. We've shown that the inequality in the problem is true without finding a general term for P_n, and without even finding what P_{15} is. Okay, now *that* was fun."

Answer to Problem 10-2

$P_{15} \leqslant 1000$ is true.

10.5.3 Using Brute Force

Tetra raised her hand. "Um..."

Miruka pointed at her. "Yes, Tetra. You have a question?"

"Well... not a question, really. I solved the problem, too, so I wanted to show my answer."

"Oh, by all means." Miruka handed Tetra the chalk as the two of them changed places at the board.

"It won't take long. I just wrote out all of the ways to pay ¥15. There were 176 of them, so my answer is this:"

$$P_{15} = 176 < 1000$$

"So, yeah, the inequality in the problem is true."

Tetra opened her notebook and showed us her work. Miruka took the notebook and skimmed through what Tetra had written:

① × 15	① × 13 + ②
① × 11 + ② × 2	① × 9 + ② × 3
① × 7 + ② × 4	① × 5 + ② × 5
① × 3 + ② × 6	① + ② × 7
① × 12 + ③	① × 10 + ② + ③
① × 8 + ② × 2 + ③	① × 6 + ② × 3 + ③
① × 4 + ② × 4 + ③	① × 2 + ② × 5 + ③
② × 6 + ③	① × 9 + ③ × 2
① × 7 + ② + ③ × 2	① × 5 + ② × 2 + ③ × 2
① × 3 + ② × 3 + ③ × 2	① + ② × 4 + ③ × 2
① × 6 + ③ × 3	① × 4 + ② + ③ × 3
① × 2 + ② × 2 + ③ × 3	② × 3 + ③ × 3
① × 3 + ③ × 4	① + ② + ③ × 4
③ × 5	① × 11 + ④
① × 9 + ② + ④	① × 7 + ② × 2 + ④
① × 5 + ② × 3 + ④	① × 3 + ② × 4 + ④
① + ② × 5 + ④	① × 8 + ③ + ④
① × 6 + ② + ③ + ④	① × 4 + ② × 2 + ③ + ④
① × 2 + ② × 3 + ③ + ④	② × 4 + ③ + ④
① × 5 + ③ × 2 + ④	① × 3 + ② + ③ × 2 + ④
① + ② × 2 + ③ × 2 + ④	① × 2 + ③ × 3 + ④
② + ③ × 3 + ④	① × 7 + ④ × 2
① × 5 + ② + ④ × 2	① × 3 + ② × 2 + ④ × 2
① + ② × 3 + ④ × 2	① × 4 + ③ + ④ × 2
① × 2 + ② + ③ + ④ × 2	② × 2 + ③ + ④ × 2
① + ③ × 2 + ④ × 2	① × 3 + ④ × 3
① + ② + ④ × 3	③ + ④ × 3
① × 10 + ⑤	① × 8 + ② + ⑤
① × 6 + ② × 2 + ⑤	① × 4 + ② × 3 + ⑤
① × 2 + ② × 4 + ⑤	② × 5 + ⑤
① × 7 + ③ + ⑤	① × 5 + ② + ③ + ⑤
① × 3 + ② × 2 + ③ + ⑤	① + ② × 3 + ③ + ⑤
① × 4 + ③ × 2 + ⑤	① × 2 + ② + ③ × 2 + ⑤
② × 2 + ③ × 2 + ⑤	① + ③ × 3 + ⑤
① × 6 + ④ + ⑤	① × 4 + ② + ④ + ⑤
① × 2 + ② × 2 + ④ + ⑤	② × 3 + ④ + ⑤
① × 3 + ③ + ④ + ⑤	① + ② + ③ + ④ + ⑤
③ × 2 + ④ + ⑤	① × 2 + ④ × 2 + ⑤
② + ④ × 2 + ⑤	① × 5 + ⑤ × 2
① × 3 + ② + ⑤ × 2	① + ② × 2 + ⑤ × 2
① × 2 + ③ + ⑤ × 2	② + ③ + ⑤ × 2
① + ④ + ⑤ × 2	⑤ × 3

$$(1) \times 9 + (6)$$
$$(1) \times 5 + (2) \times 2 + (6)$$
$$(1) + (2) \times 4 + (6)$$
$$(1) \times 4 + (2) + (3) + (6)$$
$$(2) \times 3 + (3) + (6)$$
$$(1) + (2) + (3) \times 2 + (6)$$
$$(1) \times 5 + (4) + (6)$$
$$(1) + (2) \times 2 + (4) + (6)$$
$$(2) + (3) + (4) + (6)$$
$$(1) \times 4 + (5) + (6)$$
$$(2) \times 2 + (5) + (6)$$
$$(4) + (5) + (6)$$
$$(1) + (2) + (6) \times 2$$
$$(1) \times 8 + (7)$$
$$(1) \times 4 + (2) \times 2 + (7)$$
$$(2) \times 4 + (7)$$
$$(1) \times 3 + (2) + (3) + (7)$$
$$(1) \times 2 + (3) \times 2 + (7)$$
$$(1) \times 4 + (4) + (7)$$
$$(2) \times 2 + (4) + (7)$$
$$(4) \times 2 + (7)$$
$$(1) + (2) + (5) + (7)$$
$$(1) \times 2 + (6) + (7)$$
$$(1) + (7) \times 2$$
$$(1) \times 5 + (2) + (8)$$
$$(1) + (2) \times 3 + (8)$$
$$(1) \times 2 + (2) + (3) + (8)$$
$$(1) + (3) \times 2 + (8)$$
$$(1) + (2) + (4) + (8)$$
$$(1) \times 2 + (5) + (8)$$
$$(1) + (6) + (8)$$
$$(1) \times 6 + (9)$$
$$(1) \times 2 + (2) \times 2 + (9)$$
$$(1) \times 3 + (3) + (9)$$
$$(3) \times 2 + (9)$$
$$(2) + (4) + (9)$$
$$(6) + (9)$$
$$(1) \times 3 + (2) + (10)$$
$$(1) \times 2 + (3) + (10)$$
$$(1) + (4) + (10)$$
$$(1) \times 4 + (11)$$

$$(1) \times 7 + (2) + (6)$$
$$(1) \times 3 + (2) \times 3 + (6)$$
$$(1) \times 6 + (3) + (6)$$
$$(1) \times 2 + (2) \times 2 + (3) + (6)$$
$$(1) \times 3 + (3) \times 2 + (6)$$
$$(3) \times 3 + (6)$$
$$(1) \times 3 + (2) + (4) + (6)$$
$$(1) \times 2 + (3) + (4) + (6)$$
$$(1) + (4) \times 2 + (6)$$
$$(1) \times 2 + (2) + (5) + (6)$$
$$(1) + (3) + (5) + (6)$$
$$(1) \times 3 + (6) \times 2$$
$$(3) + (6) \times 2$$
$$(1) \times 6 + (2) + (7)$$
$$(1) \times 2 + (2) \times 3 + (7)$$
$$(1) \times 5 + (3) + (7)$$
$$(1) + (2) \times 2 + (3) + (7)$$
$$(2) + (3) \times 2 + (7)$$
$$(1) \times 2 + (2) + (4) + (7)$$
$$(1) + (3) + (4) + (7)$$
$$(1) \times 3 + (5) + (7)$$
$$(3) + (5) + (7)$$
$$(2) + (6) + (7)$$
$$(1) \times 7 + (8)$$
$$(1) \times 3 + (2) \times 2 + (8)$$
$$(1) \times 4 + (3) + (8)$$
$$(2) \times 2 + (3) + (8)$$
$$(1) \times 3 + (4) + (8)$$
$$(3) + (4) + (8)$$
$$(2) + (5) + (8)$$
$$(7) + (8)$$
$$(1) \times 4 + (2) + (9)$$
$$(2) \times 3 + (9)$$
$$(1) + (2) + (3) + (9)$$
$$(1) \times 2 + (4) + (9)$$
$$(1) + (5) + (9)$$
$$(1) \times 5 + (10)$$
$$(1) + (2) \times 2 + (10)$$
$$(2) + (3) + (10)$$
$$(5) + (10)$$
$$(1) \times 2 + (2) + (11)$$

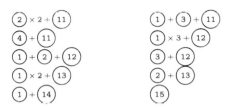

"Yep, she got every one. I'd say that Tetra wins this one through sheer effort."

"Yay! I didn't miss any this time!"

10.6 LOST AND FOUND

I didn't share Tetra's enthusiasm. I had slunk back to my homeroom to get my bag, but overcome by what had just happened, I slumped into the nearest chair and faceplanted on the desk.

Why had I become so fixated on finding a general term? The problem was given as an inequality, which should have been a big red flag. All that time I had spent trying to find a generating function had been, in the end, a gigantic waste.

Damn.

I had a problem that should have been within my grasp. I thought that I was blazing a trail toward the solution, but I had been heading in the wrong direction the whole time, blinded by my assumption that I could treat partition numbers the same way we had treated Fibonacci numbers and Catalan numbers.

Damn!

I heard footsteps at the door. Miruka's footsteps. She came closer.

"What's up?"

I kept my head on the desk.

"Well you're a barrel of fun today."

Miruka just stood there, waiting. Finally I gave in and raised my head. Her normally cheerful expression was clouded with concern. She flicked her fingers *one, one, two, three,* but I was in no mood for math gang signs.

Miruka folded her hands behind her back and looked off to the side.

"Tetra's cute, isn't she?"

I didn't respond.

"Cuter than I'll ever be."

Goin' Home played over the intercom, the signal that the school was closing.

"I couldn't solve it," I finally said. "I got lost."

"Is *that* what this is all about? Oh, c'mon. You're hardly the first mathematician to go down the wrong path. But you know what? If you don't go looking, you'll never know what you might have found. If you don't try new things, you'll never know what you're capable of. We're on a journey here. Sometimes we get tired, and sometimes we get lost. But that's no reason to give up."

"It's just... I came on like I had the whole thing down, like my generating function was going to be the answer to everything. But it didn't even help solve the problem. I looked like an idiot."

"Maybe it didn't help with this problem," Miruka said, "but I bet it would help somewhere else."

She smiled and flicked her fingers again, this time giving the *five* herself. Her hand paused in the air for a moment, then her warm fingertips came to rest on my forehead.

"If you get tired, rest. If you get lost, backtrack. That's what the journey is all about."

Miruka leaned towards me until our glasses were almost touching. I gazed into those deep eyes. She tilted her head, and came closer still.

"Good thing Ms. Mizutani isn't around," I whispered.

"Stop talking."

10.7 In Search of a Better Upper Bound

A few days later Miruka tracked me down after school.

"I found a new upper bound," she said, "way better than the Fibonacci numbers. Let's go find Tetra."

10.7.1 Starting with Generating Functions

Once we'd found Tetra we headed back to our homeroom. Miruka went to the podium and grabbed a piece of chalk. Tetra and I sat in the front row to listen to Miruka's lecture. We had the room to ourselves.

"To find an upper bound for the partition numbers P_n," she began, "means finding some function $M(n)$ such that $P_n \leqslant M(n)$. The other day we saw how the Fibonacci numbers can do that. But today I want to find an even better function."

Tetra raised her hand.

"By a 'better function,' do you mean an upper bound that's a tighter fit than the Fibonaccis?"

"Right," Miruka said, "though in this case that will only happen for large ns."

Miruka looked at me and said, "Our journey begins with a generating function.

"First off," she continued, "we need to think about the relationship between the partition numbers P_n and their generating function $P(x)$. If we keep ourselves in the range $0 < x < 1$, then we know that a P_n multiplied by an x^n will be smaller than $P(x)$." Miruka wrote on the board:

$$P_n x^n < P(x)$$

"That has to be true because $P_n x^n$ is part of the definition of the generating function. Here, let's write it out: "

$$\underline{P_n x^n} < P_0 x^0 + P_1 x^1 + \cdots + \underline{P_n x^n} + \cdots$$

"Since all the terms on the right are positive, their sum has to be bigger than any single term. But we know something else about this generating function: it has a multiplicative form." Miruka shot me another glance. "So we can rewrite the right side like this: "

$$P_n x^n < \frac{1}{1-x^1} \cdot \frac{1}{1-x^2} \cdot \frac{1}{1-x^3} \cdots$$

"Let's divide both sides of that by x^n: "

$$P_n < \frac{1}{x^n} \cdot \frac{1}{1-x^1} \cdot \frac{1}{1-x^2} \cdot \frac{1}{1-x^3} \cdots$$

"Since we know that the right side here is larger than P_n, that makes this a candidate for being an upper bound. There's a catch, though—infinite products are hard to handle. So what we want to do is put the brakes on this thing, say that we're only going to think about paying up to ∛n for now, and treat this as a finite bound. That means we'll be looking at something like this:"

$$P_n \leqslant \frac{1}{x^n} \cdot \frac{1}{1-x^1} \cdot \frac{1}{1-x^2} \cdot \frac{1}{1-x^3} \cdots \frac{1}{1-x^n}$$

"None of this has been brain-bendingly hard so far, but that right side still looks like a headache to deal with. So here's where we have to think hard. Well, I thought hard, and here's what I came up with. If a product is going to cause us problems, why not change it to a sum instead? So, class, how do we change a product into a sum?"

10.7.2 Changing Products into Sums

"You use logarithms," I said. "If you take its logarithm, then the product will become a sum."

"Exactly." Miruka pointed at the last thing written on the board:

$$P_n \leqslant \frac{1}{x^n} \cdot \frac{1}{1-x^1} \cdot \frac{1}{1-x^2} \cdot \frac{1}{1-x^3} \cdots \frac{1}{1-x^n}$$

"We want to take the logarithm of both sides of this inequality. This is a bit of a detour—we left home in search of an upper bound for P_n, but to get there we have to pass through a route that leads to finding the upper bound of $\ln P_n$. Are you following this, Tetra? Understanding all the steps isn't enough if you lose sight of the big picture."

Tetra nodded, and Miruka continued.

"When you take the log of a product, you get a sum:"

$$\ln(P_n) \leqslant \ln \left(\frac{1}{x^n} \cdot \frac{1}{1-x^1} \cdot \frac{1}{1-x^2} \cdot \frac{1}{1-x^3} \cdots \frac{1}{1-x^n} \right)$$

$$\ln P_n \leqslant \ln \frac{1}{x^n}$$
$$+ \ln \frac{1}{1-x^1} + \ln \frac{1}{1-x^2} + \ln \frac{1}{1-x^3} + \cdots + \ln \frac{1}{1-x^n}$$

"Long, ugly equations like this call for sigma notation. It won't change what the equation means, of course, but it will clean things up:"

$$\ln P_n \leqslant \ln \frac{1}{x^n} + \sum_{k=1}^{n} \left(\ln \frac{1}{1-x^k} \right)$$

"Here we hit a fork in the road. To the west, there's a hill; to the east, a forest. We need to explore both paths, but we'll be coming back here, so everybody remember where we parked:"

$$\ln P_n \leqslant \underbrace{\ln \frac{1}{x^n}}_{\text{Western hill}} + \underbrace{\sum_{k=1}^{n} \left(\ln \frac{1}{1-x^k} \right)}_{\text{Eastern forest}}$$

10.7.3 Taylor Series

"Let's go east first," Miruka said, "and mingle with the trees:"

$$\text{The forest} = \sum_{k=1}^{n} \left(\ln \frac{1}{1-x^k} \right)$$

"The eastern forest is made up of n trees, every one of them a $\ln \frac{1}{1-x^k}$:"

$$\text{A tree} = \ln \frac{1}{1-x^k}$$

"Let's see if we can find out just how big those trees can grow. To do that, we need to turn them into a function, but that will be easier if we let $t = x^k$ when we do:"

$$f(t) = \ln \frac{1}{1-t}$$

"So now we need to learn a bit more about this function $f(t)$. What do you think our first step should be, Tetra?"

"Who, me?" Tetra blinked. "Sorry, I don't really know much about logarithms."

"Look. You're faced with a function you don't know anything about. What was it you said you would never forget?"

"Oh! Taylor series!"

"Right. We need to use a Taylor series to change $f(t)$ into a power series. That takes some messy stuff like differentiating the log function and using composite functions, so for now I'm just going to skip straight to the results. Here's what we end up with:"

$$\text{A tree} = \ln \frac{1}{1-t}$$
$$= \frac{t^1}{1} + \frac{t^2}{2} + \frac{t^3}{3} + \cdots \qquad \text{for } 0 < t < 1$$

"The last thing to do is replace the ts with their original values:"

$$\ln \frac{1}{1-x^k} = \frac{x^{1k}}{1} + \frac{x^{2k}}{2} + \frac{x^{3k}}{3} + \cdots \qquad \text{for } 0 < x^k < 1$$

"We can use this to sum up our equation for $k = 1, 2, 3, \cdots, n$. In other words, we can build up the forest from all those trees:"

$$\text{The forest} = \sum_{k=1}^{n} \text{The trees}$$

$$= \sum_{k=1}^{n} \ln \frac{1}{1-x^k}$$

"So let's expand:"

$$= \sum_{k=1}^{n} \left(\frac{x^{1k}}{1} + \frac{x^{2k}}{2} + \frac{x^{3k}}{3} + \cdots \right)$$

"Clean up the infinite series with a second Σ:"

$$= \sum_{k=1}^{n} \left(\sum_{m=1}^{\infty} \frac{x^{mk}}{m} \right)$$

"Now let's switch the order of the sums:"

$$= \sum_{m=1}^{\infty} \left(\sum_{k=1}^{n} \frac{x^{mk}}{m} \right)$$

Miruka noticed my upraised eyebrow. "Yes, we can do that. Well, actually you have to be a bit careful since it's an infinite sum that we're dealing with, but just trust me that we're okay here." She turned back to the board. "Moving on, the m isn't bound to the inner sigma, so we can move the $\frac{1}{m}$ outside:"

$$= \sum_{m=1}^{\infty} \left(\frac{1}{m} \sum_{k=1}^{n} x^{mk} \right)$$

"Now we can open up the inner sigma and take another look at what we're dealing with:"

$$= \sum_{m=1}^{\infty} \frac{1}{m} \left(x^{1m} + x^{2m} + x^{3m} + \cdots + x^{nm} \right)$$

"Let's take a quick break to enjoy the scenery. Remember, we're after an upper bound, a function that will stay up above this forest. To find it, we're going to change the finite series into an infinite one, and use an inequality. That's going to let us use the geometric series formula. So let's do it:"

$$\text{The forest} = \sum_{m=1}^{\infty} \frac{1}{m} \left(x^{1m} + x^{2m} + x^{3m} + \cdots + x^{nm} \right)$$

"Now the inequality..."

$$< \sum_{m=1}^{\infty} \frac{1}{m} \left(x^{1m} + x^{2m} + x^{3m} + \cdots + x^{nm} + \cdots \right)$$

"...and the geometric series formula, with $0 < x^m < 1$:"

$$= \sum_{m=1}^{\infty} \frac{1}{m} \cdot \frac{x^m}{1 - x^m}$$

"Another quick break. Remember, we're only looking for an upper bound, so as long as we find something that we know is bigger, we're fine—we don't need to solve this last line. Now, check out the denominator there. If we can replace that $1 - x^m$ with something smaller, then we can make a new inequality. When we do that our upper bound will become a little bit larger, but at least we'll have something that's easier to work with. It's a tradeoff, but what we lose in tightness of fit, we gain in convenience. That will happen for every new inequality we make. Okay, back into the forest. Here's where we left the trail:"

$$\text{The forest} < \sum_{m=1}^{\infty} \frac{1}{m} \cdot \frac{x^m}{1 - x^m}$$

"Let's factor out the denominator:"

$$= \sum_{m=1}^{\infty} \frac{1}{m} \cdot \frac{x^m}{(1 - x) \underbrace{(1 + x + x^2 + \cdots + x^{m-1})}_{m \text{ terms}}}$$

"Now let's make this an inequality by replacing all the terms in there with the smallest term, the x^{m-1}:"

$$< \sum_{m=1}^{\infty} \frac{1}{m} \cdot \frac{x^m}{(1-x)\underbrace{(x^{m-1}+x^{m-1}+\cdots+x^{m-1})}_{m \text{ terms}}}$$

"We can rewrite those m terms as a product:"

$$= \sum_{m=1}^{\infty} \frac{1}{m} \cdot \frac{x^m}{(1-x)\cdot m \cdot x^{m-1}}$$

"Okay, ready to hear Tetra scream?"

"Why would I scream?"

"You'll see." Miruka gave a mischievous smile. "Here's what we've found so far:"

$$\text{The forest} < \sum_{m=1}^{\infty} \frac{1}{m} \cdot \frac{x^m}{(1-x)\cdot m \cdot x^{m-1}}$$

"Let's clean that up a little:"

$$= \sum_{m=1}^{\infty} \frac{1}{m^2} \cdot \frac{x}{1-x}$$

"Now we move the unbounded factor outside of the sigma—"

$$= \frac{x}{1-x} \cdot \sum_{m=1}^{\infty} \frac{1}{m^2}$$

"—and three, two, one..."

Tetra screamed. "That's the Basel problem! That's a $\pi^2/6$!"

$$\sum_{m=1}^{\infty} \frac{1}{m^2} = \frac{\pi^2}{6} \qquad \text{The Basel problem}$$

"Yep. Let us pause and give thanks to dear Euler once again. Now for some finishing touches:"

$$\text{The forest} = \sum_{k=1}^{n} \ln \frac{1}{1-x^k}$$

$$< \frac{x}{1-x} \cdot \sum_{m=1}^{\infty} \frac{1}{m^2}$$

$$= \frac{x}{1-x} \cdot \frac{\pi^2}{6} \qquad \text{from the Basel problem}$$

"And that should do it for the eastern forest—well, one more thing to make things easier down the road. Let's define t as $\frac{x}{1-x}$. Voilà."

An upper bound to the Eastern Forest

$$\sum_{k=1}^{n} \ln \frac{1}{1-x^k} < \frac{\pi^2}{6}t \quad \text{for } t = \frac{x}{1-x}$$

10.7.4 Harmonic Numbers

"We're halfway through our journey. Now we go back to that fork in the road and head off for the western hill. So let's assume that $0 < x < 1$, and take a look at $\ln \frac{1}{x^n}$. We're still keeping our definition of $t = \frac{x}{1-x}$, by the way. Since $0 < x < 1$, we know that $0 < t$, and that $x = \frac{t}{1+t}$. So let's do this:"

$$\begin{aligned}
\text{The hill} &= \ln \frac{1}{x^n} \\
&= n \ln \frac{1}{x} \qquad &\text{from } \ln a^n = n \ln a \\
&= n \ln \frac{t+1}{t} \qquad &x \text{ in terms of } t \\
&= n \ln \left(1 + \frac{1}{t}\right)
\end{aligned}$$

"Focus on $\ln \left(1 + \frac{1}{t}\right)$ for a sec. We're going to let $u = \frac{1}{t}$, and see what $\ln(1+u)$ does when u is positive—something like what we did when we were looking at harmonic numbers. When we graph it out, we see that the western hill is nice and smooth."

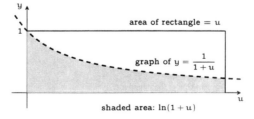

"It's easy to see that the shaded area is going to be smaller than the area of the rectangle, which gives us:"

$$\ln(1+u) < u$$

"But since we said that $u = \frac{1}{t}$, we can write that like this:"

$$\ln\left(1+\frac{1}{t}\right) < \frac{1}{t}$$

"Which gets us:"

$$\ln\frac{1}{x^n} = n\ln\left(1+\frac{1}{t}\right) < \frac{n}{t}$$

"And that's all we really need to see on the hill."

An upper bound to the Western Hill

$$\ln\frac{1}{x^n} < \frac{n}{t} \qquad \text{for } t > 0, \ t = \frac{x}{1-x}$$

10.7.5 Coming Home

"Now we scamper back to the fork in the road. When we compare our snapshots of the eastern forest and the western hill, here's what we learn about $\ln P_n$:"

$$\ln P_n < \frac{n}{t} + \frac{\pi^2}{6}t \qquad\qquad t > 0$$

"Okay, we're almost there. Let's name the right side of that equation $g(t)$, and see how small it can get when t is positive. When we find that, we'll know how to keep $\ln P_n$ in check:"

$$g(t) = \frac{n}{t} + \frac{\pi^2}{6}t$$
$$g'(t) = -\frac{n}{t^2} + \frac{\pi^2}{6} \qquad\qquad \text{differentiated}$$

"When we solve $g'(t) = 0$ we get $t = \pm\frac{\sqrt{6n}}{\pi}$, which means that while we're looking at positive ts we get a max-min table like this:"

t	0	$\cdots$	$\frac{\sqrt{6n}}{\pi}$	$\cdots$
$g'(t)$		$-$	0	$+$
$g(t)$		$\searrow$	Min.	$\nearrow$

"So here's our minimum:"

$$g\left(\frac{\sqrt{6n}}{\pi}\right) = \frac{\sqrt{6}\,\pi}{3} \cdot \sqrt{n}$$

"This is probably easier to understand if we draw a graph. We solved $g'(t) = 0$ so we could find the point where a tangent to the graph is horizontal:"

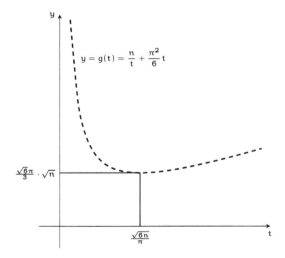

"The only thing we care about here is n, so let's just rename those messy constants as K:"

$$\ln P_n < K \cdot \sqrt{n} \qquad \text{for } K = \frac{\sqrt{6}\,\pi}{3}$$

"Remember that detour we took back at the beginning? The one that steered us into all these logarithms in the first place? Well, now we just go right back through it the other way, by inversing the log, and we're just a stone's throw from home:"

$$P_n < e^{K \cdot \sqrt{n}} \qquad \text{for } K = \frac{\sqrt{6}\,\pi}{3}$$

"It was a long trip, but that was *fun*."

**An upper bound for
the partition number P_n**

$$P_n < e^{K \cdot \sqrt{n}} \qquad \text{for } K = \frac{\sqrt{6}\,\pi}{3}$$

A map for finding $\dfrac{\sqrt{6}\,\pi}{3} \cdot \sqrt{n}$ **as an upper bound for** $\ln P_n$

$$\boxed{\ln P_n}$$

$$\downarrow \leqslant$$

$$\underbrace{\ln \frac{1}{x^n}}_{\text{Western hill}} + \underbrace{\sum_{k=1}^{n}\left(\ln \frac{1}{1-x^k}\right)}_{\text{Eastern forest}}$$

$$\downarrow$$

The hill	$\longleftarrow$	The fork	$\longrightarrow$	The forest
$\downarrow <$				$\downarrow <$
$\dfrac{n}{t}$	$\longrightarrow$	$\dfrac{n}{t} + \dfrac{\pi^2}{6}t$	$\longleftarrow$	$\dfrac{\pi^2}{6}t$

$$\downarrow \text{Min.}$$

$$\frac{\sqrt{6}\,\pi}{3} \cdot \sqrt{n}$$

10.7.6   Tetra's Notes

Miruka was right. It had been a long road, but traveling it together had been worth every moment. There were a few places I wanted to go back and check out for myself, but there would be time for that later.

I looked at Tetra, her brow furrowed in concentration.

"You okay?" I asked.

"Oh, I'm fine," she laughed. "Great, even. I haven't thought that hard in a while. I probably didn't understand half of what you said, Miruka, but that's okay. There was plenty of stuff I did understand, and it was wonderful."

Tetra showed us what she had written in her notes:

- Change finite sums to infinite sums and create inequalities
- Favor convenient forms over better upper bounds
- Use logarithms to change products into sums
- Use the formula for the sum of infinite series
- Stop forgetting to use Taylor series
- Clean up messes using new variables
- Euler's Basel problem
- Differentiation and max-min tables to find minimums

"It's like I've been given these new weapons to use," Tetra parried and thrusted with an imaginary foe, "and now all I have to do is sharpen them up and attack some problems of my own!"

10.8   GOODBYES

We kept talking all the way back to the station. From what value of n would our new upper bound give a better fit than the Fibonacci numbers? Could we, in the end, find P_n? We quickly settled into our familiar rhythm. Tetra would get excited and ask something, which I would answer, with occasional commentary from Miruka.

Finally we reached the station. This was normally the point where Miruka would split off in the other direction, but that day Tetra stuck by her side.

"This is new," I said.

"Miruka's taking me to the bookstore. Jealous?"

"Surprised. Pleasantly."

"See you tomorrow," Miruka waved.

"Yeah, let's do some more math!" Tetra added, heading off with Miruka.

I stood there, alone, watching them leave. After the energy of our conversation, the abrupt silence seemed somehow lonely.

High school was such a transitory thing, and it wouldn't be long before we each headed off in our own directions. There was a definite limit to the time and space we shared, no matter how tight the correspondence might be.

I felt a tightening in my chest.

In the distance, Tetra leaned in to whisper in Miruka's ear. They turned and looked back at me. Tetra waved in broad sweeps of her arm, while Miruka quietly raised a hand. Then they both flicked their fingers in sync. *One, one, two, three...* I laughed and raised five fingers in response.

Sure, our time together was limited. But that was all the more reason to learn together, to grow together while we could. To share our friendship, and math.

After all, mathematics is timeless.

Epilogue

A girl came bounding into the office. "Check it out! I got my year two pin!"

"Well, you're a second year student now." The answer came from a teacher behind one of the desks. "Of course you did."

"Oh, and here." She opened her notebook for him to see. "I finished the problem. All grunt work. P_{15} equals 176—waaay lower than 1000. So the answer is 'true.'"

"The brute force approach, eh?"

"My head wasn't cooperating, so I let my hands do the work. What's with the 1000? You should have said, like, 200. I was wondering though. *Is* there a general term for P_n?"

"There is... but you might not like it."

The teacher pulled out a piece of paper and wrote the equation.

Answer to Problem X

$$P_n = \frac{1}{\pi\sqrt{2}} \sum_{k=1}^{\infty} A_k(n)\sqrt{k}\, \frac{d}{dn} \left(\frac{\sinh \dfrac{C\sqrt{n - \frac{1}{24}}}{k}}{\sqrt{n - \frac{1}{24}}} \right)$$

where $C = \pi\sqrt{\frac{2}{3}}$

"You have *got* to be joking. What on earth is that?"

"An answer that Hans Rademacher came up with in 1937. Not what you'd expect, is it."

"You can say that again. Wait," she pointed at the page, "what's this here? This $A_k(n)$. I don't see that defined anywhere."

"Good catch. Nice to see you reading the equations. It's hard to give a simple explanation, but think of it as a kind of finite sum involving the twenty-fourth root of 1. I think I have the paper here somewhere..."

"Nah, I'm good."

"Well, all you need to know is that partitions of the integers still hold hidden treasures, and—"

"Hey, she's cute!" The girl picked up a picture from the desk. "She your girlfriend? Where is this, Europe?"

He took the picture from her. "That's none of your business," he smiled.

"Oooh, and a letter! From *another* girl?" She eyed the strange stamps on the envelope. "This from somewhere overseas, too?"

"It is, and I'll thank you not to rummage through my things."

"I never knew you were such a lady's man!" she winked.

He sighed. "They're friends from high school. We've been studying math together for years."

"Wow, I totally *cannot* picture you as a high school student."

"Okay, enough. Off to class with you."

"Not until I get another card."

"If it will keep you out of my papers..." He scribbled something on two index cards and handed them to her.

"Two this time?"

"One for you, and one for him."

She smiled and flicked her fingers—*one, one, two, three.* He returned the sign as she dashed out through the door.

Leaning back in his chair, he looked outside the window where a cherry tree stood in full bloom, and thought about another cherry tree long ago, its blurred pastel petals falling on a girl with long, black hair.

Afterword

The fascination one can have with mathematics is similar to the fascination a boy can have with a girl.

You try to solve a difficult problem, but you can't seem to find an answer—you don't even know where to start. But there's something about it that draws you in and won't let go. You know that something wonderful waits, if you can only coax it into sharing its secrets.

That's the kind of feeling I hope this book has brought to you.

In 2002 I began writing the stories that eventually became this book, and posted them on my website. Many people who read them sent me incredibly enthusiastic e-mails. Were it not for those e-mails, I would never have thought of turning Math Girls into the book you now hold in your hands. I therefore wish to express my gratitude to those early supporters. Thank you very much.

This book was produced using $\text{\LaTeX}\,2_\varepsilon$. The math is set in the AMS Euler font. Named after Leonhard Euler and created by Hermann Zapf for use in mathematical equations, the font's design mimics the handwriting of a mathematician with excellent penmanship.

I would like to thank Haruhiko Okumura for his book *Introduction to Creating Beautiful Documents with* $\text{\LaTeX}\,2_\varepsilon$, which was an invaluable aid during layout. I would also like to thank Kazuhiro Okuma (a.k.a. tDB) for his elementary mathematics handout macro, emath. I would also like to thank the following persons for proofreading and giving me invaluable feedback.

Hisao Aoki, Minero Aoki, Ryuhei Uehara,
Mitsuhide Uemura, Kanaya Yasoo (Gascon Labs),
Toshiki Kawashima, Hal Tasaki, Masahide
Maehara, Kiyoshi Miyake, Tsutomu Yano,
Takeshi Yamaguchi, Yuko Yoshida

I would like to thank my readers and the visitors to my website, and my friends for their constant prayers.

I would like to thank my editor, Kimio Nozawa for his continuous support during the long process of creating this book, and Ayako Nakajima for pushing me through the book's initial planning.

I thank my dearest wife and my two sons. Special thanks to my oldest son for his comments while reading the manuscript.

I dedicate this book to Leonhard Euler, our master in everything.

Finally, thank *you* for reading my book. I hope that someday, somewhere, our paths shall cross again.

Hiroshi Yuki
Spring 2007, the 300th anniversary of Euler's birth
http://www.yuki.com/girl/

Such a diversity of material might easily have grown into several volumes, but I have, as far as possible, expressed everything so succinctly that everywhere the foundation is very clearly explained. The further development is left to the industry of the readers.

LEONHARD EULER

Recommended Reading

This section is divided up as follows:

- General reading

- Recommended for high school students

- Recommended for college students

- Recommended for graduate students and beyond

- Web pages

These classifications are meant only as a guideline. Some texts may be more or less challenging depending on the level of the reader.

> [Note: The following references include all items that were listed in the original Japanese version of *Math Girls*. Most of those references were to Japanese sources. Where an English version of a reference exists, it is included in the entry.]

GENERAL READING

[1] Polya, G. (2009). *How to Solve It: A New Aspect of the Mathematical Model.* Ishi Press. Translated by Kakiuchi, Y. as *Ika ni shite mondai wo toku ka* (Maruzen, 1954).

A classic work on how to solve problems, with other topics about learning mathematics. A must-read for anyone serious about math.

[2] Yoshizawa, M. (2006). *Sansū, sūgaku ga tokui ni naru hon* [Becoming Good at Arithemetic and Math]. Kodansha.

This book discusses many topics from elementary, middle, and high school math that trip up many people. An easy-to-read, good presentation of such topics as the difference between equations and identities, absolute values, etc.

[3] Yuki, H. (2005). *Puroguramā no sūgaku* [Mathematics for Programmers]. Softbank Creative.

An introductory text on learning to think mathematically, aimed at programmers. Topics include logic, mathematical induction, sorting and combining, and proof by contradiction. http://www.hyuki.com/math/

[4] Hofstadter, D. (1985). Gödel, Escher, Bach: An Eternal Golden Braid. Basic Books. Translated by Nozaki, A., et al. as *Gēderu, Esshā, Bahha—Arui wa fushigi na kan* (Hakuyo, 1985).

A book about self-reference, recursion, representation of knowledge, artificial intelligence, and many other topics, taking Gödel, Escher, and Bach as its theme. Miruka and Ay-Ay's eternally rising infinite scale came from the discussion of Shepard scales at the end of Chapter 20 of this book.

[5] Hofstadter, D. (1985). *Metamagical Themas: Questing For The Essence Of Mind And Pattern*. Basic Books. Translated by Takeuchi, I., et al. as *Metamajikku gēmu—Kagaku to geijutsu no jigusō pazuru* (Hakuyo, 1985).

> A collection of essays from the author's column in *Scientific American*. Covers a wide variety of topics, from solving Rubik's Cube to nuclear weapons control.

[6] du Sautoy, M. (2011). *The Music of the Primes: Searching to Solve the Greatest Mystery in Mathematics*. Harper Perennial. Translated by Tominaga, H. as *Sosū no ongaku* (Shinchosha, 2005).

> Many mathematicians have been drawn in by the "music" of the prime numbers, and this book tells their story. I most enjoyed this book's discussion of the zero point of the zeta function and the prime number theorem.

[7] Fellmann, E. (translation by Gautschi, E. and Gautschi, W.) (2010). *Leonhard Euler*. Birkhäuser Basel. Translated by Yamamoto, A. as *Oirā, sono shōgai to gyōseki* (Springer-Verlag, 2002).

> A biography of Euler, describing the various fields that he worked in, and his relationship with his contemporaries.

[8] Kanagawa University Public Relations Committee (2006). *Jūnana-on no seishun—go-nana-go de tsuzuru kōkōsei no messēji* [Youth in Seventeen Syllables—Haiku Messages From High School Students]. NHK Publishing.

> A selection of haiku from submissions to the Kanagawa University National High School Haiku Competition. The haiku opening for Chapter 10 was taken from this collection. (It's interesting that $5 + 7 + 5 = 17$ is a prime...)

RECOMMENDED FOR HIGH SCHOOL STUDENTS

[9]   Nakamura, S. (2002). *Fibonacchi-sū no shō-uchū* [The Micro-
      cosmos of the Fibonacci Numbers]. Nippon Hyoronsha.

      A book on fascinating aspects of the Fibonacci
      numbers, from the very basics to advanced
      theorems.

[10] Miyakoshi, C. (2004). *Kōkō sūgaku+α: Kiso to ronri no mono-
      gatari* [High School Math and Beyond: A Tale of Basics and
      Logic]. Kyoritsu Shuppan.

      A compact summary of mathematics, from
      high school through some college-level studies.
      This book can also be read online: http://
      www.h6.dion.ne.jp/~hsbook_a/

[11] Kurita, K., Fukuda, K., and Hirata, M. (1999). *Masutā obu
      baai no kazu* [Mastering Permutations]. Tokyo Shuppan.

      A textbook on permutations. This book also
      contains many interesting problems that in-
      volve the Catalan numbers C_n. I used this
      book when writing about finding a general
      solution for the Catalan numbers to associate
      with the number of possible paths in Chapter
      7 of *Math Girls*.

[12] Shiga, K. (1994). *Sūgaku ga sodatte iku monogatari 1: Kyoku-
      gen no fukami* [The Stories that Mathematics Tells Vol. 1: The
      Deepness of Limits]. Iwanami Shoten.

      A book about sequences, limits, and power
      series. This book explains topics using not
      only problems, but also dialogues between a
      student and a teacher. A short book packed
      with deep information.

[13] Okumura, H., et al. (2003). *Java ni yoru arugorizumu jiten*
      [A Dictionary of Java Algorithms]. Gijutsu Hyoronsha.

> A dictionary of various algorithms, implemented in Java. I used this to find a recurrence relation for partition numbers.

[14] Dunham, W. (1999). *Euler: The Master of Us All*. The Mathematical Association of America. Translated by Kurokawa, N., Wakayama, M., Momotani, T., et al. as *Oirā nyūmon* (Springer-Verlang, 1999).

> This book describes the work of Euler in the many mathematical fields that he researched. A dramatic representation of Euler coming up with his unique ideas. Chapter 3, "Euler and Infinite Series," and Chapter 4, "Euler and Analytic Number Theory," were particularly useful when I wrote *Math Girls*.

[15] Kobayashi, S. (2003). *Nattoku suru Oirā to Ferumā* [Understanding Euler and Fermat]. Kodansha.

> A collection of interesting topics from number theory. Includes an explanation of methods to find the value of $\zeta(2)$ beyond Euler's initial proof.

[16] Andrews, G. and Eriksson, K. (2004). *Integer Partitions*. Cambridge University Press. Translated by Sato, F. as *Seisū no bunwari* (Suugakuk Shobo, 2004).

> A book about partition numbers. The authors are foremost experts on integer partitions, and give an easy-to-understand description of partition numbers from the ground up. The book also includes a concise summary of infinite series and infinite products in an appendix. The proof that Miruka gives in Chapter 10 for using the Fibonacci numbers as an upper limit for the partition numbers is based on the proof of this book's Theorem 3.1.

[17] Kurokawa, N. (2006). *Oirā, Rīman, Ramanujan* [Euler, Riemann, and Ramanujan]. Iwatani Shoten.

A book about the mysterious world of the zeta function, focusing on the work of Euler, Riemann, and Ramanujan.

[18] Yoshida, T. (2001). *Oirā no okurimono* [Euler's Gift]. Chikuma Gakugei Bunko.

An entire book dedicated to understanding a single equation, $e^{i\pi} = -1$. The book starts from the very basics, so that one can learn through self-study. It's somewhat rare to find a paperback with so many equations.

[19] Yoshida, T. (2000). *Kyosū no jōcho—Chūgakusei kara no zenpōi dokugaku-hō* [Emotions of Imaginary Numbers—All About Self-Study From Middle School and Beyond]. Tokai University Press.

A massive volume on becoming self-motivated in "learning by doing" from the very basics, with a special emphasis on math and physics. A wonderfully interesting book. I referenced this book when writing about the difference between equations and identities in Chapter 2 of *Math Girls*.

RECOMMENDED FOR COLLEGE STUDENTS

[20] Kanaya, K. (2003). *Kore nara wakaru ōyō sūgaku kyōshitsu—Saishō nijō-hō kara ueburetto made* [Now This I Understand—Applied Mathematics From Least Squares to Wavelets]. Kyoritsu Shuppan.

A book that teaches the mathematics required for data analysis, starting with high school math. Occasional dialogues between a teacher and a student are very helpful for understanding the content. I referred to this book when discussing topics related to the Roman and Greek alphabets in *Math Girls*.

[21] Graham, R., Knuth, D., and Patashnik, O. (1994). *Concrete Mathematics: A Foundation for Computer Science (2nd Edition)*. Addison-Wesley Professional. Translated by Arizawa, M., Yasumura, M., Akino, T., and Ishihata, K. as *Conpyūtā no sūgaku* (Kyoritsu Shuppan, 1993).

A textbook on discrete mathematics, with finding sums as its theme. I used this book as a reference for the D and Δ operators, falling factorials, convolutions, and methods for finding the general term of sequences using generating functions. Most of the topics in *Math Girls* are covered in this book in a deeper, more detailed manner.

[22] Knuth, D. (1997). *The Art of Computer Programming, Volume 1: Fundamental Algorithms (3rd Edition)*. Addison-Wesley Professional. Translated by Arisawa, M., et al. as *The Art of Computer Programming, Volume 1: Nihongo-ban* (ASCII, 2004).

A classic book, sometimes called the bible of algorithms. Section 1.2.8 introduces the use of generating functions as an effective means of finding closed forms of equations. Section 2.3.2 introduces a method for formula manipulations of derivatives. The book also discusses many other topics closely related to those appearing in *Math Girls*, such as harmonic numbers, the binomial theorem, and calculating sums.

[23] Knuth, D. (2005). *The Art of Computer Programming, Volume 4, Fascicle 3: Generating All Combinations And Partitions*. Addison-Wesley Professional.

This book introduces various algorithms related to combinations and partitions, along with their mathematical analysis. Section 7.2.1.4, "Generating all partitions," in particular the subsection titled "The number of partitions" (p. 41), was very useful when writing *Math Girls*.

[24] Matousek, J. and Nesctril, J. (2008). *An Invitation to Discrete Mathematics*. Oxford University Press. Translated by Negami S. and Nakamoto, A. as *Risan sūgaku e no shōtai* (Springer-Verlag, 2002).

A collection of fascinating problems from discrete mathematics. The "better" upper limit that Miruka found in Chapter 10 comes from the proof of Theorem 10.7.2 in this book.

[25] Euler, L. (translation by Blanton, J.) (1988). *Introduction to Analysis of the Infinite: Book I*. Springer. Translated by Takase, M. as *Oirā no mugen kaiseki* (Kaimeisha, 2001).

[26] Euler, L. (translation by Blanton, J.) (1989). *Introduction to Analysis of the Infinite: Book II*. Springer. Translated by Takase, M. as *Oirā no mugen kaiseki* (Kaimeisha, 2001).

A book about infinite series, written by Euler himself. It is a thrill to watch Euler effortlessly manipulating infinite sums and products to do his calculations. This is the book where Euler introduced e and π to the world. Experiencing Euler's work firsthand as he tackles real problems using his unique ideas is an example of mathematics transcending time in the truest sense of the phrase.

RECOMMENDED FOR GRADUATE STUDENTS AND BEYOND

[27] Stanley, R. (2000). *Enumerative Combinatorics, Volume 1 (2nd Edition)*. Cambridge University Press.

[28] Stanley, R. (2001). *Enumerative Combinatorics, Volume 2*. Cambridge University Press.

> A textbook on combinations. These books give numerous examples of applications of Catalan numbers, making it particularly good for fans of those numbers (the Catalania). See in particular pp. 219–229 of Vol. 2.

[29] Matsumoto, K. (2005). *Riman no zēta kansū* [The Riemann Zeta Function]. Asakura Shoten.

> A book about the Riemann zeta function. I used this book as a reference for multiple topics, including Nicole Oresme's fourteenth-century proof that the harmonic series diverges, and Euler's method of presenting infinite products for the $\zeta(\sigma)$ function and his proof of the infinitude of primes.

[30] Kurokawa, N. (2002). *Zēta kenkyūjo-dayori* [Communiqués From the Zeta Research Laboratory]. Nihon Hyoronsha.

> A collection of topics related to the zeta function. While this book contains difficult math, it has a fantastical feel that is wonderfully refreshing.

[31] Rademacher, H. (1937). A convergent series for the partition function p(n). *Proc. London Math. Soc.* 43, pp. 241–254.

> This is the paper in which Rademacher gave a general term P_n for the partition numbers.

WEBSITES

[32] Sloane, N.: *The On-Line Encyclopedia of Integer Sequences.* http://www.research.att.com/~njas/sequences/.

An encyclopedia of sequences. Entering a few
numbers will show any sequence they belong
to.

[33] Wolfram Research: *Leonhard Euler.* http://scienceworld.
wolfram.com/biography/Euler.html.

A simple overview of Euler. Some of Miruka's
descriptions of Euler came from this page.

[34] Tasaki, II.: *Sūgaku: Butsuri wo manabi-tanoshimu tame
ni* [Mathematics: Enjoy Learning Physics]. http://www.
gakushuin.ac.jp/~881791/mathbook/.

This page has a mathematics textbook for
students of physics, freely accessible as a PDF
file. I referenced this page for the comical
dialogue related to convergence.

[35] Stanley, R. and Weisstein, E.: *Catalan Number.* From
MathWorld—A Wolfram Web Resource. http://mathworld.
wolfram.com/CatalanNumber.html.

A web page about the Catalan numbers. This
page describes a recurrence relation, the Catalan numbers' relationship with the binomial
theorem, and examples of occurences of the
Catalan numbers.

[36] Weisstein, E.: *Convolution* From MathWorld—A Wolfram Web
Resource.   http://mathworld.wolfram.com/Convolution.
html.

This page shows convolutions as an integral.

[37] Yuki, H.: *Math Girls* http://www.hyuki.com/girl/en.html.

The English version of the author's *Math
Girls* web site.

If you're learning something because
you enjoy it, you can't let something
like school hold you back. Study as
deep, as wide, and as far as you can.

HIROSHI YUKI
Math Girls

Index

Other works by Hiroshi Yuki

(in Japanese)

- *The Essence of C Programming*, Softbank, 1993 (revised 1996)

- *C Programming Lessons, Introduction*, Softbank, 1994 (Second edition, 1998)

- *C Programming Lessons, Grammar*, Softbank, 1995

- *An Introduction to CGI with Perl, Basics*, Softbank Publishing, 1998

- *An Introduction to CGI with Perl, Applications*, Softbank Publishing, 1998

- *Java Programming Lessons (Vols. I & II)*, Softbank Publishing, 1999 (revised 2003)

- *Perl Programming Lessons, Basics*, Softbank Publishing, 2001

- *Learning Design Patterns with Java*, Softbank Publishing, 2001 (revised and expanded, 2004)

- *Learning Design Patterns with Java, Multithreading Edition*, Softbank Publishing, 2002

- *Hiroshi Yuki's Perl Quizzes*, Softbank Publishing, 2002

- *Introduction to Cryptography Technology*, Softbank Publishing, 2003

- *Hiroshi Yuki's Introduction to Wikis*, Impress, 2004

- *Math for Programmers*, Softbank Publishing, 2005

- *Java Programming Lessons, Revised and Expanded (Vols. I & II)*, Softbank Creative, 2005

- *Learning Design Patterns with Java, Multithreading Edition, Revised Second Edition*, Softbank Creative, 2006

- *Revised C Programming Lessons, Introduction*, Softbank Creative, 2006

- *Revised C Programming Lessons, Grammar*, Softbank Creative, 2006

- *Revised Perl Programming Lessons, Basics*, Softbank Creative, 2006

- *Introduction to Refactoring with Java*, Softbank Creative, 2007

- *Math Girls / Fermat's Last Theorem*, Softbank Creative, 2008

- *Revised Introduction to Cryptography Technology*, Softbank Creative, 2008

- *Math Girls Comic (Vols. I & II)*, Media Factory, 2009

- *Math Girls / Gödel's Incompleteness Theorems*, Softbank Creative, 2009

- *Math Girls / Randomized Algorithms*, Softbank Creative, 2011

CPSIA information can be obtained at www.ICGtesting.com
Printed in the USA
LVOW10*1019130515

438338LV00005B/10/P

9 780983 951315